International praise for *MARKED FOR LIFE*

"Move over, Jo Nesbø."
—*Fort Worth Star Telegram*

"A fast-paced thriller with a good blend of police procedural, the draw of a ninja-strong female lead, and enough adrenaline to make a good night's sleep a near impossibility."
—*Booklist*

"A stellar first in a crime trilogy.... Schepp couples an insightful look at the personal and professional lives of her characters with an unflinching multi-layered plot loaded with surprises."
—*Publishers Weekly*, starred review

"Intriguing...the challenging, multi-layered heroine makes it worth the read."
—*Kirkus Reviews*

"Another compelling entry into the ranks of Nordic crime fiction."
—*New York Journal of Books*

"Emelie Schepp's plot complexity is worthy of a Nesbø or Kepler."
—*DAST Magazine*

"A page-turner you can't put down."
—*TV4*

"One of the best crime novels I have ever read."
—Anna Jansson,
bestselling Nordic author of *Killer's Island*

"Captures you from the first page and never lets go. Gradually, layer after layer of human evil is revealed. An impressive debut!"
—Cilia & Rolf Börjlind,
bestselling Scandinavian authors of *Spring Tide*

"This debut novel captivates the reader from the first moment and is impossible to put down."
—*Detective Magazine*

Look for Emelie Schepp's next novel

MARKED FOR REVENGE

available soon from MIRA Books.

MIRA®

Recycling programs for this product may not exist in your area.

ISBN-13: 978-0-7783-1972-6

Marked for Life

Swedish edition © 2014 by Emelie Schepp

English edition © 2016 by Emelie Schepp

Published by arrangement with Grand Agency.

For questions and comments about the quality of this book, please contact us at CustomerService@Harlequin.com.

www.MIRABooks.com

Printed in U.S.A.

To H.

MARKED FOR LIFE

CHAPTER
ONE

Sunday, April 15

"Emergency services 112, what has happened?"

"My husband's dead..."

Alarm operator Anna Bergström heard the woman's shaking voice and quickly glanced at the corner of the computer screen in front of her. The clock showed 19:42.

"Could you give me your name, please."

"Kerstin Juhlén. My husband is Hans. Hans Juhlén."

"How do you know he is dead?"

"He isn't breathing. He's just lying there. He was lying there like that when I came home. And there's blood...blood on the carpet," the woman sobbed.

"Are you hurt?"

"No."

"Is anybody else hurt?"

"No, my husband is dead."

"I understand. Where are you now?"

"At home."

The woman on the other end of the phone took a deep breath.

"Can I have your address, please?"

"Östanvägen 204, in Lindö. It's a yellow house. With large flower urns outside."

Anna's fingers worked quickly across the keyboard as she sought out Östanvägen on the digital map.

"I am sending you the necessary help," she said in a calming voice. "And I want you to stay with me on the telephone until they come."

Anna didn't get any answer. She pressed her hand against the headset.

"Hello? Are you still there?"

"He really is dead." The woman sobbed again. The sobs immediately turned into hysterical crying, then all that could be heard in the alarm service's telephone was a long anguished scream.

Detective Chief Inspector Henrik Levin and Detective Inspector Maria Bolander stepped out of their Volvo in Lindö. The cold sea air from the Baltic caught Henrik's flimsy spring jacket. He pulled the zipper up to his neck and put his hands in the pockets.

On the paved driveway there was a black Mercedes together with two police cars and an ambulance. Some ways from the cordoned-off area stood another two parked cars, and judging by the lettering on their side doors, they belonged to the town's competing newspapers.

Two journalists, one from each paper, were leaning so hard against the police tape to get a better look that it stretched tautly across their down jackets.

"Oh hell, what an upscale place." Inspector Maria Bolander, or Mia as she preferred, shook her head in irritation. "Statuary even." She stared at the granite lions, then caught sight of the huge urns next to them.

Henrik Levin remained silent and started to walk up the lit pathway to the house at Östanvägen 204. Small heaps of snow on the gray edging stones bore witness that winter had not yet given up. He nodded to the uniformed officer Gabriel Mellqvist who stood outside the front door, then he stamped the snow off his shoes, opened the heavy door for Mia and they both went in.

Activity was feverish inside the magnificent home. The forensic expert worked systematically to find possible fingerprints and other traces of evidence. They had already lit up and brushed the doors and door handles. Now they were focused on the walls. Occasionally the flash of a camera lit up the discreetly furnished living room where the dead body lay on the striped carpet.

"Who found him?" Mia asked.

"His wife, Kerstin Juhlén," Henrik said. "She apparently found him dead on the floor when she came home from a walk."

"Where is she now?"

"Upstairs. With Hanna Hultman."

Henrik Levin looked down at the body that lay

before him. The dead man was Hans Juhlén, in charge of asylum issues at the Migration Board. Henrik stepped around the body, then leaned down to study the victim's face—the powerful jaw, the weather-beaten skin, the gray beard stubble and graying temples. Hans Juhlén had often been featured in the media, but the archive photos they used did not reflect the aged body that now lay in front of them. The dead man was dressed in neatly ironed trousers and a light-blue striped shirt. Its cotton material soaked up the growing bloodstains on his chest.

"Look, but don't touch," forensic expert Anneli Lindgren said to Henrik and gave him a meaningful look as she stood next to the large windows.

"Shot?"

"Yes, twice. Two entry points from what I can tell."

Henrik glanced around the room, which was dominated by a sofa, two leather armchairs and a glass coffee table with chrome legs. Paintings by Ulf Lundell hung on the walls. The furniture didn't appear disturbed. Nothing was knocked over.

"No signs of a struggle," he said and turned toward Mia, who was now standing behind him.

"No," Mia answered without taking her eyes off an oval sideboard. On it lay a brown leather wallet with three five-hundred-kronor bills stuck out. She felt the sudden urge to pull them all out—or at least one, but she stopped herself. In her head she said, enough was enough; she had to pull herself together.

Henrik's eyes wandered to the windows which looked out onto the garden. Anneli Lindgren was still brushing for fingerprints.

"Find anything?"

Anneli Lindgren looked up at him from behind her spectacle frames.

"Not yet, but according to the victim's wife, one of these windows was open when she came home. I'm hoping I'll find something other than her prints on it."

Anneli Lindgren continued her slow, methodical work.

Henrik ran his fingers through his hair and turned back to Mia.

"Shall we go upstairs and have a few words with Mrs. Juhlén?"

"You go up. I'll stay down here and keep an eye on things."

Upstairs, Kerstin Juhlén stared hollowly as she sat on the bed in the master bedroom with a cardigan draped around her shoulders. As Henrik entered the room, police officer Hanna Hultman took a respectful step backward and closed the door behind them.

On his way up the staircase Henrik had imagined the victim's wife as a delicate woman in elegant clothes. Instead she appeared heavyset, dressed in a faded T-shirt and dark stretch jeans. Her blond hair was styled in a blunt cut, with dark roots that revealed she was overdue for a visit to the hairdresser. Henrik's eyes searched the bedroom with curiosity. First he studied the chest of drawers and then the wall of photographs. In the middle of the wall hung a frame with a large faded photo of a happy wedding couple. He was aware that Kerstin Juhlén was looking at him.

"My name's Henrik Levin, and I'm the Detective Chief Inspector," he said softly. "I'm sorry for your loss. You will have to excuse me for having to ask you a few questions at this time."

Kerstin dried a tear with the sleeve of her cardigan.

"Yes, I understand."

"Can you tell me what happened when you came home?"

"I came home and…and…he just lay there."

"Do you know what time it was?"

"About half past seven."

"Are you sure?"

"Yes."

"When you entered the house, did you see anybody else here then?"

"No. No, there was only my husband who…"

Her lip quivered and she put her hands on her face.

Henrik knew this wasn't the right time for a more detailed interrogation so he decided to be brief.

"Mrs. Juhlén, we have some support coming for you, but I must ask just a few more questions in the meantime."

Kerstin removed her hands from her face and rested them on her lap.

"Yes?"

"You told someone a window was open when you came home."

"Yes."

"And it was you who closed it?"

"Yes."

"You didn't see anything strange outside that window before you closed it?"

"No…no."

"Why did you close it?"

"I was afraid someone might try and come back in."

Henrik put his hands in his pockets and pondered a moment.

"Before I leave you, I wonder if you'd like us to call anyone in particular for you? A friend? Relative? Your children?"

She looked down, her hands trembling, and whispered something in a barely audible voice.

Henrik couldn't make out what she was trying to say.

"I'm sorry, could you repeat that?"

Kerstin shut her eyes for a moment, then slowly raised her pained face toward him. She took a deep breath before she answered him.

Downstairs still in the living room, Anneli Lindgren adjusted her glasses. "I think I've found something," she said. She was examining the print of a hand that was beginning to take form on the window frame. Mia went up to her and noted the very clear form of a palm with fingers.

"There's another one here," Anneli pointed out. "They belong to a child."

She fetched the camera to document her find. She adjusted the lens of her Canon EOS to the right focus and was taking photos just as Henrik came into the room.

Anneli nodded to him.

"Come here," she said. "We've found some fingerprints."

"They're small," said Anneli and held up the camera in front of her face again, zoomed in and took yet another picture.

"So they belong to a child?" Mia clarified.

Henrik looked surprised and leaned close to the window to get a better look. The prints made an orderly pattern. A unique pattern. Clearly from a child-sized hand.

"Strange," he mumbled.

"Why is it strange?" said Mia.

Henrik looked at her before he answered.

"The Juhléns don't have children."

CHAPTER
TWO

Monday, April 16

The trial was over, and Prosecutor Jana Berzelius was satisfied with the result. She had been absolutely certain that the defendant would be found guilty of causing grievous bodily harm.

He had kicked his own sister senseless in front of her four-year-old child and then left her to die in her apartment. No doubt it was an honor crime. Even so, the defendant's solicitor, Peter Ramstedt, looked rather surprised when the verdict was announced.

Jana nodded to him before she left the courtroom. She didn't want to discuss the judgment with anybody, especially not with the dozen or so journalists who stood and waited outside the court with their cameras and cell phones. Instead, she made her way toward the emergency exit and pushed the white fire door open. Then she quickly ran down the steps as the clock read 11:35.

Avoiding journalists had become more of a rule

than an exception for Jana Berzelius. Three years earlier, when she started in the prosecutor's office in Norrköping, it was different. Then she had appreciated the coverage and praise the media gave her. *Norrköpings Tidningar* had, for example, titled a story about her Top Student has a Place in Court. They used phrases like *comet career* and *next stop Prosecutor-General* when they wrote about her. Her cell phone vibrated in the pocket of her jacket, and she stopped in front of the entrance to the garage to look at the display before answering. At the same time, she pushed open the door into the heated garage.

"Hello, Father," she said directly.

"Well, how did it go?"

"Two years' prison and ninety in damages."

"Are you satisfied with that?"

It would never occur to Karl Berzelius to congratulate his daughter on a successful court case. Jana was accustomed to his taciturnity. Even her mother, Margaretha, who was warm and loving during her childhood, seemed to prefer to clean the house rather than play games with her. She'd put in laundry rather than read bedtime stories, or clean the kitchen rather than tuck her daughter into bed for the night. Now Jana was thirty and she treated both her parents with the same unemotional respect with which they had raised her.

"I am satisfied," Jana answered emphatically.

"Your mother wonders if you're coming home on the first of May? She wants to have a family dinner then."

"What time?"

"Seven."

"I'll come."

Jana clicked off the call, unlocked her black BMW X-6 and sat down behind the wheel. She threw her briefcase onto the leather-upholstered passenger seat and put her mobile on her lap.

Jana's mother also frequently phoned her daughter after a court case. But never before her husband did. Such was the rule. So when Jana felt her cell vibrate again, she immediately answered as she expertly maneuvered her car out of the tight garage space.

"Hello, Mother."

"Hello, Jana," said the male voice.

Jana braked and the car jerked to a halt in the reversing movement. The voice belonged to Chief Public Prosecutor Torsten Granath, her superior. He sounded keen to hear the case results. "Well?"

Jana was surprised at his evident curiosity and briefly repeated the outcome of the trial.

"Good. Good. But I'm actually calling about another matter. I want you to assist me on an investigation. A woman has been detained after she called the police to report finding her husband dead. He was the official in charge of migration asylum issues in Norrköping. According to the police, he was shot dead. Murdered. You'll have a free hand in the investigation."

Jana remained silent, so Torsten continued:

"Gunnar Öhrn and his team are waiting at the police station. What do you say?"

Jana looked at the dashboard—11:48 a.m. She took a short breath and got her car moving again.

"I'll drive straight there."

Jana Berzelius quickly walked in through the main entrance of the Norrköping police station and took the elevator up to the third floor. The sound of her heels echoed in the wide corridor. She looked straight ahead and gave only a brief nod to the two uniformed policemen that she passed.

The head of the CID, Gunnar Öhrn, waited for her outside his office and showed her to the conference room. One long wall was dominated by windows which overlooked the Norrtull roundabout, where the lunch traffic had already become noticeable. On the opposite wall a whiteboard of considerable size was mounted, along with a film screen. A projector hung from the ceiling.

Jana went up to the oval table where the team sat waiting. First she exchanged greetings with DCI Henrik Levin, then she nodded to the technician Ola Söderström, Anneli Lindgren and Mia Bolander before sitting down.

"Chief Public Prosecutor Torsten Granath has just put Jana Berzelius in charge of the preliminary investigation of the Hans Juhlén case."

"Right."

Mia Bolander clenched her teeth, crossed her arms and leaned back. She distrusted the woman she considered her rival, who was about the same age as she. The investigation would be arduous with Jana Berzelius at the helm.

The few times Mia Bolander had been forced to work with Jana Berzelius had not made her feel friendly toward the prosecutor. Mia felt Jana just had no personality. She was too stiff, too formal. She never seemed to relax and enjoy herself. If you are colleagues, you ought to get to know one another more. Perhaps share a beer or two after work and just chat a bit. Be social. But Mia had relatively quickly learned that Jana was a person who didn't appreciate such friendly moments. Any question, no matter how small, about her private life was answered with just an arrogant look.

Mia considered Jana Berzelius an arrogant fucking diva. Unfortunately, nobody else shared Mia's opinion. On the contrary, they nodded appreciatively when Gunnar presented Jana now.

What Mia detested most was Jana's status as an upper-class girl. Jana was old money, while Mia, with her working-class background, was mortgaged. That was as good a reason as any for her to keep her distance from Jana and her airs.

Out of the corner of her eye, Jana noted the disdainful looks from the female inspector but chose to ignore them. She opened her briefcase and pulled out a notepad and pen.

Gunnar Öhrn drank the last few drops from a bottle of mineral water, then handed out packets to everyone which contained copies of everything they had documented about the case so far. It included the initial report; photos from the crime scene and immediate vicinity; a sketch of the Juhlén house where the victim, Hans Juhlén, had been found; and a short description of Juhlén. Lastly came a log with times and investigative steps that had already been taken since the victim had been discovered.

Gunnar pointed to the timeline that had been drawn on the whiteboard. He also described the initial report of the conversation with the victim's wife, Kerstin Juhlén, which had been signed by the police officers in the patrol car. They had been the first to interview her.

"Kerstin Juhlén was, however, hard to talk to properly," said Gunnar.

She had initially come close to being hysterical, had screamed loudly and talked incoherently. At one point she started to hyperventilate. And all the time she had repeatedly said she didn't kill her husband. She only found him in the living room. Dead.

"So do we suspect her, then?" said Jana and noticed that Mia was still glaring at her.

"Yes, she is of interest. We have detained her. She hasn't got a verifiable alibi."

Gunnar thumbed through the packet of papers.

"Okay, to summarize then. Hans Juhlén was murdered some time between 15:00 and 19:00 yesterday. Perpetrators unknown. The forensic experts says the murder took place in the house. That is, the body had not been transported from anywhere else. Correct?"

He nodded to Anneli Lindgren to confirm.

"That's right. He died there."

"The body was taken to the medical examiner's lab at 22:21 and inspectors continued to go through the house until after midnight."

"Yes, and I found these."

Anneli put down ten sheets of paper with a single sentence written on each. "They lay well hidden in the back of the wardrobe in the victim's bedroom. They appear to be short threatening letters."

"Do we know who sent them and to whom they were addressed?" asked Henrik as he reached across to examine them. Jana made a note about them in her notepad.

"No. I got these copies from forensics in Linköping this morning. It'll probably take a day or so before they can get us more information," said Anneli.

"What do they say?" said Mia. She pulled her hands inside the sleeves of her knitted sweater, put her elbows on the table and looked at Anneli with curiosity.

"The same message is on each one—'Pay now or risk paying the bigger price.'"

"Blackmail," said Henrik.

"So it would seem. We spoke to Mrs. Juhlén. She denies any knowledge of the letters. She seemed genuinely surprised about them."

"They hadn't been reported then, these threats?" said Jana and wrinkled her brow.

"No, nothing has been reported by the victim himself, his wife or anybody else," said Gunnar.

"And what about the murder weapon?" said Jana, switching the topic.

"We haven't found one yet. Nothing was near the body or in the immediate vicinity," said Gunnar.

"Any DNA traces or shoe tracks?"

"No," said Anneli. "But when the wife came home, a window was open in the living room. It seems fairly clear that the perpetrator gained entrance that way. The wife closed it, unfortunately, which has made it more difficult for us. But we did manage to find two interesting handprints."

"Whose prints?" said Jana and held her pen ready to note down a name.

"Don't know yet, but everything points to their being the prints of a child. The strange thing is that the couple don't have any children."

Jana looked up from her notepad.

"Is that really significant? Surely they know someone who has children. A friend? Relative?" she said.

"We haven't been able to ask Kerstin Juhlén more about it yet," answered Gunnar.

"Well, that must be the next step. Preferably straightaway."

Jana took her calendar out of her briefcase and flipped through to today's date. Reminders, times and names were neatly written on the pale yellow pages.

"I want us to talk to her as soon as possible."

"I'll phone her lawyer, Peter Ramstedt, right away," said Gunnar.

"Good," said Jana. "Get back to me with a time as soon as you can." She put her calendar back in her briefcase. "Have you questioned any of the neighbors yet?"

"Yes, the nearest ones," said Gunnar.

"And?"

"Nothing. Nobody saw or heard anything."

"Then ask more. Knock on all the doors along the entire street and in the immediate vicinity. Lindö has many big homes, a lot of them with large picture windows."

"Yes, I imagine you would know that, of course," said Mia.

Jana looked directly at Mia.

"What I am saying is that somebody must have seen or heard something."

Mia glared back, then looked away.

"What more do we know about Hans Juhlén?" Jana went on.

"He lived a fairly ordinary life, it seems," said Gunnar and read from the packet. "He was born in Kimstad in 1953, so he was fifty-nine. Spent his childhood there. The family moved to Norrköping in 1965, when he was twelve. He studied economics at university and worked for four years in an accounting firm before he got a position in the Migration Board's asylum department and worked his way up to become the head. He met his wife, Kerstin, when he was eighteen and the year after that they married in a registry office. They have a summer cottage by Lake Vättern. That's all we've got so far."

"Friends? Acquaintances?" Mia said grumpily. "Have we checked them?"

"We don't know anything about his friends yet. Or his wife's. But we've started mapping them, yes," said Gunnar.

"A more detailed conversation with the wife will help fill in more detail," said Henrik.

"Yes, I know," said Gunnar.

"His cell phone?" Jana wondered.

"I've asked the service provider for a list of calls to and from his number. Hopefully I'll have that tomorrow latest," said Gunnar.

"And what have we got from the autopsy results?"

"At the moment, we know only that Hans Juhlén was both shot and died where he was found. The medical examiner is giving us a preliminary report today."

"I need a copy of that," Jana said.

"Henrik and Mia are going straight there after this meeting."

"Fine. I'll tag along," said Jana, and smiled to herself when she heard the deep sigh from Inspector Bolander.

THREE

The sea was rough, which meant that the stench got even worse in the confined space. The seven-year-old girl sat in the corner. She pulled at her mama's skirt and put it over her mouth. She imagined that she was at home in her bed, or rocking in a cradle when the ship rolled in the waves.

The girl breathed in and out with shallow breaths. Every time she exhaled, the cloth would lift above her mouth. Every time she inhaled, it would cover her lips. She tried to breathe harder and harder to keep the cloth off her face. Then one time she blew so hard it flew off and vanished.

She felt for it with her hand. In the dim light she instead caught sight of her toy mirror on the floor. It was pink, with a butterfly on it and a big crack in the glass. She had found it in a bag of rubbish that somebody had thrown onto the street. Now she picked it up and held it in front of her face, pushed away a strand of hair from her forehead

*and inspected her dark tangled hair, her big eyes
and long eyelashes.*

*Somebody coughed violently in the space, and
the girl gave a start. She tried to see who it was,
but it was difficult to distinguish people's faces
in the dark.*

*She wondered when they would arrive, but
she didn't dare ask again. Papa had hushed her
when she had asked the last time how long they
would have to sit in this stupid iron box. Now
Mama coughed too. It was hard to breathe, it really was. A lot of people had to share the little oxy-
gen inside. The girl let her hand wander along the
steel wall. Then she felt for the soft cloth from her
mama's skirt and pulled it over her nose.*

*The floor was hard, and she straightened her
back and changed position before continuing to
run her hand along the steel wall. She stretched
out her index and middle fingers and let them gal-
lop back and forth along the wall and down to the
floor. Mama always used to laugh when she did
that at home and say that she must have given
birth to a horse girl.*

*At home, in the shed in La Pintana, the girl had
built a toy stable under the kitchen table and pretended her doll was a horse. The last three birth-
days, she had wished for a real pony of her own.
She knew that she wouldn't get one. She rarely got
any presents, even for her birthday. They could
hardly afford food even, Papa had told her. Anyway, the girl dreamed of a pony of her own that
she could ride to school. It would be fast, just*

as fast as her fingers that now galloped back up the wall.

Mama didn't laugh this time. She was probably too tired, the girl thought, and looked up at her mother's face.

Oh, how much longer would it actually take? Stupid, stupid journey! It wasn't supposed to be such a long trip. Papa had said when they filled the plastic bags with clothes that they were going on an adventure, a big adventure. They would travel by boat for a while to a new home. And she would make lots of new friends. It would be fun.

Some of her friends were traveling with them. Danilo and Ester. She liked Danilo; he was nice, but not Ester. She could be a little nasty. She would tease, and that sort of thing. There were a couple of other children on the same journey too, but she didn't know them; she had never even seen them before. They didn't like all being in a boat. Not the youngest one at any rate, the baby, she was crying all the time. But now she'd gone quiet.

The girl galloped her fingers back and forth again. Then she stretched to one side to reach up even higher, then down even lower. When her fingers reached all the way into the corner, she felt something sticking out. She became curious and screwed her eyes up in the dark to see what it was. A metal plate. She strained forward to try and study the little silver plate that was screwed into the wall. She saw some letters on it and she tried to make out what they said. V… P… Then there was a letter she didn't recognize.

"Mama?" she whispered. "What letter is this?"
She crossed her two fingers to show her.

"X," her mother whispered back. "An X."

X, *the girl thought,* V, P, X, O. *And then some numbers. She counted six of them. There were six numbers.*

CHAPTER FOUR

The autopsy room was lit up by strong fluorescent ceiling lights. A shiny steel table stood in the middle of the room and on it, under a white sheet, you could see the contours of a body.

A long row of plastic bottles marked with ID numbers were lined up on another stainless-steel table along with a skull saw. The metallic smell of meat had permeated the room.

Jana Berzelius went in first and stood across the table from the medical examiner, whose name was Björn Ahlmann. She said hello, then pulled out her notepad.

Henrik went over and stood next to Jana, while Mia Bolander stayed back near the exit door. Henrik too would have liked to have stayed at a distance. He had always found it difficult to be in the autopsy room, and he by no means shared Ahlmann's fascination with dead bodies. He wondered how the pathologist could work with corpses every day and not be affected. Even though it was also part of Henrik's job, he still found death hard to witness up close. Even after seven years on this job, he had to force himself to keep a composed face when a body was exposed.

Jana, on the other hand, didn't seem to be bothered at all. Her facial expression revealed nothing, and Henrik found himself wondering if anything at all could get her to react. He knew that knocked-out teeth, poked-out eyes, chopped-off fingers and hands didn't do it. Nor tongues that had been bitten to bits, or third-degree burns. He knew that because he had witnessed the same things in her presence, and he inevitably had to empty the contents of his stomach afterward, whereas she never seemed disturbed.

Jana's facial expressions were indeed extremely restrained. She was never harrowed or resolute; she hardly showed any emotions at all. She rarely smiled and should a smile happen to cross her lips, it was more like a line. A strained line.

Henrik didn't think that her austere personality matched her appearance. Her long dark hair and big brown eyes gave off a warmer vibe. Perhaps she was only projecting her professional side to maintain others' respect. Certainly her navy blazer, three-quarter-length skirt and ever-present high heels played into her image as a strict, nononsense prosecutor. Perhaps she let out her personal feelings outside work... Perhaps not.

Björn Ahlmann carefully folded back the sheet and exposed Hans Juhlén's naked body.

"Right, let's see. We have an entry hole here

and we have an entry hole here," said Björn and pointed at two open wounds on the chest. "Both seem to be perfectly placed, but this is the one that killed him."

Björn moved his hand and indicated the upper hole.

"So there were definitely two shots then?" Henrik commented.

"Exactly."

Björn picked up an image from a CAT scan and clipped it up on the light box.

"Chronologically, it seems that he first received a bullet in the lower part of his rib cage, and fell down. He fell backward, which resulted in a subdural hemorrhage at the back of his head. You can see it here."

Björn pointed at a black area on the image. "But he didn't die, not from the first shot or from the heavy fall. No, my guess is that when Hans Juhlén collapsed, the perpetrator went up close and shot him again. Here."

He pointed at the second entry hole in Juhlén's body.

"This shot went right through the cartilage of the rib cage and through the pericardium, the heart. And he died immediately."

"So he died from bullet number two." Henrik again repeated the pathologist's words.

"Yes."

"Weapon?"

"The cartridges that were found show that he was shot with a Glock."

"Then it won't be so easy to trace," said Henrik.

"Why?" said Jana, at the very same moment that her cell phone vibrated in her pocket. She ignored it and asked again, "Why?"

"Because, as I'm sure you are aware, a Glock is a very common weapon. So common it's used by our army and by police across the world. So I just mean it will take a while to run a check on all those on the list of people holding legitimate licences," he said.

"Then we'll have to put that task in the hands of somebody with patience," Jana answered, and again felt a short vibration in her pocket. The caller must have left a message.

"Any sign that the victim tried to defend himself?" Mia asked from across the room.

"No. No signs of violence. No scratch marks, no bruises or marks from a stranglehold. He was shot. Plain and simple."

Björn looked up at Henrik and Jana.

"The flow of blood shows that he died on the spot and his body was not moved, but—"

"Yes, Gunnar told us." Mia interrupted him from across the room.

"Yes, I talked with him this morning. But there are…"

"No fingerprints?" she said.

"No. But…"

"Narcotics then?"

"No, no drugs. No alcohol. But…"

"Broken bones?"

"No. But will you let me finish now?"

Mia became silent.

"Thank you. What does seem interesting is the path of the bullets through the body. One of the entry holes—" Björn pointed at the upper of the two "—is not out of the ordinary. The bullet went horizontally through the body. But the other bullet went diagonally, at an angle. And judging by the angle, the perpetrator must have been kneeling, lying down or sitting up when he or she fired the first shot. Then, as I said earlier, when the man fell down, the shooter went up to him and fired a final shot right through his heart."

"Execution style, then," said Mia.

"That's up to you to judge, but yes, it would seem so."

"So he was standing up when bullet number one hit him," said Henrik.

"Yes, and he was shot at an upward angle from the front."

"So somebody knelt or lay down and then shot up at him from the front? It hardly makes sense," said Mia. "I mean, it's really weird that somebody would be sitting on the floor in front of him and then kill him. Wouldn't he have had time to react?"

"Perhaps he did. Or else he knew the murderer," said Henrik.

"Or it was a bloody dwarf or something," said Mia and laughed out loud.

Henrik sighed at her.

"You can discuss that among yourselves. According to my calculations, that, at any rate, is how

Hans Juhlén died. My findings are summarized here." Björn held out copies of the autopsy report. Henrik and Jana each took one.

"He died sometime between 18:00 and 19:00 on Sunday. It's in the notes."

Jana thumbed through the report which at first sight seemed to be as comprehensive and detailed as Ahlmann was known to be.

"Thanks for the summary," she said to Björn as she fished up her phone from her pocket to listen to the voice message.

It was Gunnar Öhrn who had left a single short sentence in a resolute tone. "Interview with Kerstin Juhlén, 15:30," he'd said, and nothing more. Not even his name.

Jana put the phone back into her pocket.

"Interview at half past three," she said quietly to Henrik.

"What?" said Mia.

"Interview half past three," said Henrik loud and clear to Mia who was about to say something when Jana interrupted.

"Well, then," she said.

The medical examiner adjusted his glasses. "Are you satisfied?" he asked.

"Yes."

He slowly pulled the sheet back over the naked body. Mia opened the door and backed out to avoid brushing against Jana as she approached the doorway.

"We'll get back to you with any questions," said Henrik to Ahlmann as they left the autopsy room.

He strode in the lead toward the elevator.

"Do that," answered Björn behind them. "You know where I am," he added, but his voice was drowned out by the drumming noise from the ventilation pipes in the ceiling.

The Public Prosecution Office in Norrköping consisted of twelve full-time employees with Chief Public Prosecutor Torsten Granath in charge. Fifteen years earlier, when Torsten Granath took over as head of the office, the office went through a radical change. Under his leadership, a policy was instituted of replacing staff members who were no longer pulling their weight with a few new hires who had highly productive track records. He had thanked several longtime employees for their service while at the same time encouraging them to retire, fired lazy administrators and helped underutilized specialists to find new challenges in other areas of their profession.

When Jana Berzelius was hired, Torsten Granath had already trimmed down the organization considerably; only four members were left on staff. That same year, the office was charged with a larger geographical area, and they also had to deal with crimes in the adjacent municipalities of Finspång, Söderköping and Valdemarsvik. The recently increasing trade in narcotics also called for more employees. For those reasons, Torsten Granath had recruited new staff and now they were twelve in all.

As a result of Torsten's policy, the office could now proudly display its competence. Torsten

Granath at sixty-two ironically had slowed down a little himself and now occasionally found his thoughts wandering off to the well-kept greens on the golf courses. But his heart still belonged to his profession. Leading the work here was his mission in life and he would keep on with it until he reached pensionable age.

His office was of the homely type, with curtains draped in the window, gilded frames with photos of grandchildren on his desk and a green woolly rug on the floor. He always paced back and forth on that rug when he talked on the telephone. That was what he was doing when Jana Berzelius entered the department. She said a quick hello to the administrator, Yvonne Jansson.

Yvonne stopped Jana as she walked by.

"Hang on a sec!"

She handed over a yellow Post-it note with a familiar name written on it.

"Mats Nylinder at *Norrköpings Tidningar* wants a comment on the murder of Hans Juhlén. They've evidently found out that you're in charge of the preliminary investigation. Mats said that you owed him a few words since you sneaked out of court this morning. He had wanted a statement about the judgment and waited more than an hour for you."

Jana didn't answer, so Yvonne went on.

"Unfortunately he isn't the only one who's rung. This murder has every paper in Sweden interested. They all want something to put in their headlines tomorrow."

"And I'm not going to give them anything. You'll have to refer them to the police press officer. There will be no comment from me."

"Okay, no comment it is."

"And you can tell Mats Nylinder that too," said Jana and headed toward her office.The sound of her heels echoed as she entered the room with its parquet floor.

The furnishings were Spartan, but had a touch of elegance. The desk was of teak and so were the functional bookshelves that were filled with bound case files. On the right side of the desk was a silver letter tray with three levels. On the left side there was a laptop, a 17-inch HP. On the windowsill stood two white orchids in high pots.

Jana closed the door behind her and hung her jacket over the back of her leather-upholstered chair. While her computer started up, she studied the flowers in the window. She liked her office. It was spacious and airy. She had chosen to position the desk so that she sat with her back to the window; through the glass wall she then had full view of the corridor outside.

Jana put a tall stack of summonses to be adjudicated next to her computer.

Then she quickly glanced at her watch. Only one and a half hours before the interview with Kerstin Juhlén.

She suddenly felt tired, leaned her head forward and started to rub the back of her neck. Her fingertips slowly massaged the uneven skin there and traced over its bumps. Then she neatened her long hair to make sure it covered the back of her neck and flowed down her back.

After looking through a few of the summonses, she got up to fetch a cup of coffee. When she came back, she left the rest of the paperwork untouched.

The smallish interview room was bare except for a table and four chairs, with a fifth chair in a corner. One wall had a window with bars; on the opposite wall was a mirror. Jana sat next to Henrik with her pen and notepad in her hand as he started the tape recorder. She let him handle the questioning. Mia Bolander had pulled up the extra chair behind them. Loudly and clearly, Henrik recited Kerstin Juhlén's full name, then her personal identity number, before going on.

"Monday, the sixteenth of April, 15:30 hours. This interview is being conducted by DCI Henrik Levin who is being assisted by DI Mia Bolander. Also present are Public Prosecutor Jana Berzelius and Solicitor Peter Ramstedt."

Kerstin Juhlén had been detained as a possible person of interest, but so far had not been charged with any crime. She sat next to Peter Ramstedt, her lawyer, and placed her clasped hands on the table. Her face was pale and she wore no makeup. Her hair was uncombed, her earrings removed.

"Do you know who killed my husband?" Kerstin Juhlén asked in a whisper.

"No, it's still too early in our investigation to say," answered Henrik and looked gravely at the woman in front of him.

"You think I've done it, don't you? You think that I was the one who shot him…"

"We don't think anything."

"But I didn't do it! I wasn't home. It wasn't me!"

"As I said, we don't think anything yet, but we must investigate the circumstances surrounding his murder and determine how it all happened. That's why I want you to tell me about Sunday night when you came home to the house."

Kerstin took two deep breaths. She unclenched her hands, put them on her lap and straightened up in the chair.

"I came home…from a walk."

"Did you walk alone, or was somebody with you?"

"I walked by myself, to the beach and back."

"Tell us more."

"When I came home, I took my coat off in the hallway as I called out to Hans, because I knew that he ought to be home by then."

"What time was it then?"

"About half past seven."

"Go on."

"I didn't get an answer so I assumed that he had been delayed at work. You see, he would always go to the office on Sundays. I went straight to the kitchen to get a glass of water. I saw the pizza box on the kitchen sideboard and realized that Hans was actually home. We usually eat pizza on Sundays. Hans picks it up on his way home. Yes, well... I called out again, but still got no answer. So I went to check if he was in the living room and what he was doing and... I saw him just lying there on the floor. In shock, I called the police."

"When did you phone?"

"Straightaway...when I found him."

"What did you do then, after you phoned the police?"

"I went upstairs. The woman on the phone said I should do that. That I mustn't touch him, so I went upstairs."

Henrik looked at the woman in front of him. She looked nervous, with a shifting gaze. She fingered the cloth of her light gray pants anxiously.

"I've asked you before, but I must ask again. Did you see anybody in the house?"

"No."

"Nobody outside?"

"I noticed that the front window was opened, so I closed it. In case someone was still lurking about. I was frightened. But no, I've already told you. I saw no one."

"No car on the street?"

"No," Kerstin answered in a loud voice. She leaned forward and rubbed her Achilles tendon on one foot, as if she were trying to scratch an itch.

"Tell us about your husband," said Henrik.

"Tell you what?"

"He worked as the head of asylum issues at the Migration Board here in Norrköping, correct?" said Henrik.

"Yes. He was good at his job."

"Can you elaborate? What was he good at?"

"He worked with all sorts of things. In the department he was in charge…"

Kerstin became silent and lowered her head.

Henrik noted that she swallowed hard, he imagined, to prevent tears from coming.

"We can take a little break if you like," said Henrik.

"No, it's okay. It's okay."

Kerstin took a deep breath. She looked briefly at her lawyer, who was twirling his pen on the table, and then she started talking again.

"My husband was indeed the head of a department at the board. He liked his job and had worked his way up, devoted all his life to the Migration Board. He is…was the sort of person people liked. He was kind to everybody regardless of where they came from. He didn't have any prejudices. He wanted to help people. That was why he liked it there so much.

"The Migration Board has had to put up with a lot of criticism recently," Kerstin said, then paused before going on.

Henrik nodded. He knew the National Audit Agency had recently examined the Migration Board's procedures for arranging accommodation for asylum seekers, and they cited it for improper practices. During the last year, the board spent fifty million kronor on buying accommodations. Of that, nine million kronor had been spent on direct agreements, which are forbidden if done without the proper procedures. The Audit Agency had also found illegal contracts with landlords. In many cases no contracts were used at all. The local papers had published several articles about the audit.

"Hans was upset over the criticism. More refugees had been applying than they had anticipated. He had to quickly arrange accommodations for them. And then it went wrong."

Kerstin became silent. Her lip quivered.

"I felt sorry for him."

"It sounds as if you are well aware of your husband's work," said Henrik.

Kerstin didn't answer. She wiped a tear from her eye and nodded at the thought.

"There was the problem with improper behavior too," she said.

She quickly described how there had been assaults and thefts at the asylum accommodation center. Because of the stress of their situation, often arguments broke out among the new arrivals. The staff that had been temporarily hired to run the center found it hard to keep order.

"Which we know about," said Henrik.

"Oh yes, of course," said Kerstin and straightened her back again.

"Many of them were in poor mental condition, and Hans tried to do everything he could to make their stay as comfortable as possible. But it was difficult. Several nights in a row somebody set off the fire alarm. People got scared and Hans had no alternative but to hire more staff to keep an eye on the center. My husband was personally very committed, I can tell you that, and he put his very soul into his work."

Henrik leaned back and studied Kerstin. She didn't look quite as miserable now. Something had gradually come over her, perhaps a pride in her husband's work—perhaps a sort of relief.

"Hans spent a lot of time at the office. There were late evenings, and every Sunday he left home after lunch and didn't come back until dinnertime. It was hard to know exactly what time he would get home, what time to have dinner ready, so he always used to buy a pizza instead. Just like yesterday. As usual."

Kerstin Juhlén hid her face in her hands as she shook her head. The anguish and the misery of it all had immediately come back.

"You have the right to take a break," said Peter Ramstedt as he carefully put a hand on her shoulder.

Jana studied his touch. She knew this lawyer had a reputation of being strongly attracted to women and rarely hesitated to physically console his clients. If he got the chance, he was open to do more than that.

Kerstin raised her shoulder slightly in discomfort, which evidently made the solicitor realize that he should remove his hand. Peter pulled out a handkerchief and offered it to her. Kerstin gratefully accepted, and she blew her nose in it audibly.

"Sorry," she said.

"That's all right," said Henrik. "So if I've understood you correctly, your husband had a difficult job."

"No, I mean…yes, but I don't know. I can't really say exactly… I think…it would be best if you were to speak with my husband's secretary."

Henrik wrinkled his brow. "Why is that?"

"It would just be for the best," she whispered.

Henrik sighed and leaned forward over the table.

"What's his secretary's name, then?"

"Lena Wikström. She has been his assistant for almost twenty years."

"Of course we'll speak with her."

Kerstin's shoulders sank and she clasped her hands.

"May I ask," said Henrik, "if you and your husband were close?"

"How do you mean? Of course we were close."

"You didn't have a disagreement about anything? Argue a lot?"

"What are you getting at, Chief Inspector?" interjected Peter, leaning across the table.

"I just want to be sure we get the full picture for this investigation," said Henrik.

"No, we rarely argued," Kerstin answered slowly.

"Apart from you, who else was close to him?"

"His parents have been dead a long time, unfortunately. Cancer, both of them. He didn't have any real friends, so you could say that our social life was rather limited. But we liked it like that."

"Sister? Brother?"

"He has a half brother who lives in Finspång. But they haven't had much contact with each other in recent years. They are very different."

"In what way?"

"They just are."

"What's his name?"

"Lars Johansson. Everyone calls him Lasse."

Mia Bolander had been sitting with her arms crossed, just listening. Now she asked straight out, "Why don't you have children?"

Kerstin was surprised by the question and hastily pulled her legs back under her chair. So hastily that one shoe came off.

Henrik turned around and looked at Mia. He was irritated, but she was pleased that she'd asked. Kerstin bent down and groaned as she stretched to reach her shoe under the table. Then she sat up straight again and put her hands on the table, one atop the other.

"We never had children," she said briefly.

"Why not?" said Mia. "Couldn't you conceive or what?"

"I think we could have. But it just sort of never happened. And we accepted that."

Henrik cleared his throat and started talking to prevent Mia from asking more questions along this line.

"Okay. You didn't mix with many people, you said?"

"No, we really didn't."

"When did you last have visitors?"

"That was a long while ago. Hans was working all the time..."

"No other visitors to the house? Repairmen, for example?"

"Around Christmas a man knocked on the door selling lottery tickets, but otherwise there haven't been..."

"What did he look like?"

Kerstin stared at Henrik, surprised by the question.

"Tall, blond as I remember. He seemed nice, presentable. But I didn't buy any tickets from him."

"Did he have any children with him?"

"No. No, he didn't. He was alone."

"Do you know anybody with children?"

"Well, yes, of course. Hans's half brother. He has an eight-year-old son."

"Has he been to your house recently?"

Kerstin stared at Henrik again.

"I don't really follow your question...but, no, he hasn't been in our house for ages."

Jana Berzelius drew a ring around the half brother's name on her notepad. Lars Johansson.

"Do you have any idea who might have done this to your husband?" she said.

Kerstin squirmed a little, looked out of the window and answered, "No."

"Did your husband have any enemies?" said Henrik.

Kerstin looked down at the table and took a deep breath.

"No, he didn't."

"Nobody he was angry with or had argued with or who was angry with him?"

Kerstin didn't seem to hear the question.

"Kerstin?"

"What?"

"Nobody who was angry with him?"

She shook her head no so violently that the loose skin under her chin wobbled.

"Strange," said Henrik as he laid out copies of the threatening letters on the table in front of her. "Because as you know, we found these at your house."

"What are they?"

"The letters from your closet. We are hoping you will tell us about them."

"But I don't know what they are. I've never seen them before."

"They seem to be some sort of threats. That means your husband must have had at least one enemy, if not more."

"But, no…"

Kerstin shook her head again.

"We are very anxious to find out more about who sent these—and why."

"I have no idea."

"You haven't?"

"No, I've told you I've never seen them before."

Click-click could be heard from Peter Ramstedt's pen.

"As my client has said twice, she does not recognize these papers. Would you be so kind and note that now for the record? Then you don't have to waste time repeating the same question."

"Mr. Ramstedt, you are surely well aware as to how an interview is carried out. Without extended questioning, we won't get the information we need," said Henrik.

"Then be so kind as to stick to relevant questions. My client has clearly stated that she has *not* seen these papers previously."

Peter looked straight at Henrik. CLICK-CLICK.

"So you don't know if your husband felt threatened in any way?" Henrik continued.

"No."

"No strange phone calls?"

"I don't think so."

"Don't think or don't know?"

"No, no calls."

"You don't know anybody who wanted to warn him? Or get revenge?"

"No. But the nature of his work of course made him rather vulnerable."

"How do you mean?"

"Well…my husband thought that the decision process for asylum was difficult. He never liked having to turn away any asylum seekers, even though he wasn't personally responsible for having to tell them himself. He knew how desperate many were when they didn't get asylum here. But not everyone qualified. And no one has threatened him. Or has sought revenge, if that is the question."

Henrik wondered whether Kerstin was telling the truth. Hans Juhlén could admittedly have kept the threatening letters hidden away from her. But it did nevertheless seem unlikely that he never during all his years in the job felt frightened of somebody nor talked with his wife about it.

"There must have been a relatively serious threat against Juhlén," Henrik said to Jana when the interview was concluded. They both left the interrogation room with slow steps.

"Yes," she answered briefly.

"What do you think about the wife?"

Jana remained standing in the corridor while Henrik closed the door. "There are no signs of violence in the house," she said.

"Perhaps because the murder was well planned."

"So you think she's guilty?"

"The spouse is always guilty, right?" Henrik smiled.

"Yes, almost always. But at the moment no evidence links her to the murder."

"She seemed nervous," he added.

"That isn't enough."

"I know. But it feels as if she isn't telling the truth."

"And she probably isn't, or at least not completely, but to arrest her I'm going to need more than that. If she doesn't start talking or we can't get any technical evidence, I'll have to let her go. You've got three days."

Henrik ran his fingers through his hair.

"And the secretary?" he said.

"Check out what she knows. I want you to visit her as soon as you can, but definitely by tomorrow. Unfortunately I have four cases which I have to pay attention to, and so I am not free to go with you. But I trust you."

"Of course. Mia and I will talk with her."

Jana said goodbye and walked past the other interrogation rooms.

As a public prosecutor, she regularly visited the place. She was on emergency duty a certain number of weekends and nights every year—it went with the job. A rotating duty schedule was posted, whose main purpose was to ensure that a prosecutor was available for urgent decisions such as whether somebody should be detained. A prosecutor could keep somebody in detention up to three days without introducing charges. After that, a court hearing was necessary. On a number of occasions, sometimes late at night, Jana had been called in and, in a rush, had to make a decision about an arrest.

Today all the cells in the center were full. She looked up toward the ceiling and thanked a higher power that she wasn't on call the coming weekend. At the same time, she remembered that she would be on standby duty the weekend after that. She slowed her pace as she walked down the corridor, then stopped to sit and pull her calendar out.

She turned the pages ahead to April 28. Nothing was noted there. Perhaps it was Sunday, April 29? Nothing there either. She turned a few more pages and caught sight of the entry for the first of May. A public holiday. ON CALL. And that was the day she had agreed to have dinner with her mother and father. She felt immediate stress. She couldn't possibly be on call that same day. How had she not seen that? Of course, it was not absolutely necessary to be at her parents' for dinner, but she didn't want to disappoint her father by not coming over at all.

I'll have to swap days with somebody, she thought, as she put her calendar back in her briefcase. She got up and continued walking, wondering with whom she'd be able to swap days. Most likely Per Åström. Per was both a successful public prosecutor and a popular social worker. She respected him as a colleague. During the five years they had known each other, a friendship of sorts had grown up between them.

Per was thirty-three years old and in good shape. He played tennis on Tuesdays and Thursdays. He had blond hair, a little dimple in his chin and eyes that were different colors. He smelled of aftershave. Sometimes he tended to go on a bit, but otherwise a nice guy. Only that; nothing more.

Jana hoped that Per would swap with her. Otherwise she would resort to bribing him with wine. But red or white? She weighed the two choices in time with the sound of her heels on the floor. Red or white. Red or white.

She contemplated taking the stairs down to the garage but chose the elevator instead. When she saw that the defense lawyer Peter Ramstedt was waiting there too, she immediately regretted her decision. She stood back from him at a safe distance.

"Ah, it's you, Jana," said Peter when he noted her presence. He rocked back and forth on the soles of his shoes.

"I heard that you had gone to review the autopsy and see the victim's body at the medical examiner's."

"Where did you hear that?"

"One hears a thing or two."

Peter gave a slight smirk and exposed his whitened teeth.

"So you like corpses?"

"Not particularly. I'm just trying to lead an investigation."

"I've been a lawyer for ten years and I've never heard of a prosecutor going to an autopsy."

"Perhaps that says more about other prosecutors than about me?"

"Don't you like your colleagues?"

"I didn't say that."

"Isn't it simpler in your position to let the police do the legwork?"

"I am not interested in what is simple."

"You know, as a prosecutor you can complicate an investigation."

"In what way?"

"By calling attention to yourself."

Hearing those words, Jana Berzelius decided to take the stairs down to the garage anyway. For every step she cursed Peter Ramstedt.

The rocking had stopped. They were traveling silently, shut inside the dark container.

"Are we there?" said the girl.

Her mama didn't answer her. Nor her papa. They seemed tense. Her mother told her to sit up. The girl did as she was told. The others also began to move. There was a feeling of unease. Several others were coughing and the girl felt the warm, stuffy air as it sought its way down into her lungs. Even her papa made a wheezing sound.

"Are we there now?" she said again. "Mama? Mama!"

"Quiet!" said Papa. "You must be completely quiet."

The girl became grumpy and pushed her knees up toward her chin.

Suddenly the floor shuddered under her. She fell to one side and stretched out an arm to brace herself. Her mother got hold of her and held her close. It was silent a long, long time. Then the container was lifted up.

They all hung on tight in the cramped space. The girl gripped her mama's waist. But even so, she hit her head when the container landed hard on the ground. At last they were in their new country. In their new life.

Mama got up and pulled her daughter up too. The girl looked at Danilo, who was still sitting with his back to the wall. His eyes were wide open, and just like all the others he was trying to hear sounds outside. It was hard to hear anything through the walls but if you really concentrated then you could perhaps distinguish weak voices. Yes, there were people talking outside. The girl looked at her papa and he smiled at her. That smile was the last thing she saw before the container was opened and daylight poured in.

Outside the container stood three men. They had something in their hands, something big and silvery. The girl had seen such things before, in red plastic that sprayed water.

One man started to shout at the others. Something weird was on his face, an enormous scar. She couldn't help but stare at it.

The man with the scar came into the container and waved the silvery thing. He was shouting all the time. The girl didn't understand what he said. Neither did her parents. Nobody understood his words.

The man went up to Ester and pulled at her sweater. She was scared. Ester's mama was also frightened and didn't realize what was happening until it was too late. The man pulled Ester and held her in a firm grip around her neck as he backed away, all the time with the silvery thing pointed at Ester's mama and papa. They didn't dare do anything; they stood there completely still.

The girl felt somebody take a firm hold of her arm. It was Papa, who quickly pushed her in behind his legs. Her mama spread out her skirt to cover the girl even more.

The girl stood as still as she possibly could. Behind the skirt she couldn't see what was happening. But she could hear. Hear how the grownups started to shout. They were shouting no, no, NO! And then she heard Danilo's desperate voice.

"Mama," he shouted. "Mama!"

The girl put her hands over her ears so that she wouldn't have to hear the other children's crying and shrieking. The voices of the grown-ups were worse. They were crying and shrieking too, but they were much louder. The girl pressed her hands even harder against her ears. But then after a while, all became silent.

The girl took her hands away and listened. She tried to look out between her papa's legs, but when she moved he pressed her hard against the wall. It hurt.

The girl heard steps approach and felt her papa press her harder and harder against the steel wall. She could hardly breathe. Just as she was about to open her mouth to complain, she heard a popping sound and her papa fell down on his face on the floor. He lay there unmoving in front of her. When she looked up, the man with the scar was standing in front of her. He smiled.

Her mama threw herself forward and held on to her as best she could. The man just looked at them, then shouted something again and Mama shouted back.

"You don't touch her!" she screamed.

Then he hit her with the silver thing he had in his hand.

The girl felt how her mama's hands slipped down her tummy and legs until she lay on the floor with staring eyes. She didn't blink, just stared.

"Mama!"

She felt a hand on her upper arm as the man yanked her up. He held her arm tightly, pushing her ahead of him out of the container.

And as she left she heard the dreadful sound when they fired the silver things. They didn't have water in them. Water didn't sound like that. They shot something hard, and they shot straight into the dark.

Straight at Mama and Papa.

CHAPTER
SEVEN

Tuesday, April 17

Jana Berzelius woke up at five in the morning. She had had the same dream again; it never left her in peace. She sat up and wiped the sweat off her brow. Her mouth was dry from what she imagined was her shrieking. She straightened out her cramped fingers. Her fingernails had dug into the palms of her hands.

She had experienced the same dream for as long as she could remember. It was always the same images. It irritated her that she didn't understand what the dream meant. She had turned, twisted and analyzed all the symbols each time she fell victim to it. But that was no help.

Her pillow lay on the floor. Had she thrown it there? Presumably, as it was a long way from the bed.

She picked up the pillow and put it back against the headboard, then pulled the duvet back over herself. When she had lain there restless under the warm duvet for twenty more minutes, she realized it was pointless to try to fall back to sleep. So she got up, showered, dressed and ate a bowl of muesli.

With a mug of coffee in her hand, she looked out the window at the unsteady weather. Even though they were already halfway through April, winter still made itself felt. One day it was a cold rain, and the next it was snowing with a temperature of close to freezing. From her flat in Knäppingsborg, Jana had a view of the river and the Louis de Geer Hall. From her living room she could also see the people who visited the quaint shopping area. Knäppingsborg had recently been renovated, but the urban planners on the council had managed to retain the genuine feel of the place.

Jana had always wanted a flat with high ceilings, and when the first plans were approved for renovating the old buildings in the area, her father had put his name down to invest in a housing-association apartment for his then newly graduated daughter. As luck would have it, or thanks to a few phone calls, Karl Berzelius was given the opportunity to choose first. Of course she chose the apartment that was forty square meters larger than the others, with a total floor area of 196 square meters.

Jana massaged her neck. Her scar always became irritated by the cold weather. She had bought a cream at the pharmacy that the pharmacist assistant said was the latest on the market, but she hadn't noticed any improvement.

Jana draped her long hair over her right shoulder, exposing her neck. With a careful touch, she gently rubbed the cream into the carved letters. Then she covered her neck with her hair again.

She took a dark blue jacket out of her closet and put it on. Over that she buttoned up her beige Armani coat.

At half past eight she left the flat, walked to her car and drove in the smattering rain to the courthouse. She was thinking about the first case of the day, which concerned domestic violence. The proceedings would start at nine. Her fourth criminal case, the last for the day, probably wouldn't finish until half past five at the earliest.

It would be a long day, she knew that.

It was just after 9:00 a.m. when Henrik Levin and Mia Bolander entered the Migration Board offices. They checked in at reception and were given a temporary key card.

Lena Wikström, the secretary, was in the middle of a telephone conversation when they stepped into her outer office on the second floor. She held up her finger to signal that she would be with them in a few moments.

From Lena's office you could see straight into what had been Hans Juhlén's. Henrik noted that Hans's office looked tidy. The surface of the wide desk was uncluttered, with just a computer and a pile of folders next to it. Lena Wikström's space was quite the opposite. Papers were strewn everywhere, on the desk, on top of file folders, underneath ring binders, in trays, on the floor, in the paper-recycling box and in the wastebasket. Nothing appeared organized. Documents lay all around.

Henrik felt a shiver down his spine and wondered how Lena could concentrate in such chaos.

"That's that." Lena ended the call and got up. "Welcome."

She shook hands with Henrik and Mia, asked them to sit down on the worn visitors' chairs next to her desk and immediately started speaking.

"It's dreadful what happened. I still can't understand it. It's simply terrible. So terrible. Everybody's wondering who would do such a thing. I'm answering calls about Hans's murder all the time now. He *was* murdered, wasn't he? *Usch*, yes, it's simply too terrible, I must say."

Lena started to pick at her peeling nail polish. It was hard to say how old she was. Henrik guessed fifty-five plus. She had short dark hair and was wearing a light lilac blouse and earrings in a matching color. She almost gave an impression of elegance and affluence. If it hadn't been for the flaking nail polish, of course.

Mia took out her pen and notepad.

"I understand you've worked with Hans Juhlén for many years, is that correct?" she said.

"Yes, more than twenty," said Lena.

"Kerstin Juhlén said it was almost twenty."

"Unfortunately she doesn't really keep track of her husband. No, it's actually twenty-two. But I haven't been his assistant all that time. I had another chief first, but he retired many years ago and handed over to Hans. Hans was in charge of the accounts department before this position. We met frequently during that time since I assisted the previous chief."

"According to Kerstin, Hans was somewhat stressed recently, would you agree as to that?" Henrik said.

"Stressed? No, I would hardly say that."

"She was referring to the recent criticism that had been directed toward the department."

"Oh really? Yes, well, that of course. The newspapers wrote that we were bad at accommodating the flow of asylum seekers. But it's hard to know exactly how many will come. You just have to make an educated guess, a projection. And a projection is only that, after all."

Lena took a deep breath.

"Three weeks ago we received a large group of asylum seekers from Somalia and that meant work both before and after regular hours. Hans didn't want to risk more exposure in the local papers. He took the criticism seriously."

"Did he have any enemies?" said Henrik.

"No, not as far as I know. But you always feel a bit vulnerable in this job. There are a lot of emotions, a lot of people behave threateningly when they're not allowed to stay on here in Sweden. So if you think of it like that, then there are potentially a lot of enemies. That's why we have a security firm that always patrols here," said Lena. "But I don't think Hans felt he had specific enemies."

"Even evenings and nights?"

"Yes."

"Have you been threatened?"

"No, not personally. But the Board always has to think about security. Once a man poured gasoline over himself and ran into reception and threatened to set himself on fire if he didn't get a residence permit. They can be completely mad, those people. Yes, there's all sorts."

Henrik leaned back in the chair and glanced at Mia. She moved on to the next question.

"Is it possible to talk to the person from security who was here on Sunday?"

"This past Sunday? When he…"

"Yes."

"I'll see what I can do."

Lena picked up the phone, punched in a number and waited. Shortly after, the security firm promised to immediately send a Jens Cavenius who had worked all Sunday.

"So do you know if Hans had felt especially threatened in any way?" said Henrik.

"No," said Lena.

"No strange letters or phone calls?"

"Not that I saw, and I open all the mail… No, I haven't seen anything."

"Do you know if he had any contact with a child?"

"No. Not specifically. Why do you ask that?"

Henrik declined to answer.

"When he was here, late evenings and Sundays, do you know what he did?"

"I don't know exactly, but he was busy with paperwork and reviewed lots of documents. He didn't like the computer at all and wanted to use it as little as possible so I had to print out all documents and reports for him."

"Were you usually here with him when he was working?" said Mia and pointed at Lena with her pen.

"No, not on Sundays. He wanted to be by himself, alone, that was why he liked working evenings and weekends. Nobody was here to disturb him."

Mia nodded and wrote in her notepad.

"You said that certain persons can behave threateningly. Do you have a list of the names of all the asylum seekers that we can take with us?" said Henrik.

"Yes. Of course. For this year, or further back?"

"This year's list would suffice to start with."

Lena went into the database on her computer and ordered a printout. Her laser printer came to life and started delivering page after page with names in alphabetical order. Lena picked them up as they came out. After twenty pages, a warning lamp started to flash.

"Oh, how annoying, it's always going wrong," she said, and turned red in the face. She opened the paper tray which—to her surprise—was not empty.

"Oh, what's the matter now?" She pushed the tray back in. The printer made a noise but again the red lamp indicated that something was wrong.

"Apparatuses are best when they work properly, aren't they?" she said in an irritated voice.

Henrik and Mia just sat there in silence.

Lena opened the tray, saw that there was still some paper left and closed it again, this time with a bang. The printer started up, but no pages came out.

"Oh, why are you being so difficult!" Lena hit the start button with her fist and that got the printer to work. Embarrassed, she ran her fingers through her hair until all the pages printed out. Just then, the phone rang and in a short conversation the receptionist informed Lena that Jens Cavenius had arrived.

Jens Cavenius stood leaning against a pillar in reception. The nineteen-year-old looked as though he had just woken up. His eyes were red, and his hair was flattened on one side and untidy on the other. He was wearing a lined jean jacket and white Converse sneakers. When he caught sight of Henrik and Mia, he approached and stretched out his arm to shake hands.

"Shall we sit down?" Henrik asked.

He gestured toward a sofa and armchairs to the right of reception, which was surrounded by two-meter-high plastic Yucca palms. Some Arabic brochures were in a display on the white coffee table.

Jens flopped onto the sofa, leaned forward and despite his red-shot eyes, looked expectantly at Henrik and Mia. They sat down opposite him.

"You worked here on Sunday?" Henrik said.

"Yeah, sure," said Jens and clapped the palms of his hands together.

"Was Hans Juhlén here then?"

"Yep. I chatted a bit with him. He was the boss, like."

"What time was it then?"

"Perhaps around half past six."

Henrik looked at Mia and saw that she was prepared to take over the questioning. With a nod he let her do so.

"What did you talk about?" she said.

"Well, it was more like we said hello to each other. You could say," said Jens.

"Okay?" said Mia.

"Or nodded, I nodded to him when I went past his office."

"There was nobody else here then?"

"No, no way. On Sundays it's just dead here, like."

"When you went past Hans Juhlén's office, did you see what he was doing then?"

"No. But I could hear him using the computer keyboard. You know, you've got to have good hearing to be a security guard, so you can notice sound that might be weird or something. And my night vision is pretty good too. I was the best in the test in fact, in the selection. Not bad, eh?"

Mia was hardly impressed by Jens's senses. She raised her eyebrows to indicate ridicule and turned toward Henrik, whose gaze had fastened on one of the Yucca palms.

When she saw that Henrik appeared to be lost in thought, she thumped him on the arm.

"Hans Juhlén's computer?" she said.

"Yes?" said Henrik.

"He seems to have used it quite a lot."

"Yes, all the time," said Jens and clapped his hands.

"Then I think we should take it with us," said Henrik.

"So do I," said Mia.

CHAPTER
EIGHT

Police officer Gabriel Mellqvist was shivering. It was cold. His shoes were leaking and the cold rain trickled down from his cap onto his neck. He didn't know where his colleague Hanna Hultman was. Last he saw her, she was standing outside house number 36 ringing the doorbell. Together they had gone door-knocking at about twenty detached houses this morning. None of the residents had made any observations that were of any importance to the investigation. And not a single strange man or woman had been glimpsed. On the other hand, most people weren't even at home on Sunday. They had been at their summer cottages, on golf courses, at horse-jumping competitions and God knows what. A mother had seen a little girl go by, probably it was a playmate who was going home for the evening, and Gabriel wondered why she had even bothered to mention it to him.

He swore to himself and looked at his watch. His mouth was dry, and he was tired and thirsty.

They were clear signals that his blood sugar was too low. Even so, he went off to the next house which was behind a high stone wall.

Door-to-door canvassing was not his favorite occupation. Especially not in the rain. But the order had come from the very top of the criminal department and that meant it was best to do as he was told.

The gates were closed. Locked. Gabriel looked around. From here he could hardly see Östanvägen 204 where the murder had been committed. He pressed the intercom next to the gate and waited for an answer. Pressed again and added a "Hello!" this time. Gave the locked gates a bit of a push and they rattled. Where the hell was Hanna now? She couldn't be seen anywhere on the street. She couldn't have gone down one of the parallel streets. No, not without telling him first. She'd never do that. He sighed, took a step back and walked straight into a puddle. He felt how the cold water was sucked up by the sock in his right shoe. Oh great! Really great!

He looked up at the house again. Still saw no sign of life. He wanted most of all to give up and go off to the nearest lunch place and just get some grub. But then he saw something out of the corner of his eye. Something that moved. He screwed his eyes up a little in an effort to see what it was. A security camera! He pressed the intercom, shouted a few times to elicit an answer and managed in his enthusiasm to suppress the sensation of dizziness that gradually crept up on him.

* * *

Forty minutes and ninety-eight kronor later, Henrik Levin had eaten his fill. The Thai buffet had consisted of far too many tasty dishes. Mia Bolander had accompanied him, but chosen something lighter, a salad.

Henrik regretted his choice of lunch when he got back in the car again. He felt heavy and drowsy and let Mia drive to the police station.

"Next time can you remind me that I must have salad too," he said.

Mia laughed.

"Please?"

"I'm not your bloody mother! But all right, then. Does Emma want you to lose weight or what?"

"Do you think I'm fat, then?"

"Not your face."

"Thanks."

"She won't let you fuck her, is that it?"

"What?"

"I mean, you seem to want to go easy on the carbs, which means you want to lose weight. I read online that the biggest motivation for men to lose weight is that they want to have more sex."

"I was just talking about a salad. I just want to eat salad next time. What's wrong with that?"

"Nothing."

"Do you think I'm fat?"

"No. You're not fat. You only weigh eighty kilos, Henrik."

"Eighty-three."

"Sorry, eighty-bloody-three kilos, then. You're

a pudding, right! Why would you want to weigh any less?"

Mia winked provocatively.

Henrik remained silent and kept his real reason for wanting to eat lighter to himself.

Mia didn't need to know that seven weeks earlier he had embarked on a low-carb diet. He was also aiming to get more exercise on weekdays. But it was hard to keep to his new lifestyle choices, especially when Thai food tastes so much better with rice. After work it was simpler: home, eat, play, bath time, tuck into bed, TV, sleep. His time with his five- and six-year-old kids when he got home was pretty much routine. Admittedly, he hadn't actually asked his wife, Emma, if he could spend an hour, once or twice a week, at the gym. Hopefully she would say yes. But deep inside Henrik was afraid of what answer he would get. A firm *no*.

His wife already resented his spending too little time with the family.

But he felt that if he were in better shape, they would have better and more frequent sex. To him it was a win-win situation.

But those few times he had asked Emma for permission just to play football with the local club on a Saturday, he was turned down. The weekends were for the family, she said, and they should be out in the garden, visiting the zoo park, going to the cinema or just spending family time together. She felt she and Henrik needed to nurture their

relationship by spending more time cuddling together.

Henrik didn't particularly like cuddling. He
liked having sex. To him, sex was the greatest
proof that you loved your partner, he thought. It
didn't matter when or where you did it. Just that
you did it. That wasn't what Emma thought. For
her, it had to be pleasurable and relaxing, and you
needed lots of time and the right setting. Their bed
still remained her preference and then only when
the children weren't awake. Since Felix, who was
afraid of ghosts, insisted on going to sleep every
night between them in bed, their opportunities
for sex were few.

Henrik had to settle for the hope that things
would get better. This past month he had felt more
desire. And Emma had gone along with it too.
Once, at any rate. Exactly four weeks ago.

Henrik smothered a bit of heartburn. The next
time it would be only salad.

When Henrik and Mia entered the conference
room they were met by the news that police officer Gabriel Mellqvist had fainted while knocking on doors in Lindö. He had been found by an
elderly lady who had heard her doorbell ring a
number of times. But since she was confined to a
wheelchair, she couldn't hurry to the door. When
she finally opened it, she saw the policeman lying
on the ground.

"Luckily Hanna Hultman had come to his aid
and in Gabriel's pocket found a glucose syringe

that she jabbed into his thigh," said Gunnar. "That was the bad news. The good news is that we've found a security camera outside the lady's house. It is directed toward the street—it's positioned here."

Gunnar put an X on the map of the residential area that was hanging beside the time line posted on the wall.

The whole team was in the room. All except Jana, which pleased Mia.

"In the best case, the events from Sunday will still be on a server somewhere. I want you, Ola, to check that straightaway."

"Now?" said Ola Söderström.

"Yes, now."

He got up.

"Hang on," said Henrik. "I think you've got some more to do. We've confiscated Hans Juhlén's computer and need to go through it."

"Did the interview with Lena Wikström lead to anything?"

"She doesn't share Kerstin Juhlén's picture of Hans. According to Kerstin, Hans always worked on his computer. According to his secretary, Lena, he never did. I think it's a little odd that they would have such different impressions."

Ola, Gunnar and Anneli Lindgren agreed.

"Lena also didn't think that Hans Juhlén was as stressed as his wife claimed," said Henrik.

"But that's only what she says. I believe he was bloody worried. I would be too if there had been a lot of shit thrown at me in the newspapers and threatening notes too," said Mia.

"Exactly," said Ola.

"Lena said that there was always a security aspect concerning asylum seekers who weren't granted asylum. So we've asked for a list of all the people who have sought asylum so far this year," said Henrik.

"Fine, anything else?" said Gunnar.

"No," said Henrik. Going door-to-door hadn't produced much, except for the potential security footage.

"No witnesses?" said Mia.

"No. Not a one," said Gunnar.

"It's just bloody crazy. Didn't anybody see anything?" said Mia. "So we've got fuck-all to go on."

"For the time being we have no witnesses. Zero. Nada. So we'll have to hope that the security camera will give us something. Ola, check if we can get hold of the images right away," Gunnar said and turned to Ola. "Then you can go through Hans's computer. I'll see if the call logs from the provider are ready. If not, I'll phone and pester them till they are. Anneli, you go back to the crime scene and see if you can find anything new. Anything at all would do in the present situation."

At first the girl had cried hysterically. But now she felt calm. She had never felt like this before. Everything happened as if in slow motion.

She sat with her now heavy head bent over her thighs, her arms hanging limply from her sides, almost numb now. The engine in the van in which they were traveling growled weakly. Her thighs were stinging. She had wet herself when her captors had gripped her hard and pushed a needle into her arm.

Now she looked slowly up toward her left upper arm at the little red mark. It was really tiny. She giggled. Really tiny. Teeny weeny. The syringe was also really tiny.

The van jerked and the asphalt turned into gravel. The girl leaned her head back and tried to balance its weight so that she wouldn't bang herself against the van's hard interior. Or against somebody else. They were sitting tightly packed, all seven. Danilo, who was next to her, had cried

*too. The girl had never seen him cry before, only
smile. The girl liked his smile and always smiled
back at him. But now he couldn't smile. The silvery bit of tape was stuck hard over his mouth,
and he breathed in what air he could through his
dilated nostrils.*

*A woman sat opposite them. She looked angry.
Terribly, terribly angry. Grrrr. The girl laughed to
herself. Then she sank down again with her head
against her thighs. She was tired and most of all
wanted to sleep in her own bed with the doll that
she had once found at a bus stop. The doll with
only one arm and one leg. But it was the finest doll
the girl had ever seen. The doll had dark curly
hair and a pink dress. She missed her doll dreadfully. The doll was still back there with Mama and
Papa. She would fetch her later, when she came
back to the container.*

Then everything would be all right again.

And they would go back.

Home.

The security camera film had just arrived by mes-
senger from the security firm. Ola Söderström
opened the package and quickly inserted the little hard disk into his computer. He immediately
started looking through the images, which gave
a good overview of Östanvägen. Unfortunately
the rotating camera lens didn't reach all the way
to Hans Juhlén's house. Judging by the angle, the
camera must have been about two meters above
the ground, perhaps three, and provided an ad-
equate coverage so that you could register everything on the street. The quality was good and
Ola was pleased with the sharpness. He fast-for-
warded past Sunday morning. A woman with a
dog walked by, a white Lexus left the street and
then the woman with the dog came back again.

When the clock counter showed 17:30, he
slowed down the speed. The empty street looked
cold and windy. The overcast weather made it hard

to detect any movements and the street lighting was of poor quality.

Ola was wondering whether it was possible to adjust the brightness so that he could see the scene more clearly, when he suddenly caught sight of a boy.

He froze the image. The counter showed 18:14.

Then he let the recording continue. The boy cut across the street quickly and then vanished out of view.

Ola reversed the disk and looked at the sequence again. The boy was wearing a dark hooded sweater that hid his face well. He walked with his head down and both hands stuck inside the big pocket on his stomach.

Ola sighed. He rubbed his hand over his face and up through his hair. Just a child on his way somewhere. He let the footage continue and leaned back with his hands clasped behind his head.

When the counter showed 20:00, he still hadn't seen anything. No movement. Not a single person. Not a car had passed during those two hours. Only the boy. At that moment, Ola realized what he had seen. Only the boy.

He got up so fast from the chair that it fell backward onto the floor with a crash.

"You seem to be in a good mood."

Gunnar gave a start when he heard Anneli Lindgren's voice. She stood in the doorway with her arms folded over her chest. Her hair was tied back in a tight ponytail that accentuated her clear blue eyes and high cheekbones.

"Yes, I've just been promised the call logs," he said. "It helped when I made a fuss."

"Well now, is that all it takes to put you in a good mood?" said Anneli.

"Yes, it is, I can tell you. Shouldn't you be on your way?" Gunnar said.

"Yes, but I'm waiting for some support. It's a big house to work through. I can't get through it all on my own."

"I thought you liked working alone."

"Sometimes, sure. But you tire of it after a while. Then it's nice to have company by your side," Anneli said and tilted her head.

"But you don't have to go through everything again. Just take what's of interest."

"Well, that's obvious. What do you take me for, huh?" Anneli straightened her head and put her hand on her waist.

"And talking about going through things," said Gunnar, "I've been tidying in the storage room and found some stuff that belongs to you."

"You've been tidying the storage room?"

"Yes. What of it?" Gunnar said and shrugged his shoulders. "I needed to get rid of some junk and I found a large cardboard box with ornaments in it. Perhaps you'd like them back?"

"I can fetch them later in the week."

"No, better if I bring the box to work. Now, if you'll excuse me, I'll see if those lists have arrived as promised."

Anneli was just about to leave the room when she almost bumped right into a stressed Ola Söderström in the doorway.

"What is it?" said Gunnar.

"I think I've found something. Come and see!"

Gunnar got up from his desk and followed his colleague Ola into the computer room.

Ola, twenty years his junior, was tall and thin with a pointed nose. He was dressed in jeans, a red checked shirt and, like every other day of the year, a cap. Regardless of the temperature on the thermometer, be it minus or plus thirty degrees Celsius, he had his cap on. Sometimes it was red, sometimes white. Sometimes striped, sometimes with a check pattern. Today it was black.

Gunnar had told Ola many times that he should avoid wearing headgear during working hours, but he finally gave up because his irritating hat was trivial compared with Ola's skill with computers.

"Look at this." Ola pressed some keys and the recorded tape started to play. Gunnar saw the little boy on the film.

"He turns up at exactly 18:14," said Ola. "He cuts across the street and seems to be on his way up toward Östanvägen, toward Hans Juhlén's house."

Gunnar observed the boy's movements. Stiff. Almost mechanical.

"Play it again," he said when the boy disappeared from view.

Ola did as he was told.

"Freeze it there!" said Gunnar and moved closer to the screen. "Can you zoom in?"

Ola pressed some keys and the boy came closer.

"He's got his hands in that hoodie pocket. But the pocket is bulging too much. He must have something else in there," said Gunnar.

"Anneli did find the handprints from a child," said Ola. "Could it be this boy?"

"How old?" said Gunnar.

Ola looked at the figure. Although he was dressed in a large hooded sweatshirt, you could still make out the size of his body under it. But it was his height that decided the matter.

"I'd guess eight, perhaps nine," said Ola.

"Do you know who's got a child of that age?"

"No."

"Hans Juhlén's half brother."

"Shit."

"Zoom in closer."

Ola zoomed in another step.

Gunnar put his face right up to the screen so he could examine the bulging pocket better.

"Now I know what he's got in his pocket."

"What?"

"A gun."

Henrik Levin and Mia Bolander were driving from Norrköping toward Finspång. They sat in silence, deep in their own thoughts as they passed a road sign that told them they had five kilometers to go.

Henrik pulled over to the side of the road so he

could look up the address he wanted on the GPS navigator. The digital map showed that they had 150 meters to go to their final destination, and the navigator's voice told him to keep driving straight ahead at the next roundabout. Henrik followed the directions and approached the given address, which was in the Dunderbacken district.

Mia pointed to an empty parking space next to a recycling station that was overflowing with discarded paper and packages. Somebody had put an old radio in front of the green bins.

"So this is where he lives, the half brother," said Mia. She got out of the car, stretched and yawned out loud. Henrik got out and slammed the car door on his side.

A few people were standing and talking to each other in the grassy area between the low-rise apartment buildings. Nearby a couple of children played with a bucket and spade in a sand pit next to a set of swings. The chilly April weather had made their cheeks rosy. A man, presumably the father, sat on a bench next to them, fully occupied with his cell phone. A woman in an ankle-long winter coat was approaching them on the sidewalk with shopping bags in each hand. She stopped and said hello to a long-haired man who was unlocking a yellow Monark bicycle in a bike stand.

Henrik and Mia walked across the grass and looked for the right building number. They entered number thirty-four. A thinly-dressed man was standing in the entrance hall; he took a few steps to one side and walked back and forth, more or less as if he were impatiently waiting for somebody.

Mia glanced quickly at the list of residents next to the elevator and read the name for the third floor. Lars Johansson. Then they walked up the stairs and rang the doorbell.

Lars opened immediately. He was only wearing underpants and a pale football jersey adorned with the Norrköping team's emblem. He was unshaven and had dark rings under his eyes. While he massaged his neck, he looked with surprise at the two police officers standing in front of him.

"Are you Lars Johansson?" Henrik asked.

"Yes, what's this about?" said Lars.

Henrik introduced himself and Mia and showed his warrant to enter.

"And I was thinking that you came from one of those rags or something. Journalists have been running around here the last few days. But come in, damn it, come in! I haven't cleaned recently so keep your shoes on. Have a seat in the living room, I'll just go put some trousers on. I must go for a pee too. Are you willing to wait?"

As Lars backed away toward the bathroom, Henrik looked at Mia, who couldn't help shaking her head when they followed him down the apartment's hallway.

The bathroom was straight ahead and they could see Lars in it, picking out a pair of gray cotton trousers from the laundry basket. Then he closed the door and locked it.

"Shall we?" said Henrik and gestured politely toward Mia. She nodded and took a few steps more.

The kitchen lay to the left, and they could see it littered with piles of dirty plates and pizza cartons. A tied-up bag of rubbish sat in the sink. The bedroom that was across from the kitchen was rather small and contained a single unmade bed. The Venetian blinds were closed and Lego pieces of various sizes cluttered the floor. To the left of the bathroom lay the living room.

Henrik hesitated as to whether he should sit down on the brown leather sofa. A duvet in one corner made him realize that the sofa doubled as a bed. It smelled stuffy.

A flushing sound could be heard and Lars came into the living room wearing trousers that were five centimeters too short.

"Sit down. I'll just…" Lars pushed the pillow and the duvet onto the apricot-colored linoleum on the floor.

"There now, take a seat. Coffee?"

Henrik and Mia declined and sat down on the sofa, which made a hissing sound under their weight. The smell of sweat was pervasive and made Henrik feel a little queasy. Lars sat down on a green plastic stool and pulled his trousers up another two centimeters.

"Lars," Henrik began.

"No, call me Lasse. Everyone does."

"Okay, Lasse. First and foremost, our condolences."

"For my brother, yeah, that was bloody awful, that."

"Did it upset you?"

"No, not really. You know, we weren't exactly best buds, him and me. We were only half brothers, on our mum's side. But just because you're related doesn't mean that you spend lots of time together. It doesn't necessarily mean you even like each other, for that matter."

"Didn't you get on?"

"Yeah, or perhaps, hell, I don't know."

Lasse thought about it for a second or two. He lifted up one leg a little, scratched his crotch area and in doing so exposed a hole that was the size of a large coin. Then he started telling about his relationship with his brother. How it wasn't really good. That they actually hadn't had any contact at all this past year. And it was because of his own gambling. But he didn't gamble now. For his son's sake.

"I could always borrow money from my brother when things were really bad. He didn't want Simon to go without food. It's tough living on welfare and, you know, you've got to pay the rent and so on."

Lasse rubbed the palm of his hand against his right eye, then went on: "But then something strange happened. My brother became stingy, claimed that he didn't have any money. I thought that was bloody nonsense. If you live in Lindö then you've got money."

"Did you ever find out what happened?" said Henrik.

"No, just that he said he couldn't lend me anything more. That his old lady had put a stop to it. I had promised to pay him back, even though it wouldn't be for a while, but I promised anyway. But I didn't get any more money. He was an idiot. A stingy idiot. He could have done without a pricey steak dinner one evening and given me a hundred kronor, you might think. Couldn't he? I would have, if I were him, that is."

Lasse thumped his chest.

"Did you argue with him about money?"

"Never."

"So you've never threatened your half brother or exchanged harsh words, anything like that?"

"The odd curse word, perhaps, but I would never have threatened him."

"You have a son, right?" Mia went on.

"Yes, Simon." Lasse held out a framed photo of a smiling boy with freckles.

"Mind you, he's only five in that photo. Now he's eight."

"Have you got a better picture of him, a recent one?" said Henrik.

"I'll have a look."

Lasse reached toward a white cupboard with glass doors and pulled out a little box that was full of a jumble of stuff.

Sheets of paper, batteries and electric cables all tangled together. There was also a smoke detector, a headless plastic dinosaur and some sweet wrappers. And a glove too.

"I don't know if I've got a decent recent one.

The photos they take at school are so hellishly expensive. They charge four hundred kronor for twenty pictures. Who can order those? Bloody daylight robbery."

Lasse let the sheets of paper fall onto the floor so he could get a better look at the contents of the box.

"No, I haven't got a good one. But come to think of it, in my cell I might have one there."

Lasse disappeared into the kitchen and came back with an old-fashioned flip phone in his hand. He remained standing on the floor and pressed the buttons.

Henrik noticed that the arrow button was missing and that Lasse had to use his little finger to browse through the picture folder.

"Here," said Lasse, and held the cell toward Henrik, who took it and looked at the photo on the screen.

A low-res image showed a relatively tall and still freckled boy. Reddish cheeks. Friendly eyes.

Henrik complimented Lasse on his son's good looks, then told him to send the picture via MMS to him. Within a minute he had saved it in his image archive.

"Is Simon at school?" said Henrik when he put his telephone back in his pocket.

"Yes, he is," said Lasse and sat down on the stool again.

"When does he come home?"

"He's with his mum this week."

"Was he with you last Sunday?"

"Yes."

"Where were you between five and seven in the evening?"

Lasse rubbed his hands up and down his shins.

"Simon played his videogames."

"So you were both here, at home?"

He rubbed again.

"No. Only Simon."

"Where were you then?"

"Er…an early poker evening, you know, just down the block. You've got to join in when your mates ask you. But this was the last time. Absolutely the last time. Because, you see, I don't gamble. Not any longer."

ELEVEN

The man with the scar paced back and forth. He glared at them with a wild look in his eyes, as they stood there in a row, barefoot on the stone floor. The windows were covered but in one or two places a sliver of light shone in between the wall planks.

The girl's lips and cheeks ached from the glue of the silver tape they had slapped across her mouth. She had had difficulty breathing through her nose when they were in the van. Then, later, when they were pushed into the little boat, she had felt sick and been forced to swallow the vomit which had risen in her throat. The woman had ripped the tape off when they finally got to the big room, or hall, or whatever this place was.

The girl looked around without moving her head. Big beams supported the ceiling and she could see many spiderwebs. Was it a stable? No. It was much bigger than that. There were no rugs and no mattress to sleep on. It couldn't be some-

one's house. At least it didn't look like one, except
for the stone floor. The girl had a stone floor at
home too. But there the stones were always warm.
Here, they were icy cold.

The girl shuddered but immediately straightened up again. She tried to stand up as straight as
she could. Danilo, too, had pushed out his chest
and raised his chin. But not Ester. She just cried.
She held her hands in front of her face and refused to stop.

The man went up to Ester and said something
in a loud voice. She didn't understand what he
said. Nor did any of the other children. So Ester
cried even louder. Then the man raised his hand
and hit her so hard that she fell down backward.
He waved to the other two grown-ups who stood
by the wall. They got hold of Ester's arms and
legs and carried her out. That was the last time
she saw Ester.

The man walked slowly toward her, stopped,
then leaned forward until his face was only a couple of centimeters away from hers. With eyes cold
as ice, he said something in Swedish which she
later would never forget.

"Don't cry," he said. "Never cry anymore.
Never ever."

CHAPTER
TWELVE

Mia Bolander sat with the others in the conference room for the last briefing of the day. They were going over a number of question marks in the murder investigation of Hans Juhlén. The most important surrounded the boy whose picture was now displayed on the large screen.

Gunnar Öhrn had given high priority to the as-yet unnamed boy. He was either directly connected to the murder, or he was a key witness in the investigation. Regardless, he had to be found. That meant even more door-to-door canvassing to ask if anybody could identify the boy.

Mia was pleased that she had left that sort of drudgery when she was promoted. Questioning neighbors wasn't a challenge in the slightest. Absolutely nothing was exciting about it.

She was the first to help herself to the biggest cinnamon bun on the dish in the middle of the conference table. She was a competitive person, and could thank her elder brothers for that. In her childhood, everything had been about being first. Her brothers, who were five and six years older than she, had fought over who could do the most press-ups, who could race to the corner first and who could stay awake the longest. Mia struggled to impress her brothers, but they never let her win. Not even in something as silly as her memory.

So it had become natural for Mia to compete about virtually everything and this instinct had never waned. Since she had also been gifted with a decidedly volatile temperament, many of her classmates at school let her have her own way. Even in junior secondary school she had on several occasions been sent home for getting into fights with older pupils.

In her fifth year at the school, she had hit a classmate so hard that she drew blood. She could still remember the boy, her own age with a wide nose. He used to tease her and throw gravel at her during the PE lessons. He was also the only pupil who could run the 100 meter dash faster than she. He hadn't gone unpunished. After a lesson one day, Mia had kicked him so hard on his shin, he had to go to the school nurse and then on to the hospital to deal with a crack in his bone. That in turn had almost gotten her suspended, but she claimed it was an accident. The incident was noted on her school record by the headmaster, but Mia couldn't care less. She had run the fastest at the next PE lesson. That was all that mattered.

Mia gobbled up the rest of the bun. The granulated sugar fell onto the table and she scooped it all into a tiny mound, then licked her fingertip and used it to pick up the sugar and put it in her mouth.

Mia had almost no friends during her school years. When she was thirteen, her eldest brother died in a gang fight and she decided to go against the flow. At first she was forced to survive her tough suburban neighborhood where you were supposed to stick out as much as you could. Piercing, dyed hair, partly shaved head, no hair, tattoos, cuts, open wounds—nothing was alien. Not even for Mia, who herself had pushed a needle through one eyebrow just to fit in. But what distinguished her from the others was her attitude. She actually wanted to make something of her life. And with the help of her cocky attitude and her competitive spirit, she made it through school. She had decided that she wasn't going to be a loser like her brother.

Mia helped herself to yet another cinnamon bun, then she held the dish out to Henrik, who shook his head no.

By now they had already spent close to an hour discussing how the boy might be involved in the case. Ola showed a frozen image of the boy from the security camera file. He was slightly turned away, crossing the street.

With the help of the keyboard, Ola showed more, image after image. They appeared one by one at a slow pace. The team followed the boy's steps until the last thing to disappear was his hood.

Henrik picked up his cell and compared the images on the screen with that of Lasse Johansson's son, Simon. He remarked that any suspicions against Simon were now dismissed.

"The nephew is shorter, more muscular. The boy on the picture is thinner," he said.

"Let's see." Ola stretched to reach Henrik's phone and looked at the digital photo.

"And this Simon has reddish hair. I think our guy is darker. That's what it looks like, anyway," said Henrik.

"Okay, so we can forget Simon, but that still leaves the question—who is the boy? We must get hold of him," said Gunnar and moved on to the telephone log. Ola, who usually checked all the technical details, had been fully occupied with the security camera film so, to hurry the process along, Gunnar had chosen to check the lists himself. Now he pushed copies of the log into the middle of the table and let each of them take one.

Henrik took a gulp of coffee and looked at the first page.

"Hans Juhlén's last call was on Sunday at 18:15 to the Miami pizzeria. Ola?"

Ola got up and noted the call on the time line on the wall.

"The phone call has been confirmed by the pizzeria and they also confirmed that he picked up the pizza at 18:40. You can see the other calls on the next page," he said.

They all turned to page two.

"There weren't many," said Henrik.

"No, there are only a few. Most of them are to or from his wife. There is an outgoing call to a car service, but nothing remarkable about that," said Gunnar.

"What about texts?" said Mia.

"Nothing strange there either," said Gunnar.

Mia folded up the pages and threw them onto the table. "So what do we do now?"

"We must find that boy," said Gunnar.

"Do we know anything about the half brother?" Anneli wondered aloud.

"Not much. Mia and I just interviewed him. He is single, on welfare, he says, with some kind of shared custody of his child. And he is addicted to gambling," Henrik answered.

"Does he have a criminal record?" said Mia.

"No," said Gunnar.

"My instinct is that he isn't involved in the murder," said Mia.

"What do we think about Hans Juhlén's wife, then?" said Gunnar.

"I don't think she did it," said Mia.

"I'm not convinced either," said Anneli. "We don't have any witnesses or any decent technical evidence."

"Lasse said something interesting when we saw him. He mentioned that Hans claimed to be broke. He suddenly didn't have enough money to even lend Lasse a few kronor," said Henrik. "Since we know he had received some threatening letters, we can assume that somebody had a hold on him. Perhaps that's where the money went."

"Could Hans have had gambling debts too?" said Mia.

"Possibly, that could also explain why he seemed so stressed, at least to his wife, recently. Maybe it wasn't just the criticism his department was getting, but the threatening letters too."

"Right, we'll use that as a starting point. I want you to check his bank accounts. Ola, that's the first thing you'll do tomorrow morning," said Gunnar.

"What about the computer?" said Ola.

"The bank statements first, then the computer. Right, that's it," said Gunnar.

Henrik looked at the clock and swore to himself when he saw it was already half past seven. Overtime again. Emma would have finished dinner and the children would have already gone to sleep. Oh hell!

He sighed and drank the last of the coffee, which was now cold.

Henrik Levin tried to unlock the front door as silently as he possibly could. He opened it quickly, stepped into the hall and immediately nipped into the bathroom.

When he had finished, he washed his hands, then looked at his face in the mirror. The stubble had grown over the last three days, and it needed trimming more than he had thought. He felt with his right hand on his cheek and around his chin. He didn't want to shave now. A shower perhaps.

Henrik ran his fingers through his brown hair and noted a gray hair on his forehead. He immediately pulled it out and let it fall into the washbasin.

"Hi."

Emma poked her head into the bathroom. Her hair was clumsily done up in a bun on the top of her head. She was wearing a red velour jumpsuit and black socks.

"Hi," said Henrik.

"I hardly heard when you came in," said Emma.

"I didn't want to wake the children."

"How's your day been?"

"Okay. And yours?"

"Fine. I managed to paint the hall drawers."

"That's great."

"Yeah."

"White?"

"White."

"I thought I'd take a shower."

Emma leaned her head against the doorpost. A strand of hair fell onto her brow and she pulled it back behind her ear.

"What's the matter?" said Henrik.

"What?"

"It looks as if you want to say something."

"No."

"Are you sure?"

"Yes, sure."

"Okay."

"There's a good film on TV, I'm going to watch it in the bedroom."

"I'll come soon, just going to shower."

"And shave?"

"Yes, I'll shave."

Emma smiled and closed the door behind her.

Oh well, Henrik thought, and dug out his razor from the drawer. He'd be having a shave after all.

Fifteen minutes later, Henrik came into the bedroom with the towel wrapped around his hips. Emma seemed lost in some magnificent drama that had won more than one Oscar. Henrik feared he would be forced to watch the end of the tearful film. Fortunately there was no five-year-old in the bed.

"Felix?" he said.

"Asleep in his room. He has made a ghost drawing for you."

"Another one?"

"Yes," Emma answered without taking her eyes off the huge TV on the wall.

Henrik sat down on the edge of the bed and glanced at the couple entwined around each other on the TV. Felix was in his own bed. Now perhaps there might be a chance to...

He put the towel aside, slipped in under the warm duvet and snuggled up close to Emma. He put his hand on her naked tummy, but her eyes stayed glued to the film. He leaned his head against her shoulder and slowly stroked her thighs. He felt her hand on top of his, and they played with each other's fingers under the duvet.

"Emma," he said.

"Mmm-hmm."

"Darling..."

"Yes?"

"There's something I wanted to ask you."

Emma didn't answer. She studied the couple on the screen who were now united in a long, intense kiss.

"I've been thinking a little and you know that I'd like to start back at the gym. So I thought… if it's okay, that I…that I might go twice a week. After work."

Emma gave a start and for the first time took her eyes off the film. She gave him a disappointed look.

Henrik supported himself on one elbow.

"Please, sweetie?"

Emma raised her eyebrows. Then she demonstratively lifted Henrik's hand off her tummy.

"No," she answered briefly and returned to the end of the romantic story.

Henrik was still leaning on his elbow. Then he moved over onto his back with his head on the pillow and cursed himself. He knew better. He should have phrased his request in such a way that she couldn't say no. He stared up at the ceiling, then he puffed up the pillow and turned his back to Emma. Sighed. No sex today either. And it was his own damned fault.

It had just started snowing when Jana Berzelius and Per Åström decided to leave the local restaurant, The Colander. Per had suggested a restaurant dinner out to celebrate their judicial successes in a dirty divorce case, and Jana had finally given in. Making food alone was not exactly her favorite pastime, nor was it Per's.

"Thanks for this evening," said Jana and got up from the table.

"Happy to do it again soon. If you'd like to," said Per and smiled.

"No, I wouldn't," said Jana and refused to return his smile.

"That was a dishonest statement."

"Not at all, dear Mr. Prosecutor."

"It wasn't?"

"No."

"May I remind you that you appreciate my company?"

"Not one bit."

"A drink before we go?"

"I don't think so."

"I fancy something with gin. It'll have to be the usual. You?"

"No, thank you."

"Then I'll get two."

Jana sighed as Per vanished off to the bar. She reluctantly sat down and saw through the window how the snowflakes were slowly falling to the ground. She put her elbows on the table, leaned her chin against her clasped hands and looked across toward Per who was talking to the barman.

She caught his eye and he waved from the bar the way small children often do, by opening and closing his hand. She shook her head at him and then looked toward the window again.

The first time she met Per, she had just arrived at her new office at the prosecution department. Her boss, Torsten Granath, had introduced them to each other and Per had amicably told her about routine procedures at the office. He had given her some tips about good restaurants too. Also about music. And asked her questions about everything else that wasn't work-related. Jana had answered briefly. Some questions she hadn't answered at all. Per wasn't satisfied with the answer in the form of her sultry silence, and continued to ask various unnecessary questions. To Jana, Per's curiosity felt like a sort of interrogation and she had told him to stop. Then she briefly informed him that she did not like small talk. He had simply grinned at her, in a dreadfully stupid way, and from that day on their friendly relationship developed.

The restaurant was fully booked. The dining room felt rather squashed with all the winter coats, and the brown checkered floor was wet from the snow tracked in on the guests' shoes. The buzz of voices was loud and the clinking of glasses quiet. There were a few lamps and a lot of candles.

Jana's eyes left the window and were again drawn to the bar, past Per and on to the mirror shelf behind the barman. She looked at the selection on offer and recognized the labels like Glenmorangie, Laphroaig and Ardberg. She knew they were among the classics and were all distilled in Scotland. Her father was keenly interested in whisky and insisted on sipping a smoky sort at every family dinner. Jana's interest was limited, but she had been brought up not to say no to a glass when it was offered. She preferred a glass of white, from a well-chilled bottle of sauvignon blanc.

Per came back and Jana looked suspiciously at the large measures in the glasses he put down on the table.

"How strong?" she said.

"A single."

Jana glared at her dining companion.

"Okay, okay, a double then. Sorry."

Jana accepted his apology. She sipped her drink and made a face at the dry taste.

Somewhat later, when they had emptied the contents of the glasses, and Per had insisted on ordering two more, the conversation had turned into collegial bickering about morality and ethics in the world of law. After having discussed various stories about much-publicized cases and lawyers of doubtful reputation, the conversation turned to the problem of tired lay magistrates.

"I've said it before and I'll say it again, the lay-magistrate system should be radically changed. Instead of political nominees they should appoint people who are interested in law and justice," said Per.

"I agree," said Jana.

"You want people who are dedicated. After all, their votes on the magistrates' bench are decisive."

"Absolutely."

"Now two adolescents in Stockholm have lodged an appeal on the grounds that one of the lay magistrates had a snooze during the court proceedings."

"Yes, I heard about that."

"It's simply not acceptable that we have to incur the expense of a retrial just because a lay magistrate dozed off during the court hearing. He should be docked his pay. Unbelievable," said Per.

He took a gulp of his drink, then leaned across the table and gave Jana a serious look. Jana met his eyes. Serious too.

"What?" she asked.

"How are you getting on with the Hans Juhlén murder?"

"You know I can't say anything about that."

"I know. But how's it going?"

"It's not going at all."

"What's happening?"

"You heard what I said."

"Can't you tell me a little? Off the record?"

"Drop it."

"Is there some dirt there?"

Per smirked at Jana and his eyebrows went up and down.

"Bit of a dirty story there, right? There's usually some dirt when it's about bosses."

She rolled her eyes and shook her head.

"I interpret your silence as a yes."

"But you can't do that."

"Can't I? Cheers, by the way!"

CHAPTER

THIRTEEN

Wednesday, April 18

John Hermansson found the boy.

Seventy-eight years old and a widower for five years, John lived at Viddviken, a little village by the coast, five kilometers from Arkösund. The house was really too large for the single man and needed far too many hours of maintenance. But what kept him there was his love of the natural surroundings. Since his wife had died, he had trouble sleeping. He usually woke up very early in the morning and instead of lying in bed he would get up, regardless of the weather, and go for a long walk. Even on a chilly morning like this. He had stepped into his Wellingtons, pulled on his anorak and gone out. The sun had just started to rise and was spreading on the frosty grass in the garden. The air felt damp.

John passed the gate and decided for once to skip the forest and walk down to the sea instead. It was only a couple of hundred meters to the shore and the rocks facing Bråviken Bay. He walked down the narrow gravel lane to the water. The gravel crunched under his feet.

He followed the narrow lane that turned off to the right and after the two big pine trees he reached the sea. The water was like a mirror in front of him. That was unusual. There were usually high waves in the bay. John took a deep breath and could see it as he exhaled. Just as he was about to go back, he caught sight of something strange by the shore. Something silvery that glistened. He went closer to the ditch and bent down to look. It was a gun and it had blood on it.

John scratched his head. A bit farther away, the grass was red. But his eyes fastened on what lay next to that, under a fir tree. A boy. He lay with his face down with wide-open eyes. His left arm was bent at an unnatural angle and his head was covered in blood.

The nausea came quickly and John breathed heavily. His legs failed him and he had to sit down on a rock. He was unable to get up again, just sat there with his hand over his mouth and stared at the dead boy.

In his heart he knew that this horrific scene would be etched in his memory.

Forever.

The alarm reached the Norrköping Police at 05:02.

Thirty minutes later two patrol cars turned down the gravel lane at Viddviken. Another five minutes later the ambulance came for John Hermansson who was still sitting on the rock by the sea. A man who was delivering newspapers had noticed the old guy and asked him if everything was okay. He had pointed at the dead boy and then rocked back and forth and made a strange mumbling noise.

Just after 06:00 yet another police car turned down the lane.

Gunnar Öhrn had hurried across to the ditch closely followed by Henrik Levin and Mia Bolander. Anneli Lindgren came directly after them with a bag containing the tools necessary for a technical investigation of the finding place.

"Shot," Anneli noted and put on her latex gloves.

The boy's lifeless eyes stared at her; his lips were dry and cracked. His hooded sweater was dirty and discolored by the coagulated blood. Without a word she pulled out her mobile and phoned the medical examiner, Björn Ahlmann.

He answered after the second ring.

"Yes?"

"There's a job for you."

It couldn't be prevented. The news flash from the TT national wire service about a young boy having been found murdered near Norrköping spread at an incredible speed to all the media in Sweden, and the Norrköping police press officer had calls from a dozen journalists who wanted more details. Since it involved a minor shot to death, the entire nation was engaged, and on the morning TV shows various criminological experts expressed their views. They had found a weapon near the body. Many people assumed that the boy was from criminal circles, which sparked discussions about the level of violence among today's youth and its consequences.

When the phone rang with the news, it woke Jana Berzelius from her sleep. She got out of bed and decided to take a brisk shower to wake herself up. Since she had a bit of a hangover, she would much rather have stayed in bed. It was Per's fault. They ended up having three drinks, more than she could handle. And before that they had shared a bottle of wine with their meal and ignored the advice about drinking one glass of water for every glass of something stronger.

After the refreshing shower she took a pill for her headache and allowed herself a few moments, her hair still wet, to lie stretched out on her bed. She counted slowly to twenty, then got dressed, brushed her teeth and looked for a packet of peppermint-flavored gum. After that, she was ready for the meeting at the police station.

"We are here to summarize what we know about the boy who was found dead out at Viddviken this morning."

Gunnar used a magnet to put up the photo on the whiteboard before going on.

"Anneli, who is still out at the scene, said that the boy had been shot and that he died sometime between 19:00 and 23:00 on Sunday night. According to her, the broken vegetation indicated that the boy had been in movement and judging by the injuries to the body, he was shot from behind."

Gunnar took a sip of water and cleared his throat.

"At present we don't know whether the victim has other injuries or was sexually assaulted. The autopsy will show that and the medical examiner has given his word that he will put together a report as soon as possible. We hope as soon as tomorrow. The boy's clothing has been sent to forensics."

He got up from the chair.

"We are still combing the area around the murder scene, but as yet we haven't got any footprints or anything else from the perpetrator. The only thing that we are relatively certain about is that the dead boy at Viddviken is the same boy who was seen on that security camera footage from Östanvägen."

"And the murder weapon?" said Henrik.

"We don't know exactly yet. What we do know is that he was shot and a weapon was found near him. But the weapon has not been confirmed as the one that killed him. What we are certain about is that the weapon found near the boy was a Glock, and Hans Juhlén was killed..."

"...with a Glock." Henrik filled in the sentence.

"Exactly. The serial number is as yet unknown. I have sent the weapon to the national lab which will examine the bullets still in the gun. If they match those that killed Hans, we will have reason to suspect that this boy was somehow involved in Juhlén's murder. We've taken his fingerprints too."

"And?" said Mia.

"They matched. The handprints and finger-prints in Hans Juhlén's house match the boy's," said Gunnar.

"So he was there," said Mia.

"Yes. And my first guess says that he…"

"…is the murderer."

Jana mumbled the words and felt a creeping sensation along her backbone. She was surprised at her own reaction.

"…is the murderer, exactly," Gunnar made clear.

"But, what the hell, kids don't murder people. Not just like that. And especially not here in Norr-köping, not in Lindö. I think it's extremely un-likely that he could have done it, or done it alone," said Mia.

"Perhaps. But for the moment we don't have anything else to go on," said Gunnar.

"But then, what's the motive?" said Henrik. "Would a child send threatening letters to a head of department at the Migration Board?"

"It's up to us to find out whether the boy is the murderer or not. And we must find out who killed the boy," said Gunnar, breathing heavily.

"But who is the boy?"

"We don't know that yet either. Nor do we know why he was in Viddviken or how he came to be there. At any rate, he hasn't been lying in the water, that much is clear. He was on the shore but his back was turned against the sea," said Gunnar.

"He was running away from somebody," said Henrik.

"It seems so," said Gunnar.

"No tire tracks?" said Henrik.

"So far, we haven't found any, no," said Gunnar.

"So he came by boat, then. And the perpetrator must have been onboard," said Henrik.

"But we can't exclude the possibility that he got there by car or some other means," said Gunnar.

"Witnesses?" said Mia.

"None. But we are checking the entire coast from Viddviken to Arkösund."

"But still, who is he? The boy," said Henrik.

Gunnar took a deep breath.

"So far he isn't in any registry that we have. But, Mia, I want you to check through all cases of missing children. Check new ones as well as old, even those where the period of possible prosecution has expired. Get a photo of the boy and talk with the social services, check schools and youth clubs. We might have to ask the public for help," said Gunnar.

"Via the media?" said Henrik.

"Yes, but I'd rather not do that. There would be such a…how can I put it?…such a circus."

Gunnar went up to the map on the wall and pointed out the finding place.

"This is where the body was found. So we're looking for some sort of a boat or vehicle that passed Viddviken on the water between 19:00 and 23:00 Sunday night."

He moved his hand upwards across the map.

"We've put in a unit to go door-to-door there, and there's a dog patrol going over the immediate area."

"What shall we do about Kerstin?" said Jana. "If you can't get me more evidence, I'll have to release her early tomorrow morning."

"Perhaps she knows who the boy is?" said Mia.

"We must also ask her about her husband's financial situation," said Gunnar.

"Ola, make sure you have scoured his bank accounts. Private, savings account, investments, you name it. Check them all."

Ola nodded in response.

"Henrik, interview Kerstin again. We haven't finished with her. Not yet," said Gunnar.

FOURTEEN

It had hurt. She knew it would. She had heard it through the walls. But she didn't know it would hurt so badly.

One of the grown-ups had told her to follow him into the dark storeroom. There he had tied her hands behind her back and forced her head forward. With a sharp piece of glass he carved her new name on her neck. It said KER. From now on that was what she would be called, that was who she would become and remain so forever. While the man with the ugly scar gave her an injection, he had conveyed to her that she would never be hurt again, nothing would happen to her now. At the same time that the sense of calm spread through her body, a strength also grew within her. She didn't feel fear any longer. She felt powerful. Undefeatable. Immortal.

The grown-ups let her stay in the storeroom with her hands tied so that she wouldn't touch her *wound until it had healed. When she was finally let out, she felt weak and cold and had no appetite.*

The girl tried to see the carved letters in a mirror but she couldn't. She put her hand on the back of her neck. It stung; the skin was still sensitive. A scab had formed and the girl couldn't help fingering it, but then it started to bleed. She was angry with herself and tried to stop the bleeding by applying pressure with the sleeve of her sweater. But the red stains on the cloth grew larger each time she pressed it against her neck.

She looked at her arm in front of her. The stains were large and she turned on the tap and held her arm under it to try to get rid of the blood. But it didn't help, it only got worse. Now the sleeve was bloody and wet.

She leaned against the wall and looked up at the ceiling. The glow from the round lamp was weak and there were dead flies inside the glass globe. How would they punish her now? She wasn't meant to touch her neck. That's what they had said. The wound had to heal completely. If you touched it, it would look much worse. Ugly.

She slid down to the floor with her back against the wall. The break was soon over; she couldn't stay much longer in the toilet. How long had she been on the island? A month? Perhaps several months. The trees had at any rate lost all their leaves. She had thought that the golden-brown leaves were so lovely. At home she had never seen a tree that changed color like that. Every time she stood to attention in the yard, she wished she could cast herself into the piles of golden leaves. But she never could. She was only allowed to fight. All the time. Against the wiry boy Minos. And even against Danilo. He was bigger and stronger than she, so she hadn't been any match for him. He tried not to hit her too hard, but eventually he had to. If you didn't fight, you got beaten, beaten a lot, so Danilo hit her. At first he tried to be careful, a light thump and a slap. But then the man with the ugly scar had lifted him up so violently by his hair that he pulled some clumps out.

She had tried to defend herself; she had attacked Danilo with kicks and blows, but nothing helped. In the end Danilo had punched her so hard with his fist that he split her lip. It was swollen for three days. Then it was time for the next fight. This time she was pitted against another boy who was one year younger than her. When he deliberately aimed a blow at her painful lip, she became furious and slammed the boy on his ear so hard that he collapsed onto the floor. She kept on kicking and punching him until the man with the scar stopped her. Then he smiled. He pointed at his eyes, his throat and his crotch.

"Eye, throat, crotch," he had said. Nothing else.

The girl heard the bell ring. It was time for the next lesson.

She wrung out her wet sleeve as tightly as she could. The water dripped onto the floor and formed a little puddle. She stretched out her hand to rip off some paper and wiped up the water.

Then she got up and flushed the paper down the dirty toilet.

She rolled up her sleeve a little to hide the bloody stains, unlocked the door and went out.

Peter Ramstedt sounded grumpy when Henrik Levin phoned. His lawyerly voice was sharp and direct. Twice he repeated that he absolutely didn't have time to be present at a new interview with Kerstin Juhlén and especially not this afternoon at the time the chief inspector had proposed.

"Since my client is particularly anxious that I be with her and I am at the moment in court, it would be more suitable if we come in this evening or tomorrow morning," said Ramstedt.

"No," said Henrik.

"I beg your pardon?"

"No," said Henrik. "It is not suitable this evening or tomorrow morning. I don't know if you realize it, but we are in the middle of a murder investigation and we need to talk to Kerstin Juhlén now."

There was silence at the other end. Then the lawyer's voice could be heard again. He spoke extremely slowly and resolutely.

"And I don't know if you realize it, but as her legal representative I must be present."

"Fine, in that case you both better be here at eleven this morning."

Henrik ended the call.

At two minutes to eleven the lawyer came into the interview room to join Kerstin and the others. His face was bright red. He put his briefcase on the floor with a deliberate thud and sat down next to Kerstin. He gave Henrik and Jana an arrogant smile, put his cell phone in the pocket of his striped jacket. Then the interview began.

Henrik started by asking some direct simple questions about Hans Juhlén's financial situation, which Kerstin answered in a soft voice. But when he moved on to more specific details, she hardly had anything to say.

"Like I told you, I didn't have access to all of my husband's accounts and have no idea of the balance and thus could not say how much was in them." But she did say that his salary was transferred to a joint checking account and the payments on the mortgage and other maintenance costs came from that.

Hans had taken upon himself the responsibility for their financial situation as it was his salary that paid for their keep.

"He was the one who took care of everything," said Kerstin.

"As I understand, financially as a couple you were quite well-off?" said Henrik.

"Yes, very."

"But you said he wasn't one to waste money?"

"That's right."

"Was that why he didn't help his brother with money?"

"Has Lasse said that? That he didn't get any money from Hans?" Kerstin's voice had changed. The tone was high.

Henrik didn't answer. He stared at her pink T-shirt. The elastic of the round collar had loosened a little and a loose thread hung down from a sleeve. He had the urge to reach across the table and pull it out. How could she leave the thread hanging there, he wondered.

"He did get money from Hans," said Kerstin. "Far too much money. Hans wanted to help him but Lasse gambled it all away. Hans didn't want Simon to be affected, so in an attempt to help his young nephew, he transferred money directly into an account in Simon's name. But since Lasse was his legal guardian, he simply withdrew the money from the boy's account and lost it all on the horses. Of course my husband got angry and stopped sending any more. Perhaps that wasn't the best thing for the boy, but what could he do?"

"According to Lasse, it was you who stopped the payments," said Henrik.

"No, he got that wrong."

Kerstin put her thumb up to her mouth and started to bite a raw cuticle.

"He didn't receive any money recently, then?" said Henrik.

"No, not for the past year."

Henrik pondered this, then looked at Kerstin again.

"We're going to check into your accounts," he said.

"Why?" Kerstin met Henrik's gaze and continued biting her cuticle.

"To verify that what you've said is correct."

"You need permission," said Ramstedt, who had now leaned over the table.

"We've already arranged that," said Jana briefly and held out the signed search warrant.

Ramstedt snorted audibly, leaned back and put his hand on Kerstin's shoulder. She looked at him and Henrik noticed a nervous twitch from her left eyelid.

"Well then," said Henrik. "I have one more important question. This morning a boy was found dead. I have his photo here."

He placed two high-resolution images, one from the scene and one from the security camera, in front of her.

She gave the pictures only a quick glance.

"We must find the person who murdered your husband and that's what we are going to do, in the end," said Henrik. "But so far we have only one suspect and that is you. So if you wish to be released, you must try to think whether you have seen this boy anywhere near your house."

Kerstin sat quietly for a few moments.

"I have never seen him before," she said. "I promise, I've never seen him before. Never."

"Certain?"

"Absolutely certain."

Her headache had eased up. Even so, Jana Berzelius swallowed a second pill with a large glass of water. She had let the tap run quite a while before she considered the water cold enough.

When she was done, she put the glass down in the office sink and got to work. She had emails and calls to answer, and she was still waiting for two summonses to be approved. Now Yvonne had given her three more to deal with.

Torsten Granath stepped into the office kitchen and quickly went across to the cupboard and took out a coffee mug.

"A lot of work?" said Jana.

"Isn't there always?"

Torsten swung around to put the mug on the tray of the coffee machine, but in his eagerness he lost his grip and the mug fell.

In no time, Jana reached out with her right hand and caught hold of the mug before it hit the floor.

"Neat catch."

Jana didn't answer, just handed the cup over to her boss.

"Is that what you learned at that posh boarding school?"

Jana remained silent. Torsten was used to her taciturnity and now, carefully this time, made himself some coffee.

"If I can't even manage a cup of coffee, perhaps I should retire!"

"Or at least take things a bit more slowly," said Jana.

"No, I haven't time for that. How are you getting on with the Juhlén case, by the way?"

"I'll have to release his wife tomorrow," she said. "I've got nothing concrete to link her to the murder. That's going to please Ramstedt."

"That man! For him the law is simply business."

"And the women are his reward."

Torsten gave Jana a broad smile.

"I trust you," he said.

"I know."

Jana knew he meant what he said. He had trusted her from the very first day she came to the office. Thanks to excellent references from her trainee years, she got the much sought-after job as a prosecutor in Norrköping despite hard competition. That she was the daughter of the former Prosecutor-General Karl Berzelius might have contributed to her appointment. Her father, Karl Berzelius, had good contacts within the civil service in general, and Sweden's courts in particular. Jana had, however, managed all her university studies on her own. She had graduated in law at Uppsala University with the highest grade and her father would have felt proud when she was given her certificate. Or at least satisfied. She didn't know because he wasn't there. Instead, it was her mother, Margaretha, who told her daughter, "Your father sends his greetings and congratulations," as she handed over a bunch of carnations the color of port wine, then gave her a pat on the shoulder and a smile that said that Jana shouldn't expect more.

It had always been taken for granted that Jana would follow in her father's footsteps. To choose another career would have been unthinkable. She had heard that since she was a child. So she had also had hopes that Karl would come and congratulate her personally. But he didn't.

Jana scratched at her neck, then held her hands together over her chest. She looked at Torsten, who was still smiling, and wondered if he had had a call from her father. Karl Berzelius had retired two years earlier, but that didn't stop him from involving himself in Swedish jurisprudence. Especially concerning the cases where his daughter was the prosecutor. Twice a month he would phone Torsten and find out how she had done. This was something that her boss couldn't possibly object to. And nor could Jana.

Karl was like that.

Forceful.

Controlling.

Torsten's smile vanished from his face.

"Oh well, I must move on. I've got to go to the vet's at four o'clock. My wife is worried about Ludde. Thanks for catching the cup, that saved us having to buy a new one."

Torsten gave Jana a wink before leaving the room.

She remained standing beside the granite counter and watched him leave.

"You're welcome," she said quietly to herself.

* * *

The Juhlén bank account statements filled fifty-six pages. The bank official had been helpful and Ola Söderström had thanked him politely three times in a row.

Now he looked quickly through the sheets that showed Hans Juhlén's private account. On the twenty-fifth of every month a transfer of seventy-four thousand kronor was recorded from the Migration Board. Ola whistled when he read that impressive sum. It was a lot more than his salary of thirty-three thousand.

Two days later, on the twenty-seventh, a transfer was recorded from the same account of almost the entire balance. Only five hundred kronor were left, and that had been the pattern over the past ten months.

It was when he then started looking at the couple's joint checking account that he realized that something was wrong. That was where the money from Hans Juhlén's account had been transferred to. It wasn't in itself strange in any way. What was odd were the large withdrawals of forty thousand kronor. Once a month, that same amount had been withdrawn from the account and the withdrawals had taken place on exactly the same day of the month and at exactly the same branch.

Always on the twenty-eighth. Always at Swedbank. And always at Lidaleden 8.

The information about the large cash withdrawals reached Henrik Levin from Ola while he was in the elevator at the police building. The reception on his cell was poor, and so he had to concentrate to hear Ola's voice. He leaned against the lead-gray elevator wall and held his head at an angle so that the phone would be as high as possible. When that didn't help, he stood as close to the doors as he could. Eventually he got off the elevator and heard the message.

"So forty thousand kronor has been withdrawn from their joint account every month, on the same day and for the last ten months," he said when he stepped out of the lift.

"Yes, that is correct," said Ola. "The question is what was the money used for? To pay a person blackmailing him?"

"We'll have to find out."

Henrik ended the call, and fast-dialed Mia to ask if she wanted to come with him to visit a bank in the district Hageby.

"He's paid forty thousand a month? That's just incredible!" Mia said.

"Are you coming with me to Hageby or not?"

"No, I'm only halfway done here," said Mia and explained that it took time to go through all the current reports of missing children and adolescents. Contact with social services had led to nothing, and so far neither the residents at the Immigration Board's refugee centers nor the teachers in the junior secondary schools had recognized the boy. And if nobody could explain his identity by the end of the day, Mia would have to look farther afield and start in neighboring municipalities. In the best case she might find something there.

"But it could also be the case that this boy doesn't have any papers. That he comes from another country, and that he has come in without any contact with the Migration Board," said Mia.

"Yes, but he must have had some sort of contact since he was evidently inside Juhlén's house," said Henrik.

"True," said Mia.

Henrik walked out of the police building, unlocked his car, got in and started to drive. He was still on his phone, grateful that Sweden had yet to ban the use of cell phones while driving.

"Or perhaps it's simply a question of his parents not having noticed that he is missing. Perhaps they don't read the papers, and think their son is staying with a friend or a relative or something," Mia went on.

"Sure, but I think most parents know where their children are and would contact the police if they didn't come home in time. Wouldn't you?" said Henrik and stopped at a red traffic light at a pedestrian crossing.

A mother with two small children crossed in front of him. Both children took big steps so as not to touch the parts between the white pedestrian crossing lines. The blue bobbles on their caps bounced up and down with every step they took.

"Yes, I suppose I would, but not all parents react in the same way."

"No, you're right of course."

"But we can at least hope we soon get in a report of a missing boy. It would be very nice to
find out who he is."

"Or that we strike it lucky at one of the schools
that we still have to check."

Henrik ended the conversation, put the phone
down next to the gearshift and looked out of the
window. The mother and children had now crossed
the street and disappeared behind a house corner.

Henrik stroked the steering wheel and sighed,
his thoughts on the dead boy. It *was* weird that he
still hadn't been reported missing by anybody.
And even weirder was that his finger and handprints were found in Juhlén's house. Could pe-
dophilia be involved? A boy out for revenge who
wanted to kill the man who abused him? The
thought wasn't completely absurd, but it was unpleasant and he immediately dismissed it.

There was a lot of traffic on Kungsgatan and
Henrik drove slowly past Skvallertorget and on toward the park. He took the third exit at the roundabout and continued down Södra Promenaden.
The traffic got a bit lighter when he reached the
E22, and after a couple of kilometers he took the
exit toward Mirum Galleria.

The big parking deck was deserted, and when
he got out of the car his steps echoed against the
concrete slabs that surrounded him.

Ten minutes before closing, Henrik entered the
brightly lit Swedbank branch office. Three customers were waiting with queue numbers in their
hands. One bank official with back-combed hair

and a young look was helping customers; the other counters were closed.

Henrik showed his search warrant and was promised help if he could wait the ten minutes that remained of official hours of operation. So he sat down in an egg-shaped armchair, listened to an advertising jingle that insisted that everybody was welcome at H&M, which was located on the second floor of the mall. He studied the shoppers going past.

"Well now, Chief Inspector. Please come with me."

The bank official signaled to Henrik and showed him the way in behind the counter. They sat down beside a long table in a small conference room. The bank manager, a shortish woman in her fifties with a flowery red blouse, entered the room and joined them at the table.

Henrik explained why he was there.

"I'm grateful that you came to us in person. As you know, we are restricted by bank confidentiality. I spoke to your colleague earlier today," said the woman.

"Ola?"

"Yes, Ola, and we gave him all the details about the Juhlén account."

"I know, and it was clear that Hans Juhlén withdrew forty thousand kronor every month here, at your bank. It is extremely important that we can ascertain why he withdrew such a large amount of money."

"We rarely ask what customers are going to use

their money for, but we are most restrictive when it comes to large cash withdrawals. Customers who want to withdraw more than fifteen thousand in cash must notify us in advance."

"I understand, but in that case Hans Juhlén must have given you advance notice many times," said Henrik.

"No, he wasn't the person who did it," said the woman.

"Well, who, then?"

"It was his wife, Kerstin Juhlén."

CHAPTER SIXTEEN

Gunnar Öhrn was listening to the reporter on the car radio who announced that after an upcoming item about the history of a Swedish charity organization, he promised to play a legendary track. When the first notes came out of the speaker, Gunnar immediately recognized the voice of the singer and he drummed on the steering wheel in time to the lovely rock music.

Bruce Springsteen.

"The Boss. Oh yeah!" he called out.

Gunnar turned up the volume and drummed even harder to the refrain.

He sneaked a glance at Anneli Lindgren, who was sitting next to him in the passenger seat, to see if she was impressed by his solo on the wheel. But she wasn't. She closed her eyes and leaned her head against the headrest.

It was half past three in the afternoon. For the last ten hours she had worked at the murder scene out at Viddviken. When Gunnar had arrived, she had been standing there in wading boots with the water up to her waist. She walked back to the shore to meet him.

"How are you getting on?" Gunnar had asked.

"I've got some water samples," Anneli answered and unfastened the shoulder straps before pulling off the waders. "We've combed through the area. Not even worth thinking about shoe prints as it seems a whole lot of people walk across here."

"Have you dragged the bay?"

"Twice, but no other weapon."

"And the bullet? Did you find it?"

"Yes. And we also found something interesting. Come, I want to show you something."

Gunnar had followed Anneli away from the bay up to the gravel road. After twenty meters, she had turned off from the heavily compacted track and stepped out into the grass edging, carefully bending back some undergrowth in front of her. Gunnar then leaned forward to see what she wanted to show him. A smile immediately spread across his face.

Tire tracks were visible on the ground.

And they were deep.

Anneli had been exultant to discover the tracks. Now she sat in Gunnar's passenger seat and said nothing.

Gunnar turned the volume down. "Tired?" he said.

"Yes."

"Can you manage a briefing? I've called in everybody for 4:00 p.m."

"Sure."

"I can give you a lift home after."

"That's kind, but I've got to get my car home. Adam has his football practice at eight o'clock. Have you forgotten?"

"Oh Christ, yes, of course today is Wednesday."

Gunnar leaned his elbow against the window and put his index finger under his nose.

"But I can give him a lift too. I mean, if you want me to. We can all go together," he said.

"Yes, if you'd like to…that'd be nice."

Anneli rubbed under her eyes.

"Oh no," said Gunnar and put his hand on his forehead.

"What's the matter?" said Anneli.

"I've forgotten it again. The big box in the attic."

"It's not a big deal."

"But it's the last box with your things."

"Well, if it's been up in the attic until now perhaps it can stay there a bit longer."

"This evening I'll put it right next to the front door. Then I'm absolutely bound to remember to take it with me."

"Good idea."

There was silence for a few seconds.

"Nice that you're coming along with us this evening. Adam will be happy," Anneli said.

"I know," said Gunnar.

"I'll be happy too."

"I know."

"Won't you be happy?"

"Anneli, stop it. There's no point."

"Why isn't there?"

"Because."

"Have you met somebody?"

"No, I haven't. But we've decided to have it like this now."

"You've decided, yes. Not me."

"Okay, this time it was me. I really want it to be like this now. I think things are okay between us. That we keep it on a good level, I mean."

"On your level."

"What do you mean by that?"

"Nothing."

"I was just trying to be friendly by giving you and Adam a ride, what's wrong with that?"

"You don't have to give us a ride. We can manage well without your help."

"Okay, let's skip it, then."

"Yes, let's do that."

"Fine."

"Fine."

Gunnar muttered something, and turned up the volume on the radio just in time to hear the last tones of that damned rock track fade away.

Anneli walked a few steps behind Gunnar down the corridor. Her lips were pursed as she glared at his back. She knew that he felt her gaze, so she glared a bit harder just for the sake of it.

Gunnar stopped a moment by his office.

Anneli noticed a fax from the National Forensic Lab, SKL, in his in-tray. Probably important. But she didn't say anything, just walked straight on. She was well aware that he would immediately read the fax anyway. She went down the corridor, still with a grumpy look on her face. But as soon as she entered the conference room she straightened up and switched off her private side.

Since Anneli and Gunnar chose never to discuss their relationship with anybody, they never showed their feelings openly either. They'd been a couple before she was employed by the criminal investigation unit in Norrköping, where Gunnar was the senior officer. When the position of criminal technician was advertised on the police intranet, Anneli had compiled her CV, with her experience at SKL in Linköping, and sent in the application to the head of the department as stated, who in this case happened to be her lover. Anneli had not seen any obstacles to working together with her life partner.

Gunnar, for his part, found himself in a dilemma, and first considered setting Anneli's application aside because of a possible conflict of interest. But since Anneli's professional experience outshone that of all the other applicants, Gunnar's decision to employ her made the most sense. The fact that Gunnar and Anneli had kept the relationship secret made his decision easier, and they decided to continue to be as discreet as possible in their professional life.

But the rumor of their relationship spread anyway and some malicious gossip circulated that Anneli had landed the job by sleeping with her boss. It didn't make any difference that she had a unique talent for discovering out-of-the-ordinary evidence, such as broken vegetation or a faint tire track that others would miss. The only thing certain coworkers chose to see was that she was in a relationship with her boss.

What many people didn't know, or couldn't be bothered to find out, was that Anneli and Gunnar had an on-and-off relationship. For the sake of their son they had attempted to live together, but when the boy turned ten years old last month, they agreed to call it quits. Their commitment wasn't strong enough to stay together as a couple. Their emotions were like a roller coaster; all told they had moved in together and then separated seven times. The last stint of living together had lasted ten months. Recently it was Gunnar who told Anneli he wanted a break.

Anneli pushed aside all thoughts of Gunnar now as she said hello to Mia and Ola, who were sitting at the table.

Mia immediately said, "A witness has seen a white van at Viddviken."

Anneli was going to answer when Gunnar rushed in. He was holding the fax from SKL in his hand.

"They've identified the fingerprints on the threatening letters," Gunnar said excitedly. "Where's Henrik?"

"He's interviewing Kerstin again. Evidently she has lied about a lot of money," Ola quickly replied.

"That's not the only thing she has lied about. I must get hold of Henrik right away!"

Peter Ramstedt's neck was bright red as he stepped into the interview room for the second time that day. The lawyer swung his briefcase up onto the table, grabbed a notepad and pen out of it and then dropped the case to the floor. He unbuttoned his jacket with both hands and swept the two sides back like a cape before settling down on the chair. Now he sat there with his arms crossed and clicked his pen incessantly with his right thumb.

Henrik Levin smiled vaguely to himself. He had the trump card in his hand. The statements from the bank staff were very important, but it wasn't until Gunnar phoned him that the last bits of the puzzle had fallen into place.

"I'd like to ask you…" Henrik said to Kerstin Juhlén, who was sitting with her shoulders hunched and yellow plastic slippers sticking out under the table, "…do you normally shop with cash or a bank card?"

Kerstin stared up at him.

"Card."

"You never use cash?"

"No."

"Never?"

"Well, on the odd occasion perhaps."

"How often would you say?"

"I don't know. Once a month, I should think."

"Where do you withdraw your cash from?"

Ramstedt continued to click his pen.

Henrik wanted to grab the pen off him and squirt the ink onto the lawyer's red tie.

Kerstin interrupted his thoughts.

"Well, when I need to, I use an ATM."

"Which ATM?"

"The one in Ingelsta, next to the café."

"Do you always go to the same one?"

"Yes."

"How much money do you usually get out?"

"Usually five hundred kronor."

"You don't go to a bank teller to withdraw money?"

"No, never."

Kerstin put her little finger up to her lips and bit at her nail audibly.

"So you have never visited a bank?"

"Well, yes, of course I have."

"When did you last visit a bank?"

"Perhaps a year ago."

"What did you do when you went?"

"Perhaps it was even longer ago. I can't really remember."

"So you haven't been in a bank since then?"

Silence.

Henrik repeated the question: "So you haven't been in a bank since then?"

"No, I haven't."

"Strange," said Henrik. "We have two witnesses who can confirm that you have been seen at the bank in Hageby."

Ramstedt stopped clicking.

For a few moments there was silence.

Henrik could hear his own breathing.

"But I haven't been there," said Kerstin anxiously.

Henrik got up and walked to one corner of the room. He stood underneath a camera fastened to the ceiling and pointed at it.

"In all bank premises they have cameras like this, which register all customers who come and go."

"Hang on a moment," said Ramstedt, getting up too. "I need to have a few words with my client."

Henrik pretended not to hear him.

He returned to the table and looked straight at Kerstin.

"So I ask you again. Have you been to the bank at Hageby?"

Ramstedt quickly put his hand on Kerstin's shoulder to stop her from answering.

But she answered anyway.

"Perhaps, I may have."

Henrik sat down on the chair.

"For what purpose were you there?"

"Withdrawing money."

Ramstedt let go of Kerstin's shoulder, sighed and sat down again.

"How much money did you withdraw?"

"A few thousand. Two, perhaps."

"Stop lying now. You have withdrawn forty thousand kronor from your joint savings account each month for the past ten months."

"Have I?"

"As I said, I have two witnesses, Kerstin."

"Don't answer," Ramstedt urged her, but again Kerstin ignored him.

"Well, then I must have, mustn't I," she said quietly and with that response, her lawyer lost his control and threw his pen across the room.

Henrik instinctively ducked even though the pen passed by him at a distance. It hit the door and fell to the floor. Henrik looked at Ramstedt, then smiled to himself. He said nothing, which he knew would irritate the lawyer more than any verbal response. Instead he calmly returned to the subject.

"What did you want the money for?"

"Clothes."

"Clothes?"

"Yes."

"So you have shopped for clothes for forty thousand kronor a month?"

"Yes."

"I don't mean to be offensive, but for that much money I think you can buy considerably better clothes than a T-shirt and some plastic sandals."

Kerstin quickly pulled her feet in under the table.

"For the last ten months either you or your husband have been receiving threatening letters from somebody," he said.

"I don't know anything about that."

"I think you do."

"No, I don't. I swear. It was you who told me about the letters."

"So you have never seen the letters? Never touched them?"

"No, no, no! I haven't. I haven't."

"Okay. But now you are not telling the truth again. The fact is, we have analyzed the letters and found fingerprints on them."

"Oh yes?"

"And they are your fingerprints."

Kerstin started looking around nervously.

"May I say what I believe is the truth?" said Henrik. "I don't think you've bought clothes with that money. I think you have taken the money and given it to the person who sent the threatening letters. There were ten threatening letters and you have withdrawn a large sum of money ten times."

"No... I haven't..."

"Now you disappoint me, Kerstin. Tell the truth now. Tell us what really happened."

Ramstedt got up, adjusted his jacket and went to pick up his pen by the door. Behind Henrik's back he tried, with the help of body language, to get Kerstin to not say another word. But her shoulders were already sunk.

She swallowed.

And started telling her story.

All of it.

Henrik lingered in the interview room and stared for a minute. The interview was over, but he was still thinking. He replayed the sequence in his head. When Kerstin's lip started to tremble.

When she dried the tears on her cheeks. When she described what her husband had done.

"I don't think I ever really knew him. He was always absent in some way. He always has been… I knew that something was wrong. I knew it when he wanted me to have a pillow or something over my face when we had sex. He insisted, otherwise he would feel sick to his stomach, he said."

She sobbed.

"That was at the beginning, when we were just married. He did such strange things. I could wake up in the middle of the night and he'd be just laying there, staring at my breasts. And when he saw I'd woken up, he'd shout at me that I was a stupid fucking cunt and then he pushed in his…his…"

Kerstin couldn't get the words out. She wiped the snot from her nose on her sleeve.

"He pushed his penis so far down my throat that I'd choke and couldn't breathe. When he was finished, he said I was disgusting, that he had to go and wash himself after having been with his ugly wife."

Kerstin cried for a while, then eventually calmed down. She was silent for a while, then she started to carry on again.

"He never really wanted to sleep with me. But I thought it would get better. I told myself someday everything would get better, that it was all simply too much for him, his work I mean, and that I should feel sorry for him. But then he started to have sex with other women…and girls. He started… They must have been afraid, they must have been afraid of him. I just don't understand how he could, I…"

She cried straight out.

"He told me once how one woman screamed when he raped her on the floor. How the panic in her eyes grew when he penetrated her. How he laughed when she started to bleed from her behind. And then he'd… She was bleeding…and he…down her throat…"

Kerstin covered her face with her hands and put her head on the table.

"Oh God…" she cried.

Henrik could still hear her crying although he was now alone in the room. He looked out of the window and stared at the pale gray light. Then he got up. In half an hour, he had to be in the conference room with the team. He had to compose himself.

Henrik Levin walked slowly up the flights of stairs at the police headquarters and continued down the long and empty corridor on floor three to the conference room. He didn't look at the mail cubbies or the paintings, nor did he look in through the open office doors. He kept his gaze directed downward toward the floor and a little in front of him.

Gunnar Öhrn noted Henrik's expression and asked if he wanted to delay the briefing for an hour. But Henrik insisted on reviewing with the team the most important parts of his last interview with Kerstin. He remained standing in front of the table and his colleagues.

"Threatening letters were directed at Hans Juhlén," he began. "Hans Juhlén had sexually abused several female asylum seekers, and in return they were promised permanent residence permits. But they were never granted said permits. On one occasion he treated a young girl extremely badly, and she decided to tell her brother about him. When the first letter arrived, Kerstin realized it was written by the brother. She knew because Hans Juhlén was in the habit of boasting about his so-called conquests. About how naive the girls were. About how they had cried when he had forced them to have sex."

Anneli Lindgren felt so uncomfortable hearing this information she was squirming by the time Henrik took a short break. Then he continued.

"Kerstin made sure that Hans never saw the letters. It was she who had opened them first. She had considered going to the police to bring an end to the rapes. The only right decision would have been to get divorced, but she didn't know who she would be without her husband. Who would look after her? She didn't have any money of her own, no way to support herself. And if the story got out, it would be the end of her husband's career and then she, too, wouldn't have any money to live on. Besides, everybody would scorn her for having been married to a rapist. So she had decided to hide the letters and pay. For silence," said Henrik.

"How can you protect somebody who treats you so badly?" said Mia.

"I don't know. Hans Juhlén was really a nasty bastard. According to Kerstin, he more or less bullied her. It all started twenty years ago when he found out that she could never have a child. He reminded her of that every day. He crushed her."

"And she let him do it?"

"Yes."

"But didn't he discover that the money had been withdrawn from the account?" said Gunnar.

"Oh yes. He had asked her about the withdrawals, but Kerstin lied and said they were for purchases for their home or for a bill or a repair that must be paid. He had gotten angry, a big argument followed and he hit her. But she never changed her story. And after a while, even though her excuses never made sense, he lost interest in it and in his wife. In any event she says he stopped asking her about it," said Henrik.

"Who did the threatening letters come from?" said Mia.

"A Yusef Abrham from Ethiopia. He lives in Hageby and he shares a flat with his sister. That was why Kerstin always withdrew the money there. We'll talk to him straight after this meeting. Is it okay if I…" Henrik pointed at an empty chair.

"Of course, sit down," said Gunnar, who was used to Henrik's tactfulness. Even so, Gunnar added: "You don't need to ask permission to do that, surely?"

"No, you can just bloody well sit down," said Mia.

Henrik pulled out the chair and sat down. He immediately opened a bottle of mineral water and poured half the contents into a glass and drank it. The bubbles tickled his palate.

Jana Berzelius had been sitting in silence, observing, at the short end of the table.

She crossed her legs and said, "Has Kerstin confessed to anything else?"

Henrik shook his head.

"We still don't have anything concrete that links her to the murder, which means I must let her go."

"Kerstin did of course have every reason to want to see her husband dead, given how he had treated her. They might well have argued and she pulled out a gun and shot him," she said.

"But the gun? Where would she have gotten that from? And after shooting him, would she have given it to a child who climbed out through the window? And who would that child have been?" said Henrik.

"I don't know. Think of something yourself then!" Mia hissed.

Henrik gave her a tired look.

"Okay, now let's calm down. Jana's right, we have to release Kerstin, at least for now," said Gunnar.

"What about Lasse Johansson?" said Jana.

"He's of no interest any longer, his alibi has been confirmed by several people."

"So at the moment all we have is the boy and this Yusef Abrham?"

"And whatever is on Hans Juhlén's computer," said Gunnar.

"Right," said Ola Söderström. He shifted his weight on the chair. "It's going slowly but I've checked the hard drive. The strange, or rather revealing, thing is that someone tried to delete it."

"Delete it?" said Mia. "But you can retrieve that, can't you?"

"Absolutely, you can. Documents and cookie files can be recovered, that's no problem. As long as they haven't been bombarded with EMP."

Ola Söderström saw the questioning expressions of the team.

"That's electromagnetic pulse. It knocks everything out. There are firms that do that."

"There must have been something he wanted to hide," said Henrik.

"Perhaps. We'll have to see what I can get out of it."

CHAPTER SEVENTEEN

"I told you it was dirty."

Per Åström gave Jana Berzelius a wide smile.

They happened to have bumped into each other outside the prosecution authority's office, decided to skip the office coffee and go to the bakery café instead. The walk there had taken five minutes and luckily there was no line at the counter. Jana wondered whether she was hungry enough for a ham-and-cheddar on sourdough. In the end they had each ordered a cup of coffee and scones with jam, and then gone and sat beside the window.

The interior was typical of modern Scandinavian design, and it felt a bit like sitting in a hotel lobby. Black leather chairs were squeezed into round oval oak tables. Armchairs with high backs stood in pairs in the corners. Lamps of different sizes in black-and-red cloth hung from the ceiling, and a pleasant aroma of newly baked bread permeated the room.

"I regret I said anything to you about the investigation," Jana said to Per.

She had told him in confidence about Hans Juhlén's darker side.

"Actually it's rather fascinating. After all, just think what it'll be like when the media get wind of the fact that the boss at the Migration Board has abused asylum-seeking women and girls," Per said and smiled.

"If you don't keep your voice down, the papers will find out extremely quickly."

"Sorry."

"It's a complicated investigation."

"But tell me more?"

"Not a word to anyone about what I say." Jana gave Per a piercing look. "Okay?"

"I promise."

"Now listen. Hans Juhlén was shot. In his house the police find handprints with fingerprints from a child. The same child is found shot to death with a gun that turns out to be the same type of gun that killed Hans Juhlén. And then this business with the girls…"

"The dirty…"

"Call it what you like. But can you explain to me how it all fits together?"

"No."

"Okay, thanks."

"You're welcome."

Jana lifted the coffee cup up to her lips. She looked at Per, at his stylish shirt and blazer and trim-fitting trousers. So well dressed. Per had

been single for as long as she could remember.
He had a couple of longish relationships behind
him but didn't really feel comfortable living with
anyone.

"Better alone on your own, than alone in a relationship," he had said a couple of years ago.

Jana knew that his work and his commitment
to working with adolescents took up all his time.
It was not in her interest to try to interfere with
anybody's life. Not even Per's.

Even though the conditions at times might have
been right, things had never clicked between them.
For Jana, Per was merely a friend and a colleague.
Nothing more.

"I need your help," said Jana and put her coffee cup on the table.

"But I don't know how everything fits together," said Per.

"I don't mean with the investigation. I need to
switch work days with you."

"Why?"

"Dinner with Mother and Father on Tuesday,
the first of May holiday."

Per angled his head to one side and whistled.

"Fine, that's fine."

"I'll give you a nice bottle of wine as compen-
sation. Red or white?"

"Neither. I'll do it for you if you tell me more
details about that filthy man Hans. I'm thinking of
selling the story myself. I can get a bundle for it!"

"You're just hopeless."

Jana forced a smile and took a bite of her scone.

* * *

Makda Abrham saw them coming from the kitchen window. She knew right away it was about that man at the Migration Board. She had anticipated that this day would come when she would be forced to tell them all about the evil that she had been subjected to.

The worry grew in her tummy and when she opened the door the pressure was so hard on her diaphragm that she had to support herself against the wall. She couldn't really grasp the names of the police officers and she didn't even look at the ID cards they showed.

"We're looking for Yusef Abrham," said Henrik and put his ID away. He studied the woman in front of him. Young, perhaps twenty, dark eyes, slim face, long hair, a cloth bracelet and a sweater with a low neckline.

"Why?" she said.

"Is he at home?" said Henrik.

"Me…sister. Why?"

Makda found it hard to formulate the words. Why her brother? Weren't they going to talk with her? Why did they want to talk with Yusef?

She swept her dark hair behind her ear and revealed a long row of pearls on her earlobe.

"We just want to talk with him about Hans Juhlén."

The policeman said his name.

The name of the filth.

Of the revolting man whom she hated above all else.

"Yusef? Police!" Makda called out into the flat.

She stepped aside and let Henrik and Mia enter the ground-floor apartment, and then she moved to the left. She knocked carefully on a closed door.

Henrik and Mia waited in the hall.

There was a traditional Swedish woven mat on the hall floor and an empty yellow hat rack on the wall. On the floor were three pairs of shoes, two of them white and presumably newly purchased sneakers. They were of a well-known brand and Henrik knew that they were expensive. Otherwise there was nothing in the hall, no drawers, no pictures or anything to sit on.

Makda knocked again on the closed door and said something in a language that Mia thought sounded like Tigrin.

She smiled at the police officers as a sort of apology, and knocked again.

In the hallway, Henrik and Mia decided to step in and help Makda, who seemed to be growing more and more anxious. They walked into the apartment and stood beside her at the bedroom door. From there they could look right into the kitchen, which had its own back door. A fan was on and an ashtray on the table was full of cigarette butts. In the other direction was a bathroom, a second bedroom and a living room. There was almost no furniture at all.

"Yusef, open the door. We just want to talk with you a little."

Henrik banged on the bedroom door but there was no answer.

"Open the door now!"

He banged harder. Several times.

Then he heard a creaking sound from inside the room.

"What was that?" Mia wondered out loud, having also reacted to the creaking sound.

"It sounded like a window that…"

That very same moment she caught sight through the kitchen window of a dark-skinned, barefoot man moving quickly through the back-yard.

"Damn!" Mia shouted and ran to the back door and into the yard.

Henrik came after her.

Mia saw how the man running ahead of her forced his way through some bushes and disappeared from view.

"Stop!"

Mia ran after him through the bushes just in time to see him veer off into a playground. In a few quick strides he crossed the sand pit and jumped over the fence beside the swings. Mia was not far behind. She shouted to the man again to halt. She jumped over the fence and followed him into a narrow bicycle path, not too many meters behind. She would soon catch up. Nobody could beat her.

Nobody.

Mia tensed her muscles and closed the gap. By the time they reached the end of the path, she had caught up and felled him with a well-directed tackle. They both rolled over in the snow. Mia quickly got a firm hold of the man's left arm as he lay facedown on the ground beneath her and she bent it up onto his back. Then she caught her breath.

Henrik came running up, pulled out a pair of handcuffs and locked the man's arms behind his back. He forced him up onto his feet and showed his ID card before leading the man to the car.

Makda had also run after them but had given up in the playground. When she saw her brother come back between the police officers in hand-cuffs, she slapped her hands over her mouth and shook her head. She went up to her brother and shouted loudly and accusingly at him in Tigrin as she gripped his neck.

Mia pulled her away.

"We're just going to talk with him," said Mia in a calming voice and led her away to the swings.

"He needs to come with us to the station. Don't worry."

Mia stopped, put both her hands on Makda's shoulders and looked her in the eye.

"Now listen to me. We will be talking with you, too, about what has happened. About what was done to you. I'll send a woman who knows your language and who you can talk with privately."

Makda couldn't understand what the woman police officer had said. But she could see in the woman's eyes that it was something good. She nodded. Mia smiled and left the playground. Makda didn't know where she should go. So she just stayed there.

Anxious.

And completely lost.

They had hardly sat down in the station before Yusef Abrham claimed, in poor English, that he didn't know a word of Swedish. Henrik Levin and Mia Bolander had struggled for more than forty minutes to get hold of an interpreter. When the interpreter finally came, Yusef claimed he couldn't talk because he had a throat infection. That was when Mia lost her temper. She threw the threatening letters down onto the table and let fly a long harangue with expletives that the interpreter then repeated in Tigrin but without the same anger. Yusef just glared at her, scornfully.

After a few more expletives from Mia, he sighed loudly and finally started to talk about Hans Juhlén. About how Hans had abused his sister. One cold January evening Juhlén had come to the apartment and asked to be let in to speak with Makda about her residence permit.

"She was alone at home, she didn't want to let him in, but he had forced his way in and raped her in the hall," said Yusef. "And when I came home, she was in her room sobbing. I wanted to help her, but she told me not to say anything to anybody about what had happened."

He rolled his eyes and said that his sister's naive hope of getting a residence permit meant that she continued to open the door every time Hans Juhlén rang the bell.

Yusef had kept his word about keeping the sexual encounters secret, but his suspicion that Juhlén had lied about his sister's residence permit had been gnawing at him.

"Juhlén seemed to be an idiot, and you shouldn't trust idiots."

When three months had passed and Makda still hadn't received a positive answer from the Migration Board, Yusef decided to use the same blackmail techniques as Juhlén. But instead of sex, he used money. One time he hid and documented Juhlén's visit and his degrading act with his cell phone. Afterwards, he sat down and wrote the first threatening letter and mailed it to Juhlén's wife. A couple of weeks later he was contacted by Kerstin Juhlén. She had beseeched him to withdraw the threat, but Yusef refused.

"He abused my sister, so I felt I could abuse him. And if his wife didn't pay, I would leak the photos to the media!"

Kerstin realized he was serious and a day later she delivered the money.

"But I didn't say anything to Makda—I kept the money for myself. So Makda knows nothing of my blackmail scheme. If my sister wanted to fuck him for nothing, then she could just go ahead."

"So you wrote the threatening letters yourself?" Henrik asked.

"Yes."

"So you do know Swedish?"

Yusef smirked.

After that, he answered all the questions in fluent Swedish.

Yusef had been living in Sweden for a year and a half and had learned the language fairly quickly. He was born in Eritrea and grew up there, but had left the country on account of the troubles with Ethiopia.

"We were lucky," he said. "Lucky that we could make our way here. That we survived the whole journey. That we didn't end up in a ghost container."

"What do you mean by ghost container?" said Henrik.

"It's one of the common ways of traveling to a new country these days and it isn't safe. Especially not for illegal refugees. You know, many die on the way. Sometimes they all die. That's happened in Afghanistan, Ireland, Thailand. Even here."

"Here?" said Henrik.

"Yes."

"In Sweden?"

"Yes."

"That's strange. Wouldn't we know if that were the case?" asked Mia.

"You don't see everything that happens. Anyway…my parents are going to come here too," said Yusef.

"When?" said Henrik.

"Next year I think. It's dangerous to stay in Eritrea."

"Indeed," said Henrik. "But back to the threatening letters. Have you told anybody about them?"

Yusef shook his head no.

"You know you have committed a crime?" said Mia.

"It is only a letter, not a real threat."

"Oh yes, it is. And making threats against people is a very serious crime in this country. You will probably end up in prison for it," said Mia.

"It was worth it," he said.

Yusef didn't protest when the policemen took him away to a cell. He walked slowly and seemed relaxed, as if he were relieved at having told the truth.

Ola Söderström stared at the computer screen, the only source of light in the room. He was going through the files he had found on Hans Juhlén's computer. Now and then you could hear the muffled sound of the lift going from floor to floor. The ceiling fans hissed and the hard drive made an angry buzzing sound as he hunted down the deleted files. But then it went silent. Ola had gone through everything.

Now we'll see, he thought. He knew there must be something interesting somewhere. There always was. In every computer. But you had to look in the right place. Computers hid more than people knew, and often you had to search through the files several times to uncover everything, or use special software.

He started by looking through Hans Juhlén's cookie folder to see which sites he had visited. Headlines from the national newspapers showed up, and Ola glanced at the articles about the Migration Board. Most of them were about the board's illegal contracts with landlords and other suppliers of housing. A series of reports questioned whether management knew about the principle of public access to official records, and one journalist had investigated the government procurement processes at the board and for which Juhlén was ultimately responsible. The board was severely criticized and had often been asked why it took so long to improve their routines when it came to finding and paying for accommodations for asylum seekers. Hans was quoted as saying that there was "a difference between buying a photocopier and buying accommodation."

Juhlén was under pressure, Ola thought, and he moved ahead with the cookie folder. Four sites turned up about ships, and another one was about transport containers. Then he came upon a long list of sites with pornographic content, mainly featuring dark-skinned women.

Ola straightened his back and let the computer work its way through these hidden folders and files. "Statistics 2012" said one of them. Ola opened that and checked a comparative diagram showing the number of refugees in 2011 and 2012. One table showed the fifteen countries from which most of the refugees came. During the first months of the year, the largest number of residence permits had been granted to people from Somalia. After that came Afghanistan and Syria.

Ola opened a folder with information material and standard forms. He went through reports that dealt with special themes such as Athletics and Migration, the European Refugee Fund, and Labor Immigration. He quickly checked folders with conference material and government instructions for the board's activities, reports and fact sheets, laws and legal information. Three of the folders on the hard drive were unnamed. It was in one of these that he found a key document.

It apparently had been deleted on Sunday at 18:35. He clicked on the file to open it, and the page that appeared was a surprise. It was completely blank except for a few lines with capital letters and numbers.

There were ten lines in all:

VPXO410009
CPCU106130
BXCU820339
TCIU450648
GVTU800041
HELU200020
CCGU205644
DNCU080592
CTXU501102
CXUO241177

Ola Söderström wondered what these letters and numbers were.

He copied the top line and pasted it into the search field, but it didn't match any document. He repeated the procedure with each of the other lines, but met with the same result for all of them.

He tried writing just the letters, but that led to similar dead ends. His first guess was that each line was a sort of code. A personal code perhaps. Could it mean something else? Names, perhaps? Were they the first numbers in a personal ID? Year, month and day representing birth date? He dismissed that idea too, and felt stuck.

It was almost midnight by now, but the mystery remained unsolved as he worked through the night.

EIGHTEEN

The sweat dripped from her brow.

The girl fought as hard as she could.

Right fist forward, duck, left fist forward, kick, kick, kick. The man with the ugly scar pointed at his eyes, his throat and his crotch.

"Eye, throat, crotch!" he shouted.

She shouted after him:

"Eye, throat, crotch!"

Right fist forward, duck, left fist forward, kick, kick, KICK!

"Attack alert!"

The girl froze in her movement. The man disappeared from her field of vision.

No, she thought. Not a surprise attack! She hated them. She had no problem with close combat; she was really good at it. She had good instinct and a well-developed ability to react. Especially with a knife. She knew where to put her weight to get the blade as close to her attacker's throat as possible. It was a question of first getting her challenger off balance and then down onto the ground. It often worked with just a few well-directed kicks to the knees. If that didn't suffice, or if she met with hard opposition, she elbowed or kneed her challenger in the head several times.

Against Danilo, or Hades, as it was carved on his neck, she usually used direct blows and clenched her fist just before her hand reached his throat. When he bent forward from the pain, she would get hold of his head and knee him in his face until he fell down. But he could often out-wit her and get her down on the ground first, and there he would sit astride her on her chest with his hands around her throat. Sometimes she would black out, but that was a part of the training. She was meant to be hurt. She had to learn never to give in, not even when it got dark.

She had become physically stronger, and more and more often she escaped from such a position and herself gained the advantage. With a well-directed knee into Hades's back or kidneys, she could get loose. If she then managed to get a kick in his face, she might even win the fight.

The kicks were important in close combat. She had practiced getting the right movement of her hip so as to get more power in her leg. Rotating movements demanded balance and she had practiced with particular attention to finding the center of gravity in every position. She knew that it was a matter of life and death that she master the techniques to perfection, and when she was falling asleep in the evening, she would often re-

*hearse them in her head. Back leg forward, raise
knee, rotate, kick.*

The endurance exercises weren't so bad either.
She had learned to ignore the pain of the cold
snow that she had to crawl naked in. Running or
doing interval training up a hill wasn't so bad either. What she disliked most was performing the
attacks because of the surprise element. She had,
of course, trained attack and defense many times
before. She had trained standing, sitting and lying
down. Even against weapons and against several
opponents in the dark, in confined spaces and in
stressful situations. But she still couldn't get used
to the sudden pounce.

Now she focused her gaze on a point on the wall
and listened for the slightest sound. She would
probably have to stand there a long time. That
was also a part of the training. Once she had been
forced to stand at the ready for seven hours before
she was attacked. Her arms and legs had been
shaking on and off, and she had felt dehydrated.
But by then she had turned off all emotions, didn't
feel the pain any longer. She was Ker after all.
Goddess of Death. The one who never gave up.

Then she suddenly heard the sound of a small
stone crunching, as if somebody were creeping
up. And she was right. Somebody was approaching her. From behind.

She tensed her muscles and, with an aggres-
sive roar, jerked around. The man with the ugly
scar was close, and the girl saw the knife leave
his hand at high speed. She watched it, lifted her

hand and caught the knife by the handle in a swift movement. She squeezed the handle hard in her hand as she met the man's eye. He crouched, then pounced. Quick as a flash, she shifted her weight and used all her strength to get her heel up and direct a kick at him. It hit the mark perfectly.

The man collapsed onto the floor and she was there in an instant. She put one foot on his chest and leaned over him with the knife against his brow. Her dark eyes burned. Then she raised the knife a little and threw it to the ground. It landed two centimeters from the man's head.

"Good," he said, and gave her an encouraging look.

She knew that she had to say it.

But she found it hard.

"Thank you, Papa!"

CHAPTER
NINETEEN

Thursday, April 19

Her running shoes drummed against the asphalt. Jana Berzelius veered off toward Järnbrogatan and exchanged the hard surface for the gravel footpath next to the waterway. She had done stretches at home and then had gone out for a refreshing run. She still hadn't really warmed up, and she felt how the chill pierced her black leggings. She was lightly dressed, but after a kilometer she knew she would start sweating.

All winter she had enjoyed jogging and running outdoors. Her will to train had not been dampened by snow, slush and cold winds. She ran the same round in all weather, following Sandgatan to the town park, on to Himmelstalund and then back. She preferred an urban setting to a hilly landscape; she didn't want to have to drive out of town just to be able to run on a special path. It was a waste of time, driving. When she exercised she wanted to get going directly.

And going to a gym wasn't an alternative for her either; no way was she going to join an aerobics group. She liked to be on her own, and so for her running was the optimal exercise.

Bodybuilding didn't require visits to a gym. In her apartment she had her own equipment and always finished her ten-kilometer run with push-ups and sit-ups. And before showering she usually stood in front of her chin-up bar and did lifts. She liked how she had full control of her body when she did that, and counted to twenty before she would sink down to the floor, exhausted.

It was now 06:57, with plenty of time left in the morning. She checked her pulse. When it had come down to normal range, she got up and pulled off her clothes.

She showered for twenty minutes, after which she picked out a matching set of underclothes, then looked in her walk-in closet for a sheer blouse to go with her deep blue pants and jacket.

She fried four slices of bacon and two eggs and ate her breakfast just in time to watch the morning news on TV. After a long report from a foreign correspondent, an item about the dead boy who was found outside Norrköping came on. He was still unidentified despite a comprehensive investigation. The picture of a smiling Hans Juhlén was shown, and the reporter was asking himself whether there was a link between the two victims and added that the answer would probably come at the press conference that the county police authority was holding at nine that morning.

From the weather report she heard that a new storm was on its way across the North Sea. The girl spoke clearly and with a friendly smile when she warned that there would be chaotic snow conditions in central Sweden. So far in April there had already been a record amount of snow, and now more was expected. Jana turned the TV off. She put on some light makeup, brushed her teeth and combed her hair. When she checked herself in the mirror, she was not completely satisfied with what she saw and so put on another layer of mascara. Then she let her jacket hang over her arm as she went to the garage.

Because of the morning mist and the icy roads, it took fifty-five minutes, instead of the normal forty, to drive to the forensics center in Linköping. The traffic was crawling along and Jana had to concentrate to keep on the correct side of the divide. In the vicinity of Norsholm the mist lightened somewhat and when she got to the exit for Linköping North, visibility was normal again.

Jana walked toward the main entrance and the office of the medical examiner, Björn Ahlmann. Although there were still fifteen minutes left before their meeting, DCI Henrik Levin and DI Mia Bolander were already sitting in the visitors' armchairs there. Long rows of medical books were perched on the birch shelves on the wall, and in the window hung light green curtains with white swallows on them. The desk was a light birch wood and above it hung a bulletin board with various phone numbers and photos from holiday trips.

When Björn Ahlmann had first studied medicine at Linköping University, he had planned to specialize in neurology, but along the way he had become interested in forensic medicine and he finally chose that field as a specialty. Although the work was mentally demanding and the days were filled with independent work, he felt satisfied. He had a good reputation based on his qualified analyses and informed judgments. He knew that his conclusions had a great influence on the lives of individuals, and that his autopsy results were of crucial importance in any court proceedings. Even though he was by far the most qualified person in the department, he didn't regard himself as the expert he was.

Björn got up from his ergonomically designed office chair and greeted Jana with a firm handshake when she entered the room.

Jana then nodded to the two waiting officers.

"I did as promised," said Björn. "The report is ready, although we're still waiting for a few analyses of samples. I'd like us to go and look at the body—there's something interesting I want to show you."

One of the ceiling lights flashed on and off as they stepped out of the elevator into the basement corridor.

On the way down the hall Bjorn chatted with Henrik about his eldest grandchildren, who were ten and thirteen years old, and their various sporting activities, swimming and football. He had proudly told Henrik about how he was going to take them to the weekend competitions in Mjölby and Motala.

Neither Jana nor Mia listened as they were fully occupied with avoiding each other's gaze.

Björn unlocked the fire door and turned on the lights in the sterile room.

Mia as usual stood back to keep her distance from the autopsy table, while Jana and Henrik stood right next to it.

Björn washed his hands thoroughly, put on latex gloves and folded back the white sheet. The naked body only filled about two-thirds of the bench. The boy's eyes were closed, his face white and stiff. His nose was narrow, his eyebrows dark. His head had been shaved and the exit hole in his forehead was visible. Clearly he was shot from behind.

Jana reacted when she saw all the bruises covering his arms and legs.

Henrik too.

"Are those bruises from when he fell? When he was shot?" said Henrik.

Björn shook his head.

"Yes and no. These are," said Björn and pointed at large dark areas on the boy's outer thigh and hip. "Here there are also wounds on the inside, bleeding at various depths of the muscles."

Björn pointed at the muscular arms.

"But many of the bruises are from earlier, that is, before he died. He has previously been subjected to brutal violence, especially to his head, his throat and around his genitals. And his legs, I might add. I would say that these have been caused by kicks and blows. Perhaps by a hard object."

"Such as?" said Henrik.

"A piece of iron tubing, perhaps, or hard shoes. Not easy to say. I'll have to wait and see what the cell-tissue samples can tell us."

"And regularly, you said?"

"Yes, he has several old scars and some internal bleeding which would indicate that his body had been abused over a lengthy period of time."

"Assault, thus?"

"Yes, very serious assault, I would say."

Henrik nodded slowly.

"No sign of any sexual abuse, however, no sign of sperm, no red areas around his anus," Björn continued. "No sign of a stranglehold either. He died from a shot to the back of his head. The bullet is still being analyzed."

"Type of weapon used?"

"Not confirmed yet."

"When will you get the results of the bullet analysis and the tissue samples?"

"Tomorrow, or perhaps the day after."

"The boy's age?"

"Nine or ten years. Hard to be more exact."

"Okay, anything else?" said Henrik.

Björn cleared his throat and went and stood at the end of the table, next to the boy's head.

"I've found traces in his blood of drugs that depress the central nervous system. So he was under the influence of narcotics. A rather large dose."

"Which substance?"

"Heroin. He has repeatedly injected, or someone has injected him, through the veins in his arm. Look here."

Björn showed them the festering skin in the crook of the boy's arm, then twisted the arm and showed a large inflamed area.

"There is a very advanced infection on the underside here. Presumably the deceased missed the vein when injecting so that the solution had ended up in the tissue outside and not in his blood."

The skin on his arm was red and swollen and there were small wounds everywhere.

"If you press here it feels as if…how shall I explain? It feels like clay and that means the arm is full of pus. This is the sort of infection you can get when you use intramuscular injections, and are not to be played with. I've seen horrific examples where parts of the body have simply rotted through with infection. Large holes straight into the skeletal bone are not unusual, nor is sepsis, blood poisoning. Some veins can be completely smashed from all the injections, especially in the groin. In the worst cases, amputation of an infected limb is the only treatment."

"So what you are saying is that this nine- or ten-year-old was an addict?" said Henrik.

"Most definitely. Yes."

"A dealer?"

"That I don't know. I'm not the right person to make that judgment."

"A runner perhaps?"

"Could be." Björn shrugged his shoulders.

"Now let's see… This is what I wanted to show you."

Björn turned the boy's head to one side so more of his neck was exposed, then pointed to a specific area.

Jana could see letters carved into his flesh. They were uneven and looked as if they had been cut with a blunt object. Jana saw that they spelled out a name, and the ground began to rock beneath her feet. She gripped the edge of the table with both hands so as not to fall.

"Are you all right?" said Henrik.

"I'm fine," Jana lied and couldn't take her eyes off the letters.

She read the name again. And again. And again.

Thanatos.

The god of death.

CHAPTER

TWENTY

Gunnar Öhrn was browsing the internet edition of the local papers. He leaned his head back while he looked at the sports pages. He always read the sports before the news. Always the financial pages before politics. And always the arts pages before the auto section. Blogs and family pages—he never touched those.

During the month since he and Anneli had separated most recently, Gunnar established his own routines that suited him perfectly. He got up at half past six, ate breakfast and drove into the police station. He was often home by six in the evening and would eat something, then go into town and do his errands if his son was not with him. By eight o'clock he was home again and would read or be on his computer until midnight. If the weather was decent, he might consider going out for an hour's walk, but not often. Anneli had always insisted he needed to get more exercise and when they lived together she would drag him off on a walk. On his own, he could decide himself how fast he would walk, and he preferred a leisurely pace.

Gunnar left the sports pages and clicked his way to the local news, where he read about a fifteen-year-old trumpeter who had been awarded a music scholarship of two thousand kronor. The boy wore braces on his teeth and reminded him of his son, Adam.

Two days a week Adam would come for dinner, if his sports schedule allowed. They would go out for pizza and sometimes a movie. Gunnar had thought about volunteering to be an assistant coach for his son's team, but he had already missed the single pre-season training session. Maybe next time, he thought as he saw the picture of himself appear on the computer screen. The photograph had been taken at the morning press conference.

After the boy had been found dead, a horde of print, TV and radio journalists had besieged the press conference and they had been forced to move to a bigger space. The largest conference room in the police building had to be opened and that too became overcrowded. The air was filled with the buzz of voices and radio equipment being tested. Gunnar Öhrn and the county police commissioner, Carin Radler, had first welcomed everybody and then turned it over to the press officer, Sara Arvidsson. She had described the murder of Hans Juhlén but played down the murder of the boy. She had also made a point of informing them that Kerstin Juhlén had been released from custody but that she was still helping them with their inquiries. It had been one hell of a press meeting. Short, intense but necessary, according to Carin Radler. It was always better to gather the press and feed them some tidbits than let them speculate wildly because of a lack of information.

Sara Arvidsson answered most of the journalists with a brisk "No comment!" She hadn't said much at all about the investigation, which was now in its fourth day and had aroused considerable attention.

Gunnar opened another news website and saw a photo of himself. In profile. On a third site you could only see half his body. Instead the photographer had focused on Sara.

"Good thing," he muttered and closed his computer. He didn't like being at press conferences while an investigation was still going on. There was always a risk that somebody would reveal more than necessary. Investigative journalists also had a knack of asking trick questions and making false claims that were later transformed into absolute truths by other writers who didn't restrict themselves to reliable sources. And it wasn't nice to always have to repeat "No comment," but it was necessary. Especially in this case.

Gunnar sincerely hoped that the letters and numbers that Ola Söderström had shown him that morning would lead to something.

The team would be meeting again at twelve

o'clock. He looked at the silver watch on his wrist. Half an hour to go. He decided to grab some lunch from the cafeteria beforehand.

Jana's hands shook as she unlocked the door.

Once she was inside her apartment, she kicked off her shoes and sank down on the floor with her back to the door. She remained sitting like that a while. Getting her breath back.

Everything that had happened was like a fog. She had made her apologies and said she had an urgent meeting with a client, then she left the forensics center as fast as possible. She could hardly remember how she got home. Her driving must have been careless because on one occasion she had only just avoided crashing into another driver, who had been traveling below the speed limit. She couldn't remember even where she had parked, nor how she had made her way upstairs.

Now she slowly got up, tripped over the threshold of the bathroom and stopped herself from falling by catching hold of the washbasin. Her entire body was trembling as she looked for her pocket mirror in the bathroom cupboard. Irritated when she couldn't immediately locate it, she knocked all the contents of one drawer onto the floor. A bottle of perfume smashed, and its sweet scent ran out over the floor tiles. She pulled out another drawer and rummaged carelessly among all the things inside, but still no mirror.

Jana stopped for a moment to think. Her handbag! It was in her handbag. She went back into the hall and opened the wardrobe. There, in the corner of her dark blue purse, lay the round pocket mirror.

She took it out and hurried back into the bathroom. Then she stood in front of the wall mirror and hesitated. Her heart was thumping, her body trembling. With shaking hands she pulled her hair to one side, angled the little mirror toward her neck and held her breath.

She didn't dare look. She shut her eyes and counted to ten. When she opened them again, she saw the reflected letters.

K-E-R.

KER.

"The god of death," said Mia.

"What?" said Henrik.

"*Thanatos* means god of death."

Mia zoomed in on the text displayed by the digital encyclopedia.

They had left Linköping and were on their way back to Norrköping in a hurry. The meeting with Björn Ahlmann had gone on longer than expected and now they would be hard-pressed to get to the update briefing at noon.

Mia was reading aloud from the passenger seat.

"Now listen to this. Thanatos is a god of death in Greek mythology. He was extremely fast and strong. If you saw Thanatos with a torch pointing downwards, it meant that somebody would die. But if the torch was pointing upwards, that was a sign that there was still hope."

"Do you believe in all that?" said Henrik.

"No, but what the hell, the kid had the name on his neck. That must mean something."

"Or perhaps it was just what he was called."

"Or wasn't."

"He can't have carved it himself, at any rate. That's for certain."

"Perhaps with the help of a mirror."

"No, it's impossible to get the letters so straight."

"But who would write a god's name on a child's neck?"

"Don't know."

"Some crazy bastard."

"Or friend. Perhaps he belongs to a gang?"

Mia deleted the name and entered a new word in the search engine.

Henrik signaled to change lanes.

A traffic sign showed that they only had ten kilometers to the exit to Norrköping South. Mia was absorbed online and Henrik's thoughts wandered initially to the dead boy and then to Jana Berzelius. During the autopsy she had suddenly made her excuses and quickly left. She was always the one who stayed longest and who asked extra questions or even challenged Björn Ahlmann's conclusions. Today she hadn't asked a single question during the examination of the boy's body.

Henrik wrinkled his brow. Of course it had been dreadful to see such a little body on the pathologist's table. Was it when she saw the letters on the boy's neck that her face first turned a bit pale? Or had he imagined it? Why was he questioning her behavior?

He and Mia stepped into the conference room thirty seconds before the meeting was due to start, and Jana was already there with her usual focus. Next to her sat Anneli, all her concentration on the local paper. Ola and Gunnar sat with their heads close together, talking quietly.

Mia flopped down onto her usual chair and stretched out to reach the coffee thermos on the table. Henrik sat down next to Jana.

Gunnar got up from his chair and said, "Okay, everybody. It's time to get to work. We'll start straightaway with Henrik and Mia. You've been to forensics, can you tell us what you know about the boy's injuries?"

Henrik nodded, clasped his hands on the table and leaned forward.

"Björn has confirmed what we already know. The boy was shot from behind and it seems that he was brutally assaulted before, although not sexually, and that he was under the influence of drugs, heroin to be exact."

"How old was he?" Gunnar asked.

"Around nine or ten, and apparently already an addict—he had sores and infections on his arms."

"Pitiful."

"Yes, it's uncommon to find such a young addict," said Gunnar.

"Once you start, you are hooked, regardless of age. Heroin is an extremely addictive drug," said Ola.

"But it's uncommon to find such a young addict," said Gunnar.

"So we think he was at Hans Juhlén's house possibly to steal money for his addiction?" said Mia.

"Well, that's one theory," said Gunnar. "We must get a better idea of who the boy was, whether he was a member of a gang, a dealer, an addict, who he bought the stuff from, sold to, and so on."

"We need to reach out to all the heroin addicts and dealers we know." Gunnar walked up to the window.

"Selling often takes place in deprived areas," said Mia as she brushed the palm of her hand back and forth across the table.

"But drugs are a problem in all classes of society, aren't they?" said Henrik.

Mia looked over at Jana and smiled.

"Only in rich areas it is better hidden," said Mia.

"But what would make children sell drugs?" said Henrik.

"Money, of course," said Mia quickly. "If there were summer jobs for all teenagers, they wouldn't need to push drugs."

"So you're saying that they start selling drugs because the council doesn't give them summer jobs?" said Jana. That was the first time she opened her mouth at the meeting. She leaned across the table and glared at Mia. "Allow me to smile at that. A job is something you find yourself, it's not something you're given."

Mia clenched her teeth, and folded her arms over her chest.

That prosecutor could go to hell. "But we're talking about a ten-year-old here, and ten-year-olds don't have summer jobs," said Henrik.

Mia gave him an irritated look.

"But why would a ten-year-old be involved in drugs? Could he have been forced into it?" said Ola.

"Forced to deal? That's very likely," said Henrik.

Gunnar pulled his chair out but didn't sit down. "Let's skip the speculation and concentrate on something else. The tire tracks next to the crime scene at Viddviken come from Goodyear. Marathon 8. We don't know for certain whether the tracks are from the white van that the witness had seen. Incidentally, have we got any more on that?"

"Yes, I spoke to Gabriel and according to the witness it seems the vehicle was an Opel," said Mia.

"Model?"

"He didn't know."

"Well how did he know that it was an Opel?"

"I suppose he recognized it."

"But not the model?"

"No, not the model."

"How big?"

"He described it as a little van."

"And what is the witness's name?"

"Erik Nordlund."

"Where does he live?"

"Jansberg. He was doing some forestry work out there and saw the van driving at high speed outside his house. He lives close to Arkösund Road just a couple of kilometers before the turning down to Viddviken."

"Ask him to come down right away. He must surely know which type of van he saw. Print out pictures of all the Opel models and put them in front of him. We must find that van. Even if it isn't connected with the murder, the driver might have seen something that's important."

Gunnar walked back and forth in front of the map on the wall, then picked up a red marker and wrote on the whiteboard: *Opel.*

They were still nowhere with this investigation, and it was extremely frustrating. He sat down and tried to pull himself together.

"You said the van was driving fast," Henrik said to Mia.

"Yes, according to the witness, it was," said Mia.

"Are there any speed cameras on Arkösund Road?" said Henrik.

"Yep."

"Perhaps it was caught by the camera?"

"Good point, Henrik. Check with the department of transportation up in Kiruna. They'll be able to tell us if their cameras registered any car that violated the speed limit that evening," said Gunnar.

Ola raised a finger. "I'll do that," he said. "But

have you abandoned the theory about the boy coming by boat?"

"No, but nobody has seen or heard of a boat in the area at that time. So we'll concentrate on the van first."

Gunnar nodded to Ola. "Okay, over to you."

"Right-o."

Ola pressed a few keys on his keyboard and opened the document with the letters and numbers; he started the projector but the screen showed nothing.

"Now what's wrong?" he said and got up from his chair. "Is it the light or what?"

Ola adjusted his cap and then climbed up onto the conference table to reach the apparatus hanging from the ceiling.

Jana glanced at him as she took short shallow breaths. Ever since she had left home she had been struggling to retain her composure. Her calm was only surface-deep, and she couldn't really control her nerves. Several times she had to remind herself to focus. She stretched out to reach the coffee thermos, which was in front of Mia. Even though her insides felt like one big raw nerve, her movements didn't betray that.

Mia glared at Jana as Jana pulled the thermos across the table.

Ola was still busy up by the ceiling and the rest of the group was silent, deep in their own thoughts.

Jana took a sip of coffee.

Ola broke the silence. "That's it. It should work now."

He climbed down from the table and woke the computer up from sleep mode. The screen showed the image of the strange combinations of letters and numbers.

Jana looked up at the enlarged image. Her eyes opened wide, as her heart beat rapidly. She could hear a rushing sound in her ears; the room was rocking. She immediately recognized the first line. She had seen it before. In her dream. The one that recurred time after time.

VPXO410009.

"Right, I found these combinations in Hans Juhlén's computer. I've gone through every single folder and file and document on his hard drive and this document is the only one that looks weird. Hans Juhlén used these combinations for something several times and saved the document with the same name over and over. But I've no idea why. Nor do I know what the numbers and letters mean. Does anyone here have any ideas?"

They all shook their heads. Except Jana.

Ola went on: "I've searched online, but haven't gotten anywhere."

Ola scratched his head on the outside of his cap again.

"Perhaps his secretary knows? Or his wife?"

"Henrik, check with Lena. Mia, you can ask Kerstin. Also check whether Yusef knows anything. We'll have to ask everybody. Right, Jana?" said Gunnar.

Jana was caught unawares.

"What?"

"What do you think?"

She forced herself to smile and answered:

"I agree. We'll keep at it."

TWENTY-ONE

The steel was cold in her hand.

The girl swallowed and looked up at the man with the ugly scar standing in front of her.

They were in some sort of cellar. Usually it did service as an isolation cell. They were put there if they had failed some exercise or command, if they didn't finish their food or hadn't shown enough endurance when running. Sometimes simply because the older ones felt like it.

She had been locked up in there twice before. The first time she had misunderstood the routines and had gone to the toilet without permission. She was locked up in the room with no light for three days and was forced to defecate on the floor. The stench was as bad as in the container. That seemed to be the only thing she still remembered from the journey with her mother and father. The memory of them faded with every day that passed. But using a stone, she had carved their faces on the wall next to her bed. Hidden behind a small cupboard so no one else could see—but every evening she pushed the cupboard to one side and said good-night to her parents.

The second time the girl had been forced down into the isolation cell was when she had picked at the carvings on her neck. The man with the ugly scar had found the bloodstains on her sleeve and pulled her by her hair across the yard. Five days, that was how long she had to stay there that time. The first day she slept almost the entire time. The second day she thought about trying to escape; and the third day she had trained herself how to kick hard and attack with a knife. She had found a little piece of wood on the floor and used it as a knife. On the last two days she explored the room in all its darkness. She rarely left the rooms in which they trained so being down in the cellar was both unpleasant and exciting. In her curiosity she examined every object she could find. She particularly liked the old workbench that stretched along one wall, with its tin cans of paint and various plastic containers. The girl examined them all as best she could in the dim light. On the second wall were two shelves with cardboard boxes and newspapers. A rusty bicycle stood leaning against the wall under the stairs and a brown suitcase stood in front of that. An old door was propped up against the stair railing, with a stool next to it. The girl noted that nobody had moved anything since she had been there.

"It's time," said the man with the ugly scar and gave her a gun. "Now is the time for you to prove

to me that you deserve to be my daughter. The target is not the usual one."

The man nodded to the woman who was standing against the wall on the top stair. She opened the door and let Minos in. He slowly walked down the steps and tried to accustom his eyes to the dark.

"This is your new target," the man said to her.

When Minos heard those words, he stopped short on the stairs. In that same instant he forgot everything he had learned. Panic took over, and he tried to dart back up toward the door. But the woman who stood there pulled out her gun, pointed it at his head and forced him down the steps again.

Minos begged for mercy.

He threw himself at the man's feet and screamed.

The man kicked him away. "You're a loser. If you had done as you'd been told, you would be standing here instead of Ker. It is only the strongest who survives, and she is one of them."

Minos's eyes rolled with fright. He was kneeling now on his bare knees and shaking.

The man went up to the girl and grabbed her hair and forced her head back. He pulled hard to show that he was serious, and looked her straight in the eye.

"Soon you'll be in complete darkness. So you will have to make use of your other senses. Do you understand?"

She understood. Her heart started pounding.

"Make me proud!" the man whispered.

The stairs creaked as the man and the woman climbed back up and left the cellar. When the door was shut, the girl held the gun tightly and immediately raised it.

The dark surrounded her. She didn't like it and her breathing became rapid. She wanted to scream but knew an echo would be the only reply. An empty echo. Her heart was thumping and the darkness began to voluntarily release its hold.

Now she heard Minos as he bumped into the bicycle. She assumed he had crawled in under the stairs. She tried to calm herself. Breathe deeply. She could manage this; she would conquer the darkness. She gained control of her breathing, inhaling slowly and deeply and exhaling through her nose. She concentrated and listened. Silence. Numbing silence.

The girl took one step forward, stopped and listened again. Then another step, and then one more. After three more steps she knew she would reach the staircase and would have to step to the side to get past them and reach the area where Minos was.

She stretched out her hand to feel the staircase railing and counted the steps in her head: One, two, three. Now she felt the cracked railing in her hand. After three more steps, she let go of the wooden rail and blindly felt for something with her hand in front of her. With her next step, she kicked the suitcase on the floor; the sound gave her a start. At the same time she heard Milos crawling up through the space near her. Pointing the gun in front of her, she followed his sound from right to left. But it disappeared just as quietly as it had come. The movement had made her breathe faster, and she closed her mouth again so she could listen. Where was he now? She slowly turned her head so that she could hear her target. She searched her memory. Could he be sitting under the workbench?

Or next to the shelves?

She stayed where she was, silent and not moving. Waited for a signal, a breath or a sense of movement from him. But all she could hear was silence.

She knew there was a risk she would be ambushed.

Perhaps Minos was already standing behind her back?

That thought made her turn around. Her brow became sweaty and her damp hands warmed the steel. She must do something. Couldn't just stand there waiting for him.

The earth floor was uneven and she put one foot forward to keep her balance. Let the other foot follow after.

Then she stood completely still again. Hesitating. One more step forward, then another. She turned to the right and the left, all the while with the gun pointing forwards. Her senses worked hard to compensate for her eyes.

She stretched out one hand in a sweeping movement and felt the hard surface of the bench. She knew it was two meters long and she felt her way alongside it with her hand. When she reached the end, she stopped.

Then she finally heard it.

A breath.

The signal.

She reacted instinctively and pointed the gun in the direction of the sound. And then she was hit by a hard blow across her arm. She lost her balance and concentration. A second blow was more painful, straight to her head, and she put up her arms to shield herself. She mustn't drop the gun.

Minos was close, dangerously close. His anger was dreadful. He hit out again. And again. The girl tried to keep her footing, to focus. When Minos tensed up for a final blow, she reacted. She threw a punch in the dark, and hit her mark. Minos grunted.

She hit out again. This time with the gun. The third time she hit his forehead and heard the heavy thud as he fell to the ground.

She put both hands on the gun and pointed it down to the floor.

Minos was whining. His voice felt cold as metal and cut like a knife through the darkness.

A sense of calm immediately settled over her. She felt strong, with a greater presence than ever. She was no longer afraid of the dark.

"Don't do it," said Minos. "Please, don't do it. I'm your friend."

"But I'm not yours," said the girl and fired the gun.

CHAPTER TWENTY-TWO

When Erik Nordlund went in through the main door to the police station, he hoped the meeting would take about ten minutes at most.

In the reception area he met with a whole crowd of people. Most of them were applying for passports.

The uniformed woman behind the counter recorded his name, picked up a phone and called Henrik Levin.

Within one minute, Henrik was down in reception.

"Detective Chief Inspector Henrik Levin. Hello. Thank you for coming."

They shook hands and took the elevator up to the third floor, walked down a corridor and into the office.

"Coffee?"

"Yes, that would be nice."

"Milk, sugar?"

"Sugar."

"Meanwhile take a seat, I'll be back shortly."

Erik sat down and looked around the area through the other side of the glass wall. About ten police were sitting at separate desks working away. Telephones were ringing, conversations were going on, photocopiers were buzzing and keyboards clicking. He had no instinct for desk work and suddenly felt a strong urge to get back to his duties in the forest.

He wondered whether he should hang up his warmly lined jacket, but decided not to, it would only be a short visit. Tell the policeman what he saw, and then leave.

In the distance he could see the chief inspector approaching with two cups of coffee. As he came into the room, a drawing taped onto the wall fluttered from the draft. A green ghost, drawn by a child. Erik immediately thought of his three grandchildren, who sent him drawings every week, squeezing them into an envelope that was far too small. They mainly drew suns and trees, flowers and boats. Or cars. But never ghosts.

He took the cup that Henrik offered him, and immediately sipped some coffee. The steaming liquid burned his throat.

The detective inspector sat down and pulled out a notepad. The first question he asked was about Erik's profession, and he talked about felling trees.

"Most trees have a natural fall direction." Erik put his cup down and gesticulated. "And the direction of the fall is influenced by whether the tree leans to one side, the extent and form of its branches and the direction of the wind. A lot of snow and ice in the crown can easily weigh a ton, and can make it hard to judge which way the tree will fall, and this winter has been bloody cold."

Henrik nodded in agreement. It had been an exceptionally cold winter and close to record snow depths in many parts of the country.

Erik went on in an enthusiastic voice: "The basis of safe tree felling is the width of the holding wood, the bit between your front wedge and your back cut. This is the 'hinge,' and if your hinge is too wide it will be a heavy and clumsy fall. But if the hinge is too narrow that's even worse because it might give way and then the tree would fall out of control. You can really hurt yourself if you don't do it properly. You can't mess around with nature. Bang!" Erik clapped his hands together. "You can end up under a tree trunk with a broken leg or worse. One of my coworkers was knocked out by a birch that splintered. He was out cold for several minutes before we managed to bring him back to consciousness."

Erik picked up the cup and took another sip of coffee.

Henrik then began to steer the conversation toward what was important.

"You saw a van?"

"Yes."

"On Sunday?"

"Yes, at about eight in the evening."

"You're sure about that? And the time too?"

"Yep."

"According to Gabriel and Hanna, who visited you yesterday, you said it was an Opel. Is that correct?"

"Yep, to be sure."

"And you are quite certain that it was an Opel?"

"Absolutely. I've owned one myself. See!"

Erik unhooked a bunch of keys from his belt and showed Henrik a metal key ring with a symbol.

"Opel. And I've got one of these too." Erik picked out a Volvo symbol from the bunch, that too in metal.

Henrik nodded.

"Where did you see it? The Opel?"

"On the road outside my house. It was going very fast."

"If I get a map, can you point out exactly where you saw the van and which direction it was traveling in?"

"Of course."

Henrik Levin went off for a few moments and came back with a map that he unfolded on the desk.

Erik took a marker, looked for his house on the map and put a red cross and arrow on the road shown by a brown line.

"This is where I saw it. Right here. And it was heading for the coast."

"Thank you. Did you catch a glimpse of the driver?"

"No. I was blinded by the headlights. I couldn't see anything except the color of the van."

"License plate?"

"I couldn't see that either."

"Did you notice any other vehicle?"

"No. At that time of day the road is usually empty. Except for the occasional truck."

Henrik fell silent. The man in front of him seemed credible. He was wearing red work clothes and an orange over-the-jacket fluorescent vest.

Henrik folded the map and picked up a pile of printouts of pictures of Opel vans.

"I know you can't remember which model of van it was, but I want you to look through these pictures and see if there is anything that reminds you of the van you saw."

"But I didn't see…"

"I know, but look at the pictures and take your time. Give it the time it needs."

Erik sighed. He unzipped his jacket and hung it on the back of the chair.

It wasn't going to be a quick visit.

Jana Berzelius was still feeling slightly nauseous. She rested her head in her hands and tried to gather her thoughts. She was shaken.

The lettering on the boy's neck had affected her in a way she had never previously experienced. She knew what the name meant. But that he should have just that particular name, that wasn't possible.

It couldn't happen.

It wasn't allowed to happen.

She sat on the edge of her Hästens bed. The room suddenly felt small. Shrinking. Stifling.

She tried again to gather her thoughts but realized she was in a state of mental paralysis. Her brain refused to function. When she finally made her way to the kitchen, her hands shook. A glass of water didn't make things better. And nothing in the fridge could help. The nausea was too strong and Jana dismissed the idea of having something to eat. Instead she turned on the espresso machine.

With the cup in her hand, she went back into the bedroom and sat on the bed again. She put the cup on the bedside table, opened the cupboard underneath and took out one of the black notebooks she had there. She slowly looked through her notes, at the images and symbols she saw in her dreams. Arrows, circles and letters of the alphabet in neat rows. Here and there a drawing. Some of them were dated; the very first date noted under a sketch of a face was September 22, 1991. She was nine years old and for therapeutic reasons had been encouraged to keep notes about her recurring dreams. She had told her parents of these experiences, about her horribly realistic dreams, but her mother and father, Karl and Margaretha Berzelius, had thought they were far too imaginative. Her brain was playing a trick on her. They had brought her to a psychologist to help her to get past the "phase," as they put it.

But nothing helped. The dreams continued to trouble her so much that she tried everything she could to stay awake. The never-ending anxiety, with difficulty breathing and sense of despair that she felt was breaking her down. When her parents said good-night in the evening, she had immediately opened her eyes again and thought about how she could stay awake all night long. She liked games in the dark and she often passed the time by galloping with her fingers across the covers and bunching up the filling in the duvet into small obstacles that her fingers could jump over.

She also moved around inside the room, in the dark, or sat in the deep window bay and looked out over the garden. She stretched up to be as tall as possible in the three-meter-high room, or crouched down making herself as small as possible under the wide bed. The psychologist had told her she should let things take their time, and that the dreams would eventually disappear.

But they didn't.

They only got worse.

And after yet another two weeks of dramatic nights, her father had thought about whether they should start giving her medicine. He wanted to solve her silly ideas once and for all. Sleep was one of our primary needs, and any idiot at all could do it.

He had finally taken her along to the hospital and a doctor had given him a jar of sleeping pills.

The effect of the sleeping pills was short-lived, and unfortunately the side effects were serious. Jana lost her appetite as well as her concentration, and finally her teacher, in a confidential conversation with her mother, had said that Jana had fallen asleep in two lessons. She also said that it was completely hopeless to try to have a discussion with the girl. If they asked her to solve a mathematical formula, she would simply mumble in reply. Considering the educational ambitions that Karl and Margaretha had for their daughter, they really must do something about it. And straightaway.

Jana found the drowsiness terrible. She couldn't think straight and she did everything in slow motion. So it was a victory when they stopped the medication. Since Jana never wanted to visit a hospital again to talk to a psychologist, she lied to her parents and told them that the dreams had disappeared. Even the psychologist had been fooled. Instead she clenched her teeth. Every evening she trained how to smile in front of the mirror. She masked her own personality by copying the gestures of others, their body language and their facial expressions. She learned the social game and its rules.

Pleased with the improvement, Karl Berzelius had patted her on the head and believed there was hope for her. With the lie about everything now being fine, she never needed to worry again about having to visit analysts.

But she dreamed.

Every night.

The keys clinked against the letterbox when Mia Bolander unlocked it. She took the pile of letters and quickly browsed through them. Only bills. Mia sighed and relocked the box, ran quickly up the stairs to her flat on the second floor. Her steps echoed in the stairwell. The door to her flat creaked. In the hall, she opened a drawer and put the letters on top of the pile of unopened bills. She locked the door, pulled off her boots and threw her jacket onto the floor.

It was seven o'clock. They would be getting together at Harry's in an hour.

Mia went straight into the bedroom and got undressed. She picked out a dress she had bought at the Christmas sales three winters ago.

It would have to do, she thought.

Then she went into the kitchen and opened the fridge. With a grim look on her face, she noted that there was no booze left. She looked at her watch again. The liquor store was closed. Oh, fuck!

She quelled an impulse to go down to the supermarket and buy the low alcohol beer. Instead she searched through all the cleaning material under the sink, in the cupboard with the cups and saucers and among the vases. She even opened her microwave in the hope of finding something. In the end, in the pantry behind a loaf of bread in a plastic bag she found one can of Carlsberg. It had already passed its best-before date, but only by a month or so and in the lack of anything else it would have to do. She opened the can and drank straight out of it with her mouth around the edge to stop the froth from dripping onto the floor. Sour and cardboardy.

Mia wrinkled her nose, wiped her mouth with her naked arm and went into the bathroom. She twisted her hair into a ponytail and took another gulp of the beer, then decided to put on some heavy makeup. Two shades of blue eye shadow and black mascara. With the stiff rouge brush she chased the last of the powder left in the compact. She worked up a dark tone under her cheekbone and liked the way it narrowed her face.

She picked up the can of beer and went into the living room to wait. Forty minutes to go.

Suddenly she thought about money. Today was the nineteenth. Almost a week before she got paid again. Yesterday she had seven hundred left in her account. But that was before she went out.

And how much did she spend during the evening? Two hundred?

Entrance, a couple of beers, a kebab.

Perhaps three hundred?

She resolutely got up from the sofa, drank the last of the beer and set the empty can down. She put on a pair of shoes from the hallway, picked up her jacket and went downstairs to the lobby.

The cold wind stung Mia's bare legs as she walked in the dark past the blocks of apartment buildings. She could have taken the tram, but she saved over twenty kronor by walking. From where she lived at Sandbyhov, it was only a fifteen-minute walk to the center.

Her stomach was rumbling as she passed the Golden Grillbar. She read the signs outside. Hamburger plate, sausage with bread, chips…

She cut across the double tramlines. At the corner of Breda Vägen and Haga Gatan she found an ATM. She checked her balance and saw that she had only three hundred and fifty kronor. She had spent more than she thought yesterday. She'd have to go easy this evening. Just one more beer. Perhaps two, at the most. Then she'd have some money left over for tomorrow. *Otherwise I'll have to borrow from somebody*, Mia thought. *As usual*.

She crumpled the ATM printout and threw it on the ground and continued to walk toward the center.

The notebook had two hundred pages. But that was only the first. In her bedside table there were twenty-six more. One year of dreams in each. Jana turned to the final page, to a drawing she had done when she was young. It showed a knife with the edge of the blade colored red.

Jana closed the book and stared out of the window with a thoughtful gaze. Then she opened the book again and turned to a page with a combination of letters and numbers. VPXO410009. That was the exact same combination that Ola Söderström had shown her. Had shown the team.

Jana got up with the notebook in her hand, went into her study and unlocked a door that led to a little storeroom. She had transformed the storeroom into a place where she could collect everything that might help her to understand her background. Up to now she had only had the help of her dreams.

Jana turned on the ceiling light and stood there in the middle of the room. Her gaze was directed at the walls. The room was about ten square meters. Two walls consisted of bulletin boards, and these were completely filled with images, photos and sketches. On one wall there was a whiteboard and that was covered with penned notes. Under it was a small desk and a chair. There was a safe next to that. There was no window in the room, but the light diode up on the ceiling lit up all the surfaces.

She had never shown this room to anybody; her parents would probably try to get her hospitalized if they found out. Nor did Per have any idea of her research. She had never uttered a word about it to any of them, and she never would do. This was her business, and hers alone. Everything in the room was about her earlier life as a child.

The truth was—and she had realized this a long time ago— she liked digging into the past. She had done it for as long as she could remember. It gave her a bit of a kick of satisfaction, like a complicated game, only it was about her, herself. And now another player had joined the game. It felt completely absurd, unreal.

Jana put the notebook down on the table, went up to one of the notice boards and looked at the various bits of paper attached to it. At the very top was a picture of a goddess. She had found it in a book that she had happened across in one of Uppsala's antique shops in her student days, and she had bought it for just over fifty kronor.

In that old university city she had used the public library as well as the university library. But the law department library became her natural refuge. She always sat in the same place in the Loccenius room, right in the corner with her back to a bookcase and with a high narrow window on her left side. From there she could see the entire reading room and all the students who came and went. There wasn't much room on the reading desk and the green reading lamp wasn't very bright. Her law books didn't take much space, but the ones on Greek mythology were large and unwieldy.

At the main university library they had, over the centuries, acquired large and valuable collections. Jana had found literature that described mythology in general and goddesses in particular. She had been especially interested in goddesses of Death, and when she had come across texts of importance in her research, she copied them and later put them on a bulletin board in her student apartment. Titles such as *The Goddess*, *Imaginary Greece* and *Personification in Greek Mythology* were obvious choices for her private reading in the evenings. She wrote down all the texts that interested her and made copies of all the important illustrations. She tried to understand all the links she could find.

What all these hours of research had in common was a single name.

Ker.

Jana had devoted all of her free time to trying to solve the mystery of the strange carving on her neck, but she got nowhere. The first time she looked up the name, she read that it meant the goddess of violent death.

Jana remembered that she had first found that explanation in an old encyclopedia. Now she looked across at the row of books neatly lined up with their spines in order of height. Roughly in the middle she found the encyclopedia, pulled it out and opened it at the page with the yellow Post-it sticker. She ran her index finger along the lines that had been marked with a weak cross. "Ker," it said. Jana went on reading. "Greek mythology. The goddesses of Death (or more correctly, of violent death) in Ancient Greece. Hesiodes, however, only mentions one Ker, the daughter of the Night and the sister of Death (Thanatos)..."

Jana stopped reading.

Thanatos!

She sat down and put the book on the desk. She stretched out her arm, took a sheet of paper down from one of the notice boards, and read what was on it. The heading was: Greek Mythology—Gods of Death. There were about thirty names on the list and on the third line was the boy's name.

She felt her nausea rise again.

Jana leaned back in the chair and took a deep breath.

After a short while she got up and went across to the other bulletin board. On an otherwise empty sheet of paper there was a list of combinations. Letters of the alphabet and numbers in large print and next to this a picture of a transport container.

In her earliest memory she had recalled a name plate and at the same time she had seen a blue container in her mind's eye. But she didn't know how they were connected. She had assumed that the combination was associated with the container and had tried to find it on one of all the millions of internet pages out there but that hadn't led to any result. She had then convinced herself that it had all been a meaningless dream and at that point her efforts to try to understand who she was had come to a dead end.

She hadn't been in the secret room for too long a time. She had decided to leave things as they were, not to go on looking for answers. Anyway it had felt hopeless. Now she had to deal with a strange thought. Was it time to get an answer once and for all? The boy was an important piece of the puzzle. When she saw the name carved on his neck she had been frightened, but now, afterward, she realized that the name could help her get an answer to the riddle that had dominated her entire life. The combination was an important piece of the puzzle too. Would one of them lead her to the truth? Or perhaps both together?

Jana stopped her musings. The thought that the police had the same combination of letters and numbers in their hands was rather disconcerting. She didn't really know how to deal with that. Should she be grateful to get help? Should she open up to them and tell them about her own investigations? Show them the drawings? The name on her neck? No. If she as much as uttered a word about her having personal reasons for leading the investigation, she would immediately be taken off the case.

Jana sat down again. She didn't know what to do. Her thoughts were whirling around. She must let the police take care of the investigation. But she couldn't just stand on the sideline and passively watch. She had to do something with the pieces of the puzzle that had come to light. She had to get an answer. It was now or never.

But how should she proceed? Which lead should she follow first? The boy or the combination? She had to make up her mind.

Jana got up from the chair, locked the storeroom and went into her bedroom.

Then she got undressed, climbed into bed and turned the light off. The decision had come to her and she was content with it.

Very content.

CHAPTER
TWENTY-THREE

Friday, April 20

It was early in the morning when Mats Nylinder hurried to catch up with Gunnar Öhrn outside the police station. During the windless and clear night, frost had formed and created a pattern on the paving stones by the entrance that looked like snowflakes. The ice crystals had gathered in clumps on the office windows and the bare branches that stuck up from the border underneath were silvery white.

Mats Nylinder was a general reporter with *Norrköpings Tidningar* and Gunnar thought he had an exaggerated interest in news. His way of going about things was nerve-racking and fiery, and the impression he gave could be compared with a rodent from the animal world. In appearance, however, he was more like a hard-skinned member of a motorbike gang. He was short, had a ponytail and wore a brown leather waistcoat. Around his neck hung a camera.

"Gunnar Öhrn, wait! I have a few more questions. How exactly was the boy murdered?"

"I can't go into that," Gunnar answered and increased his pace.

"What weapon was used?"

"No comment."

"Had the boy been sexually abused?"

"No comment."

"Are there any witnesses?"

Gunnar didn't answer, and pushed open the door in front of him.

"What do you think about how Hans Juhlén had been exploiting asylum seekers?"

Gunnar stopped, his hand still on the door. He turned round.

"What do you mean?"

"That he forced women refugees to have sex with him. That he demeaned them."

"That is not something I want to comment on."

"There'll be a scandal of enormous proportions when the story gets out. You must have some comment?"

"My job is to investigate crime, not worry about scandals," said Gunnar authoritatively and disappeared inside.

Gunnar made his way up the stairs and went straight into the office kitchen area. After pushing a button, he had a steaming cup of coffee in his hand and he continued down the corridor toward his office.

A new pile of documents had come from the

National Forensic Lab and were waiting for him to examine.

"Did you bring the box with you?"

Anneli surprised him. She stood leaning against the wall with one leg crossed in front of the other. She was wearing beige chinos, a white top and a white cardigan. On her wrist she had a twined gold bracelet that Gunnar had given her for her birthday.

"No, I forgot it again. Can you pick it up at the house?"

"When?"

Gunnar put his coffee down and started to thumb through the documents on his desk.

"When can I fetch it?" Anneli repeated.

"The box?" he said, without taking his eyes off the papers.

"Yes. When can I fetch it?"

"Whenever it suits you. Anytime."

"Tomorrow?"

"No."

"No? But you just said…"

"Well, okay…or, I don't know. But do you know what this is?"

He waved the papers in front of Anneli's face.

"No."

"This is finally progress in the investigation, I can tell you. Progress!"

"But can you tell me what they mean?"

Mia Bolander gave secretary Lena Wikström a pleading look.

"No, I've no idea. What is it?"

"That's what I want you to tell me."

"But I haven't seen those numbers before."

"And the letters?"

"No, nor those. Is it some sort of code or what?"

Mia didn't answer. For more than twenty minutes she had tried to get Lena to explain the weird combinations they had found in Hans Juhlén's computer. She thanked Lena for her help, even though she hadn't got any, and left the Migration Board.

In her car she thought about how tired the secretary had looked. Her face was pale, the area around her eyes was a purple-blue color. With slow movements, she had pushed around the documents lying spread out on her desk. Mia had asked how things were, and Lena had answered that she was depressed.

What a pathetic woman, Mia thought. Bloody useless that she couldn't tell us anything!

On her way back to the police station, Mia got caught in the long line of cars on Ståthögavägen. The traffic was crawling along and that irritated her even more. But what made her most angry of all was that she was broke. Yesterday's evening out had cost more than she had intended. And she had treated too. Two beers for some bloke she didn't even know. Somebody who on top of it all was married.

So unnecessary. So. Bloody. Unnecessary.

Her mobile suddenly made a shrill noise.

It was Ola Söderström.

"How did it go?" he said.

"It didn't. She didn't know anything about the combinations."

"Oh, great."

"Yes, isn't it just!"

Mia became silent. She pinched her upper lip with her index finger and thumb.

"But Ola," she then said, "I thought that perhaps, have you tried turning the numbers around?"

"No. But I have tried combinations with the numbers first and the letters afterwards."

"But if you reverse them, what then?"

"You mean I should search on 900014 instead of 410009?"

"I don't have the combinations in front of me, but it sounds like you get what I mean."

"Hang on…"

Mia heard how Ola pressed the keyboard. She turned her head back to see if she could change to the left lane. But the cars there were going just as slowly. She sighed out loud just as Ola's voice came back.

"All I get is pages with ISO 900014, that's international standards. And a report about X-rays from Harvard."

"But what about the other combinations?" said Mia.

"Let's see, 106130 becomes 031601. No, that's a hex code. 933028 is a hex code too, but I don't think he was interested in colors on the internet."

"No, nor am I."

Mia tried to get a glimpse of how many cars there were in front. The queue was hopelessly long.

"How did you get on with the department of transportation and their cameras?" she said.

"Still waiting. It all depends on whether the driver exceeded the speed limit or not. If he did, then there will presumably be an image. And then that image will be compared with photos on passports and driver's licences. If it can be matched, then we'll have an identification. If not, then at least we shall have the name of the owner of the van and we can hope that it's the same person who drove where the boy was found," said Ola.

"But that depends on whether he or she drove too fast," said Mia.

She straightened her back in the driver's seat and put her hand on the wheel. The traffic had started to move.

"Yes, the cameras only react to speed violations and the department of transportation are now checking their logs. The information must be decrypted first before we can get it. If there is any, that is."

"Jesus, what now…!"

"What's the matter?"

"The traffic! I hate lines. Get a bloody move on!"

Mia banged her hand against the steering wheel and then gesticulated wildly at the driver in front who had stalled his engine.

"And you're in a good mood today?" said Ola.

"None of your fucking business."

Mia immediately regretted her harsh words.

"Okay," said Ola. "It's none of my fucking business but you might be interested to know that we've got an answer from the National Forensics Lab."

Ola was in a bad mood too, she could hear. She didn't say anything and let him go on:

"The boy was shot with a .22 Sig Sauer. The gun has not been used in any criminal activity in Sweden earlier. But only the boy's fingerprints were found on the Glock that was found next to him. All technical evidence points to him being the person who fired the gun that killed Hans Juhlén."

Ola ended the call abruptly.

She had irritated him and now she was sitting here in a lousy mood and he was in a lousy mood. Useless fucking morning, Mia thought.

TWENTY-FOUR

There were seven of them in the beginning. Now only Hades and she were left. She had shot Minos, and Hades had killed his opponent in the cellar. One boy had got a deep knife wound between his ribs during an exercise and he died some days later from his injuries. One girl had tried to escape and then been locked up in the cellar, and when they opened it again she had starved to death.

A weakling, that's what Papa had called her.

Then there was Ester, who disappeared when they got to the farm. But it was her own fault. If only she had listened to Papa and done as he had said, then she would certainly have still been with them. Alive.

The girl stroked her head with her hand. She had no hair. The trainers had shaved her. It was so that she would create a stronger identity of her own, they had said. Hades, too, had a shaved head and he rubbed the bare top of his head, back and forth. They were sitting opposite each other in the middle of the stone floor and staring at one another. Neither of them said anything, but Hades smiled at her when her eyes met his.

Spring had come and the rays of the sun sought their way in through the cracks between the wall planks. They had been given a new set of clothes but the girl wasn't interested in that. She was longing to get her hands on the weapons that lay in front of them. The sharp blade glistened now and then, reflecting the sharp light that came from outside. Next to the knife lay a gun, and the girl had never seen it as well polished before. Hades had done a good job with that. He must have polished it for hours.

Hades had once been extremely fond of technology. On the garbage heap he had found lots of broken machines and tried to repair them. He had dreamed of finding a telephone. But he never did.

She knew that, because she had helped him go scavenging.

The girl's thoughts were interrupted by the door being opened. In came Papa, closely followed by the lady trainer and another man whom they didn't know. Papa stopped in front of them, bent down and examined their shaved heads. With something that resembled a look of satisfaction, he stood up and ordered the girl and the boy to do the same.

"Well," he then said. "Now it's time. You're going on a mission in Stockholm."

TWENTY-FIVE

Jana Berzelius remained sitting in her car in the dock area with the engine running. She had spent several hours planning her work, considered and dismissed various methods until she had reduced them to a selection of realistic scenarios to choose from.

She had finally decided that her private investigation must fulfill certain conditions. She must never be linked to the actions she carried out. She must be wary of telephone calls and email. She had to be extremely thorough in everything she did. Absolutely never act on impulse. If it came out that she was carrying out a private investigation parallel with that of the police, then not only would she be suspended, but her name—Ker— would be the object of the next investigation. That would presumably mean the end of her career.

She had nevertheless decided to proceed and to start with the boy. The carvings on his neck were not there by chance. The letters had a purpose and the name had the same connotation as hers, death. But during the morning she had come to the conclusion that it was better to start by investigating the number and letter combinations that Ola Söderström had found in Hans Juhlén's computer. It could hardly have been a coincidence that she had seen the combination together with a shipping container in her dreams, and she had made her final decision to visit the docks.

It was, however, difficult to find a way to visit as discreetly as possible. She would presumably be seen by people who passed by, or by dockworkers or others employed there. But if anyone were to recognize her, she would explain that she wanted to be a step ahead in the investigation. And as the prosecutor in charge, she had every right to try to hurry things along.

Jana sat quite still on her leather-upholstered driver's seat. She ran through the whole situation in her head.

From her pocket she pulled out the list of combinations. She looked through them all and wondered how she should present her interest in them. She would have to weigh her words carefully. Not reveal too much. A minute later she folded the piece of paper and put it back in her pocket. She stepped out of the car.

The entrance to the docks office was dark and the doors were locked. The sign displaying the operating hours revealed that the office had closed an hour earlier.

She felt the door handle again, but nothing moved. She took a step back and peered up at the office windows that looked like empty black holes in the yellow building. A cold wind made her shiver and she pulled her leather gloves out of her pockets.

Then she walked along toward the terminal and realized that they had stopped working there too. The dark, lively water broke against the concrete edge. Two huge cranes towered over a freighter berthed by the quay. A bit further away were another two ships. Trucks were parked in a fenced-off area, and large batches of timber had been stacked beside the wall of a hangar. The spotlights cast long shadows on the warehouse and the asphalt.

Jana was just about to return to her car when she caught sight of a light coming from a shed right at the end of the dock area. Despite her gloves, her hands were still frozen and she pushed them into the pockets of her trench coat, resolutely approaching the shed. Her heels clapped against the concrete surface. Her footsteps joined the noise from the traffic from the port bridge behind her. She glanced at the warehouses where the light from the spotlights didn't reach. She was still alone in the dock area.

The shed was close now, and she slowed her step. She really hoped somebody would be there. Anybody at all, somebody to ask. With only a couple of steps to go, the sound of music reached her ears. The door was ajar and a sliver of light shone out through the narrow opening.

Jana raised her hand and knocked. Her glove dulled the sound so she knocked again, only firmer this time. Nobody opened. She stood on tiptoe and looked in through the window but couldn't see any movement in the shed. She pulled the door open and looked inside.

A coffee machine was bubbling away on a cabinet. Two folding chairs stood next to a table. An old mat covered the floor, and a strong lightbulb hung from the ceiling. But nobody was there.

A loud noise startled her. She turned round and tried to localize it. Then she saw that the big doors to the closest hangar were open.

"Hello?" she called out.

No answer.

"Hello?"

She closed the shed door and went toward the hangar and the more deserted part of the dock area. She remained standing in the entrance. It was bitterly cold in the large space where various machines and smaller cranes were parked. Different sizes of tools rested on the floor, and shelves along the walls were filled with spare parts such as tires and truck batteries. Cables hung down from the ceiling and a lifting mechanism to repair vehicles was stationed at the far end of the hall. On the right side was a sort of side room, almost corridor-like, which led to a gray steel door.

A man was crouching down and working on a truck with his back to her. She knocked on the metal wall next to the entrance so that he would notice she was there, but he didn't react.

"Excuse me!" she said in a loud voice.

The man lost his balance and only just got it back by supporting himself with one hand on the floor.

"Oh hell, you gave me a scare!" he said.

"Sorry. But I need to talk to somebody in charge."

"The boss has gone home."

Jana stepped into the hall and took her hand out of her pocket to greet him.

"I'm Jana Berzelius."

"Thomas Rydberg. But, sorry, I don't think you want to shake hands with me."

Thomas got up and showed her his oily hands.

Jana shook her head, put her glove back on and looked at the man in front of her. He was well built, with dark eyes and a wide chin. A knitted gray cap covered the top of his head, and under his jacket you could just glimpse a pair of suspenders holding up his trousers. She guessed that he must be approaching retirement. A dirty polishing rag stuck out of one pants pocket and Thomas tried to clean his fingers on it.

"I wonder if you can help me?" she said.

"With what?"

"I'm investigating a murder."

"Shouldn't the police be doing that? You don't look like a police officer."

She sighed.

Her plan of not revealing too much was already going wrong. She had to rewind the tape a little.

"I'm the prosecutor investigating the murder of Hans Juhlén."

Thomas stopped cleaning his hands.

Jana went on.

"We've found a list of combinations of numbers and letters that we know are significant but we can't fully understand. We have reason to believe that they are a sort of code for shipping containers," she said and unfolded the sheet of paper with the combinations on it.

Thomas took the paper out of her hand.

"What've you got here...?"

His facial expression changed. He immediately refolded the sheet and gave it back to Jana.

"I've no idea what these mean."

"Are you certain?"

"Yes."

Thomas took a step back. And yet another.

"I need to know what the combinations stand for," said Jana.

"No idea. I can't help you."

Thomas looked at the steel door and then looked back at Jana again.

"Do you know anybody who can?"

He shook his head. Took another step back, two, three...

Jana realized what he was going to do.

"Wait," she said, but Thomas had already turned round and started to run toward the steel door.

"Wait," she shouted again, and ran after him.

When Thomas saw that Jana was following him, he grabbed at the tools as he passed, and turned and threw them at her as a warning. But nothing hit her and she continued the chase. He finally reached the door and tried to pull at the handle but realized that the door was locked. Panicked, he pulled harder on the handle and threw his weight against the door—but it was pointless. He couldn't get out.

Jana came up behind him and stopped about three meters away. He was standing still now, breathing heavily. His head angled from side to side as he tried to find another escape route. But there weren't any.

He saw a large adjustable wrench on the floor, quickly bent down and picked it up. He turned around and aimed it toward her. She didn't move a muscle.

"I don't know anything!" he shouted. "Get out of here!"

He raised the wrench again to show that he meant it. That he would hurt her. Badly.

She realized that she ought to do as he said. That she should leave. It had gone too far. She took a step back, and saw that Thomas smiled when she did that. She took a few more steps back, tripped and was caught by the wall.

He was there straightaway, and stood in front of her.

Close. Too close.

Now she was the one who was trapped.

"Wait a moment," she said.

"Too late," said Thomas. "Sorry."

Jana immediately felt as if she had been transformed. A sense of calm took over. She stared right into his eyes. Focused. Stretched out the fingers of her right hand.

Thomas suddenly let out a roar and swung the heavy tool in his hand at her. She ducked and he missed. He swung again but she nimbly jumped to one side. He renewed his grip on the wrench and tensed his muscles. Then Jana took a quick step forward, raised her hand and hit him.

Eye, throat, crotch.

Bang, bang, bang.

And then a kick. Back leg forward, rotate, kick. Hard.

She kicked him right on his forehead.

Thomas collapsed and ended up lying by her feet.

Lifeless.

At that very same moment she realized what she had done. The adrenaline boost turned immediately into horror. She put her hands over her mouth and took a step back. What have I done? She removed the hand from her mouth, held it in front of her and saw it shaking. How did I...? Now she became aware of her surroundings. What if somebody had seen her? Twice she looked round to make sure she was safe. Nobody could be seen. The hangar was empty. But what should she do now?

A vibrating sound came from the lifeless man's

clothes. It developed into a ringing sound that got louder.

Jana bent down and checked one of his pockets, but found nothing. She pushed him over to get her hand into the other one, and there she found his cell. "Missed call" it said on the screen. Hidden number.

She decided to take the phone with her. She threw a quick glance at the lifeless body, took off her gloves, turned round and walked out.

The dark shadows hid her as she made her way to where she had parked. The docks were just as desolate as before.

When she got into her car she immediately opened Thomas Rydberg's phone and went through the list of calls received. Hidden number several times. Then there were a couple of complete numbers and she quickly wrote those down on a parking receipt. In the list of outgoing calls, there were numbers connected to names, and Jana made a note of these too. Nothing seemed weird or out of the ordinary.

It wasn't until she checked the list of outgoing text messages that she found something strange. In one of them it said: Del. Tues. 1. That was all.

She stared at the short message, wrote it down, as well as the date it was received. Since an active phone can be traced with simple means, she quickly slid out the SIM card and put the telephone in the glove box.

She took a deep breath and leaned her head against the neck-rest and felt calm again.

It shouldn't be like this, she thought. I ought to react, scream, cry, shake. I've just killed a man!

But she didn't feel anything.

And that worried her.

TWENTY-SIX

Saturday, April 21

The children usually woke up as early as six, as they did this Saturday morning too.

Henrik Levin stretched and yawned widely. He looked at Emma who was still asleep. The children were making quite a noise upstairs and Henrik decided to get up. He checked his mobile but no new messages had come during the night.

His pajamas were comfortably warm as he went up the stairs to the children's room. Felix had tipped the whole box of Legos over the floor and smiled happily when he saw his dad in the door. Vilma was sitting on her bed and rubbing the sleep out of one eye.

"Well now, what do you think? Breakfast?"

With whoops of joy Felix and Vilma ran down the stairs and into the kitchen. Henrik followed after them. He closed the door to keep the sound down and laid the table with bread, butter, ham slices, juice, milk and yogurt. Vilma opened the pantry cupboard and reached out for the box of cereal.

Out of the ordinary, Henrik boiled two eggs for himself and during the time that took he buttered bread for the children, adding spread or ham to each slice according to their wishes. Felix managed to turn the cereal box upside down and transformed the kitchen table into a buffet with the colorful fruity rings.

Henrik sighed. There was no point getting out the vacuum cleaner. That would wake Emma and she deserved to sleep in for a change. But he couldn't let the kitchen look like a battlefield.

Henrik poured out the boiling water from the pan and let the eggs cool under the cold water tap. Then he bent down and tried to pick up all the cereal. He managed to tread on some of them under the table and the crumbs fell into the gaps in the rush matting. He hated crumbs. He considered it a cardinal sin to leave a table with crumbs on it. It must be left clean. Wiped down, and preferably sparkling clean.

He looked out through the window. Today he would try to find time for a run. If he got the children ready with breakfast, getting dressed and brushing their teeth, then Emma would surely let him take half an hour to get some proper exercise. Besides, he had let her sleep in. So he should be on her good side.

Felix pushed some cereal off the edge of the table. Vilma's joyful laughter encouraged him to do it again. He pushed off a green ring, then an orange one. With his index finger he flicked one that landed in the flower pot. Vilma laughed out loud and Felix flicked off yet another, and one more after that.

"Stop it. That's enough," Henrik said.

"All right then," said Vilma.

"All right then," said Felix.

"Stop copying me," said Vilma.

"Stop copying," said Felix.

"You're stupid."

"Stupid is stupid."

"Stop that now," said Henrik.

"It was him," said Vilma.

"It was her," said Felix.

"Now stop that."

"Stop it yourself."

"All right, now we're finished."

Henrik was just about to pick up the eggs from the cold water when he heard his cell ringing.

"Good morning! Sorry to call so early," said Gunnar Öhrn in a clear voice.

"That's all right," Henrik lied.

"We've had a call from a witness who saw Hans Juhlén a few days before his death. We ought to check that. Can you come?"

"Can't Mia take it?"

"I can't get hold of her. She's not answering."

Henrik looked at Felix and Vilma.

He sighed.

"I'll come."

* * *

The loaf of bread had gone moldy. Mia looked at the green fungus that was growing threadlike on the slice of bread. She threw the whole bag into the waste bin and thought of an alternative for breakfast. She had heard her cell ring, but didn't bother to look it up. She didn't want to talk to anybody. She wanted to eat. The fridge didn't have much to offer her, nor the freezer compartment. The pantry cupboard had long since been emptied of everything edible except for a packet of fusilli. She pulled out a saucepan, measured a liter of water and threw in a couple of handfuls of the twisted pasta. Boil for twelve minutes, it said on the packet. Far too long, Mia thought, and turned the timer to ten minutes.

She went into the living room and flopped down on the sofa. With the remote in her hand she surfed between the channels, trying to choose between various repeats from the previous week. *Garden Wednesday*, *Wilderness Year*, *Spin City* and *Border Guards*.

Boring shows.

Mia sighed and threw the remote aside. What she needed now was a good film channel. But then she'd need a new TV too. With a really good picture. Plasma. Or LCD. With 3D. Henrik had bought one, a 50-inch model and Mia had been green with envy. A friend of hers had also bought a huge flat thing. Everybody had one. Except her.

The gray weather outside the window meant you could hardly tell it was daylight, even though the dawn was several hours ago. She hadn't come home until four in the morning and she had fallen asleep with her clothes on. When she woke up she had her phone in her hand and the battery was dead.

It had been a good evening out in other words, one of the better ones for a long time, and Mia had got talking to a guy who was nice as well as generous. But she nevertheless declined his invitation to go home with him. Now she regretted it. If she'd been at his place, she would certainly have been given a decent breakfast with freshly squeezed juice. Then they would have been able to lie closely entwined in front of his big-screen TV. She assumed he had one. It would all have been better than sitting alone staring at her old TV.

She considered going off to the Ingelsta shopping mall and checking the price of a new one.

She had two kronor left in her account. At least she was in the black. And she didn't actually have to buy one today. She could just go and look at what was available.

The timer buzzed in the kitchen. Mia went in and took the pasta off the hotplate. I'll just go looking, she thought.

Just looking.

Not buying.

Jana Berzelius took an extra long shower and let the hot water loosen up the last of her tension from the night before. She had hardly slept, but had gotten up at dawn and run fifteen kilometers.

Too far, too fast. It was as if she was trying to run away from what had happened. But she couldn't. The image of the dead man came back to her. For the last kilometer she had run so fast that her nose started bleeding. But even though the blood was dripping onto her windcheater she had sprinted the last hundred meters. Back in her flat, she had in some strange way felt strong and she managed to do twenty-three chin-ups on her bar. She had never managed that before.

Now she stood in the shower and thought about Thomas Rydberg. What was it about those combinations that had made him so desperate? Something had obviously caused him to panic.

Her thoughts moved on to the sudden attack that she made on him. She had reacted so coldly and instinctively, and that perplexed her. The way she had hit out had come just at the right moment. From inside her. Almost practiced. And besides, her blows had struck home perfectly, and even more remarkable was that the violence had made her feel good.

Who am I? she wondered.

Karl Berzelius stood by the window in his study, the telephone in his hand. The display had long since turned itself off. The voice at the other end was silent. His white shirt was buttoned up to his neck and tucked into the neatly pressed trousers. His hair was gray, thick and combed back.

Outside, the rays of the sun had pierced the

heavy clouds. Like spotlights on a stage, all the light fell on a single point, a tree with buds.

But Karl didn't see the sun. He didn't see the tree. He had his eyes closed. When he slowly opened them, the light was gone. Only grayness was left.

He wanted to move, but was unable to do so. It was as if the parquet floor was ice and his feet had frozen in it, and he was a prisoner of his own thoughts. He thought about the conversation he had just had with Chief Public Prosecutor Torsten Granath.

"It's a difficult investigation," Torsten had said with the sound of his car engine in the background.

"I understand," Karl had answered.

"She'll manage it."

"Why shouldn't she?"

"It's taken a turn."

"Yes?"

"The boy…"

"I've read about him, yes. Go on."

"Has Jana told you about him?"

"She never tells me anything, you know that."

"I know."

Torsten had then told him in detail where the boy had been found dead. He had described an arm at a strange angle, a gun and all the rest of what was in the police report. After a thirty-second pause, his voice sounded troubled. The background noise got worse and Karl had to concentrate to hear what he said.

"The strange thing is that everything points to him."

Karl had scratched his forehead and pressed the phone even harder against his ear.

"It seems as if he is the perpetrator. And that it was he who killed Hans Juhlén."

"What do you think?"

"I don't think anything. But what is even more remarkable about this boy is that he has something carved on his neck. It's a name, a name of some god, a god of death."

Karl's heart started to race. He found it hard to breathe. The floor rocked. Torsten's words echoed like a shout from a deserted tunnel.

A name.

On his neck.

He opened his mouth but couldn't recognize his own voice. It was alien, distant and cold.

"On his neck…"

Then he fell silent. Before Torsten could say anything else, he ended the call. He had never before hung up in the middle of a conversation. But nor had he ever before had such a suffocating feeling.

I must get some air, he thought now, and pulled open the top button on his shirt. The cloth seemed to cling to him as he struggled with the next button. He tugged so hard that it came loose and fell to the floor. He inhaled deeply as if he had been holding his breath.

The thoughts whirled around inside his head. He saw the picture of a neck, with light skin and black hairs in vertices. He saw letters, pinkish-red deformed letters. But he didn't see the picture of a boy.

He saw the picture of a girl.

The picture of his daughter.

The child had been nine years old and completely bothersome. She hadn't slept at night and at breakfast had talked about dreams which could only have been pure lies and the product of a sick imagination. He quite simply didn't want anything to do with her flights of fancy, and one morning he had had enough. He got hold of her thin arms and demanded that she should be quiet. She did become quiet. Even so, he had taken a firm grip of her neck to force her into her room. That was when he had felt the uneven skin. He pushed her hair aside to see what it was, and the sight of those three letters was something he would never forget. He had swallowed. He felt sick.

Just as suddenly as now.

Karl shut his eyes.

He had insisted that she should get the scars removed. He had visited dermatologists and even tattoo parlors and been told that it would be difficult to remove them. They couldn't say in advance how many treatments would be necessary. And all of them wanted to see the scars first. Karl hadn't dared say that it was a name carved into the skin. Let alone dare show his daughter's neck to anybody. What would people think?

He opened his eyes.

He had decided that the carved letters would

have to stay. With harsh words he had told her never to show them to anybody, and he ordered Margaretha to buy Band-Aids and polo sweaters. Her hair was to be worn long, and not be put up. After that they never spoke about it again. It was over. It had been dealt with. And that was that.

Now there was a boy with a name carved on his neck.

Should he say anything to Jana? And what would he say? They had already dealt with this issue between them years ago. Filed it away. There was no more to add. It was her own private business now. Not his.

Karl's heart beat fast.

The telephone vibrated in his hand and Torsten's name appeared again in the display. He didn't answer.

Just squeezed the telephone and let it go on ringing.

Nils Storhed stood on the port bridge walkway holding his little dog in his arms. To Henrik Levin, who was walking toward him, he looked like a Scot with his tartan beret, lace-up shoes and dark green overcoat.

"He looks like he comes from Scotland," said Gunnar, who was walking next to Henrik.

"My thought exactly," said Henrik and smiled.

The port bridge was a heavy concrete construction which linked Jungfrugatan to Östra Promenaden across the water. There was always a lot of traffic on the major road across the bridge, and this day there were lines of Saturday motorists. The noise from the traffic and the shrieking of the seagulls could be heard together.

Nils Storhed leaned against the railing with a view of the rowing club and the bustle of the city behind him. In front of him lay the docks and on his left side the district heating power station towered up against the gray sky.

The little dog in his arms panted heavily and its winter coat was shedding. It left lots of white hairs on Nils's coat.

"Is your dog tired?" said Gunnar after they had introduced themselves with their full names.

"No, she's freezing. Her paws don't like the cold," said Nils.

Neither Henrik nor Gunnar had time to say anything before Nils went on. "Yes, well, I'm sorry. I know I ought to have called you sooner."

"Yes, right…" said Gunnar.

"I didn't think it was so important but now I realize it is, and yes, my wife's been nagging me all week saying I should phone, but I've had lodge meetings here and dinners there, so it wasn't until this morning I pulled myself together. One doesn't want to hear any more nagging either, if you know what I mean," said Nils and gave them a wink.

"Okay, then…" said Gunnar.

"Yes, so I called in and said how it was."

"You saw Hans Juhlén?" said Gunnar.

"The very same."

"Where did you see him?" said Henrik.

"Over there."

Nils pointed toward the dock area.

"In the docks? You saw him there?"

"Yes, and I saw him last Thursday, more than a week ago."

"And you are certain that it was him?" said Gunnar.

"Oh yes, I'm certain it was him. I knew his parents. His dad and I were in the same class and always said those were the days."

"Okay, but can you point out the exact place where you saw him?" said Gunnar.

"Of course, come with me, boys."

Nils let his dog down and brushed the hairs off his overcoat. Gunnar and Henrik followed Nils across the bridge toward the dock parking lot.

"It's hard to grasp that he's dead. I mean, who can do something so evil?" said Nils.

"We're trying to find out," said Gunnar.

"That's good. Yes, I hope I can be of some help."

He slowly led them across the lot and up to the yellow main building where they stood outside the locked doors.

"He was walking along here. He was on his own. And seemed angry."

"Angry?"

"Yes, he looked very angry. But he acted as if he knew where he was headed."

Gunnar and Henrik looked at each other.

"You didn't see anyone else nearby?"

"No."

"Did you hear any voices or other sounds?"

"No, not that I remember."

"Did he have anything in his hands?"

"No, I don't think so, no."

Henrik looked up at the main building and the dark office windows.

"What time was it?" he said.

"Yes, well it was in the middle of the afternoon, around three, I think. That's usually when we take her out for a walk."

Nils looked at his dog and smiled.

"That's what we usually do, isn't it, old girl? Oh yes. We usually do that. We do, don't we?"

Gunnar pushed his hands into his pockets.

"Do you know if he had his car parked here?"

"No idea."

"We've got to try to get hold of somebody in the office."

Henrik phoned the police communication center and asked the operator to immediately contact the managing director of the Norrköping Docks.

"Shall we look round for the time being," Gunnar wondered aloud and nodded in the direction of the big warehouses some distance away.

Henrik nodded in response, while Gunnar thanked Nils for his cooperation and the information he had supplied them with.

Nils raised his cap.

"Glad to be of help. I don't suppose you gentlemen have anything against my following along with you? I know a lot about the port here."

Nils immediately started to tell about the history of the port and what it looked like on the quay in the old days. While they walked, he rambled on about the surface materials, warehouses that protected goods from the elements and the flexibility of the cranes. When he started talking about the rail cars and how they linked with the mainline, Gunnar silenced him with a polite thank-you.

"Hans came walking along here, you say?"

"Yes, he came from here."

Nils pointed at the halls that they were now approaching.

"So perhaps he hadn't been in the office building?"

"I don't know. I said I saw him outside, not that he was in there."

Henrik's cell phone rang. It was from the station telling him they couldn't reach the managing director and asking if they should try the person on call instead. Henrik said yes.

Gunnar took the lead as they crossed the asphalt area, and looked with curiosity between the warehouses they passed.

Henrik was not far behind, and after him came Nils with his panting dog at the end of an outstretched leash.

Gunnar saw a shed a bit further along and went toward it. He opened the door and looked in. Tables, folding chairs, a coffee machine, some cupboards and an old mat on the floor. The ceiling light was on, and the news was on the radio.

Henrik, still standing on the quay, looked around. His gaze fell on some containers far away that were lined up in a depot next to a couple of tall gantries that lifted them onto ships.

"Would you believe those metal things are transported around the world?" said Nils who had now come up beside Henrik.

"They carry anything you want... Iron, gravel, garbage, toys."

Gunnar closed the door to the shed and noticed that the sliding door to a warehouse was open. He motioned to Henrik, trying to attract his attention. But it was futile. Henrik was focused on Nils, who carried on about the contents of the containers: "machines, timber, cars, clothes..."

Gunnar slid open the door to one side and went inside. He cast a glance at the large space. The ceiling was lighted by fluorescent lights, and the walls were steel-clad with storage shelves and cupboards lined up against the back wall. Forklifts and trucks were parked on one side, and on the floor lay...a man.

Henrik was still standing on the quay with Nils, who wouldn't stop talking.

Then, as if his prayers had been answered, Henrik's phone started to ring. The station got hold of an emergency number and was now putting the call through. While he waited for someone to pick up, Henrik excused himself and walked toward the area where Gunnar had been standing a moment ago.

He peered into the shed first, but Gunnar wasn't

there. Suddenly he heard Gunnar shout: "Henrik! Come here!"

Henrik ran toward the warehouse from where Gunnar's voice had called. He found his boss leaning over the body of a man.

Dead.

"Phone forensics!"

Henrik immediately dialed the station.

Jana Berzelius felt clean again.

She brewed a cup of coffee, made some oatmeal and squeezed some oranges for juice. It took her fifteen minutes to eat her breakfast. She thumbed through the morning paper without much interest before going into her study. She started up her computer and then unlocked the secret storeroom. She had hidden Thomas Rydberg's telephone and SIM card in a box. She knew that she must get rid of both right away. The box also contained the ticket with all the numbers she had found in the cell phone. She took the ticket and went and sat in front of the computer.

She nimbly keyed in the first number on the home page of the search engine and that led her to a company that sold spare parts.

The next search provided information about a lunch restaurant. The next two were a private individual and an inspector at Norrköping Docks. When she checked all the numbers Rydberg had called, she didn't find anything remarkable.

Jana fingered the parking receipt and wondered

about the abbreviation in one of the outgoing text messages. Del.Tues.1.

You only wrote as cryptically as that if you had something to hide.

The message had been sent on April 4 and presumably it ought to mean Delivery Tuesday 1. But what did the 1 stand for? Was it how many? Or the date perhaps?

Jana glanced down at the right-hand corner of the computer screen. Today was April 21. Ten days to the first of May. She entered the telephone number that the text message had been sent to on the search engine. In less than a second she had an answer. The result surprised her. Could it really be correct?

She read the name again.

The Migration Board.

CHAPTER
TWENTY-SEVEN

They sat in silence in the back of the van. The vehicle shook and it was very noisy inside the small space. The girl tried to brace herself against the sudden rocking.

Hades sat next to her with a dogged look on his face. His gaze was locked on a point straight in front of him.

The girl was falling asleep when the van finally stopped. The driver told them to do it quickly. Not to waste any time, just complete the mission and then come back out again.

The woman sat opposite them and fidgeted with her necklace. A thin gold chain, with a name engraved on a small ornament that hung from it. The girl couldn't stop staring at the chain. The woman twirled it between her fingers, stroked and fingered the shimmering ornament. The girl tried to read the name but it was hard to see the letters between the woman's fingers. She saw M... A... M.

The van jerked to a stop. That same moment she

*saw the last letter and she put them all together
in her head to form a word:* Mama.

*The woman gave the girl an irritated look. She
didn't say anything but the girl understood that
the time had come.*

Now they would leave the van.

And carry out their mission.

TWENTY-EIGHT

The police crime-scene tape vibrated in the wind. The dock area had been cordoned off and a lot of people had gathered, curious to catch a glimpse of what was happening on the other side of the police tape.

Anneli Lindgren was there working methodically in the chilly hall. Gunnar Öhrn had called in another two forensic experts one of whom had come from Linköping, and they now sat beside the dead man. They had been working with the body for two hours.

Gunnar and Henrik stood outside, freezing. They hadn't even considered taking their hats with them—they thought they were only going to talk with a witness. But they had discovered a dead man instead, and their mission at the docks had changed.

"I'm finished," Anneli eventually called out and waved to them to come back in. "As far as I can see, he died here. He suffered powerful blows to the throat and head. I'll let Björn Ahlmann take over from here."

She pulled off her gloves and looked directly at Gunnar.

"The third one," she said.

"I know. I KNOW. Do you think they are related? Any similarities?" he said.

"Maybe related, but no similarities as to manner of death. Hans Juhlén and the boy were both shot, but by different weapons. This man has been beaten to death. A heavy blow to the head. Traces of bruising around his neck."

"The boy had that too."

"True, but apart from that there are no similarities. Unfortunately."

Anneli pulled out her camera.

"I just need to take some pictures of the area," she said.

Henrik nodded and looked at the man on the floor.

"He's around sixty," he said to Gunnar.

"We've asked the manager to come to the station and identify him," said Gunnar.

"Now?" said Henrik.

"At four."

"We'll have a briefing after that. I must get hold of Ola first. And Mia. She never answers."

Henrik's shoulders sagged.

The rest of Saturday was wrecked.

The price was 12990 kronor. In installments. No interest. No charges the first six months. Perfect.

Mia Bolander folded the receipt and smiled at the shop assistant, then maneuvered her 50-inch

TV with 3D out of the store. It even came with a special digital-TV package. That alone was worth 99 kronor a month. The contract was for 24 months. It was worth it. Now at last she had a state-of-the-art flat screen and all the film channels. She could just about fit the carton into her wine-red Fiat Punto if she left the hatch open. On her way home, Mia wondered whether she might invite a couple of friends over for the evening to celebrate. If she provided the venue, perhaps they could be persuaded to bring along booze and nosh. She felt in her pocket for her phone but the pocket was empty. The other one was as well.

Back in her flat she found her cell with no charge under one of her pillows in her unmade bed. She dug out her charger and plugged it in. Before she could phone her friend, the telephone vibrated in her hand.

It was Gunnar Öhrn.

"Mia will soon be here," said Gunnar and looked up at the little group of people seated around the conference table in front of him.

Henrik Levin had a grim expression. He was clearly affected by the discovery of yet another murder. Anneli Lindgren looked tired, too.

Ola Söderström, however, looked alert, almost upbeat as he drummed lightly on the table.

Only Jana Berzelius seemed her regular self. She sat ready with her notepad and pen. Her long hair was neatly blown dry and down as usual.

Gunnar started by welcoming them all, and apologized for having had to mobilize the whole team this late on a Saturday.

"Mia is on her way, but we can start without her. The reason for this meeting is Thomas Rydberg, who was found murdered today at 08:30 in the docks."

He paused. Nobody asked any questions.

"This is the third person found dead in a week."

Gunnar went up to the whiteboard where photos of all three victims had been posted, and he pointed to one of them.

"Here we have Hans Juhlén, shot in his home on Sunday evening, April 15. No sign of a break-in. No witnesses. But on a security camera we saw this boy…"

Gunnar moved his finger from the portrait to an enlarged still from the security camera footage.

"…who, on Wednesday morning, April 18, was discovered dead at Viddviken, also shot, but by a different weapon. Everything seems to point to him, however, as being the perpetrator who murdered Hans Juhlén. But why? That we don't know."

Gunnar put his finger on the third photo. "And today we found Thomas Rydberg. He has been identified by staff from the docks. Sixty-one, married, two grown-up children who live on their own, he's worked in the docks all his life, and lives in Svärtinge.

"Apparently he had a bit of a temper when he

was young and had been convicted of assault and threatening behavior. For the last few years he has been sober. The forensic team says he was beaten to death and that his body had been in the warehouse a while, which means the murder probably took place yesterday afternoon or evening."

"But how do we know that this murder is connected to the other two?" Ola wondered out loud.

"We don't," said Gunnar. "At the moment we know very little. But the murder has landed in our lap. And the one connection we do have is that Hans Juhlén was also in the docks area a few days before he was murdered."

Gunnar looked gravely at the team.

"We've got a lot to do, to put it mildly. The boy is still unidentified, and nobody has reported him missing. We've asked the Migration Board to check the asylum seekers' centers and every single school, but he is as yet unidentified. Nobody has been reported missing either. Our next step is to use Interpol."

Anneli nodded slowly as she started speaking.

"As Gunnar reported, there is at this time no similarity between these three murders. The cause and means of death differ among all three," she said.

"Several perpetrators, you mean?" Henrik clarified.

"Yes."

"If it is the boy who killed Hans Juhlén, we

still have at least one if not two other perpetrators out there. And the clock is ticking," said Gunnar.

Jana swallowed and looked down at the table.

"But the question is whether the murder of Hans Juhlén is connected with the blackmail letters and with the information we gathered from Yusef Abrham," said Gunnar. "What connection could there be between Yusef and the boy we are calling Thanatos because of his carvings?"

"Are you suggesting that the boy could have carried out the murder on the orders of Yusef?" said Henrik.

"It's just a theory. But the boy and the victim Thomas Rydberg could be part of a drug ring. The drug angle is a weak link, I know that, but it's still a link."

"And we did find narcotics at the docks. Five bags of a white powder on a shelf under a storage cupboard," said Anneli. "One could well imagine that it's all connected to some drug dealings."

"Heroin?" said Ola.

"We assume. We've sent the bags for analysis," said Gunnar.

"The boy was doped with heroin," said Ola.

"But where does Hans Juhlén fit into all this? Was he also selling drugs?" said Anneli.

A murmur could be heard from the team.

"Right, then," Gunnar cut in. "I know it has been long hard days for most of you, and there's still a lot to be done. I've worked with you for several years and I know what you can achieve. I want you to find any possible links between these victims. For instance, between Hans Juhlén and Thomas Rydberg. Were they born in the same town? Did they go to the same school? Cross check their relatives, friends, everything."

Gunnar wrote *Links* on the whiteboard.

"We must investigate all the known heroin addicts in town. Ask all the contacts we know of. Get at every dealer, big or petty, every snitch, addict."

He wrote *HEROIN* on the board.

"Ola, here's the number of Thomas Rydberg's cell phone."

Gunnar pushed across a piece of paper toward Ola.

"Make sure I get a list of all the incoming and outgoing calls. Check if he had a computer, if he did, get it and examine it."

Next, Gunnar wrote *Call logs* on the whiteboard and underlined the words. Jana froze. She thought about the cell she had at home. "Did you find anything at the crime scene?" Jana said briskly.

"No, nothing besides the heroin," Anneli answered.

"Nothing else?"

"No, no tracks, no prints."

"Security cameras?"

"No, there wasn't any."

Jana sighed with relief internally.

"The narcotics unit should be able to analyze the heroin and trace it back to whoever is selling it. Henrik, will you follow up on this?" said Gunnar.

"Yes, sure," said Henrik.

"Fine."

The meeting lasted thirty minutes. When it was over, Jana pulled out her diary and thumbed through it to give the team time to leave the conference room before she did. When they had all left, she went up to the whiteboard and stopped in front of the photos of the victims. She studied each of them in detail. Her gaze fastened on the boy. His throat was blue. A mark of extreme violence.

She found herself instinctively putting her hand on her own throat. It was as if she could feel a hard pressure there…as if there was something familiar about it.

"Did you find something?"

She gave a start on hearing Ola Söderström's voice.

He came in through the open door and went up to the table.

"I forgot my notes," he said and stretched after a pile of papers that still lay in the middle of the table. Then he came and stood beside her.

"Feels a bit panicky all of a sudden."

He pointed toward the photographs. "That we still have little to go on, I mean. Feels a bit desperate, this narcotics angle."

Jana nodded.

Ola looked down at his notes.

"And these letters and numbers," he said. "I just can't get my head round these!"

Jana didn't answer. She just swallowed.

"Have you any thoughts about what they could mean?"

He held up the notes with the combinations in front of her.

She glanced at them, screwed her eyes and pretended to be thinking.

"No," she lied.

"But they do mean something," said Ola.

"Yes, I agree."

"They must have a purpose."

"Yes."

"But I can't figure it out."

"No."

"Or I'm interpreting them wrongly."

"Perhaps."

"Frustrating."

"Yes, I realize it is."

Jana went to the table, picked up her briefcase and her diary and took a couple of steps toward the door.

"Better to be a prosecutor, right?" Ola said. "And avoid this sort of riddle?"

"Be seeing you," she said, as she left the room.

In the corridor she broke into a half run. She wanted to get away from the police building as quickly as possible. It was extremely uncomfortable lying to Ola. But it was necessary.

Jana took the elevator down to the garage and walked quickly across the concrete floor to her car. Her telephone started ringing just as she sat down behind the wheel. When she saw her parents' home number, she felt like ignoring the call. But at the sixth ring she lifted the phone to her ear.

"Jana," she answered.

"Jana, how are things with you?"

Margaretha Berzelius's voice sounded a bit uneasy.

"Just fine, Mother."

She started the car.

"Are you coming for dinner next week?"

"Yes."

"It's at seven."

"I know."

She looked in the side mirrors and started reversing out of the parking space.

"I'm making a roast."

"Lovely."

"Your father likes it."

"Yes."

"He wants to talk to you."

Jana was surprised. That was unusual. She stopped the car and heard her father clearing his throat at the other end of the phone.

"Any progress?" he said. His voice was deep, dark.

"It's a comprehensive investigation," said Jana.

He remained silent on his end.

She didn't say anything either. Her eyes were wide with anxiety. Something about this case seemed to have caught his attention.

"Well then," he finally said.

"Well then," she repeated slowly.

She ended the conversation, pressed the phone

to her chin and thought about what he might have wanted to say. That she wasn't doing a proper job? That she wasn't clever enough? That she would fail?

She sighed and put the phone down on the passenger seat. She didn't see the little wine-red car coming into the garage and pulling behind her until suddenly she heard the screech of tires and a long beep of a car horn. She pressed the button on the car door to lower the window, looked behind her and saw Mia Bolander behind the wheel of her Fiat.

Mia rolled down her window furiously.

"Can't you see anything when you're in a car like that?" she hissed.

"Oh yes, the visibility is good," said Jana.

"But didn't you see me?"

"Yes," Jana lied and smiled to herself.

Mia's face turned darker.

"A pity you didn't back out quicker—you could have crashed into me."

Jana didn't answer.

"Quite a fancy car you got there. Comes with the job, does it?"

"No. It's my personal one."

"You must earn plenty?"

"I earn the same as other prosecutors."

"Evidently pretty good."

"The car says nothing about my salary. It might have been a gift."

Mia Bolander laughed out loud.

"Oh yeah, right!"

"By the way," said Jana. "You're too late, the meeting is already over."

Mia clenched her teeth, swore out loud, then pressed the accelerator hard and shot off with her tires screeching.

CHAPTER
TWENTY-NINE

The man was lying there asleep when they climbed in through the window. Hades first, then the girl after him. They moved nimbly and silently. Like shadows. As they had been taught to do. They crept up on either side of the wide bed. At first listening for sounds, but the silence of the night was evident.

The girl carefully loosened the knife that was fastened to her back and held it in a firm grip. Not shaking. Not hesitating. She looked at Hades. His pupils had dilated, his nostrils too. He was ready. And at the agreed signal the girl took a quick step forward, climbed up onto the bed and cut perfectly across the man's throat. The man gave a start, he made a noise, was choking, struggling for breath.

Hades stood still, studying the jerky movements. He let the man feel mortal dread and panic a moment. The man opened his mouth as if screaming, his eyes wide open. He stretched out one hand in a desperate attempt to get help.

But Hades just smirked. Then he raised his gun and peppered the man with all the bullets in the magazine. He shouldn't have done that. That wasn't the order. He should just keep guard. Protect her. But he shot anyway.

The girl looked at the man who lay lifeless between them. A bloodstain gradually spread across the white sheet. From the slash in his throat, the holes in his chest, stomach and brow.

Hades was breathing heavily, a dark look in his eyes.

The girl knew that what he had done was wrong, he had broken the rules, but still she smiled at him. Because it felt good. When they stood there in the half-dark bedroom and looked at each other they were both filled with a euphoric feeling of being part of something bigger. Now they were the tools that they had so long been trained to be.

At last.

Together they climbed out through the window and made their way back to the van. The woman was waiting for them there. Her face still showed nothing. Showed no pride at all. Instead she herded them brutally into the empty back of the van and the girl immediately sank down on the floor. Hades sat down too. He sat directly opposite her, with long outstretched legs, and his gaze fixed on the ceiling.

The woman closed the doors and ordered the man who was driving to immediately take them away.

The girl leaned forward and took the bloody

knife from the holder on her back. She pulled her legs up to her chin and looked closely at the blade. With her index finger she pushed the red blotches back and forth across the shiny surface. She had managed it, the first mission had been accomplished. Now they would return. Home.

And be rewarded with the white powder.

Henrik Levin and Mia Bolander parked outside the pizzeria for a quick dinner. They both assumed they would be working all evening. Henrik ordered a salad and Mia asked for a calzone.

"So it could be a settling of accounts?" Mia said.

"Yes," said Henrik. "After all, as recently as last year two people suffered gunshot wounds in a gang fight in the district Klinga. Everything pointed to it being about the drug monopoly in the town."

"But where does Hans Juhlén fit in? Do you see him as some sort of gang leader?" said Mia. She didn't give Henrik time to answer, but went on: "I think it's more like a contract killing ordered by someone who wanted to be rid of Juhlén, someone who let the boy carry out the murder."

Mia took a large bite of her calzone.

"I'm still not convinced he was murdered by the little boy," said Henrik.

"What would convince you then? Everything

points to it being the boy who killed Juhlén. Absolutely everything," said Mia. "The murders can in some way be explained as settlements ordered by gangs, but carried out by children."

She looked at Henrik.

"You're sick in the head," said Henrik "Children killing… It's not…"

Henrik became silent.

Mia stared at him. "But it does happen. And now if you'll excuse me while I eat more of my calzone."

Henrik leaned over the table. "What I mean is, *how* do you get a child to kill somebody? And who turns a child into a murderer?"

"Good questions," said Mia.

They ate in silence a while.

"Perhaps it's all just a coincidence. I mean the murders might not be connected at all," said Henrik and wiped his mouth with a serviette.

"Drop it, can't you?"

Mia shook her head, ate up the last of the calzone, then pushed the plate to one side. "Shall we be off?" she said.

"Yes. We just have to pay first."

"Oh yeah, shit. I've forgotten my wallet at home. Can you cover me?" said Mia with a big ingratiating smile.

"Of course," Henrik answered and got up from the table.

It was ten o'clock on Saturday evening and Gunnar had completely run out of steam. He sat in his office and pondered the murders, the damned investigation. However he looked at all the motives, he couldn't piece it together. Juhlén, the unidentified boy and Thomas Rydberg. The blackmail letters, the deleted documents and the number and letter combinations. The heroin. The letters carved into the boy's flesh.

Gunnar sighed.

When they had gone door-to-door in the area near the docks, a witness said he had seen a dark car in the parking lot at around five o'clock on Friday.

At first he had claimed that it had probably been a black BMW, one of the bigger models, and Gunnar had immediately started a comprehensive check of all the X-model BMWs in the town. But then the witness changed his mind and started to say that it could just as well have been a Mercedes or a Land Rover, so Gunnar stopped the check. When the witness then changed his mind again and said that the car wasn't dark at all, he had dismissed the information completely.

Gunnar then phoned Henrik who told him that they had had no results after reaching out to the known heroin addicts in town. Nor had the conversation with Thomas Rydberg's wife led to anything that could help them in the investigation.

Now Gunnar had 42 unanswered emails and nine voice messages on his cell. All from journalists who had questions—and expected answers—about the entire investigation. Directly. Now.

Gunnar had no answers to give them, and he

ignored everybody who had tried to reach him. He actually thought about going home. It wouldn't be bad at all to stretch out on the sofa with a cold beer in his hand. But it would be even nicer if he had some company.

He got up from the chair, turned off the office light and walked across to the elevator. He thought about phoning Anneli. When the doors opened again down on the ground floor, he was standing with his cell in one hand. She might get the wrong idea. Like that they should start over again. No, no, no, he wasn't going to phone.

He put the cell back in his pocket, then he pressed the button for floor 3 again and went back up to the office. No point in going home really; he could just as well keep on working.

He walked down the corridor to his room, turned the light on and started to write a letter with an appeal for help.

It was addressed to Europol.

THIRTY-ONE

Sunday, April 22

Jana Berzelius woke up lying on her back, her right hand tightly clenched. She started to loosen up her fingers, closed her eyes and consciously tried to relax. There had been something different about her dream last night. A picture of something she had never seen before. But she couldn't quite pinpoint it.

She dragged herself out of bed and went to the bathroom. Once up, she felt a sudden shudder go through her body.

The wind was roaring outside and the rain was beating against the window. She wondered what time it was. Because of the dark she couldn't really tell whether it was still night or early morning.

She went back into the bedroom and sat down on the edge of the bed. The covers lay in a pile on the floor, as usual. When she reached down to pick them up, she tried again to remember again what had been new in her dream.

She lay down and shut her eyes. The images immediately came back. The face. The scarred face and the voice that shouted at her. He held her in a firm grip. Hit her. Kicked her. Shouted at her again. He had a tight grasp of her neck, she couldn't breathe. She fought to come out of his grip, to get some air, to survive. He just laughed at her. But she didn't give up. She had a single thought. To never give up. And just as everything started to black out, she saw the detail that hadn't been there before.

A necklace.

A shining, glimmering necklace lay by her side. She reached out for it. Something was written on it. A name. Mama. Then everything went black.

Jana sat up and immediately pulled out the notebooks that lay in the cupboard of the bedside table. She spread them out across the bed. Then she thumbed through them back and forth, from notebook to notebook to try to find anything she had written about a necklace or an image of a necklace. But she searched in vain. Then she did something she hadn't done for ages.

She turned to an empty page, picked up a pen and started to draw.

For the greater part of the night, Henrik Levin had lain awake pondering the investigation. When the clock struck six, he got up, made some coffee and ate a bowl of yogurt with some sliced banana. He wiped the sink draining board and the kitchen table down twice, then brushed his teeth before waking up Emma to say that he must work yet another Sunday. When he opened the front door, he heard the children waking up and hurried out so he wouldn't have to see their disappointed faces.

One of the leads that he was busy following, and which he had been thinking about during the sleepless night, concerned the drugs that the forensic team had found in the docks. He thought that a larger search of the dock area was needed, and that they ought to immediately interview the staff.

Henrik felt how cold it was when he placed his bare hands on the cold steering wheel. As soon as he turned the key in the ignition, the CD player started at full volume. Markoolio's voice sang joyfully about Phuket, about summer all year round and then "Thai, Thai, Thai." Henrik immediately turned the CD off and backed out from the drive.

In the silence he thought about the previous evening. After the pizza stop and before they called it a day, he and Mia had managed to start up a conversation with yet another couple of known heroin addicts. They had even spoken to a man who had been of use in earlier investigations about narcotics and who had given them important information that eventually led to them catching underage dealers. Henrik had hoped that this time too he could get the man to talk. But just like the other heroin addicts, he had been extremely taciturn.

"But bloody well tell us if you know anything," Mia had said three centimeters from the man's face. After that she had threatened him with various nasty consequences if he didn't give them information that would help the investigation.

Henrik had got hold of her arm and made her sit down on a chair. Then she had calmed down. Most of all they wanted names. But to snitch in the underworld after all meant virtually signing your own death warrant.

Stopped at a red light, Henrik found himself thinking that he ought to put more emphasis on the weapons that had been noted in the investigation, a Glock and a .22 Sig Sauer. Besides, he must phone the transportation department and remind them to hurry along with trying to identify any vehicles that the speed cameras might have caught on the road in the area where the boy had been found dead.

Henrik felt energetic. He was hoping for a productive day.

When he got out of his car in the police garage, it was half past seven. He saw there was a light on in Gunnar's room and he soon saw Gunnar sitting in front of his computer, fingers tapping away keenly on the keyboard.

"Did you have trouble sleeping, too?" said Henrik.

"Oh no. It was just a bit awkward trying to fit on a sofa here in the office," Gunnar answered without taking his eyes off the screen in front of him.

Henrik smiled. "I thought I'd go through the

files again. I just can't fathom these murders,"
he said.

Gunnar whirled around on his chair and looked
at him.

"Do go through it all. I'm just going to forward
some emails from curious reporters to the press
officer. Twenty-two left."

Gunnar whirled back and went on writing.

Henrik went to the conference room, turned on
the lights and looked down from the window at the
empty roundabout. Norrköping had not woken up
yet. On the large table he laid out the files which
summed up the cases with Hans Juhlén, the unknown boy with carving in his neck they were
calling Thanatos, and Thomas Rydberg, and sat
down to look through them all.

The file about Thomas Rydberg still consisted
mainly of thirty or so pictures that Anneli had
taken at the scene the day before. The last four pictures were taken outside in the docks area. Henrik
looked at them absentmindedly and felt a tiredness
creep up on him. He closed the ring file noisily
and wandered off to the kitchen where he drank a
large glass of water. A thought suddenly occurred
to him that he had seen something on the photos.

He banged the glass down and hurried back into
the conference room and opened the Rydberg file
again. Once more he looked through the photographs, page by page, photo after photo. He was
close to giving up again when he got to the very
last photo. It was an overview of the crime scene,
and Anneli had probably been kneeling when she

took the photo. The wide-angle showed forensics busy working. In the background through the open doors of the hall you could see the container depot. Several different-colored containers stood there.

He tried to see what was written on them. But it was too small to see. Instead he quickly got up, ran down the corridor to Gunnar's room.

"Have you got a magnifying glass?"

"No, look in Anneli's room."

Anneli's office was in perfect order and every item had its given place. Henrik opened the desk drawers, one after the other. In the bottom one he found what he was looking for and hurried back to the conference room. Now he could see the details he needed on the photo. The picture was taken from too far away for him to be absolutely certain, but on one container there were some letters and numbers.

Henrik immediately opened the Juhlén file and got out the list with the ten combinations. He started to compare them and suddenly gave a start. The combination had the same format: four letters and six numbers.

At a quarter to eleven Henrik Levin and Gunnar Öhrn got in the car to drive to the docks. They had arranged to meet the harbor director who would show them round the container depot.

When they turned in to the parking area a man of short stature with reddish hair and black glasses was standing there waiting for them. He was wearing a blue checked shirt and light jeans. He gave them a friendly smile and introduced himself as the managing director, Rainer Gustavsson. He asked if they wanted some coffee, but Henrik politely declined and asked instead to be taken directly to the container area. Rainer Gustavsson took the lead.

They were just loading a large ship, container after container lifted up by the gantries on the dock. Metal hit against metal, cranes were moved and trucks driven in an endless line. Several longshoremen in blue overalls with company logos were standing on the deck. They were all wearing safety helmets. Two men checked that everything was safely stowed and fastened. They knocked on the steel wires and now and then one of the men pulled out a spanner to tighten them.

Henrik looked up at the hull where the containers towered five high.

"It requires a lot of working hours to load a ship," said Rainer. "And it must all be done quickly. If something goes wrong and delays the ship, money starts ticking away directly. Efficiency is everything in the freight world."

"How many containers can you load on a ship?" Henrik asked.

"The largest ships that come to us can take six thousand six hundred containers. But there are ships in the world that can take more than eighteen thousand containers. If you lose one minute for every container, then that would mean more than three hundred hours delay. That's why the loading is very important and in recent years we have made wide-ranging investments in the docks to improve the logistics. Now we have a complete system to deal with everything from notification, in-delivery, examination, estimates, repairs and out-delivery. Thanks to our two new ship-to-shore gantry cranes we can also handle larger and larger container ships," said Rainer.

"What sort of goods do you handle?" said Gunnar.

"Every type imaginable." Rainer straightened his back as he said that.

"How do you check the contents?" said Gunnar.

"Customs does that. But sometimes it's hard to determine who is responsible for the freight."

Rainer stopped and looked at the two men.

"We've had quite a few investigations here over the years. The local council as well as the Environmental Protection Agency have stood in front of fully-loaded containers, looked inside and tried to work out what they contain."

He took a deep breath and lowered his voice a little. "Not long ago we had three people from Nigeria who had filled a container with scrap from old cars. They wanted to send it from here to Nigeria because they thought the scrap was valuable. What we regard as scrap here, can be useful there. But they didn't know about documentation. That meant that the council had to take over the case and the entire container had to be emptied to evaluate its contents. Some car parts were confiscated as they were seen as hazardous waste. I don't know what happened to the container after that."

Rainer started walking again.

Henrik and Gunnar came up on either side of him.

"But how often does that happen? That you have to empty a container?" said Henrik.

"Not so often. Freight is governed by customs formalities. The seller is obliged to declare the goods for export and the buyer must declare for import. There's a whole set of regulations for sea freight. Sometimes the parties to an agreement don't even know the delivery conditions in the other party's home market. Then things can go wrong."

"How so?" said Gunnar.

"Confusion can arise as to who will pay for insurance, when the risk is transferred from the seller to the buyer and so on. There are international regulations, but discussions can nevertheless arise about legal responsibility," said Rainer and threw out both hands. "Here we are!"

The containers were piled like enormous building blocks of metal. On the right stood three orange-colored ones on top of each other. After them another three were stacked in the same way. Gray, rusty and with the name Hapag-Lloyd on the sides. Fifty meters further on there were another 46 containers. Blue, brown and gray, mixed together.

The wind found its way through the narrow space between them, resulting in a weak howling sound. The ground was damp and the dark clouds looked threateningly dark.

"Where do the goods come from?" said Henrik.

"Mainly from Stockholm and the Mälardal region. But also from Finland, Norway and the Baltic states. And of course Hamburg. Most of the goods from abroad are reloaded there and then they come to us," said Rainer.

"We found narcotics in the place where Thomas Rydberg was murdered. What would you know about that?"

"Nothing."

"So you have no idea whether there is any drug trade in the docks?"

"No."

Rainer answered quickly, looked down at his shoes, stamped on the ground.

"But of course I can't be certain it doesn't happen. But if that sort of illegal trade took place on a large scale, then I think I would have noticed it."

"Has there been any other illegal trade? Like liquor?"

"Not any longer. A lot of ships here have even forbidden consumption of alcohol onboard."

"But earlier?"

There was a little delay before he answered.

"We've had problems with ships from the Baltic states. They were selling bootleg liquor and we caught youths buying vodka directly from the ships."

"But now have you discovered any trading at all?"

"No. But it's hard to prevent, we have six thousand meters of quays to keep an eye on, and we can't have staff just patrolling the docks. We don't have the resources for that."

"So there could be drug trading going on here?"

"Yes, you can't categorically say that there isn't any."

Henrik walked up to a blue container and studied the length of it. Drops of water were running down its corrugated metal side. He then went round to the doors. There were four galvanized lock mechanisms from the top down, and in the middle was a box covering a sturdy padlock. On the right-hand door there were numbers and letters.

He immediately recognized that type of combination.

"It's been confirmed that Hans Juhlén, who was the head of the Migration Board's asylum department, was here in the docks," said Gunnar.

"Oh yes?" said Rainer.

"Do you know what he might have been doing here?"

"No, I don't. No idea."

"Do you know if he met anyone?"

"You mean like a relationship?"

"No, I don't mean anything. I'm just trying to find out what he was doing here. So you don't know if he was acquainted with someone employed here?"

"No, but of course it's possible."

"In Hans Juhlén's computer we found ten different combinations with numbers and letters. They look roughly like this." Henrik pointed at the door and then pulled out the list from his pocket. "Can you tell me what these mean?"

Rainer took the list and pushed his spectacles up to the root of his nose.

"Yes, they are numbers for containers. That's how we identify them."

Jana Berzelius thoroughly wiped Thomas Rydberg's cell with a cloth and some degreasing cleaner and then put it inside a 3-liter freezer bag that she placed on the table. She worried about how she could get rid of the phone. Her first thought was to burn it. But where? In the flat it would set off the fire alarm, and even if she took the battery out, it would probably smell of smoke and burned plastic out in the hallway and stairwell. Another idea was to throw it into the Motala Ström River and let it sink to the bottom. That seemed to be the best alternative, she thought. She must throw it in from a place where she couldn't be seen. She thought about places where you could access the river, but none of them were suitable and deserted.

She decided to go out and check for herself if there was a hidden place next to the river.

She put the bag with the cell in her handbag and left the apartment.

Gunnar Öhrn and Henrik Levin sat in the dock office and eagerly watched as Rainer Gustavsson typed at his computer. They had left the container depot in a hurry.

"Okay, shoot!" said Rainer, his reddish eyebrows rose above his glasses and his brow became furrowed.

Henrik unfolded the sheet of paper in front of him and read out the first combination on the list.

"VPXO."

"And then?"

"410009."

Rainer punched the keyboard.

There was a slight buzzing sound as the computer searched the web-based international register of shipping containers. It barely took one minute but for Henrik it felt like an eternity.

"Ah, right. This container is no longer in the system. It must have been scrapped. Shall we check the next one?" said Rainer.

Henrik was squirming on his chair.

"CPCU106130," he read out.

Rainer entered that.

"Nope, that's not there either. Next one?"

"BXCU820339," Henrik read out.

"No, the system says that it isn't in use. They've probably all been scrapped."

Henrik felt a stab of dejection. A moment ago they had a decisive lead in their hands, and now they were again back at square one.

Gunnar rubbed his nose in evident irritation.

"Can you see where the containers came from?" he asked.

"We can look here. This one came from Chile. I'll see where the other two...yes, they were from Chile too," said Rainer.

"Who scraps them?" said Gunnar.

"The company that owns the container. In this case it's Sea and Air Logistics, SAL."

"Can you check where the other containers came from? And who owns them?"

Henrik put the list down on the table. Rainer entered the fourth combination and made a note. The same with the fifth. And the sixth.

When the tenth and final combination had been checked, the pattern was clear.

All the containers came from Chile.

CHAPTER THIRTY-TWO

"*Stop!*" the woman shouted.

"*Now?*" wondered the man who was driving.

"*Yes, now! Stop!*" she shouted out again.

"*But we've got a long way left. This isn't where...*" said the man.

"*Shut up.*" The woman cut him off. "*I'm going to do it, and I decide where. Not you and not him.*"

The man braked and the van came to a halt.

The girl immediately understood that something was wrong. Hades reacted too and straightened his back.

The woman glared at the girl.

"*Give me the knife!*"

The girl obeyed her immediately and handed it over.

"*And the gun. Give it to me!*"

Hades looked at her when he handed the gun over. The woman grabbed it from his hand and checked the magazine.

It was empty.

"You weren't meant to shoot," said the woman with a hard voice.

Hades lowered his head.

The woman opened a box in the corner of the driver's cab and pulled out a full magazine which she loaded the gun with. Then she pulled the firing mechanism as far back as she could, let go and pointed the weapon at the girl.

"Out," she said.

They stepped out of the car and into the forest. The silence was like a lid. The late night was just turning into day and the first rays of the sun were appearing between the fir trees. The woman pushed her along with the gun pressing against her back. Hades went first. He was hanging his head as if he had done something wrong and was ashamed.

The path they were walking along was narrow. Now and then she stumbled on the roots which stuck up from the soft ground. The branches scratched her arms and wet the thin cotton of her sweater. The further they went into the forest, the weaker became the headlights from the van.

One hundred and fifty-two steps, she counted silently and continued counting as they approached a dip in the terrain.

The dense forest opened up in front of them.

"Keep on walking!" said the woman and pushed the weapon hard between her shoulders. "Move on!"

They went down into the dip using their hands to push away thick branches.

"Stop there!" said the woman and took a firm grip on her arm.

She pushed the girl toward Hades and put them next to each other. She gave them a last glance before walking round them and disappearing behind them.

"You thought you were immortal, didn't you?" she said.

She hissed the words.

"You couldn't have been more wrong. You are nothing, just so you know. You are completely worthless little insects that nobody wants! Nobody wants anything to do with you! Do you hear me? Not even Papa cares about you. He needed you to kill, nothing else. Didn't you know that?"

The girl looked at Hades and his eyes met her panic-stricken look.

Please smile, she thought. Smile and say that it's just a dream. Let that little dimple on your cheek become even deeper. Smile. Just smile!

But Hades didn't smile. He blinked.

One, two, three, he indicated with his eyelids. One, two, three.

She understood what he meant and blinked back, in confirmation.

"Of course you didn't grasp that. You're totally brain-dead. Programmed. But now it's over."

The woman spat out the words.

"Now it's over, you damned monsters!"

Hades blinked again. Harder this time. One, two, three. And then again. The last time. One. Two. THREE.

They threw themselves backward. Hades got a firm hold of the woman's arm and twisted it to make her drop the gun. The woman was caught unawares and instinctively pulled the trigger. A shot went off. The sound echoed between the trees.

But then she couldn't resist the pressure from Hades any longer and shrieked with pain when he forced her arm back.

The girl got hold of the gun and immediately pointed it at the woman. Then she saw Hades sink down on the grass. He had been hit.

"Give me the gun," snarled the woman.

The girl's hands shook. She stared at Hades who was lying still in the grass. His throat was bare and he was breathing heavily.

"Hades!"

He turned his head toward the girl and they looked into each other's eyes.

"Run," he whispered.

"Come on now, give me the gun," shouted the woman.

"Run, Ker," Hades whispered again and coughed violently.

"Run!"

The girl backed a couple of steps.

"Hades..."

She didn't understand. She couldn't just run off. Couldn't leave him.

"Run!"

Then she saw it.

His smile.

It spread right across his face. And that very same moment she understood. That she must.
So she turned around and ran.

CHAPTER
THIRTY-THREE

Jana Berzelius drove alongside the Motala Ström River for more than thirty minutes without finding a single appropriate place. People were around at every potential site and it would presumably have been regarded as odd if she had gone to the water's edge and thrown a mobile phone straight into the river.

She maneuvered the car into a parking space on Leonardsbergsvägen and turned the engine off. She thought about how she could get rid of the phone. A feeling of frustration grew inside her and finally it bubbled over. She hit the steering wheel. And again. With both hands.

Hard.

Harder.

Then she leaned her head back and caught her breath. She put her elbow against the car door and the fist of her right hand against her mouth. She sat like that a long while and just looked out across the barren landscape. Everything was gray.

Depressing. The trees had no leaves, the ground was brown from the dirty snow that had recently melted. The sky was just as dark gray as the asphalt on the road.

Then an idea started to take form inside her head. Jana opened her handbag and pulled out the plastic bag with the mobile in it. Why hadn't she thought of this before!

She sat up properly in the driver's seat and put the phone next to her bag. The number that the text message had been sent to belonged to the Migration Board. That much was clear. But she hadn't bothered to try to phone the number—yet.

She started the car, absolutely certain she would make the call. But first she had to buy a prepaid card.

She quickly turned out from the parking space and set course for the nearest petrol station.

Mia Bolander sat rocking on the chair in Henrik Levin's office. She was biting her thumbnail while reading the list with the combination numbers.

Gunnar stood in the middle of the room, Henrik sat at his desk.

"SAL manufactures containers in Shanghai, China," said Henrik and adjusted the desk pad so that it would be parallel with the edge of the table.

"They own, or rather they owned, the first three containers on Juhlén's list and they have been scrapped."

"What about the others?" said Mia.

"Four of the others were owned by SPL Freight

and the rest by Onboardex. The strange thing is that they have all been scrapped. So we must find out what the containers were filled with. Henrik, you take SAL, Mia, you take SPL and I'll take Onboardex. I know it's Sunday but we can surely get hold of somebody. We must get an answer to why Juhlén had combinations for scrapped containers in his computer."

Gunnar strode with decisive steps out from Henrik's office.

Mia slowly got up and left the room dragging her feet. Henrik sighed and suppressed a strong desire to tell her to get a move on.

He put the landline phone in front of him, and dialed the number to SAL in Stockholm. He was automatically connected to an exchange abroad where a digitally recorded voice said in English that the telephone wait time was five minutes. Eventually he heard a male receptionist answer in English with a German accent.

Henrik explained what he wanted in rather limited English and was connected to a female administrator in Stockholm with a drawling voice.

After briefly introducing himself, Henrik got to the point.

"I want to check a couple of shipping containers that you owned in the past."

"Have you got their identity numbers?"

Henrik slowly read out the combinations and heard how the woman clicked the letters and numbers on her keyboard.

Silence followed.

"Hello?"

"Hello, yes?"

"I thought you had hung up."

"No, I'm waiting for an answer from the system."

"I know that the containers were scrapped by you, but I want to know what sort of goods they contained."

"Well, as far as I can see they weren't scrapped."

"They weren't?"

"No, they aren't in the system at all."

"What do you mean?"

"They're missing."

"All three of them?"

"Yes, all three. They have disappeared."

Henrik immediately stood up and looked straight at the wallpaper.

His thoughts were whirling around.

He thanked her for the information with a stuttering voice, then left his office and in five quick strides was in Mia's room.

She was just putting the phone down.

"That's odd," she said. "According to SPL they have never received those containers. They've vanished without trace."

Henrik went straight into Gunnar's room and almost bumped into him in the doorway.

"Well," Gunnar started.

"Don't say anything," said Henrik. "The containers are missing, aren't they?"

"Yes, how did you know?"

* * *

The pay-as-you-go SIM card cost fifty kronor.
Jana Berzelius paid with the exact change and
said no thanks to the receipt that the assistant offered her. She left the little kiosk and had to walk
sideways so as not to bump into the display shelf
with all the candy and chewing gum.

She chose the place to purchase the card carefully. She considered going to a gas station at first,
but then changed her mind. Gas stations had security cameras and she didn't want to risk being
recorded.

Once she was back in her car, she pulled off her
gloves, opened the envelope with the SIM card
and put it inside Thomas Rydberg's cell phone.
Then she turned the phone on and remained sitting
with it in her hand for quite a while before dialing
the number that the text message had come from.
She waited to see if the call would go through.
She had expected that the person she was ringing
wouldn't answer, that the phone would have been
turned off, or the number was no longer in use.

When she heard the first ring she was genuinely
surprised. Her heart started to beat faster. She put
one hand on the steering wheel and squeezed it
hard. Suddenly she heard a voice with a name.

The name astounded her.

The temperature in Henrik Levin's office had
gone up a couple of degrees. Gunnar Öhrn sat
with a sheet of paper in front of him. Mia Bolan-

der was leaning against the wall, and Henrik sat on a chair, one leg crossed over the other.

"So no company had received the containers. They are all missing?" said Mia.

"Yes," said Henrik. "But that isn't so unusual. Shipping freight containers can fall overboard in heavy seas and the risk is greater if the crew hasn't secured them properly. Or if they've been loaded wrongly."

"Evidently a lot of containers are lost every year. It's hard to get any exact figures but I heard that it can be between two thousand and ten thousand," said Gunnar.

"That's quite a wide range," said Mia.

"Yes," said Henrik.

"And the companies didn't seem especially concerned," said Gunnar.

"No, it's evidently quite normal," said Henrik.

"They will be well insured," said Mia.

There was silence in the room for a few moments.

"Okay, so if these containers, the ones we've been looking for, are somewhere on the seabed, then that isn't particularly strange. The strange thing is why Hans Juhlén had the combinations in his computer," said Henrik.

"What did they contain? I mean, they must have contained something," said Mia.

"Nobody can tell us that either. All they know is that they all came from Chile and that they arrived via Hamburg, were reloaded here in Norr-köping and then shipped back to Chile again. But they never arrived back home; they disappeared somewhere on the way back across the Atlantic," said Henrik.

"So there's a whole lot of valuable goods lying on the seabed, in other words? I ought to become a diver," said Mia.

"The first container on the list was recorded as missing in 1989," said Henrik. "Another two went missing in 1990 and 1992. The last one disappeared a year ago. In between, the others went missing. So why did Hans Juhlén have these ten container combinations, all of them missing, in his computer?"

He recrossed his legs and sighed silently.

Mia Bolander raised her shoulders in a gesture of helplessness. Gunnar scratched his head just as Ola Söderström appeared at the door. He came in and leaned up against the wall with the ghost drawing on it. The drawing fell to the floor. "Sorry," said Ola.

"Doesn't matter," said Henrik, as Ola picked up the drawing and handed it to him.

"Nice ghost," Ola said.

"My boy is in a difficult period right now. Everything is about ghosts."

Henrik put the drawing on his desk and went back to his musings.

"Ghosts?" said Mia.

"Yes, he dreams about ghosts, draws ghosts, watches films about ghosts," said Henrik.

"No, I mean…ghosts! When we questioned

Yusef Abrham he said something about ghost containers, didn't he?" said Mia.

"Yes," said Henrik.

"That illegal refugees die en route. Sometimes all of them."

"But the containers were on their way from Sweden, not to Sweden."

"Yes, you're right," said Mia.

"But what could have been inside them?" said Ola.

"It's almost impossible to get any information about that," said Henrik.

"Perhaps they were empty?" said Ola.

"That doesn't seem likely. Why would Juhlén keep the numbers then, since most of them disappeared years ago?"

He got up from the chair and went on: "The document was deleted Sunday evening, correct? Ola?"

"Yes, at 18:35," said Ola.

"Hang on a moment… What time did he pick up the pizza?"

"At 18:40 if I remember right," said Ola.

"How far is it between the Migration Board and the pizzeria that we're talking about?"

Mia pulled out her phone and entered the addresses in a map app.

"Eight minutes by car."

"But that assumes one is already sitting in the car, doesn't it?"

"Yes…"

"Then it is impossible that Hans left his office,

got into his car, drove to the pizzeria in just five minutes, isn't it?"

"Yes..."

"So somebody else in his office must have deleted the document," said Henrik.

"I don't know how we could have missed this. But now it is clear that Hans Juhlén himself could not have been able to delete the document from his computer," said Henrik into the phone.

Jana regretted that she had answered when Henrik called. He just went on and on.

"He died some time between seven and eight in the evening. The document was deleted at 18:35. So somebody else did it."

"Yes."

"We must find out who."

"Yes."

Jana was silent for a moment or two, then she said, "The young security guard who worked at the Migration Board on Sunday...why don't you phone him again. Ask him if he saw anybody else in the building at the time. And now you'll have to excuse me. I'm busy."

"Okay," said Henrik. "I just wanted to let you know."

Jana Berzelius ended the conversation and stepped out of her car. She had parked a bit out of the way and could see the terraced house she was going to in the distance.

She crossed the street with quick strides and kept away from the street lamps as best she could.

Now and then she looked over her shoulder to ensure that nobody noticed her.

She checked the windows but there was no
movement from the curtains. She was grateful for
the darkness when she entered through the white-
painted fence and went up to the front door. The
letterbox outside had the number 21 on it. And a
name. Lena Wikström.

Mia Bolander took a noisy bite of the juicy pear
she had found in the fruit bowl in the staff kitchen.

Henrik had tasked her with immediately phoning the security company that patrolled the Migration Board. She took another big bite while she
punched in the number. A receptionist answered
immediately at the other end of the line.

"Mia Bolander, Norrköping CID."

But the words were hard to distinguish with a
piece of pear still in her mouth. Mia swallowed
and started again.

"Hello, this is Mia Bolander, detective inspector. I need to get hold of…"

She stretched across to reach the carelessly
scribbled name on the notepad and read it out loud.

"…Jens Cavenius. It's urgent."

"One moment please."

Mia waited thirty seconds and managed to eat
the rest of the pear.

"Unfortunately Jens Cavenius is not working
today," said the receptionist.

"I must get hold of him immediately. Make sure

he phones me, otherwise I'll trace his number my-self. Okay?" said Mia.

"Yes, right."

She gave the receptionist her number and thanked her for her help.

It didn't take more than five minutes, and then Jens Cavenius phoned.

Mia got straight to the point.

"I need to know about your observations from Sunday, so think carefully. Did you really see Hans Juhlén?"

"I went past his office."

"Yes, but did you *see* him?"

"No, not exactly, but the lights were on in the room."

"And?"

"I heard him typing on the computer."

"But you didn't see him?"

"No… I…"

"So somebody else could have been there?"

"But…"

"Think a bit *more* now, did you see anybody else in the office, did you notice any detail, item of clothing or anything else?"

"I'm trying to think."

"And I'm trying to get you to think quicker."

"I believe I saw an arm through the crack in the door. A lilac arm."

"And if you think a bit more, who might have such an arm at the office?"

"I don't know…but perhaps…"

"Yes?"

"Perhaps it could have been his secretary, Lena."

Lena Wikström was feeling uneasy. She fingered her gold necklace and bit her lip. She felt sick when she thought about Thomas Rydberg not being there any longer. That he had been murdered. In the docks. By whom?

She felt even more sick when she looked at her cell which still lay on the bed on top of the blanket. Two lamps on the dresser were turned on, and light fell on the three frames which were placed between them. Happy children's faces with midsummer garlands, a reminder of the last summer. Small imitation crystals hung from a white enamel ceiling light.

Who had phoned?

She let go of the necklace and opened one of the wardrobe doors, pulled out a suitcase and put it next to the phone on the bed.

She had never before been called on that number. She was the only one who initiated the communication. Nobody else. That was the arrangement. The others were only allowed to text messages, which were memorized by the recipient and deleted forever. Nobody ever phoned. That was how it worked. Now the rule had been broken.

By whom?

She hadn't recognized the number. Now she didn't dare touch the phone. Just let it lie there on the bed.

Lena unzipped the suitcase. Her instinct was to just run away. Of course it could have been a wrong number. A mistake. But she wasn't really convinced. The worry of being exposed was simply too great for her to just let the call pass.

She opened another wardrobe door and picked out three cardigans, a blouse and four tops. She didn't bother about underclothes, just packed what was on top in the drawer.

She could buy some new clothes wherever she went. She had often thought this day would come some time; she *knew* it would eventually come. Even so, she had no idea where to go. Where she could run to.

Suddenly the doorbell rang.

Her hands froze on the suitcase. She wasn't expecting a visitor.

Lena looked out through the bedroom window, which faced the front door. But she couldn't see anybody.

With a growing sense of unease, she tiptoed out from the bedroom, through the living room, past the bathroom and into the hall. She looked through the peephole in the door but her eye only met with darkness.

With both hands she unlocked the door, then the two extra locks and looked out through the narrow chink.

A woman was standing there outside.

"Hello, Lena," said the woman and put her foot in the door.

* * *

"What have we got on Lena?" said Gunnar
Öhrn.

They were all standing around the conference
table. Everybody felt the tension in the room.

"She is 58 years old, unmarried, two adult children, her son lives in Skövde and her daughter in
Stockholm. No criminal record," Ola Söderström
read out.

"So what do we do now?" said Mia.

"We must bring her in for questioning," said
Henrik.

"But so far all we have is a scatterbrained teenager who thinks he might have seen her in Juhlén's
office that Sunday," said Mia.

"I know, but for the moment that's the most important lead we've got," said Henrik.

"Henrik's right. It's important that we follow
up on this. Straightaway!"

Gunnar looked serious. He pointed a finger at
himself.

"I'm going there. Henrik and Mia, you're coming with me."

He left the room and Henrik and Mia were right
behind him.

Ola was left on his own.

He knocked on the tabletop, absorbed the news
that the investigation had at last gained some mo-
mentum, and went into his room to start up the
computer. Then he took his lunchbox into the staff
kitchen and put it in the fridge.

On his way back, he just happened to notice a bundle of papers in Gunnar Öhrn's in-box. He picked up the bundle to see what they were. They were conversation logs from a mobile operator. The number belonged to Thomas Rydberg.

Ola had a quick look at the lists. When he came to the page with outgoing text messages, he was astounded. Then he suddenly found himself in a hurry, ran across to the lift and frantically pressed the button to catch up with his colleagues.

Lena Wikström didn't have time to react when Jana Berzelius pushed her way in and closed the door behind her. It wasn't very light in the hall, but Jana could see some china figures and an embroidered cloth above a sideboard. A mirror with an ornamental frame. A frosted shade on the ceiling light.

Jana stood absolutely still on the mat in the hall. There was something familiar about the woman in front of her. She didn't know what.

"Who are you?" Lena said and riveted her eyes on Jana.

"My name is Jana Berzelius. I'm investigating the murder of Hans Juhlén."

"Indeed? But what are you doing inside my home at this time of day?"

"I need some answers."

Lena stared uncomprehendingly at the woman in high-heeled shoes and a dark trench coat.

"I can't help you."

"Oh yes, you can," said Jana and went straight into the kitchen.

"You can't just come in like this," said Lena.

"Yes I can, and if you object then I'll issue a search warrant. Then I'll have every right to be here."

Lena sighed.

"Okay, what do you want to know?"

"Hans Juhlén was murdered in his home," Jana said.

"That's not a question."

"No."

Lena walked up to the front door and locked it. She carefully opened a drawer and slowly lifted out a gun, which she pushed inside the waistband of her trousers. Then she put her sweater over it and that nicely hid the bulge. Then she went into the kitchen with a forced smile on her lips.

"So, what's the question?" Lena said.

"Hans Juhlén was murdered at approximately 7:00 p.m. When the police went through his computer they found some identification numbers for shipping containers. The combinations were deleted from the computer at half past six. So he couldn't have done that himself. Was it you?"

Lena was at a loss for what to say. She suddenly felt pressure over her chest.

Jana went on: "I have an important reason to find out what was in those containers."

"I'm sorry, but I must ask you to leave."

"I just want to know."

"You will leave my home."

Jana remained standing by the table while Lena slowly moved her hand behind her back, toward the gun.

"I'll stay until I get an answer," said Jana. She had seen Lena's hand had started to move behind her back and made herself ready for what might come next.

The very moment Lena took the gun up from her waistband, Jana threw herself forward, hit Lena against her kidneys with the side of her hand, then kneed her in the stomach. Lena lost her grip on the gun and groaned from shock as well as the dreadful pain.

Jana checked the gun, which was loaded, cocked the trigger and crouched down in front of Lena. She could see something glimmer around Lena's neck.

Something goldish.

The floor rocked when she saw what it was. Everything started swimming before her eyes, and she heard a roaring in her ears. Her temples ached and her pulse was so high, it hurt.

A necklace.

With a name.

Mama.

The elevator descended extremely slowly. At least it felt like it did.

Ola Söderström stared at the display as the elevator passed each floor. When the elevator stopped and the doors opened, he ran out as fast as he could into the garage to find his colleagues. He heard a car door slam and walked rapidly toward the sound. He heard another door and stretched to see over the tops of the parked cars.

Then he saw Gunnar Öhrn's silhouette disappear into a car and the sound of yet another car door echoed in the garage.

"Stop!" shouted Ola.

The red brake lights lit up in front of him.

Gunnar opened the door and stuck his head out.

"What's the matter?"

Ola caught up with the car, rested one arm on the door and tried to get his breath back.

"We've...got...hold...of the call logs," he said.

He gave Gunnar the lists.

Mia and Henrik looked at each other.

"Thomas Rydberg's...cell. Check page eight. His...texts."

Ola leaned against the door and took three deep breaths while Gunnar found the right page. On line two there was a text that was extremely strange. Del.Tues.1.

"Has Thomas sent this?" he said.

Ola nodded briefly.

"To whom?"

"The phone is registered with the Migration Board."

"Hans Juhlén?"

"Yes, or perhaps his secretary Lena?" said Ola.

Gunnar nodded slowly, then closed his car door and drove off in a great hurry.

CHAPTER THIRTY-FOUR

It seemed like Lena Wikström was still in pain. She pressed her right hand against her kidney and glared at Jana Berzelius who was standing in front of her with the loaded gun. She had stood there a long time, her eyes just staring.

"The necklace," Jana whispered.

She was suddenly hit by the incredible force of a memory. With a girl, a boy and a woman. *The woman had a gun and she and the boy threw themselves backward. He got a firm hold of the woman's arm and twisted it to make her drop the gun. A shot went off. The sound echoed between the trees.*

The woman shrieked with pain when the boy forced her arm back.

The girl got hold of the gun and immediately pointed it at the woman. Then she saw the boy sink down on the grass. He had been hit.

And the girl…was me.

It was me!

Jana felt dizzy and had to hold on to the kitchen table to support herself.

"Hades," she said slowly.

Lena gasped.

"You! You killed him!" said Jana. "I saw it. You killed him right in front of my eyes!"

Lena was silent, her eyes turned into narrow slits and she examined Jana from top to toe.

"Who are you?" she then said.

Jana's hands started to shake. The gun vibrated. She held it in both hands to keep it still, to keep her aim on Lena.

"Who are you?" Lena repeated. "You can't be the person I think you are."

"Who do you think I am?"

"Ker?"

Jana nodded.

"It can't be true…" said Lena. "It can't be."

"You killed him!"

"He isn't dead. Who has said he's dead?"

"But I saw it—"

"Don't believe everything you see," Lena cut her off.

"You know what's inside those containers, don't you?" Jana said slowly.

"Yes. You ought to know too," said Lena.

"Tell me!" said Jana.

"You don't know? Can't you remember?"

"Tell me what was in them!" Jana insisted.

Lena got up with some effort from the floor, sighed heavily and sat with her back against the kitchen cupboards.

"Nothing remarkable…"

Lena winced with pain, pulled up her sweater and looked at the red mark that Jana's blow had left.

"Go on!" Jana said.

"About what?"

"What was in them? Narcotics?"

"Narcotics?" said Lena. She looked with surprise at Jana and smiled.

"Yes, exactly," she said and nodded. "That's right, narcotics. We…"

"Which we! Tell me!"

"Pah, there isn't so much to tell…it started mainly by chance, one could say, but then it got more…organized."

"Do you know why I have a name carved on my neck?"

Lena didn't answer.

"Tell me!"

Jana took a step forward and pointed the gun right at Lena's head. Lena played it cool and shrugged her shoulders. "It was his idea. Not mine. I had nothing to do with it. I just…helped a little."

"Who is *he*? Tell me!" screamed Jana.

"Never," said Lena.

"Tell me!"

"No! Never, never, never!"

Jana held the gun in a new grasp. "And Thomas Rydberg, what did he do?" she said.

"He knew when the containers were on their

way. Then he informed me. First by calling, later by sending me a message. Stupid, really."

Lena took a deep breath.

"But he paid well," she said.

"Who? Thomas? Who paid well?"

Jana suddenly heard the sound of a car braking.

"Are you expecting anybody?"

Lena shook her head.

"Get up. Be quick! Up!" Jana ordered when she heard car doors slamming. She held the gun against the back of Lena's head and pushed her toward the window.

"Who is it?"

"The police!"

"The police?" Jana thought. *What are they doing here? What do they know?*

She bit her lip. They must immediately leave the house. But what should she do with Lena? She smothered a vengeful impulse to kill her. Killing Lena was of course absurd. Lena was an important source and for the moment she was the only one who could say who was responsible for everything that had happened and why. But what should she do? Tie her up? Leave her be? Knock her unconscious?

Jana swore to herself. She put her hand into her pocket and pulled out Thomas Rydberg's phone and placed it in front of Lena.

"Using texts these days isn't stupid at all," she said. "In fact it was extremely well done. Do you know what this is? It's Thomas Rydberg's cell."

"Why have you got it?"

"That doesn't matter, but now I know how to get rid of it."

Jana nodded to Lena.

"Move!"

Footsteps could be heard outside the door.

Jana held the gun pointed at the back of Lena's head and pushed her toward the bedroom.

When she saw the open suitcase on the bed, she told Lena to sit down next to it. She wiped the mobile and pressed Lena's fingers on it.

"What are you doing? What do you think you're doing!?"

She put the mobile in the suitcase.

"The police are here. You will confess everything to them. That it was you who was behind the murder of Hans Juhlén and Thomas Rydberg."

"You're crazy. Never."

"I see you've got children. Grandchildren too. I shall kill them, one for each day that passes, until you confess."

"You can't do this!"

"Oh yes, I can. And you know I can."

"It won't end here. It will never end. Never!"

"Yes, it will."

"You'll get caught for this! I'll make sure you're caught, Jana, just so you know!"

"You know what? I don't think anybody will suspect a prosecutor. And as for that, you and I will meet in court. In about two weeks I'll charge you for murder. Murder gives the highest penalty in Sweden. So, yes, it will end here. It's over. For you, *Lena*."

When there was a ring on the door, Jana left the bedroom.

She silently unlocked the back door. The garden was embedded in a darkness that embraced her when she stepped out.

THIRTY-FIVE

She tasted blood in her mouth. She was completely exhausted.

The girl threw herself to the ground and crept up to a rock. The pine needles pricked her through her trousers and here and there you could see small red stains of blood. The branches had cut up her legs when she ran.

She tried to hold her breath so that she could hear any sound. But it was hard. She was completely out of breath. Her heart was thumping away from the effort and her head throbbed from the pulsating blood.

She pushed away a strand of hair that had fastened on her sweaty forehead. Tried to straighten her fingers, which had a clamplike hold on the gun. There were seven bullets left in the magazine. She put the gun down on her lap.

She sat there for two hours. Against the rock.

Then she started to run again.

CHAPTER
THIRTY-SIX

Monday, April 23

Lena Wikström had been arrested on suspicion of murdering Thomas Rydberg. Jana Berzelius had asked the court to detain her in custody and there would be a hearing later the same day. Lena would be interrogated, and Gunnar was looking forward to that.

He whistled where he stood waiting in the stairwell. The elevator was in use and the button with the upward-pointing arrow lit up. Even so, he pressed the button a second and third time. As if the elevator would come faster for that.

He felt happy and somewhat relieved over having achieved a breakthrough in the investigation. They had visited Lena Wikström on routine business and quite unexpectedly found they now had a major suspect for the murder of Thomas Rydberg—at any rate she was involved in the murder. Finding Rydberg's mobile in Lena's house was a circumstance they couldn't ignore.

The news about the phone had leaked out to the media during the morning and at a quarter to two in the afternoon Gunnar managed to leave the press conference.

At that, the police press officer had tried to keep to short answers to general questions about Lena Wikström and tried to completely ignore questions of her involvement in the murders of Juhlén and the unidentified boy. Gunnar had hoped that the statement would give the impression that the investigation was moving forward all the time and that thanks to the breakthrough with Lena they could hope that it would all soon be over. But when press officer Sara Arvidsson concluded her short announcement, keen hands shot up into the air followed by a shower of questions. *Is she guilty of the murder of Hans Juhlén? Has she killed the boy too? Can you confirm that she sold drugs?* Arvidsson gave the vaguest answers she could, and mentioned that the investigation was at a sensitive stage, then thanked those present and left.

Gunnar took the elevator up to the police center and grabbed something to eat in the cafeteria. It would be a little while before they started questioning Lena. Feeling hungry, he went straight to the vending machines and selected a chocolate bar and gobbled it down where he stood. Out of the elevator came Peter Ramstedt, in a shiny suit, orange shirt and spotted tie. His hair was backcombed and surprisingly blond. He must be Lena's lawyer too, Gunnar thought.

"Eating on the sly, Gunnar? Doesn't Anneli keep track of you?"

"No," said Gunnar.

"Are you still a couple these days or what? One hears so many rumors."

"You shouldn't believe rumors."

Peter smirked widely.

"No, no, of course not," he said and pulled up his jacket sleeve to see what time it was. "We start in ten minutes. Who's the prosecutor?"

That very same moment the elevator doors opened again and Jana Berzelius stepped out. Today she was wearing a knee-long skirt with a high waist, a white blouse and colored bracelets. Her hair was dead straight and her lips a pale pink.

"Speak of the devil," said Ramstedt loudly. "Shall we?"

Gunnar led the way down the corridor.

Peter Ramstedt walked side-by-side with Jana Berzelius.

He glanced at her.

"Yes, well, you haven't got much of a case," he said.

"No?"

"No technical evidence."

"We've got the phone."

"That doesn't tie my client to the crime."

"Oh yes, it does."

"She isn't going to confess."

"Oh yes, she is," said Jana and walked into the interview room. "Believe me."

* * *

Mia Bolander stood with her legs apart and her arms folded. Behind the mirror window she had a good view of the interview room.

Lena Wikström sat huddled up, her eyes fixed on the table top and her hands folded on her lap. The lawyer sat down, whispered something to her, and she nodded in answer without looking up at him.

Opposite them sat Henrik Levin. Mia saw when he said hello to Jana Berzelius, who put her briefcase down on the floor, pulled out a chair and settled down. She looked her usual alert self. Elegant. Superior. Fucking hell.

The door opened behind Mia, and Gunnar Öhrn came in. He checked that all the technical equipment was working. It was controlled from a few switches and the system allowed them to record on several different media at the same time. It had a function for two cameras that recorded simultaneously so Mia and Gunnar could follow Lena and Henrik on the same screen.

Gunnar went and stood by the window.

At exactly two o'clock, Henrik started the tape recorder and began questioning Lena. Her eyes didn't leave the table when Henrik asked the first questions. She just mumbled her answers.

"We understand that you deleted a list of number and letter combinations from Hans Juhlén's computer on Sunday, April 15. Why?" said Henrik.

"I was told to do so," said Lena.

"By whom?"

"I can't say."

"Did you know someone named Thomas Rydberg?"

"No."

"Strange. Because he sent a text message to you."

"Did he?"

"Don't play stupid now. We know that he had."

"Well, then I suppose he had then."

"Good, so now you can explain what Tues. 1 means?"

"No."

"You don't know or you won't tell?"

Lena didn't answer.

Henrik fidgeted.

"But you do confess that you deleted the file which contained the combinations," he said.

"Yes."

"Do you know what the combinations mean?"

"No."

"I think you do."

"No."

"According to our information, you deleted identity numbers. For containers."

Lena huddled slightly more.

"We need your help to find these containers," said Henrik.

Lena remained silent.

"It's important that you tell us where those containers are."

"It won't be possible to find them."

"Why not? Why won't it be…"

"It won't," she cut him off. "Because I don't know where they are."

"I'm convinced you are not telling the truth."

"Perhaps my client is simply saying what she knows, nothing more," said Peter Ramstedt.

"I don't think so," said Henrik.

And nor do I, thought Mia behind the mirror. She scratched herself under her nose with her index finger and then folded her arms again.

"We'll be sitting in this room until you tell us where the containers are," said Henrik. "So tell us now."

"But I can't."

"Why not?"

"You don't understand."

"What is it we don't understand?"

"It isn't so simple."

"We've got all the time in the world to listen. Tell us now what…"

"No," she cut him off again. "Even if I tell you, you won't be able to get at them."

The room fell silent.

Mia looked at Jana who had fixed her gaze on Lena.

Henrik leaned back on his chair and sighed.

"Okay, then we'll talk about something else meanwhile, about you," he said. "Can I ask…"

Now it was Jana who cut him off. She had leaned forward slightly. Her dark eyes met Lena's uncooperative look.

"How many children do you have?" she said slowly.

Oh, right, she's going to ask the questions now too, thought Mia, irritated. She looked at Gunnar, who stood next to her. He was deeply engrossed in the interview and didn't notice her eyes on him.

"Two," whispered Lena and looked down at the table. She swallowed.

"And what about grandchildren? How many grandchildren do you have?"

"But…" was heard from Peter Ramstedt.

"Let her answer," said Jana.

Mia rolled her eyes and gave a bit of a grunt. She looked at Gunnar yet again. But he didn't notice her demonstrative body language. He just stared at Jana. Of course he thought she was pretty with her long dark hair and everything. If dark hair could be called pretty. Which in fact it wasn't. It was bloody ugly with dark hair like that. And long.

Mia touched her own blond hair and watched Jana who still sat there and waited for an answer from Lena.

"The prosecutor asked how many grandchildren you have," said Henrik.

But what the hell? thought Mia, and took a step back from the window. It looks as if…yes, it looks as if she…

Lena's lips quivered. She nervously clasped her fingers together. Then she raised her head and looked at Jana, at Henrik and Jana again.

A tear fell slowly down her cheek.

"The containers are off at Brandö Island," she said slowly.

Two hours later, Gunnar Öhrn and Henrik Levin had a long and heated discussion with the county police commissioner Carin Radler where they had described their progress in the investigation. Carin listened patiently while they recounted the interview with Lena Wikström.

"You could say that it is of utmost importance that we salvage those containers," said Gunnar.

"And how many people know about her involvement?" said Carin.

"So far, only the team. We must work quickly before the media get wind of all this."

"And how will you explain the salvage operation?"

"We'll cover it."

"But I consider a salvage operation to be irrelevant. The containers you talk of might not even exist."

"I believe they do, and we must find out what they contain."

"But I'm the one who makes the decision in this case."

"I know."

"Putting resources into such an operation is very costly."

"But necessary," said Gunnar. "Two people and a boy have been murdered. Now we must find out why."

Carin thought a while.

"What do you want?" Gunnar had asked.

"I want a solution."

"Good, we do too."

Carin nodded briefly.

"Okay. I'll rely on your judgment. The salvage operation can start tomorrow. Phone the docks."

THIRTY-SEVEN

It was early morning when she got back to Stockholm.

The girl stumbled along on the cobbled street, supporting herself with one hand against the rough façade of the buildings. The shop window glass reflected her mirror image but she did not care. Her little hand touched the locked doors as she passed by. She was looking for a place to hide. Somewhere she could rest. The gun rubbed uncomfortably against her tummy; she had to stop it falling out from her waistband so she used her other hand to keep it in place.

A pedestrian tunnel appeared in front of her. She staggered down the stairs and when she was on the bottom step she met an elderly couple. They stopped and stared at her. But she just kept on going.

The girl felt dizzy. Her legs suddenly gave way and she thrust out her arms to break the fall when she landed on the hard concrete floor. She got up again. Took one step at a time. Supported her-self with one hand on the tiled walls. She looked straight ahead and counted every time she put one foot down in front of the other. She had to keep focused. At the end of the tunnel she saw a barrier; she tried to get through but the doors wouldn't budge. So she sank down on the floor and crawled under it. Then she heard a female voice behind her.

"Hello there! You must pay!"

But the girl didn't listen. Kept on going.

The voice got louder.

"Hello you! You must pay if you want to travel through here!"

She stopped, turned round and whipped the gun out from her trousers. A woman in uniform be-hind her immediately held up her hands and took a step back. The girl balanced the gun's weight in her hands; it felt dreadfully heavy. She could hardly hold it up.

The woman looked frightened. So did the other people who passed by. They all stopped in their tracks and stood completely still.

She waved the gun in front of her and backed toward the stairs. When she reached the top step she turned round and ran down as fast as she could. Her arms shook. She had trouble holding the gun up. She counted as she walked straight ahead 32 steps, and then she lost her footing on the last one. She twisted her ankle in the fall; the pain was intense. Still she didn't show any emotion.

She got up again and limped across to a gar-

bage can. A metallic sound could be heard when the gun landed on the bottom. She shuffled on, relieved that she no longer had to carry the heavy weapon. Now she felt all right. And she would feel even better if she could only get some sleep. Just a little.

Exhausted, she hid in a little space behind a bench, flopping down with her back against a concrete wall. The hard surface pressed against her backbone. Her ankle was throbbing but she didn't care. She found herself in a borderland state between dream and reality.

Then she fell asleep. Sitting in the underground station.

THIRTY-EIGHT

Tuesday, April 24

Henrik Levin wrapped his arms around himself against the cold. His down jacket wasn't much help. The merciless Baltic wind seemed to find its way through the zipper of his coat. He had tried to layer himself, but three hours out in the bitter cold had taken its toll. He looked around to see if there was anywhere he could seek shelter. Ahead of him lay the open sea, and the waves washed against the slippery rocks.

Brandö Island was as far out as you could go in Arkösund. The tourist boats flanked the idyllic spot in the summer and the archipelago line passed close by. Now those summer months felt far away.

His scarf fluttered in the wind and Henrik wound it yet another time round his neck to keep out the draft. He contemplated sitting in the car and looked across to the cordoning tape where a total of fifteen police cars were parked.

The cordoned-off area was all of 500 square meters, and the harbor staff worked methodically so that they could start the salvage process.

It had taken a long time to locate the containers. They had to map the sea floor in the specified area repeatedly with echo sounding. Every response was followed up by divers. The process had taken time, and delayed things by more than two hours.

Around the area they had cordoned off a safety zone and had forbidden other boat traffic. They had a floating crane in place as well as a freight barge for the containers.

Henrik looked at his watch. Ten minutes, they'd said. Then the lifting would start.

Jana Berzelius listened to the radio. As in all complex operations, somebody always revealed more than necessary. Who leaked? The salvage work had attracted an enormous amount of attention and been the most important news item all morning.

Jana turned down the volume and looked out through the windshield. She didn't feel at all like getting out of the car and joining the shivering police officers who were next to the cordon.

Farther away stood Henrik Levin, and he also looked frozen. His shoulders were hunched and his scarf tightly wound round his collar. Now and then he wrapped his arms around himself, trying to get warm.

She turned up the heat in the car—to 23

Celsius—before she pulled out her mobile and downloaded the last hour's emails. There were eight of them, most about additional material for one case or another. One question asked about protecting a witness; another was about a future trial that would take place on May 2. The charge was arson, and the victim was a young woman who fortunately had escaped with her life, but suffered severe burns to her face.

Jana put the phone down in her lap and felt it vibrate. She saw her parents' number on the display. She wondered why they were phoning. Again. Three times in just over a week was out of the ordinary.

At the same time, someone knocked on her windshield.

Mia Bolander waved lazily. Her nose and cheeks were red from the biting wind.

"We're about to start now," she mimed through the glass and went straight off toward Henrik.

Jana nodded and silenced the call.

The dockworkers started moving. Someone waved his arm, another one half ran toward the rocks. A bearded man talked into a walkie-talkie and pointed out to sea.

Jana stretched up in the front seat to try and see what was happening. But she still couldn't. She would have to get out of the car. She put her cell in her pocket, unbuttoned the top button on her parka, turned up her collar and left the car. Her checked cap and long matching scarf kept her warm as she resolutely walked into the cordoned area.

Henrik noted her presence when she came and stood beside him.

The bearded man received a message on his radio and answered.

"You can go ahead now," he said, before turning to Henrik and Gunnar. "Here comes the first one."

Jana looked out across the sea and the safety zone. She screwed up her eyes as she watched the floating crane work. Slowly, slowly, a steel cable was winched up. The waves hit against the barge. The wind howled. Then a dark gray object broke the surface and a container became visible. The water poured down on the sides. The container rotated half a turn and was then lowered cautiously onto the barge.

The second container to be lifted up was blue. When that broke the surface, Jana became rigid. She saw the combination code. And recognized it. Paralyzed, she watched the container's rocking movements before it landed on the barge. When the third container came up, she immediately felt impatient. She wanted to see what was in them. Now!

The salvage operation took one and a half hours. One by one, the containers were lifted from the barge onto land.

Jana put her weight on her other leg, to relax.

Mia Bolander jumped up and down and wound her arms round in large circles.

Anneli Lindgren and Gunnar Öhrn stood next to Ola Söderström and chatted.

Henrik helped to direct the crane operators until all ten containers were lifted into place.

"We'll start with this one," Gunnar shouted and pointed at an orange-colored container that had emerged from the water as number four.

They gathered together outside the steel, moon-shaped doors. The bearded dockworker stood in the middle, in front of the locking mechanism.

"When we open, we've got to be very careful. I want you all to move to a safe distance. The containers will contain a lot of water," he said.

"I thought they were watertight," said Henrik.

"Oh no, believe me, they're not."

Henrik's spirits sank drastically. The hope of finding something important was immediately dampened. Water was a great enemy that could eliminate important evidence. Often very quickly.

"Go back!" the dockworker shouted out.

Jana took several steps backward.

Gunnar got hold of Anneli's arm and pulled her along, as if he wanted to protect her.

Henrik and Mia came after them. From twenty meters, Henrik looked questioningly at the dockworker.

"Go further back!" he shouted.

At fifty meters they stopped. The dockworker gave a thumbs-up sign and then looked closely at the doors. He felt the locking rods and checked the locking mechanism. With the help of a hefty tool, he forced open the lock and set it down. He thought for a few moments about how he could avoid getting caught by any water that might be inside. He steadied himself, put his hand on the metal handle and pulled. His hand slipped. It was like holding a cake of soap. He tried again. Took a firm grip with both hands, tensed his muscles and pulled as hard as he could. The doors opened and water gushed out with enormous power. The dockworker was caught by the flow and landed hard on his back. The water washed over him and he spat and hissed. He tried to wipe his face with his wet jacket, but it didn't help, so he tried to sit up.

But something else came gushing out of the container.

He tried to dry his eyes again so he could see what it was that had landed next to him. Something round and covered with algae. He gave it a slight poke and felt something stick on his hands. He poked again and then rolled the object to one side. He immediately pulled back at the dreadful sight that met him.

It was a decomposed head.

Jana stood stock-still. Her face revealed nothing as she looked across the wet ground. Body parts were strewn everywhere. Rotting arms and legs. Clumps of hair. The stench was awful.

Henrik Levin held his nose as his stomach cramped. He struggled not to vomit.

Anneli Lindgren was very cautious when she documented the head. The face had dissolved, the eye sockets seemed to have grown bigger and what was left of the eyes hung out.

"One year," said Anneli and got up. She estimated roughly one year that they had been in the water. "We can thank our cold climate for the bodies being so well preserved."

Henrik nodded and felt queasy and swallowed several times to get rid of that.

Mia Bolander's face had turned white. She had already used up a whole year's supply of expletives.

Jana Berzelius remained standing at a safe distance. Immobile.

Anneli carefully went up to one of the rotting bones, bent down and took a series of photographs. The skin hung down off the bone like bags of water. When she touched the surface, the skin fell off and stuck on her latex gloves. The bone had penetrated the skin at several places. Anneli got in close with her camera to catch all the details.

"Shall we open the next container?"

Henrik nodded, but he could no longer keep the contents of his stomach down.

It took a relatively long time before the next container could be opened. Because of the macabre contents found in the first one, they had to take rigorous safety precautions. Anneli Lindgren had discussed different methods with the dock manager Rainer Gustavsson. They decided they would pump out the water before the doors were opened. But so as not to risk the contents of the container being sucked out, they needed a mechanical filter and the necessary equipment was only available in Linköping. Bringing it to their location further delayed the process. It took two hours before three technicians arrived with the special pump. They set up the filter unit, fit in the filters then inserted a large valve to regulate the flow of the water.

Henrik Levin left all this to the specialists. Even though the outdoor temperature had fallen during the afternoon, he was no longer freezing. He just wanted not to vomit again. He had emptied his stomach three times, and that was three times too many. He wasn't the only one. Even Mia Bolander got sick. She stood next to him now and looked pale.

"We'll start the pump now," said one of the technicians.

The water poured out from the container into a large tank. The emptying took place in silence. The rotted bodies had left everyone shocked and stunned. Henrik thanked the powers above that the cordoning had kept the journalists at a distance. Anneli had called in reinforcement, and five police officers were now following her instructions and gathering together the body parts for transport to forensics. Henrik looked from a slight distance at the rust that climbed up the blue steel wall of the container.

Jana Berzelius stood behind him. She didn't

see the rust. She saw the numbers. And letters. The combination.

Just like they had looked in her dream.

"I think we are going to find more bodies inside there," said Mia.

"Do you think so?" said Henrik.

"Yes, I fucking bet there'll be corpses in all of them," said Mia.

"I hope not," said Henrik dejectedly.

"Ready!" called out one of the pump technicians.

"Who's going to open it?" Henrik called back.

"Not any of my workers. The last one is at the clinic getting his stomach pumped. He swallowed a bit too much water. And other stuff. You open it."

"Me?" said Henrik, surprised.

"Yes? Open it now."

Henrik went up to the doors and felt them. They were slimy. He pulled one rod toward him but the door didn't budge. He took a deep breath. He separated his legs far apart to give himself leverage, then got a harder grip on the rod and gave a sudden pull. The door creaked as it slowly opened.

Inside the container was dark. Completely black and totally impossible to see inside. Dripping water echoed as it hit the hard floor. The space sounded empty.

"Lights!" he said.

Mia Bolander rushed off to a car and got a large torch from the trunk. She hurried back to Henrik.

"Can someone see that we get some more lights!" she shouted. "We must be able to see!"

Henrik took a large flashlight and turned it on. The ray of light worked its way over the dark floor. He took one hesitant step forward, and then another. The light traveled across the floor from one side to the other, up to the ceiling and across it and finally back down into the floor of one of the far corners.

He caught sight of something in there. He lifted the flashlight and held it as steadily as he could while pointing it there. Then over to the other corner. Something was there too. A heap of some sort. Two more steps and he was inside the container. He made his way slowly forward, inch by inch so as not to risk treading on anything. He kept the torch pointing just in front of his feet on the floor to make sure nothing was in the way. Then up again and into the corners. Now he was halfway inside the container. And he saw the heap.

Of skulls.

That same moment the whole interior was lit up by a car headlight. Henrik blinked in the strong beam, he turned round and saw Mia give him a thumbs-up sign. He did a thumbs-down.

"You were right, Mia. There are more here."

Mia Bolander went quickly up to the opening and looked in.

Jana Berzelius followed closely after her.

Side by side they stood and looked at the corner that Henrik Levin was pointing toward.

"Here," he said.

"But what's that?" said Mia and nodded into the container. In the middle lay a rusty object with a pink frame.

"That's a mirror," said Jana slowly.

She recognized it. It was familiar. As if she had had one like it. And she had too. Of course she had. With a crack in it. Like this one. *But...if this was mine, what was it doing here?*

Jana held her breath. The hairs stood up on her neck. On her arms. She slowly looked toward the heap of bones that lay in both corners. She understood what they were. That they were all that was left.

Of some people she once knew.

"Damn and blast, right, from now on I want a 24-hour watch on the docks!"

Gunnar Öhrn slammed his fist on the plastic table. He was bright red in the face and looked at the group of tired people sitting round the table.

Henrik had dark rings under his eyes.

Mia had a vacant stare and Ola was yawning widely.

The only one missing at this briefing was Anneli—she was still documenting the remains of the bodies from the first container. She was being helped by five forensic experts from Linköping and Stockholm. A team from Örebro was on its way.

Because of the advanced state of deterioration the work was very arduous. It was almost impossible to lift up body parts with your hands. They used special lifting gear and soft bases so that the skin wouldn't fall off during the move. They had opened all ten containers and in every one had found human remains. There were only bones left, except in one, and that was the first container which had only been on the seabed about one year.

It was now just before 9:00 p.m. The team had been on Brandö for eleven hours. What had at first been a technical salvage operation had been transformed into a seething workplace for a lot of police officers, trainees and forensics. The work would go on all night. Perhaps for several days.

Gunnar got even redder in the face thinking about it.

"Not a single container must be emptied without supervision. Is that clear? We must check everything that comes into the docks. And I really mean everything."

They all nodded.

On the table was some takeaway food well packed in aluminum dishes. Nobody had touched it. The stench from the decomposed body parts still hung over the area and because of that they all had a nonexistent appetite.

"The combinations on the containers are the same as those that Juhlén had in his computer," said Ola.

"And that Lena Wikström deleted," said Mia.

"Why did she do that?" said Ola.

"She had been given orders by somebody," said Henrik.

"And we're going to find out who. We'll make her tell us," said Gunnar.

"We're talking about loads of corpses here, there's like ten mass graves…" said Mia. "Who are these people? Or were?"

"Hans Juhlén must presumably have known," said Henrik.

"And Lena Wikström must know his role in it all, they were working in the same department."

They all nodded again.

"Are there any similarities between the containers?" said Gunnar.

"Well, all the containers were from Chile," said Henrik.

"Yes, but apart from that. In which city were they loaded? Who loaded them?" said Gunnar.

"We'll find out," said Henrik.

"According to the call log for Thomas Rydberg's mobile, it would seem that another load is to be expected. In a text he sent to Lena he wrote: Del. Tues.1," said Gunnar. "She won't say what that means, but I'd guess that it's about a delivery due on Tuesday the first. Next Tuesday is the first of May and so I think we must check every nook and cranny on all freight ships that are going to dock here in Norrköping then," said Henrik.

"But the message could just as well mean that there's a delivery to a house which is number one, or that it's a delivery to a person, or that the ship is number one, or…" said Mia.

"We get your point," said Gunnar.

"But I'm just saying that perhaps we ought to widen the approach a little," said Mia.

"Yes!"

"Were there any more texts? Similar ones I mean," said Henrik.

"No, not from Rydberg, and nobody else either," said Ola.

"Right then," said Gunnar. "We'll interrogate Lena again. Get her to talk. Find out in what way the Migration Board is involved. Check all the employees."

He rubbed his face and went on. "And check Lena's cell. Texts, conversations—everything! Then I want you to look for all the people who have ever had any contact with her. Classmates, boyfriends, aunties, uncles—all of them," said Gunnar. "And ask Rainer to write down the ships that are going to dock there. Talk to every captain and ask them to start to open the containers onboard."

"But it's impossible to open the containers onboard, a ship can carry more than six thousand," said Henrik.

"And out at sea there can be high winds or storms," said Mia.

Gunnar rubbed his hand over his face again.

"Well then, we'll simply have to open them all when they reach the port. The most important thing is to nail the people who've done this. And nobody, NOBODY, can let up until we've found the bastards!"

CHAPTER THIRTY-NINE

Phobos drew the gun from his hip. He got a good grip on the weapon. As always. With an accustomed hand he put the gun back into his waistband and covered it with his jacket. Then he drew it again. And again.

It was important to quickly switch from normal to emergency. Especially when he was on guard. Anything could happen, he had learned that. And it wasn't only darkly dressed men who were difficult. Even a lightly dressed woman could be a big problem.

On the roof he had a good view of the back street. He was only on the second floor and stood leaning against the concrete façade of the next-door building.

The premises under him were locked up, hidden behind a curtain of metal. A vertical advertising sign spread its flickering light over the cobbles. The fabric from a torn awning fluttered in the wind. An empty tin can noisily rolled along the pavement edge. Phobos had his gaze directed toward a steel door. The windows next to it had bars on them. Nobody could imagine that there was trade going on behind them. But there was. And it had been going on for four hours. That was how long he had been standing there. In the dark.

As soon as the business was finished he would make sure that what he was protecting would be safely conveyed. But it would probably be at least another hour. Hopefully it would be quicker than that.

Phobos sincerely hoped so.

Because he was freezing.

So he drew his gun to keep himself warm.

He had been thinking of her all day.

Karl Berzelius sighed, turned off the television and went across to the window. Tried to look out over the garden. But out there it was as dark as down a deep well.

Karl met his mirror image in the mullioned window. He was in a somber mood and wondered why she hadn't answered.

It was silent in the house. Margaretha had gone to bed early. He had silenced her at dinner, hadn't been able to talk. Even less able to eat. Margaretha had looked at him in astonishment. Her short and sinewy body had squirmed. She had fiddled about with her steel-rimmed spectacles. Taken small bites of food.

There was nothing that Margaretha needed to know. Absolutely nothing, he now said to himself.

He looked down at his hands and felt deep remorse.

Why hadn't he dealt with those carved letters straightaway? Why had he let the child keep them on her neck? He knew why—it had been too hard to explain to somebody why she might have had them or where they came from. If it had come out that she had marks carved on the flesh of her neck, she might have been called a freak. There would have been gossip. *Berzelius has adopted a freak.* She would probably have been classified as one of those people who cut themselves. Perhaps there would even have been talk of an institution for people with destructive behavior.

Karl felt how his anguish turned into anger. It was as if history was about to repeat itself. Again she would risk not only his good reputation, but also her own. Accursed child, he thought. It was all her fault!

He immediately became thankful that she hadn't answered the phone. He didn't want to talk to her any longer. From now on he would not take any steps to have contact with her again.

He nodded slowly, satisfied with that fateful decision.

He remained standing by the window quite a while. Then he turned off the table lamps in the living room, went into the bedroom and lay down beside Margaretha to sleep. After just over an hour he still lay there awake. He got up and put on his dark blue dressing gown and wide slippers. He shuffled across to the sofa, sat down with difficulty and started watching TV again.

The little wine fridge held twelve bottles.

Jana Berzelius grasped one of them, pressed the electric corkscrew and filled a crystal glass to the brim. She took a gulp and felt how the light yellow liquid ran down her throat.

It had been necessary to leave the salvage site. She had stood there a short while and looked into the container, then she had told Henrik she had to go. She quickly walked across the area, got into her car and drove home.

She couldn't stand still, had to occupy herself with something. She opened the big fridge and pulled out a cluster of tomatoes. With a knife in her hand, she started to cut them up, slowly cutting through the thin skin, putting the slices in a bowl, and swallowed yet another gulp of wine. Took out a cucumber, rinsed it and put that under the knife too. She thought about the container. Deep inside she had known that its contents would be important for her. The dream had shown the numbers, letters, the combination. She had seen it and known. But she had had no idea that she would find the mirror in there. She cut slice after slice of cucumber. *How could she know it was her mirror?* The knife worked faster with the cucumber. *Had she been inside it? She must have been inside it.* The slices were coming all the faster. *She had been inside it!* Now she was violently hacking away at the cucumber. Then she raised the knife and stabbed it right into the chopping board. The blade sank deep into the wood.

Jana thought about it from different angles. Started thinking about the carved name on her neck. *Why did she have a name carved there? Why had she been marked in that way?* She really did want an answer to all her questions. But there was nobody to ask. Except Lena. Jana immediately dismissed the idea of visiting Lena at the detention center. Someone could overhear the questions she would ask. Perhaps start to suspect something, or even find out that Jana was carrying out her own investigation on the side. She didn't want to risk anything, not unnecessarily. She took a deep breath. There really was nobody else to turn to. Nobody at all. Unless... Jana looked up and saw the knife sticking straight up from the chopping board. No...there was nobody. Or was there? Well, perhaps there was one person. A single person, but he wasn't alive. If he had been alive he would certainly have been able to tell her everything. But he wasn't alive, of course. *Was he? Could he...? No...or?*

Jana grasped the wineglass and went to her computer. She emptied the glass in one gulp, sat down in front of the computer and went to a site where you could search for companies and people throughout the country. She hesitated a moment, then wrote the name *Hades* and pressed Enter.

Lots of company names showed up, but not a single person. She opened another search engine and wrote the same name. The search gave thirty-one million results.

She sighed. It was hopeless. He wouldn't be still alive. He couldn't be. It was simply impossible. But why had Lena implied that he was?

She changed her search to "Hades as a name" but that too resulted in a hoard of pages. She tried every possible combination of the name to try to find something that would lead to him.

She was close to giving up when it suddenly struck her. If you really wanted to find somebody then you ought to look in the police computers.

She needed to get into those databases.

And she needed to get into them without being found out.

CHAPTER
FORTY

Frederic "Freddy" Olsson drummed on the garbage trolley. The music pumped away in his earphones. A rasping voice at high volume.

Billy Idol.

"Hey little sister, what have you done?"

Freddy nodded in time and sang along with the lyrics.

"Hey little sister, who's your only one?"

It was just before midnight and there was nobody on the platform.

Freddy parked his trolley routinely in front of a waste bin, opened the lid and lifted out the bag of rubbish. He had to exert himself, the bag was heavy.

Goddam, so much rubbish, he thought before he tied the bag and let it join the others on the trolley.

He got out a new bag, turned up the volume on his Walkman and sang: "It's a nice day to start again."

Then he stopped, drummed on the trolley and bellowed out: "It's a nice day for a white wedding."

He smiled to himself, lined the bin with the new bag and locked the lid with a click.

When he steered the garbage trolley toward the next rubbish bin he caught sight of a leg sticking out from a little space behind a bench. He went up to it and saw a little girl sitting there, leaning against the wall. She was fast asleep.

Freddy looked around as if he was looking for her parents. But the platform was empty. He slowly took off his earphones, went up to the girl and prodded her.

"Hey," he said. "Hey, you!"

She didn't move.

"Hey little girl, wake up!"

With his fingers he prodded her cheek. Once again, a bit harder. Her dark eyes stared straight into his, and in a fraction of a second she was on her feet. She shouted and waved her arms, trying to get away from him as quickly as possible.

"Easy," said Freddy.

But she didn't listen. She backed away from him.

"Hey, stop there," he said when he saw where she was going.

"Stop! Oh hell! Watch out!"

The girl continued to back away.

"Stop! Watch out!" he shouted and threw himself forward to catch her.

But it was too late. The girl stepped right over

the edge onto the track. The last thing she saw was Freddy's terrified look.

Then everything was black.

CHAPTER FORTY-ONE

Anneli Lindgren took off her gloves. She was feeling rather faint. It had been an incredibly demanding day and she hadn't eaten anything all those hours she'd been working. She longed to get home to her flat and to get some sleep. But first she'd have to pick up her son from her mother's; Anneli had had to call her in to look after him when she realized how much work she had ahead of her.

It was eleven in the evening when the last marks had been made in the area and in the containers. The camera contained more than one thousand photos and the battery was almost empty. The team had left the salvage site, there were just a few uniformed police officers left, and Gunnar Öhrn.

He came up to her.

"Time to call it a day?" said Gunnar.

"Yes."

"Can I give you a lift?"

She looked at him with suspicion.

"You look tired," said Gunnar.

"Thanks."

"No, I didn't mean it like that…"

"I know. I'm tired and I just want to get home but I've got to go to the station first and leave the camera there and some other stuff."

"Then we'll drop in there on the way."

"Are you sure?"

"Yeah, sure. Come on."

Jana Berzelius stood close to the wall with her briefcase in her hand and looked out over the open office landscape. There was just one woman sitting at one of the desks typing away with her eyes fixed on the screen in front of her. The office was otherwise empty. It was 11:00 p.m. and presumably the rest of the night shift was out on calls. Or they had been sent to the salvage site.

Perfect, Jana thought.

Thanks to the lie about having to visit the detention cells, it had been easy to get into the police building. She walked determinedly toward the woman who immediately looked up from her work when she heard Jana approaching. She was young, twenty-something. Blue eyes, pearl earrings.

"Hello, I'm Jana Berzelius. Prosecutor."

"Hi, I'm Matilda."

"I'm working with Gunnar and his team and we usually meet in here," said Jana and pointed toward the conference room.

"Oh yes?"

"And I need your help. During our last meeting

I happened to leave my notebook in the conference room and I wonder if you could open it for me."

Matilda looked at the clock and then at Jana, hesitant.

"I'm going to the arrest unit," Jana explained. "And I've got to have something to write my notes on if somebody is arrested tonight."

Matilda swallowed the lie, smiled and got up from her chair.

"Of course I can open it for you."

Matilda got up.

Jana glanced quickly at her computer screen and saw that the police register was open. So Matilda was logged in.

She followed her down the corridor to the conference room. Matilda opened the door with her key card and held it open for Jana.

"Here you are."

"Thank you," said Jana. "Now I'll manage."

"Close the door after you when you've found your notebook."

"Yes, of course. It must be here somewhere," said Jana and stepped into the room.

She heard Matilda returning to her desk and computer, and walked round the conference table to make the search more credible. Then she opened her briefcase, took out her notebook and closed the door behind her.

"Here it is," she said when she went past Matilda. "Thanks for your help."

"You're welcome. No trouble," answered Matilda

and waved absentmindedly to the prosecutor when she left the office landscape.

It was silent again around Matilda. Now the hard disk sounded loud and the ceiling fan buzzed.

She liked working on her own and especially at night when you didn't risk being interrupted by questions from colleagues or being disturbed by all the telephones ringing that could be heard throughout the day.

She heard the ping from the lift and how the doors closed again.

She picked up her cell and was just about to phone her boyfriend when she heard something. It sounded like metal, and it came from the kitchen. She listened carefully to see if she could hear it again. Had she imagined it? No, there it was again.

She got up to go and see what it was. With her phone in her hand she walked toward the kitchen, turned on the light and glanced around at the sink and the dining table. It was cold in there and she wrapped her arms around herself and shivered. The sound returned. She turned her head toward the windows and saw that one of them was open. She relaxed and went across to close it. The very moment she shut the window, she heard a loud noise behind her. She was scared and it gave her a start. The kitchen door had slammed shut.

"Oh, it's only the door, from the draft," she mumbled to herself when she felt how fast her heart was beating.

She pressed the handle on the window frame to the locked position. She glanced at the well-filled fruit basket on the sideboard but decided she'd rather have something sweet. In a striped tin she found what she was looking for and immediately popped a round biscuit into her mouth. With another one in her hand, she closed the lid and decided to go back to work. She took hold of the kitchen door handle but...nothing happened. It wouldn't budge. The door was locked! Hell!

She felt the door handle again. How could it lock itself? She couldn't fathom it at all. She knocked lightly on the door but realized immediately that it was a waste of time.

She was the only person in the department.

Jana Berzelius heard Matilda knock on the door when she quickly sat down on the office chair and pulled the keyboard toward her.

Now she would have to work quickly.

Gunnar Öhrn opened the door for Anneli Lindgren who yawned widely. She had dozed off during the drive from the salvage site to the police building.

"Are we already there?" she said.

"Yes. Shall I take it all up for you?"

"No. I'll come with you."

Gunnar opened the boot, lifted out a large, heavy bag and grasped the camera bag too, which he handed over to Anneli.

She hung it over her shoulder and yawned widely again. Then they walked side-by-side to the lifts, pressed the button and waited to go up to the third floor.

Matilda didn't know what on earth she should do. She pounded on the door. Felt the handle again and tried to push against the door with all her weight. But it didn't help. She banged on the door, once, twice and a third time.

"Hello!" she called out. "Hello!"

Yet again she reminded herself that there wasn't a single person in the department apart from her. Then she realized she had her mobile in her pocket. But who could she phone? Her first thought was to ring her boyfriend. But he wasn't authorized to get into the police building, she almost laughed at the silly idea. The reception? They could send somebody up, a maintenance man or something. But then she remembered that she only had her private mobile in her hand. And that she didn't have any direct numbers or internal numbers to the various departments.

"Oh Christ, this is so stupid," she said out loud and kicked the door.

Jana heard how the elevator started up. And how Matilda hit the door. Although it sounded more like a kick.

She had done the search but...nothing. No results when she tried "Hades." What else could she try? She thought frantically. Think up something! Think! Think! Think!

The elevator had stopped. Probably on the floor below but just as she sighed with relief she heard it starting up again. On the way up.

Jana was still thinking. What else could he be called besides Hades? What? She bit her lip, her thoughts spun round. Then a name floated up from her memory. Something beginning with Dan…

She wrote "Dan" and got lots of entries for various people with that name. But it didn't feel right. Dano… Daniel… Danilo… Danilo! She immediately entered that name.

The elevator was close now.

Come on! Give me something!

Jana looked up over the screen then quickly down again. Then she saw the result. There were several Danilos. But her eye fell on Danilo Peña. In Södertälje.

Jana pulled out her mobile, took a picture of the screen and then immediately exited from the register. Then she grabbed her things, quickly took off her shoes and ran in her stockinged feet with them in her hand toward the elevator. She pressed the button and the doors opened immediately. She sneaked up to the staff kitchen, carefully pulled the chair away from under the door handle, before rushing back to the now open elevator, and pressing the button for the garage.

The doors closed slowly and just as they did so she heard the neighboring elevator give a ping as the doors opened and somebody stepped out.

* * *

The heavy bag rubbed against his hip, and Gunnar changed his hold on it when he entered the lift.

Anneli went in after him.

The department was empty and silent, as it usually was at night. They both went along to Anneli's room, turned on the light and left the two bags inside.

"Hello!" Matilda called out. "Is someone there? Hello?"

She banged on the door and felt the handle which…easily went down. She pushed open the door and almost bumped into an astonished Gunnar.

"Oh, God!" said Matilda. "Lucky that you're here. I've been locked in."

"What did you say? Locked in?" said Anneli who had just come out from her room.

"Yes, in the kitchen! The door locked itself. I couldn't get out."

Gunnar went up to the door and felt the handle. Up and down, no problem at all.

"Strange. This door can't lock itself. You can't lock it at all," he said.

"But… I couldn't get out," said Matilda.

"Well, how did you open the door now?"

"Well, I…opened…"

"So it was unlocked?"

"No, it was locked. I couldn't open it."

"But then you could."

"Yes."

Matilda felt like an idiot. How could she explain to them? She *had* been locked in! But now she couldn't face having to explain the whole thing to them.

"Well I couldn't get out," she mumbled to herself and walked off with a grumpy expression back to her desk.

CHAPTER FORTY-TWO

Wednesday, April 25

Henrik Levin woke up. Didn't know where he was, but realized after a few seconds that he'd fallen asleep on the sofa in the living room. It was pitch black in the room. He picked up his mobile; the display said it was 02:30, so he had only slept a couple of hours. The display turned off and it became black around him again.

At seven o'clock he woke up to the sound of a smothered ringing tone. He had dropped the phone in his sleep and now he had to look on the floor to find it. It was under the sofa, and when he reached it he turned the alarm off, stretched out and felt that he had had far too little sleep.

After a quick breakfast with Emma and the children, he drove to the station. Gunnar Öhrn was the first to meet him and they made their way together to the conference room.

"It seems as if everyone in the containers has

been shot. There are marks on the skeletons to indicate that," said Gunnar.

"So they were killed and then dumped into the sea," said Henrik.

"Yes."

"But why were they killed? Was it about money? Drugs? Were they refugees who didn't pay? Did somebody betray them? Were they smugglers?"

"I don't know, but I'm thinking along the same lines. Above all I can't really see what role Hans Juhlén had. Why was he murdered?"

"Ought we to bring in his wife for questioning again?"

"Perhaps, but I think we can get some more out of Lena. To be honest, Henrik…"

Gunnar stopped and looked in both directions. Then he looked at Henrik. Sighed.

"This has turned into an extremely complicated series of events. I don't know any longer what we should concentrate on. First Hans Juhlén, then the boy and last Thomas Rydberg. And then this mass grave at sea—it's rather hard to digest. And hardly something we can make public. Yet Carin is on me like a polecat."

"She wants a press conference?"

"Yes."

"But we've got nothing concrete to give them."

"I know, and we must tone it all down. It already feels as if this is getting too much for us. I might have to ask the National Crime Squad for help and you know what I think about that."

A shadow fell across Gunnar's face.

Henrik pondered.

"Wait until we've questioned Lena again," he said.

Gunnar looked at Henrik as he said that. His eyes were red, shiny. He threw out his hand.

"Okay, I'll wait until we know some more."

At a quarter to seven, Jana Berzelius drove down the slip road to the E4, the motorway to Stockholm.

The sun was up and it dazzled her from the east. The music on the radio was interrupted for news and weather reports and the meteorologists warned about black ice on the roads.

The traffic got heavier after Nyköping and the sun disappeared too. The sky turned dark gray and the temperature went down to zero. The hard rain beat against the asphalt. She stared straight ahead on the wet road. Listened to the noise inside the car. The forest dashed past on both sides of her. The fencing was rubbed out in the periphery. Taillights turned into red streaks.

At Järna the lines started. While she waited for the traffic to start flowing again, she opened an app on her mobile and entered the address for Danilo Peña. She couldn't use the car's own GPS—it would have been extremely risky as her journey could easily be tracked should anyone do a check.

The app presented a clear route and she could see that she was only ten minutes from her destination. The rain stopped but the heavy gray clouds remained. She turned off the motorway and drove toward the center. A right turn and she was in Ronna. Here were blocks of flats with green, blue and bright yellow balconies. On the streets there were lots of neon-colored signs with handwritten texts in languages other than Swedish.

A gang of five youths sat in a smashed bus shelter, an elderly lady stood some way away supporting herself with a brown stick. A car with a punctured tire, a bicycle with the front wheel missing and an overflowing wastepaper bin.

She looked for number 36 and found it far down along Smedvägen. She parked on the street and considered putting money in the parking meter, which was covered with graffiti, but it was out of order. On her way to the high-rise building, she passed several cars, all with crosses or icons hanging from the rearview mirror by the windscreen. By taking small steps she avoided the pools of water that had formed on the ground.

In the entrance hall sat three ladies with shawls, chatting to each other. They stared quite openly and disapprovingly at Jana when she came in through the door. A child's scream, loud voices and the banging of doors echoed in the stairwell. It was cold and damp. Smelt of cooking.

The list of tenants showed that she would have to go to the eighth floor, so she took the lift. When the lift doors opened again she looked out cautiously. On the door closest to the stairs it said D. Peña.

She stepped out of the lift and raised her hand to knock on the door but that same instant discovered that it wasn't properly shut. She gave it a push and the door swung open.

"Hello?" she called out and stepped into the hall.

No furniture at all, just an old mat on the floor and yellowy-brown wallpaper.

She called out again and got an echo in answer.

For a moment she hesitated, but then felt bolder and stepped straight into the living room. A ripped-open sofa, a little table in front of it, a television, a mattress without any sheets, a pillow and a checkered blanket. The wind howled through the crack in a window.

She went through the living room toward the kitchen. Stopped, held her breath and listened for any sound.

She stood like that for a few seconds, then stepped through the doorway into the kitchen. That same moment she saw a fist coming at her and the blow knocked her to the floor. She saw the fist again and immediately raised her forearm to shield herself. The other forearm came up, the blow hit her wrist and the pain was intense.

Up, she thought.

I must get up!

She twisted her body toward the left, quickly put her right hand in under her chest and pushed herself up.

Then she saw a man and what he had in his hand.

"Don't move," he said. "If you want to live."

*T*he girl tried to swallow but her tongue felt numb. She tried to open her eyes but couldn't. As if in a tunnel, she heard a voice talk to her but she couldn't grasp the words. Somebody touched her and she tried to hit the hand away.

"Calm down," said the voice.

When she lifted her hand to hit out again she felt an intense pain in her head, which forced her to remain still. In the end she opened her eyes and met with a strong light.

She blinked several times until a stranger appeared in front of her. A white-dressed man was leaning over the bed she lay in.

"What's your name?" he said.

The girl didn't answer.

She screwed up her eyes to accustom them to the light. The man had blond hair, spectacles and a beard.

"I'm Doctor Mikael Andersson. You are in hos-

pital. You've been in an accident. Do you know your name?"

She swallowed again, searched her memory for an answer.

"Do you remember what happened?"

She turned her head and looked at the doctor. The pain pulsated in her bandaged head. She shut her eyes for a few moments, and then opened them again slowly. She didn't know how she should answer. Because she couldn't remember.

She couldn't remember anything at all.

FORTY-FOUR

Phobos fidgeted with his gun. He knew that he had carried out the mission most satisfactorily. And it was a simple task to shoot that man who hadn't paid in time.

A single shot sufficed. In the back of his head. One hole. Blood on the floor.

It was better to sneak up on the victims and shoot them from behind, then they didn't have time to react and there was less risk of opposition. They just fell forwards. Most of them died straightaway. Others shook. Made a noise.

The water broke against the boat and it rocked heavily. Even so, he felt relaxed and satisfied. Because he knew he would get his reward.

At last he would get the dose he deserved.

The gun was two centimeters from Jana Berzelius's cheek.

The man in front of her quickly wiped a drop

of saliva from the corner of his mouth. He had long dark hair, brown eyes and an angular face.

Who was he? Was it Hades?

"Who the hell are you?" said the man and pushed the gun even closer to her cheek.

"I'm a prosecutor," she said and wondered quickly about possible escape routes.

They stood in the kitchen; the living room was behind her, the hall in front. Two escape routes, one of which required more time. She could knock him out but he had the advantage with the gun.

She looked across at the kitchen table. No knives.

"Don't try," said the man. "Tell me instead what you as a prosecutor are doing in my place."

"I need your help."

The man laughed.

"Oh really? You don't say. How interesting. And what can I help you with?"

"You can help me to find out something."

"Something? And what is this *something* about?"

"My background."

"Your background? How could I help you with that when I don't even know who you are?"

"But I know who you are."

"Really? Who am I then?"

"You are Danilo."

"Brilliant. Did you work that out all by yourself, or did you perhaps read my name on the door?"

"You are someone else too?"

"You mean I'm a schizo?"

"Show me your neck?"

The man fell completely silent.

"You've got another name written there," said Jana. "I know what it says. If I guess right then you must tell me how you got it. If I guess wrong then you can let me go."

"We'll change the agreement a little. If you guess right then I'll tell you. Sure, that's no problem. If you guess wrong, or if I don't have a name on my neck, then I'll shoot you."

He cocked the gun, took a couple of steps back from her and stood with his legs apart ready to shoot.

"I can report you for attempted murder," said Jana.

"And I can report you for breaking in. Now guess!"

Jana swallowed.

She was pretty sure it was him.

But would she dare say the name?

She shut her eyes.

"Hades," she whispered and heard a shot go off.

CHAPTER FORTY-FIVE

The girl sat before her on the hard chair with her eyes on the floor. She hunched up and her hands were hidden under her thighs.

She just sat there.

Silent.

Welfare officer Beatrice Alm looked up over her reading glasses and delicately shut the folder lying on the desk.

"Well now," she said and leaned forward and folded her hands. "You are one lucky girl. You are going to get a mommy and a daddy."

CHAPTER FORTY-SIX

Jana opened her eyes.

The man was still standing in front of her with the gun lowered. For a brief second she felt her body to see if she had been hit. She hadn't. The bullet had gone right past her and left a hole in the wall behind.

She fixed her eyes on the man. He was breathing heavily.

"How do you know?" he asked with his jaws tightly pressed together. "How the fuck do you know? Tell me!"

He went up to her and stood with his face against hers.

"How the fuck did you know that? Tell me now!"

He grabbed her hair and forced her head back. Brutally. Then he hit her on her forehead with the gun and pressed it against her temple.

"I'll shoot again. And this time I promise it'll go right in here. So tell me. Spit it out!"

Jana made a face.

"I've got a name too," she said roughly.

He immediately thrust her head to one side. Pulled at her hair, scratching the skin. She felt her neck exposed to him and began to panic. She quickly got out of his hard grip. She backed a few steps and looked up at him.

He shook his head.

"It can't be true, it can't be true. It can't be you."

"Yes, it is me. And now you'll explain to me who I am."

It took Jana Berzelius ten minutes to tell the brief story of her life. She sat next to Danilo on the thin mattress in the naked living room. Both with their knees drawn up and with their heads bent down.

"So you were adopted?" he said.

"Yes, I was adopted. Jana is my first name now. Berzelius my surname. My father is the Prosecutor General but now he's retired. What he wanted most of all was a son who would follow in his footsteps. Instead, I got to do that."

They studied each other. Both uncertain how to react.

"I remember nothing from the accident. I've been told that I had fallen down onto a rail track in the underground and hit my head so hard that I lost my memory. Nobody could tell me how I came to be there on the track or who I was. I was alone. There was nobody who asked about me, or who came looking for me after the accident."

Jana stopped speaking.

"So you can't remember anything at all?" Danilo said.

"Some fragments or images can come to me in dreams, but I don't know if they're real memories or pure fantasies."

"Do you remember your real parents?"

"Did I have any?"

Danilo didn't answer.

The wind howled loudly from the crack in the window. The room immediately felt cold. Jana wrapped her arms around her knees.

"Can't you tell me something about your life?" she said.

"There's nothing to tell."

"I dreamed that you were murdered."

Danilo squirmed uneasily.

"I escaped. Okay? I got a bullet in my shoulder," he said, and pulled down his sweater to reveal a large scar on his right shoulder. "When you ran away I just lay there completely still, played dead. When Mama ran after you I got up and ran off too. And here I am now. End of story."

"But didn't they find you?"

"No."

Jana pondered.

"Is that what she was called?"

"Who?"

"Mama, was she called that?"

"Yes."

"Did I say it too?"

"Yes."

Danilo's shoulders sank somewhat.

"Why are you here? Why are you raking up the past?"

"I want to know who I am." Jana bit her lip. "Can I trust you?"

"How so?"

"Can I tell you secrets without you spreading them?"

"Hang on. Who has sent you?"

"Nobody. I'm here entirely on my own and for purely personal reasons."

"So what do you want me to do?"

"I've got to a point where I need answers. And I need to find out things without involving the police."

"But you're a prosecutor. Surely it's the police you should talk to?"

"No."

"Okay, okay. First I want to know what this entails before I decide if I want to help you or not."

Jana hesitated.

"I promise I'll keep quiet about everything you tell me."

He sounded convincing and for the time being Jana didn't have anyone else to turn to. She had to trust him.

So she told him.

It took more than an hour to describe all the intricate details in the investigation. She told about Hans Juhlén, about the boy with the name carved on his neck who had been found dead out by the coast at Viddviken. She told about Thomas Ryd-berg but left out the detail that it was her who had killed him.

When she came to explaining the salvaging of the containers, Danilo became pale in the face.

"Oh, fuck," he said.

"In one of the containers I found a mirror. I think it belonged to me. Now you must tell me— have I been in there?"

"I don't know."

"Please, tell me if I've been there."

"You haven't. Get it!"

"I just want to know who I am. You are the only person who can help me. Tell me who I am!"

Danilo got up. His face had become dark.

"No."

"No?"

"You're welcome to dig into the past, but I don't want to do it."

"I don't usually ask for favors, but please, help me."

"No. NO!"

Danilo looked out through the window.

"Please!"

"No!" Danilo turned quickly toward Jana. "Never. I'm not going to do it. Get out of here now!"

He pulled her up from the mattress. She fought her way free.

"Don't touch me!"

"Never come here again!"

"I won't. I can promise you that."

"Good. Get out!"

She remained standing where she was. Looked at Danilo a last time before leaving the flat. She cursed herself. For having told him everything. Having opened up. She should never have done it.

Never.

Henrik Levin looked at the clock. 15:55. Five minutes to go before the interview with Lena Wikström was to begin.

Jana Berzelius was late. She had never been late before.

Henrik scratched his head and wondered how he should handle the questioning without her by his side.

Mia Bolander noticed his worry.

"She's bound to turn up," she said.

That same moment, Peter Ramstedt came in.

"Oh I see," he said. "So the prosecutor doesn't want to join the interview in time? That is rather problematic."

He laughed aloud.

Henrik sighed and looked at the clock again. One minute left. He was just about to close the door to the little room when he heard quick steps in the corridor.

Jana Berzelius ran across the stone floor. She had a large plaster on her brow.

"You're late," said Mia triumphantly when Jana reached them.

"No, I don't think so. You can't be late to something that hasn't even started," said Jana and slammed the door right under Mia's nose.

* * *

The interview had gone on for two hours.

Now Henrik Levin knocked lightly on Gunnar Öhrn's office door.

"Nothing," he said.

"Nothing?" Gunnar repeated.

"She refuses to say who gave her the order to delete the file with the container combinations, or what the text she got from Thomas Rydberg means."

"And what does she say about the containers?"

"She says that she doesn't know anything about them either."

"But that's not true. I mean she knew where we could find them."

"I know."

"So what do we have?"

"She won't admit to anything and I can't actually see what we can prove."

Gunnar sighed loudly and breathed in through his nose.

"Time to go home," said Gunnar.

"I will. What about you?"

"I'm going to finish soon too."

"Plans for the evening?"

"I'm having company. Female company."

Henrik whistled.

"No, not that sort. It's only Anneli, who's going to fetch a carton with some stuff in it. And you?"

"Thought I'd surprise the family with dinner."

"Exciting."

"I don't know whether McDonald's is so exciting."

Gunnar gave a little laugh.

"See you tomorrow," said Henrik and walked with light steps toward the lift.

When Jana Berzelius sat down at the table for two at the local restaurant, The Colander, she was already irritated by her colleague Per Åström. For more than twenty minutes he had talked nonstop about his results in a tennis tournament that had been arranged the weekend before. His company had never bothered her earlier, but now she had to struggle not to open her mouth and tell him to close his!

Jana had long since realized that she didn't feel comfortable in social relationships and she had organized a life for herself as a hermit. She was satisfied with that. Of course, her work demanded a whole lot of social interaction with people but they were always superficial contacts and that was something that suited her perfectly. And besides, it was arduous and time-consuming to get to know another person. And she hated it too when people got nosy about her private life, and asked questions that she didn't want to answer. Per Åström often got on her nerves with his questions, but for some strange reason he hadn't given up like all the others when Jana had declared that she wanted to be left in peace. On the contrary, he had liked her cold attitude and over the years had learned to interpret her vague looks.

Per fidgeted with his wineglass.

"What's the matter?"

"What do you mean?"

"What's the matter, I can see there's something."

"It's nothing."

"Has something happened?"

"No."

"Are you sure?"

"Yes, I feel fine."

She met his gaze. It felt strange to lie to him. She had nobody else she could have a conversation with, and she would very much have liked to tell him everything. But how would he react if she said she had murdered Thomas Rydberg? What would he say when she admitted to having sought out an old friend whom she thought was dead but who was very much alive? And how could he even begin to understand when she explained that she would do anything to find out about her background? Her hidden background? There was no point in saying anything. Not to anybody.

"Is it something you need help with?"

Jana didn't know what she should say. Instead she got up and left the restaurant without saying goodbye.

She walked down Kvarngatan, cut across Holmen Square and then the market square at Knäppingsborg. Inside her apartment, she took off her coat, pulled off the high-heeled boots and went into the bedroom where she immediately took off her trousers. When her sweater was over her head she heard her cell ringing. She went into the hall only wearing silk underwear. She looked at the display.

Hidden number.

It must be Per. He always used a hidden number to prevent clients from getting the idea of ringing to his private telephone.

She answered.

"I don't want to know how tasty the food was," she said.

There was silence at the other end.

"Hello?"

She was just about to end the call when she heard a voice which said: "I'll help you."

The hairs on her neck stood up.

She recognized the voice.

It belonged to Danilo.

"Meet me in the town park in Norrköping tomorrow. At two o'clock," he said.

Gunnar Öhrn freed himself from Anneli Lindgren's arm.

They were sitting on the dark brown leather sofa in the living room, each with a glass of wine. The room was lit low with a 3-way lamp in one corner. One wall had bookcases and a liquor cabinet. A few paintings waiting to be hung were leaning against another wall. Two wine bottles stood on a glass table. Both were empty.

"This isn't a good idea," said Gunnar.

"What?" said Anneli.

"What you're trying to do."

"It was you who said I should come over."

"To pick up the carton, yes. Not…"

"What?"

Anneli put a hand on Gunnar's leg.

"Don't do that."

Anneli moved closer and gave him a light kiss on his throat.

"That's better."

Anneli slowly unbuttoned her blouse.

"That's actually rather nice."

"And this?"

She took her blouse off, and climbed astride him.

"That is really nice," said Gunnar and suddenly pulled Anneli toward him.

CHAPTER FORTY-SEVEN

Thursday, April 26

Jana Berzelius followed the instructions she had been given and directed her steps across the wide gravel path. Daffodils as well as lilac crocuses stood high in the borders. There was a smell of wet ground and soil. She turned off beside a large rock and followed the gravel path for about one hundred meters. When she saw the little hot-dog stall she slowed down, looked at her watch and saw she was on time.

At the stall she ordered a hot dog, paid twenty kronor and then continued along the gravel path until she came to the green park bench, which had seating facing both ways. She sat down on the right, next to an anarchist symbol that had been carved on the seat.

Jana took a bite of her hot dog and looked out across the park. Two park benches away sat four local dropouts with a bag of beer cans. Their worries seemed to have vanished as they exhibited their loud and shrill delight for passing families who were on their way to the playground. Two girls were competing to see who could swing the highest, and a little boy sat at the top of the slide hesitating as to whether he dared slide down.

She had just taken another bite of her hot dog when she heard a voice behind her.

"Don't turn round. Pick up your phone."

She felt his presence.

His back was against hers.

She put the mobile up to her ear.

"Hold the phone all the time so it looks as if you're talking on it."

"Why did you want to meet in Norrköping?" said Jana.

"I had some business here."

"Why did you change your mind? Why do you want to help me?"

"That doesn't matter. Do you still want to do this?"

"Yes."

"But you'll have to do the heavy work yourself."

"Okay."

"I can't give you everything."

"Well, what can you give me?"

"He's called Anders Paulsson. You'll find him in Jonsberg. Ask him about the transports."

"Which transports?"

"That's all I can give you."

"But what sort of transports are they?"

"Ask him."

"Is he the man behind it all?"

"No. But enough."

"How do you know that?"

"I just know. Believe me. See you."

"But…"

She turned round.

Danilo had gone.

Danilo hurried from the park. He knew Jana would seek out Anders Paulsson. He smiled to himself. He knew that she would go straight to him, knew too that that was the last thing she would do in her life.

He picked up his phone and texted: Expect company.

Gunnar Öhrn stepped quickly out of the shower and wrapped a towel around his hips.

In the bedroom, Anneli had just finished fastening her bra and she was talking to her babysitter on the phone. She ended the conversation and threw the phone onto the bed.

Gunnar looked at the clock. He was late for the press conference which would start at 13:00 hours.

"Now how can I explain this?" he said to Anneli.

"Say that you were out on a call or something. You're a policeman, damn it!"

Gunnar threw himself onto the bed and moved across to Anneli, supporting himself on his elbows.

"If we've just separated we shouldn't have sex with each other. Especially after a month."

"You're right."

"This mustn't become a habit."

"No."

Anneli got up, pulled on her jeans and blouse and buttoned it.

Gunnar followed her to the hall. He lifted up the big cardboard box that stood next to the front door.

"Don't forget this," he said. "Do you need help getting it to the car?"

"I'll take it this evening," Anneli answered and closed the door behind her.

Gunnar was left alone with the box in his arms. He smiled.

Anders Paulsson drove home a lot faster than the speed limit allowed. He cut corners and let the van go well over the middle of the road into the opposing lane.

When he reached the little locality in Jonsberg, he turned off from the 209 and saw a black BMW pulled off to the side of the road. He pressed the clutch down hard and struggled to engage third gear.

Four hundred meters further on, he suddenly braked and skidded to a halt outside his red house. The blinds were down in all the windows. Not to stop people from looking in—the nearest neighbors were quite some distance away—but because he generally didn't like the daylight. There was rubbish everywhere in the house. Cardboard boxes piled up high. Old newspapers in heaps, old paper plates with the remains of food on them, bottles, beer cans and cartons from various fast-food outlets. There was a rancid smell, shut-in and rotten, but that didn't bother Anders. He didn't really care about anything. Not about his home, not about himself. He had cared once about a woman but she died a long time ago from cancer. After it happened, he had not been capable of looking after the house. The years passed and it got harder and harder to deal with one thing and the other. It was simpler to give up. Not to care at all.

Anders unlocked the door and went straight into the kitchen with his shoes on, managing to avoid the hardened excrement that one of his cats had deposited a week or so ago. That had driven him to such a rage that instead of cleaning up the shit, he had decided to clean up what caused it. He didn't know which cat was guilty, so he punished them all. The damned creatures protested and clawed him, spitting and hissing, but he nevertheless managed to get them all into the big freezer in the cellar.

Now he stood and looked quizzically at the knife block. It was empty. Strange. He pulled out a kitchen drawer. No knife there either. The unease crept up on him. He opened a kitchen cupboard and felt with his hand on the top shelf.

Empty!

Then he immediately put his hand on his hip and felt the little sheath in his waistband. At least I've got that, he thought.

"Are you looking for something?"

Anders was frightened by the sudden voice behind him. He froze, his eyes like saucers.

Jana Berzelius stood in the doorway. She had a gun in her hand.

"Is this what you're looking for?" She flipped the safety catch, holding the gun in a firm grip with her gloved hands.

"Don't turn round!"

Anders started to laugh. A hollow and affected laugh. He shook his head and looked down at the kitchen worktop, still with his hand on his hip.

"How did you know where it was?" he said.

"I had time to check the house before you came home."

"How did you get in?"

"I like windows."

"Who are you?"

"I don't like questions."

"So I can't even ask you what you are after."

"I'm here to ask you about your container transports," she said.

"Which container transports? I don't know what you mean."

"I think you do."

Anders sighed, he looked up at the pine-paneled ceiling and then down again.

"What are they?" she said again.

He straightened his back.

Jana noticed the slow tensing of the muscles on his forearm and just had time to lean her head to one side before she felt the whoosh of the sharp blade. Quick as a flash, he had turned round and the knife was now embedded in the wall a couple of centimeters from her head.

She pointed the gun at him.

"You missed," she said.

Anders looked all around him trying to find an object to defend himself with. He glanced quickly at the black toaster.

"Please. Don't kill me."

"I'm going to ask you again. What did you transport?"

He glanced at the toaster yet again and in a fraction of a second grabbed it and hurled it at Jana with such force that she dropped the gun. It landed on the floor.

She looked at him.

He looked at her.

They both had the same idea.

The gun!

They threw themselves to the floor the very same moment but she was a fraction quicker to get her hand on the magazine. He tried to pull it out of her grip. He hit her on her side with his elbow so that she'd release her hold. But she retained her clamp-like grasp on the gun. He hit her again, but she clenched her teeth and put all her force behind a single blow. The muscles in her back were tensed, in her shoulders too, and she hit back as hard as she could. Her hand found its way in between his ribs, and he suddenly dropped down onto his knees, gasping for breath.

She held the gun against him. He looked down at the floor. His breathing became all the heavier and then turned into sobbing. After a brief moment she realized he was crying.

"Don't kill me," he said. "Don't kill me. Nobody was to know... I should never have done it."

He looked up at her.

"I should never have done it." He lowered his head again and sniffled loudly.

"Please, don't kill me. It wasn't me that hurt them. I just drove them to where they were going. They were ordinary transports. To their missions."

Jana furrowed her brow.

"What did you transport?"

"The children."

Anders hid his face in his hands. He sobbed loudly.

She lowered the pistol.

"Which children?"

"The children... I fetched them when they were...ready. And when they had carried out their missions then I...took them back again. Then I saw the grave. I saw...they stood there..."

She stared at him, thought she had heard wrong.

"I didn't do anything. I just transported them to where they were going. To the training and then back from there. But it wasn't me who killed them."

Jana was speechless. She looked at the man kneeling in front of her. They looked at each other. His eyes were red. Saliva was dripping from the corners of his mouth onto his bleached sweater.

"I didn't kill them. Not me. It wasn't me, I didn't do anything. I promise, I just drove the van. Nothing happened, I just drove, and they didn't know anything anyway."

"I don't understand," she said.

"They must die. All of them. Him too…"

"Who? You mean…?"

"They've got their own names… Thanatos…" Anders whispered. "He was really special. He was really…"

Anders started to shake.

"It wasn't meant to be like that. I didn't know. He ran."

"Was it you who killed the boy, was it you who killed Thanatos?"

"I had no choice. He tried to escape from the boat."

"The boat?"

Anders became quiet.

He looked at a point far in front of him. Blinking.

"The boat…"

"Which boat?"

"The boat! He tried to escape! I had to stop him. He had to go back to the island, but he ran."

"What's the island called?"

"He didn't want to die."

"Tell me what the island's called!"

"It hasn't got a name."

"Where is it? Tell me where it is!"

Anders went quiet, as if he suddenly became aware of the situation he was now in.

"Near Gränsö Island."

"Are there children out there now?"

He shook his head slowly.

"Who are you working for?"

He looked up at Jana again.

"I've told you too much," he said.

"Who are you working for? Give me a name!"

Anders opened his eyes wide.

Tensed himself.

And then he cast himself against Jana. Tried to knock the pistol out of her hands.

She was caught by surprise but kept her hold.

He put his hand on the pistol and pulled hard, put all his weight onto her arms and roared loudly.

Jana's index finger was pressed hard against the trigger guard. The pain was intense. She concentrated all her strength; she mustn't lose her grip. Her arm trembled. The adrenaline was pumping. She struggled as hard as she could. But she couldn't keep it up. Her finger was stuck. It felt as if it would break off.

He pushed up again and her index finger was forced up in a U-shaped arch.

She had to let go.

When the bone cracked she let go.

Anders got hold of the pistol and immediately pointed it at her. He took small, short steps backward. "It's all over now. I know it is."

He was sweating, his hands trembled, his eyes were darting here and there.

"I'm already dead. It's over. He is going to come. I know he will. It's over."

Anders raised the pistol.

Jana realized what was about to happen.

"It isn't over. Wait," she said.

"It's over now. That's just as well," said Anders and put the barrel in his mouth and pulled the trigger.

Torsten Granath lay on a leather sofa outside his office at the Prosecution Department. He looked up when Jana Berzelius came walking along the corridor.

"What's happened to you?" he said and nodded toward the plaster on her forehead.

"It's nothing. Just a graze. I fell when I was out running," she lied.

"You strained your finger too?"

She nodded and looked at her index finger. It wasn't very painful but it swelled a lot.

"It's still very slippery at some places." Torsten sighed and stretched out at full length again.

"Yes."

"Ice isn't good. You've got to think about your hip joints. Especially at my age. I'm thinking about buying those studs you can put on the soles of your shoes. You ought to get some. For when you're out running, I mean."

"No."

"No. I know. They are actually rather silly."

"Why are you lying here?"

"My back, you know. It's only problems with old men. Time to take it a bit easy."

"That's what you usually say."

"I know."

Torsten pushed himself up into a sitting position. He gave Jana a serious look.

"How are you getting on with the investigation? I've got a feeling it was wrong to let you take care of this," he said.

"It's going fine," she said briefly.

"Have you charged anybody?"

"Yes. For the death of Thomas Rydberg. But our suspicions about the perpetrator Lena Wikström are based on assumptions and a few witness statements. She hasn't confessed to the murder of Rydberg yet. As the prosecutor I'm concerned about actually making the charges stick and being able to prove anything."

"And then you've got Juhlén, the boy and the containers. How many murders are we actually dealing with here?"

"It's unclear. We haven't counted all the victims yet. The state of decomposure of the bodies is making it difficult."

"So there will probably be dreadful statistics in other words?"

"Yes."

"Oh heavens above. An enormous murder case to unravel, involving multiple victims, perhaps the largest ever in this country…"

Torsten got up and rolled his shoulders to release some tension.

"Gunnar Öhrn isn't entirely convinced that you're on the right track as far as Lena is concerned."

"He isn't?"

"No, he thinks she's keeping back some important information, but not that she is the brains behind this horrible business."

"Has he said that?"

Torsten nodded.

"And he thinks you're a bit too silent to be the investigating prosecutor," he said.

"Oh, indeed?"

"Yes, it might be a good idea to take the lead a bit more."

Jana gritted her teeth.

"Okay."

"Don't take it so personally."

"No, it's all right."

"Good."

He patted her on the shoulder before moving along to his office on his stiff legs.

She disappeared immediately into her own office and closed the door behind her. She would have to have a talk with Gunnar!

Gunnar Öhrn leaned back in his office chair and rubbed his eyes. The press conference was over and the reporters had asked an overwhelming number of questions about the salvage work. But the press officer, Sara Arvidsson, had only revealed that the police didn't want to comment on anything specific. It was only a question of time before the media fathomed the extent of the crimes and got hold of the pictures of all the dead bodies found in the containers. Then it would no longer be possible to answer as evasively. He had a strange feeling that he was being observed, and he twisted round on his chair.

Jana Berzelius stood in the doorway.

"Oh, you gave me a fright," he said.

"I have been informed that you think I am weak as the investigating prosecutor," she said.

"I…"

She held up her hand and cut him off.

"It would be more suitable if you made your constructive criticism known to me directly, instead of talking to my boss," she said.

"Torsten and me, we're old colleagues."

"I know. But if it's about me then you ought to talk with me first. Not with him. So you think I'm doing a bad job as the prosecutor in this investigation?"

"No. You're not a bad prosecutor. I just consider that you ought to be more active than you are. You seem to be absent and… I don't know… perhaps not really committed."

"Thank you for your opinion. Was that all?"

"Yes."

"In that case I'll say what I really came for."

"Which is?"

"I want to check out an island."

"Why?"

"I have received some information that something is going on there that has to do with the investigation."

"Such as what?"

"That's what we will have to find out."

"What's the island called?"

"I don't know exactly. It's somewhere off Gränsö Island."

"How do you know something's going on there?"

"I received a tip."

"Hang on a moment. You got a tip about an island you don't know the name of. From whom?"

"Anonymous."

"So you've had an anonymous tip about an island?"

"Correct."

"When did you get it?"

"An hour ago."

"How?"

Jana swallowed.

"It doesn't matter, I got a tip," she said quickly.

"Was that when you got that cut on your forehead?"

"No, that happened when I was out running," she said, hiding her throbbing index finger behind her back.

"And you've no idea where the tip came from?"

"No, it was anonymous like I said."

Gunnar became silent a moment, and looked at Jana.

"Did it come from a man or a woman?"

"The voice was deep, so presumably a man."

"And how come this man contacted you and not the police directly? How did he know you were involved and get your number?"

"No idea, all I know is that we ought to check out that island."

"But I want to know why. And what can we

expect out there? Perhaps it's a trap? A criminal gang that wants to sabotage the investigation? We're on the track of something enormously nasty here, Jana."

"Listen," she said. "This is the first time I've received an anonymous tip and I take it very seriously, and you should too."

He nodded slowly and sighed.

"Okay," he said. "I'll send Henrik and Mia."

"I'll go with them. Then I'll be a more active prosecutor," said Jana and went straight out.

FORTY-EIGHT

Friday, April 27

Henrik Levin, Mia Bolander and Jana Berzelius drove out to the archipelago in silence. Jana looked at the barren landscape. The closer they came to the coast, the more the rocky landscape dominated the view outside the car windows. When they arrived and got out of the car she could breathe in the fresh sea air.

Arkösund was a small coastal locality which attracted tourists who come by car as well as those with boats. There was a service center, a general store, a gas station and several boat-building firms. A hotel had recently opened and there were a couple of pubs and restaurants to choose between. A town bulletin board announced the upcoming First of May celebrations to be held in the village. A bonfire was promised as well as a traditional procession with torches from one of the harbors for visiting boats. A fireworks display and a speech, evidently by a local politician, would end the evening. The bulletin board also had a poster with a picture of a musician and the details of when he would be performing at the local outdoor theatre. The lines from the flag-poles chattered in the wind. Though the boat season wasn't in full swing yet, already three plastic boats were by the jetty.

Jana looked across the marina and could see a short man walking toward them with one hand on his cap to keep it from blowing away. The man introduced himself as Ove Lundgren and said he was the harbormaster. He was the man who kept an eye on all the moorings and did the regular maintenance work for all four small marinas. He had on rubber boots and a wind jacket. His face was tanned and weather-beaten. He helped the three of them onboard a Nimbus boat he had borrowed for the day. He talked warmly about the archipelago boat lines while he maneuvered the boat between the high waves.

"There are lots of islands out here," he said. "And I'm not sure but I think that your Gränsö Island is a couple of nautical miles off the Kopparholm Islands. For fifty years it was forbidden to visit the islands, it was a restricted area and only the army was there. But we're going even further out."

"Are we?" Mia squeaked, and took a firm grip of the railing so as not to slide back and forth on the seat in the choppy sea.

The boat went quite fast and passed several islands, some of them with gigantic summer houses that belonged to various business leaders and people who had inherited property. Ove knew the names of all the owners.

The islands became more spread out and the grand buildings now lay way behind them.

Mia was feeling seasick and doing her best to smother the impulse to retch. Her skin became pale and clammy. She gulped in the sea air and looked straight out over the railing at the horizon.

They passed several islands. Big and small. Some were deserted and barren. Others were inhabited and full of birds.

She felt some dry heaves and tried to squelch her nausea. She closed her eyes for a brief moment and when she opened them, she saw Jana opposite her. Jana wasn't bloody fucking bothered at all by the rough sea. Mia muttered to herself and turned her head away. She wasn't going to let Jana see her discomfort. Hell no.

After following the charts for a couple of hours they had reached the open sea. Finally they caught sight of a relatively large and tree-covered island that Ove pointed out named Grimsö, and he steered in that direction. When they got close to the rocks he slowed down.

Mia lifted her head to see the island better, but because of all the vegetation and especially the fir trees it was impossible to say whether there were any buildings there.

Ove saw a rock jetty and expressed his surprise that anybody had bothered to build one this far out in the archipelago. He maneuvered the boat to the side of the jetty and helped Henrik and then Jana and Mia to climb out.

Mia still had her hand over her mouth and as soon as she got off the boat she vomited.

"Let's go," said Henrik. Mia waved in an attempt to say *You go ahead.*

"You go on, I'll look after her," said Ove.

"Shall we?" said Henrik, and Jana nodded in answer. They climbed up the rocks.

"So you got a tip?" he said to her after a while.

"Yes," said Jana.

"Totally anonymous?"

"Yes."

"Weird."

"Mmm."

"And you've no idea who it was?"

"No idea."

Henrik took the lead along a narrow path and they walked in silence through a grove of trees and thick brushwood. The path opened up a little and then divided into two. They chose the path that looked the most used, and turned to the right.

Henrik had his hand on his holster, looked around several times and listened intently for any sound. The trees thinned out as they went down the path, and when they went round a large rock they caught sight of a house.

Jana stopped and immediately took a step back. She was terrified.

Henrik stopped too with a surprised look on

his face. He looked at her, then at the house, then back at her again.

"What's the matter?" he said.

"It's okay," she said and her facial expression immediately became its old self again.

She walked past Henrik with determined steps. She saw that he raised his eyebrows and felt how he watched her as she strode toward the house.

She had a weird feeling in her body, as though she was shut in behind some thick glass, as if she had stood still and watched herself walk up the gravel path to the house...as if her body reacted but not her being.

Her legs were taking her in the direction of the house.

Mechanically.

Then suddenly she had the urge to rush forward and yank open the door. Something about the house was familiar to her. It was... What was it?

She came to a halt.

Henrik stopped too, right behind her.

She looked up at the house and felt an equally strong urge to turn around and run back to the boat. But she couldn't do that. She had to control herself now. She looked down at the gravel and picked up a few of the small stones. In her memory some vague images appeared and she saw now how, as a little girl, she had struggled with her small feet in the gravel. And she remembered how painful it had been when she fell on it. She held the gravel in her open hand, looked down at it and then squeezed it tightly with her fingers. She clenched her hand so hard that her knuckles went white.

Henrik cleared his throat.

"I'll go ahead," he said and walked past her. "Stay here. I'll make sure it's safe first."

He walked quickly across the grassed area and stopped a few meters from the front steps. He noticed no movement inside the house. He walked slowly up the rotting wooden steps, pulled out his gun and knocked on the door with its peeling paint. He waited but there was no answer.

At the side of the house, rainwater dripped into an overflowing barrel from a crooked and rusty drain pipe.

He walked all around the house and stopped at every window, but couldn't see a living soul. But he did discover a barn a bit further away.

He signaled to Jana then disappeared behind the corner in the direction of the red barn.

She stayed where she was for a few moments with the gravel in her hand. Silence surrounded her. Her muscles relaxed, the blood came back into her hand and she let the gravel fall to the ground. She slowly walked up toward the house and stopped in front of the steps. Then she went to the side of them, closer to the cracked wood-paneled façade, and crouched down by the base of the building to look in through a dirty, narrow cellar window. She saw a small room. The ceiling was low. There was a workbench along one side, two shelves with cardboard boxes and newspapers. Some stairs, a stair railing and a little stool.

Like a pressure wave, another memory came flooding back to her. She immediately realized that she had been inside there. In the dark. And somebody had been inside there with her.

Who was it?

Minos…

"Have you found anything?"

Mia Bolander had arduously made her way along the gravel path. Her earlier face, so pale, was now bright red. She must have run to catch up.

Jana got up from the cellar window.

"Where's Henrik? Has he checked the area? Is he inside the house?" Mia said.

Jana had no desire to talk with Mia. And she certainly didn't want to examine the area with her or anyone. Another unsettling feeling welled up inside her. In some inexplicable way she felt an enormous need to protect the place. To drive Mia and Henrik away. They had no right to be here. It was her house. Nobody else should go inside. Nobody should nose around here. Nobody. Only her.

Mia came closer.

Jana tensed her muscles and lowered her head. Made herself ready to defend.

To fight.

Then Henrik came running. He ran in panic with eyes like saucers and his mouth half open.

When he saw Mia he shouted as loud as he could: "Call for backup! Get everybody here, everybody!"

* * *

Phobos was barely nine years old, but even so he was an old hand.

He washed the bend of his arm with soap and water. Then he used gravity to get the blood to the right place. He swung his arm and clenched his fist. Sat down on the floor and tied the compress hard.

The needle hit his vein with the angular filed edge upwards. It was the same vein, the same procedure, in the same room, in the same building. As usual. Everything was as usual.

He drew the syringe handle back and saw the dark red and thick blood flow into the syringe. He immediately released the tie around his arm and slowly injected the rest of the drug.

When there was one unit left in the syringe, he started to feel it. It wasn't the same feeling. He immediately pulled the needle out of his arm. Two drops of blood ended up on his trousers.

The last thing he remembered was that he shouted out with an unrecognizable voice. His heart rushed. His head spun round. Suddenly he couldn't see, couldn't hear, couldn't feel. The pressure over his chest was enormous. He gasped for air. Tried desperately to stay awake.

Slowly, slowly he came back.

And when his vision returned, he saw Papa in front of him.

"What the hell are you doing?" Papa said and hit him hard on the cheek.

"I…"

"What?"

Yet another slap.

"I just wanted to sleep," Phobos mumbled. "Sorry... Papa."

The grave was oblong and looked like a ditch. The children had been cast down there like animals. They lay there in several layers, tightly packed together and covered with what was presumed to be their clothes.

"There are about thirty skeletons," said Anneli. "But here are also bodies that have been buried about one year."

From the bottom of the ditch she looked more like an archeologist than a forensics expert. She had come by helicopter as had most of the other police officers and forensics who were now on the island.

The house was being examined in great detail.

"What do we do?" said Gunnar, overcome by resignation, from the edge of the ditch.

"Every skeleton must be taken up one at a time, examined, photographed, weighed and described," said Anneli. "The bodies must be taken to the pathology lab."

"And how long will that take?"

"Four days. At least."

"You've got one day."

"But that's impossible..."

"No buts. Make sure you get help and do it. We must act quickly now."

"Gunnar? Can you come here?"

Henrik Levin came out from the barn and waved toward his boss with both hands.

"And call Björn Ahlmann right away. Make sure he prepares the lab immediately!" he said over his shoulder to Anneli while he strode across toward the entrance to the barn.

It was damp inside and it took a while for his eyes to adjust to the dark. He blinked a few times before he could look around.

What he saw, confounded him.

A gym. About 100 square meters.

Gunnar let his gaze sweep the premises. A rubber mat on the floor, a banister along one side and a punching bag hanging from the ceiling. In one corner lay ten-kilo weights on top of each other with a thick rope next to them. On the left was a shabby storeroom with old furniture and next to that a door which looked as if it hid a lavatory. At the far end was yet another door with a lever tumbler lock. Here and there, rain water had seeped in and together with the dirt on the floor formed brown pools. It smelt of fungus.

"What the hell is this place?" he said.

Jana Berzelius had come to the interior staircase in the house. She stopped there a few moments. She felt nauseous, uncertain. Should she go up and look or not?

"Just don't touch anything," said police officer Gabriel Mellqvist who was standing by the entrance.

Something about his facial expression seemed

to question her actions, but Jana pretended not to notice.

The house was deserted and would soon be examined by the forensic team. She knew that. She also knew that she really shouldn't be inside there. But still she quickly went upstairs. On her way up she noticed that there was hardly any dust or spiderwebs on the banisters, and she had the impression that somebody had been in the house recently. She shivered as she turned to the left at the top of the stairs, and entered a large room. The planks of the wooden floor were damp and had warped. Four single beds with steel frames were placed close to each other. The mattresses had holes with batting coming out and rat droppings everywhere. A broken lamp hung from the ceiling; the walls were a sad gray color.

Jana's gaze fastened on a chest of drawers next to one of the beds. She went up and pulled out the top drawer, which was empty. Then she pulled out all the others, and they were empty too. Then she used both hands to pull the chest away from the wall as quietly as she could. She leaned down and looked at the wall. Two faces were scratched on the wallpaper; they showed a man and a woman. A mama and a papa. Carved by a child's hand.

Carved by her.

FORTY-NINE

Saturday, April 28

She could remember it so clearly now, could see everything before her every time she closed her eyes for a few moments. It was as if somebody had given her a good shaking. She remembered the container, that she was dragged out of it, that she was taken away in a van, trained hard and then that she fled away from it all.

From Papa.

At the same time, she realized that every single detail, every note and every image in her notebooks were from the same reality. So they hadn't been dreams; they had been memories. Nobody had believed her either. Her father and mother had tried to silence her with medication and psychologists.

Sitting in her car, Jana hit at the steering wheel.

She shut her eyes and roared out loud. Then she became quiet. Breathed deeply. And suddenly, behind her closed eyes, she saw Papa before her.

* * *

*He stood over her, watched how she tensed up.
The terror had grown in her eyes. The hate in his.*

*And when he gave her the knife, she had realized what she was forced to do. She was forced
to kill so as not to be killed. So she turned round
and let the knife in her hand slowly sink between
the ribs of the boy who lay beside her.*

*He, too, with tape over his mouth, and panic
in his eyes.*

It had been beautiful, in a horribly dreadful
way.

When Jana opened her eyes again, for a brief
moment she experienced the feeling of carrying
out a required task for Papa. But then she slowly
returned to the horrific reality.

She started the car and drove out onto the motorway. When she passed the sign that welcomed
her to Linköping, she increased speed and felt
how the adrenaline ran through her. Outside the
forensic center she adjusted her jacket and ran her
fingers through her hair.

She was back in her role as prosecutor.

Medical examiner Björn Ahlmann was leaning
over the little girl who lay on the bench. Her body
was partly decomposed from lying in the grave.
Her eye sockets were holes.

Björn had the girl's hand in his and took her fingerprints. When he heard somebody in the doorway, he looked up and saw Jana Berzelius.

"Can you identify them?" she said.

"Let's hope so. For their parents' sake," said Björn.

"They're not alive," Jana said briefly.

"The parents?" said Björn.

"No, they are dead too," said Jana.

"How can you know that?"

"I assume it."

"An assumption is only a guess. As prosecutor you must be certain."

"I am."

"Certain?"

"Yes, I believe the children's parents were in those containers that were salvaged."

"To believe is also a guess."

"Match their DNA with the children's and you'll see."

"You know that means a lot of work."

"Yes, and the possibility to be able to identify them."

Björn Ahlmann was just about to open his mouth to say something when Henrik Levin and Mia Bolander entered the room. Mia furrowed her brow when she saw the corpse on the bench and stopped a few meters away.

"She's not very old, is she?"

"About eight years," said Björn.

"What do we know?" said Henrik.

"Shot," said Björn. "They were all shot."

"All of them?" said Henrik.

"Yes, but the entry holes are different," said Björn.

"Did the children die where they were found?" said Henrik.

"In the ditch, yes. It seems so. They have presumably stood naked on the edge and been shot."

"Presumably is only a guess," said Jana and winked.

Björn cleared his throat.

"And there is reason to believe that the children belong to the people who were found in the containers," Henrik said.

"Yes, and the prosecutor has initiated such a DNA match attempt," said Björn.

Henrik ran his fingers through his hair and then left his hand on his neck a few moments.

"Fine. See if you can match them, straight-away," he said.

Björn nodded in answer.

"Anything else?" said Henrik.

"Yes, I found something interesting on the girl's neck," said Björn.

He turned her head to one side and exposed her neck.

The letters *E-R-I-D-A* were carved in the skin below her hairline. Erida.

Mia immediately pulled her cell out of her pocket and did a search for the name on her network.

"It must be the same person who has carved the name on the boy we found out at Viddviken," said Henrik.

"Yes," said Mia without taking her eyes off her telephone.

"So it's the same murderer," said Henrik.

"The goddess of hate," said Mia. "Erida stands for the goddess of hate and that too is a name from Greek mythology. Like Thanatos."

The room fell silent.

All you could hear was the sound of the fans.

"One more thing," Björn said finally. "The girl's head was shaved, but I found several long strands of hair on the girl. They are dark and thick and definitely not hers."

"Send them straight to the National Forensics Lab," said Henrik.

"Already done," Björn answered.

The team sat in the conference room waiting for the briefing to begin. Gunnar Öhrn thumbed through a pile of papers. Anneli Lindgren was fidgeting with her hair; Henrik Levin leaned back in his chair with his arms folded over his chest. Mia Bolander also leaned back balancing her chair on its back legs. Jana Berzelius was leaning forward over the table with her notepad in front of her.

"First," said Gunnar. "I've just spoken to Björn Ahlmann, who confirms that several of the murdered children have the same DNA profile as the remains of those adults who were found in the salvaged containers. Which means they are relatives."

"So presumably they are their parents," said Henrik.

"Yes, it seems so," said Gunnar. "We can reasonably assume that the children must have been originally in the containers, then were taken out and brought to the island. The parents were shot and dumped in the sea."

"The containers came from Chile, right? Could this have been human trafficking?" said Henrik.

"Yes. I would guess this is about illegal refugees from Chile," said Gunnar.

An oppressive silence spread around the table.

Gunnar went on, "The children that Björn Ahlmann has been able to perform an autopsy on have all had names carved on their necks. The names come from Greek mythology. Marking children is like giving them an identity. Carving into their flesh is beyond barbaric."

"Marking is common among gangs. Think tattoos, emblems," said Mia.

"But this has been systematic. Deliberate kidnapping."

"But that's just crazy," said Anneli.

"The toxicological analyses tell us that a couple of the children had drugs in their blood," said Gunnar. "Our boy, Thanatos, was also drugged. My guess is that the children sold drugs or were used as couriers in the drug trade."

"So we should look for a drug dealer," Henrik noted.

"Or several, who are interested in Greek mythology," said Mia.

"Okay, but we should try to find out how it all fits together…" said Gunnar. "Lena still hasn't told us how she knew about the containers or who gave her the order to delete the file in Juhlén's computer. And this makes me wonder: Why delete a file? You do it to hide something. Hans Juhlén didn't delete it himself. It must be Lena who has something to hide."

"But did Juhlén know about the containers?" said Henrik.

"Yes, but we don't know what he knew about them, perhaps he didn't know the truth."

"You mean about the drug dealing with children involved?"

"Exactly."

"So the containers also may have contained drugs?" said Henrik.

"I don't think they'd smuggle drugs as well as illegal refugees. But sure, it's a theory."

"Okay, but if they got rid of the adults, why keep the children?"

"Their being under age for criminal responsibility," said Mia triumphantly. "And they tend to be loyal to their taskmasters…"

"On the island a sort of training center with quite a lot of weapons had been set up," said Henrik. "Do you think the children were trained to…"

The room fell silent. Henrik went on. "I believe Hans Juhlén found out about all this. That's why he was in the dock area with Thomas Rydberg. And Rydberg was scared he would be discovered, and he told Lena, who then deleted the file in the computer. She also gave somebody the order to kill Juhlén and then Rydberg."

"We do actually have another interesting name

to add to the investigation," said Gunnar. "According to Björn Ahlmann a few strands of hair were found on one of the children, and the DNA analysis shows that the hair comes from this man."

He reached out to pick up the remote and started the projector, which showed a picture of a dark-haired man with a broad nose and a large scar across half of his face.

"Christ, just look at him!" said Mia.

Jana was just about to open her mouth to shout out: "That's him!"

But she stopped herself and instead sat uncomfortably still on her chair.

"Gavril Bolanaki. Evidently he is called Papa," said Gunnar. "I want you, Ola, to check what links exist between this man, Thomas Rydberg and Lena Wikström. Check if they share a past. Company? Schoolmates? Anything."

"What do we know about this Gavril?" said Henrik.

"Not much. Born 1953 on the island of Tilos in Greece. Swedish citizen since 1960. Did his military service in Södertälje. Some military equipment was stolen in the mid 70s and for a lot of reasons he was at first suspected, but then was found not guilty on what was described as dubious grounds," said Gunnar.

"Do we know which weapons disappeared?" said Henrik.

"No," said Gunnar.

"Where is he?" said Jana with an exaggeratedly soft voice.

"We've put him on the national Wanted List, and informed all police authorities. Let's hope that will help us to arrest him quickly," said Gunnar. "I think we're on the right track now."

I think so too, Jana thought to herself.

"In the first investigation of the island they found some food which leads us to believe that someone has been there recently. We don't know yet whether that would be Gavril or someone else. I'll get a dog handler to go over the area and I want you, Henrik and Mia, to come with me and Anneli to the island again. We're leaving in ten minutes."

Mia Bolander was seasick again.

She tried to fix her gaze on just one place in the distance when the coast guard launch bobbed up and down on the big waves. She had eaten breakfast only half an hour earlier, before they had left the station. She had managed to persuade a trainee to treat her to a sandwich.

Today was the twenty-eighth. Only three days since she had received her salary and already she was broke. A whole month until the next payment. And today was Saturday too, and that always meant going out somewhere. Mia wondered how she'd be able to afford a beer.

Mia put a hand over her mouth, then leaned over the railing and vomited.

The search led to results. The police dog had found an underground concrete bunker quite close to the barn. The entrance was well hidden by bushes.

Gunnar went in first. It wasn't very big and he stopped after about three meters. The ceiling was low and he had to keep his head down when he looked around. There were two empty bags on the floor. A large number of guns hung on the walls. Gunnar immediately recognized the AK-47s, Sig Sauers and Glocks. Lots of ammunition lay sorted in various plastic containers. There were five smallish knives and several silencers too.

Gunner turned round and went out. He was met by Henrik Levin's and Mia Bolander's questioning gazes.

"It's a weapons stash. The biggest I've ever seen," said Gunnar.

"Could they be from Södertälje?" said Henrik.

"Very likely. There are some older weapons as well as newer ones."

"So it could be that this Gavril, in some way, smuggled weapons out from the barracks in Södertälje and built a weapons store here," said Henrik.

"There are several Glock pistols in there and that is one of the most common weapons in the army," said Gunnar.

"And one was used to murder Hans Juhlén," said Henrik.

Gabriel Mellqvist had only one hour left of his watch by the jetty. He stamped his feet in turn to try to keep them warm. He scanned the horizon again. Just at that moment he caught sight of a boat heading toward the island. He looked through his binoculars at the railings to see if any of his colleagues were on board.

The boat slowed down, seemed to almost come to a stop and then suddenly turned sharply and drove off.

Gabriel grabbed his radio.

No time to lose.

Henrik Levin was just on his way down into the bunker when police officer Hanna Hultman came running.

"An unknown boat has been sighted, it's driving fast away from the island."

Henrik Levin ran as fast as he could to the jetty and jumped up onto the coast guard launch.

Mia Bolander was right behind him.

"After it!" he shouted. "Don't wait for Gunnar. Go ahead!"

Henrik waved to the coast guard officer, Rolf Vikman who quickly steered the launch out from the jetty and followed the boat that Gabriel Mellqvist had seen. It had disappeared from sight and Rolf increased speed in the direction it had last been seen, while he radioed in to the county communication center.

Henrik also stared into the distance. They had reached 30 knots and the launch threw up cascades of water around it. When they approached a little island they slowed down, but the boat still couldn't be seen anywhere. Henrik turned his head in all directions.

Mia too. They listened for the sound of an engine but couldn't hear anything except the noise of the launch they were sitting in.

When they reached the next island, Rolf slowed down a little and Henrik's gaze swept over the jagged rocks. The wind whistled in his ears. Two seagulls circled high above them, with a shrill squawking.

Mia stood on her toes to be able to look over the railing. They slowed down a bit more, and Rolf zigzagged among the waves to stop them from drifting into land.

"Go on ahead," said Henrik, and they rounded the island. Rolf increased the speed again and the wind caught Henrik's jacket. A feeling of doubt was beginning to grip him. No boat to be seen.

"There!" shouted Mia suddenly and pointed eagerly with her hand. "There! There! I can see it!"

Rolf immediately steered in the direction she pointed.

"A Chaparral," he shouted out. "A fast vessel I'm afraid."

The Chaparral sped off, as if the driver had seen the coast guard launch. Henrik drew his gun and Mia did the same. Rolf increased the speed of the launch and slowly got nearer to the boat.

"Police!" Henrik shouted and showed his weapon. "Stop!"

His words drowned in the noise from the engines.

The Chaparral went off at full throttle and increased the distance between them.

"He's trying to get away," Rolf shouted and followed at the same speed.

The chase continued at high speed. Henrik's jacket flapped wildly in the wind stream. The cold bit into his cheeks and his hair stuck out behind.

"Police!" shouted Henrik even louder when they got closer to the boat.

He just managed to catch a glimpse of the driver before he sheered right in front of them. A dark-haired man, oldish, dark hair under a rough cap.

"Hell," shouted Rolf, and sheered too.

They clipped the waves fast. The cascades got higher and higher.

The Chaparral slowed down unexpectedly.

Henrik raised his pistol without letting go of the railing.

"Stop!" he shouted to the driver.

But the boat sheered again and raced off.

"After him, Rolf! After him!"

Rolf opened the throttle and followed closely behind. The boat in front of them slowed down yet again. Then sheered and pulled away at a high speed.

Jana Berzelius knew that she shouldn't do it. Nevertheless, she sat there with the phone in her hand and wrote a text message to Danilo. She tried to compose it as cryptically as possible. She had bought a new telephone and a prepaid SIM card and knew that would never give her away, but she was still not entirely convinced.

So she wrote: A gave me the place. Papa soon home.

She was just about to send the text when her private telephone started ringing in her pocket. She picked it up and saw that it was a hidden number. She sincerely hoped it was Danilo phoning, and she immediately answered.

It was Henrik Levin.

"We've got him," he said in a calm and controlled voice.

Jana held her breath.

"We got him after a one-and-a-half-hour boat chase," said Henrik.

"At last," whispered Jana.

"We need a hearing. Immediately."

"I'll arrange it. And the interrogation?"

"That will start tomorrow morning."

Jana ended the conversation with a brisk "see you!" She was trembling. With shaking hands she again picked up the newly bought phone and deleted the last part of the message. Instead she wrote: A gave me the place. Papa is home.

Then she pressed the button and sent the message.

Danilo stared at his cell.

"Hell," he shouted as loud as he could. "Bloody hell!"

He banged his fist against the wall with all his strength.

"Fuck, fuck, fuck, FUCK!"

He was in a rage. Absolutely mad. How could he have let it go so wrong? Anders should have killed her! Anders was an idiot, a failed fucking idiot who never did a single fucking thing right in the whole fucking world. First he fails to take the boy to the island, and then he fails to deal with Jana.

Danilo sighed. He was forced to deal with it himself. As usual. It was always him who had to sort everything out. And everything was a bloody mess just now.

"Fuck!" he shouted out yet again.

He thought of different ways of dealing with Jana. Forever. Or was there a chance she could be used in some way? Could he make use of her instead?

A smile spread across Danilo's face.

The more he thought about the possibility of using Jana, the clearer his strategy became.

After ten minutes he knew exactly what he would do. She only had herself to blame. She was the one who started stirring the shit, and once you'd done that you had to accept the consequences.

Whatever they may be.

Sunday, April 29

Gunnar Öhrn stood with a cup of coffee in his hand, and looked at the extra news bulletin on the TV which was about the arrest of Gavril Bolanaki.

The county police commissioner had demanded that the press officer should issue a press release and the news was spread within an hour of the man's arrest.

"Does it feel okay?"

Anneli Lindgren lay on one side of the bed with a sheet wrapped around her naked body.

She too had listened to the news bulletin.

"Yes, it feels good that we caught him. He's going to be interrogated tomorrow. Will there be time to search the whole island before that?"

Anneli lay on her back and stretched out on the mattress.

"Yes, we've got several forensics working there today, and there must be lots of places we can take samples for DNA testing. At least I hope so."

"Me too," said Gunnar and took yet another gulp of coffee, just as the telephone rang.

It was Ola Söderström.

"Now listen to this, we've finally got an answer," he said. "The department of transportation has managed to identify the driver of the van that the witness Erik Nordlund thought he saw on Arkösund Road. The van belongs to an Anders Paulsson, fifty-five. He worked as a loader for DHL for twenty years. Now he's got his own firm, in the transport sector too. What's most interesting is that he was married to Thomas Rydberg's sister. She died of cancer ten years ago and he doesn't seem to have anyone new."

"So Rydberg and Anders are linked to each other," Gunnar noted. "Where does he live?"

"In Jonsberg, Arkösund," said Ola.

"That sounds most interesting. I'll put Henrik and Mia on it straightaway," said Gunnar and put the phone down.

Mia Bolander was drinking a cup of coffee. It was still too hot and she sipped it slowly while she examined herself in the car mirror. During the night the mascara had formed tiny, tiny black dots around her eyes.

"Oh, fuck!" she swore out loud.

"Hard night?" said Henrik.

"As if you'd know what that means."

"I know quite a lot about parties."

"Children's parties, or what?"

"No."

"When was the last time you boozed so much that your head exploded?"

"So that's what you've done, is it?"

"Yep. I have. And fucked too. And it was damned nice!"

"Well, thank you, but that was more information than I needed."

"Don't ask so much then!"

He sighed and checked the speedometer to ensure he was going at exactly the permitted speed.

Mia went back to trying to rub the mascara from around her eyes.

They had about ten kilometers left to Jonsberg where Anders Paulsson lived. Fifteen minutes later they arrived outside the red detached house. In the yard outside stood a white van, an Opel. The garden was not cared for, and the blinds were pulled down inside. The corners of the building that had once been white were now discolored and gray.

Henrik drove slowly past, parked some way away, turned off the engine and got out. Mia downed the last drops of the coffee. As she put the mug in the holder between the seats, she saw that Henrik's wallet lay there. She acted quick as a flash, got hold of the wallet and opened it and took a one-hundred kronor bill, shoved it into her pants pocket, then put the wallet back. Then she broke into a smile, opened the car door and stepped out.

Henrik had by now snuck up to the house and was crouching down next to the back wheel of a parked van. His eyes glistened with enthusiasm when Mia approached.

Together they went up to the house and stood on either side of the front door. Mia placed a foot against the door to prevent anyone from knocking it open.

Then they rang the doorbell. The sound echoed from inside. They waited thirty seconds. Then rang again. Still nothing. They exchanged looks and rang the bell once more. Still nothing happened.

Mia went around the side of the house and saw that all the windows had their blinds pulled down. Everything was quiet. On the other side of the house she discovered an open window. She called to Henrik to come as she got a firm grip on the window frame and then hoisted herself up with one leg closely followed by the other. With a less than gracious jump, she disappeared into the house.

Once inside, she was hit by the dreadful stench of excrement. She immediately put one hand inside her jacket and pulled the cloth over her nose. She looked down at the floor and discovered heaps of shit and dried-up stains of urine.

There was rubbish everywhere. Cardboard boxes piled on top of each other. Old newspapers in heaps, moldy remains of food on paper plates, empty bottles, beer cans and fast-food cartons. An old radiator was on a sofa. The carpet was rolled up. The table had a big crack in it, and the wallpaper was ripped.

Henrik looked in through the open window and the acrid smell of feces immediately made him nauseous. He pulled his head back and retched.

Mia took a couple of cautious steps forward with her drawn weapon, maneuvered her way between the piles of shit and all the rubbish.

"Police!" she called out, but her voice was drowned by a feeling of queasiness.

Mia came into a hall and saw the door to the kitchen. The hall too was in an awful mess, and she could hardly discern the wallpaper pattern because of all the rubbish piled up against the walls. She went into the kitchen and was met by an even worse stench. It came from a man who lay in a strange position. His mouth was open wide, his eyes staring blankly, and Mia could quickly see that he was dead.

CHAPTER FIFTY-ONE

Monday, April 30

Jana Berzelius wanted to delay the planned morning trial, but there wasn't any legal possibility to do so. For the first time in her professional career as a prosecutor she had also hoped that one of the parties who were called to court would have given due notice of inability to attend. If one of the witnesses had suddenly fallen ill, or there had been serious disruption to public transport, or for some other unpredictable reason had not been able to come to the court, then they would have had to postpone the hearing. But unfortunately all the parties were present, as were the lay magistrates and the judge, and Jana's spirits deflated a little. The trial would start at the designated time.

She sighed and opened her red folder with the evidence she was going to present in court. The charge was arson. She looked at the clock. In five minutes the trial would start. And in five minutes they would start questioning Gavril Bolanaki at the police station. She had been in touch with Henrik Levin by phone and told him to start the interview without her. She hoped the trial would be over within an hour and then she would hurry to the detention center to confront him, confront Papa.

She tidied her hair. Let her hand stop on her neck. Felt the carved letters.

The time has come, she thought.

At last.

Henrik Levin looked up at the man who sat in front of him. Black shirt with rolled-up sleeves. His hair was dark, longish and combed back. His nose was wide and his eyes dark, framed by bushy eyebrows. The scar on his face went from his forehead down to his chin; it was hard to stop staring at it. Henrik fixed his gaze on the other half of the man's face and started to speak: "What were you doing out at sea?"

Silence.

"Why did you flee from us?"

Silence.

"Do you live on the island?"

Still silent.

"Have you seen this boy before?"

Henrik showed him a photo of Thanatos.

The man raised one corner of his mouth in what resembled an arrogant smile.

"I want a lawyer," he said slowly.

Henrik sighed.

He had no choice but to obey.

* * *

After two hours, the trial was about halfway through. Jana was frustrated. The injured party and the accused had been interrogated to establish facts and after the break the witnesses and the written evidence would be dealt with. She got up from the prosecutor's bench and left the courtroom. After a quick visit to the restroom, she pulled her phone out of her pocket and saw that she had missed a call from a hidden number. A recorded message said that Henrik Levin had tried to get hold of her, and she immediately phoned him.

"How are things going?" she said when he answered.

"Nothing yet," he said.

"Nothing at all?" said Jana.

"No. He's saying nothing. He's demanding a lawyer."

"Then he'll get one. But I want to talk to him first."

"It's pointless."

"But I want to try."

She looked at the clock and went on: "In three hours the trial here ought to be over. Then we can start questioning him again."

"Okay. The interview room at two o'clock again," said Henrik.

"Without a lawyer."

"We can't do that."

"Yes, we can. I'm the prosecutor and he's my client and I want to talk with him."

Jana savored the words: *my client.*

"I'll see what I can do."

"Just five minutes. That's all I ask."

"Okay."

When the conversation ended, she remained standing there a while with the phone pressed to her chest. She felt exhilarated in some way.

Almost happy.

Mia sat leaning well back in the chair with her arms crossed over her chest. Henrik had left the interview room in a hurry to answer a call from Jana Berzelius and meanwhile she sat there and kept an eye on the suspect. The man in front of her half smiled all the time. His head was lowered and the lamp cast shadows over the scar on his face.

"Do you believe in God?" said Mia.

The man didn't answer.

"Your name, Gavril. It means God is…"

"My strength," he filled in. "Thank you, I know what it means," he said.

"So you believe in God?"

"No, I am God."

"Oh yeah? That's nice."

He smirked at her. She felt uncomfortable. Squirmed. Gavril did the same. Copied.

"A god doesn't kill," said Mia.

"God gives and takes."

"But he doesn't kill children."

"Oh yes, he does."

"So you've killed children?"

Gavril smirked again.

"What the fuck are you smirking at?"

She leaned back in the chair. Gavril too.

"I haven't killed any children," he said. "I've got a son myself; why would I want to kill such small creatures?"

"But we fucking well found your hairs on a little girl who lay in a mass grave on an island which you were on your way to!"

"But that doesn't mean I've killed her, does it?"

Mia glared at Gavril. He glared back. She refused to look away.

"But I wonder," he said slowly. Still glaring hard at her. "If I knew who has killed them and if I tell you, what would you do for me?"

"Yes, what would we do for you?"

Gavril heard her sarcasm. He clenched his teeth, hissed.

"I don't think you understand what I mean. If I tell you who did it, what do I get in return then?"

"This isn't a fucking negotiation. Don't you…"

"I want you to listen very carefully."

Gavril leaned forward. Came close to Mia. Unpleasantly close.

She didn't look away. She couldn't lose.

"If you lock me up, I want you to remember my face for the day I get out. Do you get what I mean?" he hissed.

Then he calmed down, leaned back on the chair and said: "You'll be making a big mistake if you lock me up. That's why I'm making my offer. I can easily name several key people who govern the Swedish drug trade today. I can point out places and persons. But I think you are most interested in the children's role in all this. I'm right, aren't I?"

Mia refused to answer.

"So if I tell you how it all fits together, what will you do for me? I'm not going to confess to anything about myself, but I can tell you everything I know about the others. If that is of interest, I mean. But I think it is."

Mia bit her lip.

"I have a suggestion," said Gavril. "If I tell you everything then you must protect me and my son. If you lock me up now, you won't get to know anything and I can guarantee that more children will die. I am the only one who can put a stop to it. I want to have the best possible protection too. From the highest levels. Otherwise I won't say anything. So — how do you want it?"

Mia lost. Her gaze left his. She looked down at the table, then straight into the mirror in the window. She knew that Gunnar stood there behind it, and she knew that he was just as uncertain as she was.

What the fuck should they do now?

It was 13:42. The trial was over and Jana Berzelius gathered up her papers and left the courtroom in a hurry. As usual she went straight to the emergency exit and pressed the white fire door open with her hip. With quick steps she ran down the stairs to the heated garage down below. And while she maneuvered her car out of the parking place, she phoned Henrik Levin to persuade him to prepare the second interview with Gavril. But the number was busy.

She drove quickly out of the garage and made another attempt to reach Henrik, but even though she heard it ringing this time, he didn't answer. She thought every traffic light changed to red as soon as she approached. The pedestrians took an exaggeratedly long time to cross at the zebra crossings and the other motorists drove unusually slowly in front of her. When she did finally reach the police station, all the parking spaces were occupied too, and she had to drive round three times before she found a small space in which to park.

She could hardly open the door without it touching the car next to hers, and she had to pull in her stomach and hold her breath to get out of the car. She half ran across to the stairwell where she pressed the button to summon the lift. She waited and waited but according to the display the elevator was only going up and down between the higher floors. In the end she took the stairs.

She was out of breath when she got to the department and made an attempt to compose herself before she opened the door to the interview rooms. There was frantic activity in there, and the first person she met was police officer Gabriel Mellqvist.

He immediately held up his hand.

"This is a prohibited area."

"I have a meeting with my client and I'm a bit late," said Jana.

"What is your client's name?"

"Gavril Bolanaki."

"I'm sorry, you can't come in."

"Why not?"

"The case is closed."

"Closed? How can it be closed?"

"I'm sorry, Jana, you must leave."

Gabriel pushed her out through the door and closed it in front of her. She remained standing in the corridor, surprised and angry.

She pulled out her phone and rang Henrik again. No answer. Rang Gunnar. No answer.

She swore out loud and then ran down the stairs to the garage.

Lena Wikström sat in her cell and banged her head against the concrete wall. The only soft thing in the cell was a mattress with a plastic cover and yellowish faded sheets, and she sat crouched up toward the end of the mattress with her arms clasped around her legs. On the wall was an oval-shaped white lamp and next to that somebody had used a black object to misspell Fuck and instead written Fukc. Some weak light came in between the bars in the window. The cell was eight square meters and besides the bed contained a sort of wooden desk with a built-in and very solidly anchored chair, also of wood.

Lena had been in the detention cells for seven days. She had dealt with it without great problems since she—deep inside—had hoped she would get out. But this particular day her hopes had been dashed. In the line to lunch she had heard the news that Gavril had been arrested and was also in the detention center. She left her food untouched on the tray. She hadn't even been able to drink the milk she had been served. It had been *him* who was going to help *her* out. But now he too was locked up, in a cell close to hers.

It's over now, she thought and banged her head harder against the wall. Now everything is over, and I'm finished too. I just have to accept that. There is nothing more I can do. Just one thing remains. And that is that I must get away from here.

From this life on Earth.

Torsten Granath stood beside his desk wearing a beige coat and was just putting a folder in his briefcase when Jana Berzelius stormed into his office. She stood in the middle of the room, putting her weight on one leg, with her arms folded.

"What's happening?" she said.

Torsten looked up at her, a question mark on his face.

"I must go home. My wife phoned, and there are problems with Ludde. He has been eating his own excrement the last 24 hours. We must take him to the vet's."

"I mean Gavril Bolanaki. What's happening?"

"Ah yes, that. We were going to inform you."

"Why is it finished? He's my client."

"The case is closed. The Security Service has taken over. Nobody can talk to him. Not even you."

"Why not?"

"He's going to be an informer."

"What do you mean, informer?"

"He's going to help the police in their mapping of the drug trade in Sweden. Because of the threatening picture for him, both he and his son are now in the care of the Security Service and they will be moved from the detention center tomorrow morning at nine."

"Does he have a son?"

"Evidently he does."

"Where are they going to move him to?"

"That's confidential, Jana. You know that."

"But…"

"Drop it now."

"But we've got him…"

"As prosecutor it isn't about convicting people, but about finding out the truth."

"I know."

"And now the police will have the best possible insight into the drug trade. That was the only good thing to come from this."

No, it wasn't, Jana thought and turned on her heel and stormed out again.

Jana Berzelius was resolute. Her eyes had narrowed; she felt like killing somebody…in particular the person who had decided that Gavril Bolanaki would get protection. Gavril had manipulated the police, she knew that. He had led them to believe that he was just a minor figure with good insight in what had gone on. Now he would avoid everything, the hearing, the trial and conviction. He would get away!

She squeezed her hands around the steering wheel, slowed down and opened the side window. She quickly drew the parking card in the reader and then drove into the garage with screeching tires. She parked at her reserved place and slammed the car door behind her. In the stairwell she took two steps at a time up to her apartment. With a firm grip she put the key into the lock, opened the door and stepped into the hallway. She was just about to close the door when she saw a hand grasp it from the outside. She didn't have time to react before a darkly clad figure pushed his way in behind her.

His face was well hidden with a large hood. Then he held up both hands, showing his empty palms to her.

"No fighting, Jana," said the man and she immediately recognized the voice.

It belonged to Danilo. He pulled off the hood and exposed his face.

"You ought to be more careful," he said.

Jana snorted at him and turned on the ceiling light.

"Sending a text wasn't the smartest thing to do," Danilo went on.

"Why not? Are you hiding from somebody?" said Jana.

"No, but you are."

"The police can't trace a prepaid SIM."

"You never know."

They both fell silent and looked at each other from top to toe. Danilo broke the silence after a few moments.

"So he's been caught, then?"

"Yes. Or perhaps..."

"What do you mean?"

"Come in and I'll tell you."

FIFTY-TWO

Henrik Levin woke suddenly. He had had a short snooze. And that was hardly surprising. The day's events had demanded total concentration and he wasn't only exhausted mentally, his body too was aching with tiredness.

Henrik looked up from the pillow. On his stomach lay a book about a teddy bear. Vilma lay on his arm. Her little body was quite still. Felix lay close to him on the other side. He was breathing deeply. Henrik tried as carefully as he could to get his arm out from under Vilma, but she moved and pushed even closer. Henrik looked at his daughter's sleeping face. He pressed his nose against hers and then freed his arm. Felix didn't move a muscle when the other arm, under him, disappeared too. In his sleep, he opened his mouth out wide like a baby bird in a nest. Henrik stroked the boy's cheek. Then he delicately started to maneuver himself out from the narrow bed and after a couple of attempts he had to clamber over the high edge of the frame. The heat from the children's bodies had made him sweaty. He pulled the sticky shirt away from his skin and decided that the children could stay on in the same bed for the night.

He turned off the moon-shaped bedside light and quietly closed the door to Felix's room.

It took him fifteen minutes to brush his teeth, use floss and then rinse with exactly the recommended amount of mouth-rinse. He studied his face in the mirror and noticed that another couple of hairs on his left temple had turned gray. But he didn't bother to remove them. Was too tired for that. So he left the bathroom and went into the bedroom.

The TV had been turned off. Emma lay in bed in a pink T-shirt with the covers up to her waist, deeply involved in a book. Henrik got undressed, folded his clothes and put them on the chair next to his side of the bed. With a yawn, he sunk down with his head on the pillow, put one arm under his head and looked up at the ceiling. The other arm was under the covers and his hand felt its way into his underpants and grasped his intimate bits. As if to make them comfortable.

Emma put her book down and looked at him. He felt her gaze. It hit him like an electric prod.

"What is it?" he said.

She didn't answer.

He pulled his hand out from his pants and lay on his side next to her.

"Well, we haven't…" she started.

"What haven't we?"

"Had sex so much lately."

"No."

"And it isn't because of you."

"Okay?"

"It's because of me."

"But it doesn't matter," said Henrik and immediately wondered why on earth he had said that. It certainly did matter. It mattered an awful lot. In fact it was everything.

She leaned forward and gave him a long kiss. He responded likewise. They kissed again. A bit predictable one might say. His hand on her breast. Her hands on his back. She scratched him a little. Then harder and Henrik got the feeling that this was an invitation. At last, he thought, and pulled Emma closer to him. But then he remembered the words she had only just a few moments earlier uttered. That there was something that had made her not want to as much as before. With a gentle hand he pushed her away. She looked at him with her big blue eyes and her gaze was full of desire.

"I'm just wondering what the reason was," said Henrik. "You said it was because of you."

Emma smiled and the lines of laughter around her eyes showed up immediately. He loved every one of them.

Then she bit her lip, still with the smile there. She had a mischievous look. Her fingers played over the sheet and drew an invisible heart.

Afterwards he had wanted to freeze that moment. He would have given anything for time to have stood still, just there and then. Because she looked so happy.

Then she said it.

"I'm pregnant."

He immediately regretted having asked. Why hadn't he just given his desire a free rein, and they could have got on with it? Why had he been so stupid and asked?

Emma cast herself over him.

"Isn't it wonderful?"

"Yes."

"It is, isn't it?"

"Yes, really."

"Are you pleased?"

"Well, yes. I'm pleased."

"I hadn't wanted to say anything. You've been so busy at work and there simply wasn't a good occasion. Until now."

Henrik didn't move. He lay there under Emma, as if he had turned into stone. She moved slowly, rubbing her body against his. His thoughts spun around and around: pregnant? Pregnant! Now there would be no more sex at all. Not for nine months. That's what it had been like when she was pregnant with Felix and Vilma. Then he hadn't wanted to at all. It hadn't felt right to do it with Emma when she had a baby in her tummy. And now she had one again.

A baby.

In her tummy.

Yet again, he pushed her away.

"What's the matter," she said. "Don't you want to?"

"No," he answered curtly and held up his arm against her. "Come on, lie down here."

She looked at him with surprise.

"Come on," he said. "I just want to hold you a while."

She lay her head on his chest. He let his arm sink down onto her shoulders.

"So you're pregnant." He looked up at the ceiling. "Great. Really great."

Emma didn't answer.

Henrik knew that she was disappointed that they weren't having sex. Now she could presumably feel what he had felt every time she hadn't wanted to. Now the roles were reversed, he thought, before he closed his eyes. He wasn't going to fall asleep, he knew that. And he was right.

He didn't get any sleep at all that night.

"So he's going to be moved tomorrow," Danilo repeated. He stood in the middle of Jana's living room with his arms folded and his eyes fixed on a point far away outside the window.

She sat on the couch with her hands cupping a glass of water. It had taken her twenty minutes to tell Danilo what had happened. The whole time, he had stood up in the same position.

"Where is he going to be moved to?" he said. "Do you know?"

"No, I've no idea," said Jana.

Danilo paced back and forth over the floor.

"What a fucking mess," he said.

"What should we do?"

Danilo was silent, pacing all the faster. Then he suddenly stopped and looked at Jana.

"So you've no idea about where they're going to put him?" he said.

"No, like I said. It's confidential," said Jana.

"Then there's only one way to find out."

"What's that?"

"With a tracking device."

"That's a good plan. Really."

"I'm serious. A GPS tracker is the only alternative."

"Or we could simply follow the police cars? What do you think about that? A bit simpler perhaps?"

"And risk being seen? I don't think so. With a tracker we can follow them from a distance."

"But we still risk being discovered."

"Not if we do it right."

"How do we get hold of a tracker?"

"I'll fix it."

"How?"

"Trust me."

"But haven't you forgotten an important detail? Like that Gavril is locked up? In the detention center? How do you think you're going to install a tracker on him?"

Danilo sat down beside Jana.

"I'm not going to do it," he said.

"You're not?"

"There's only one person who can fasten it on him. One who can always get inside the detention center. One who the police will never suspect."

"Who is that?"

"You."

FIFTY-THREE

Tuesday, May 1

The corridor seemed to go on forever. Her heels echoed all around her. To maintain her focus, she counted her steps. She had been counting ever since she stepped out of the elevator on the floor with the detention center, and now she was up to fifty-seven. She looked at her Rolex.

08:40.

She fixed her gaze on the door and squeezed the handle of her briefcase. Seventy-two steps in all, she thought as she put her briefcase down on the floor. She rang the bell to be let in and then heard a voice telling her to say her name to the microphone on the wall.

"Jana Berzelius, the prosecutor's office. I'm going to have a talk with my client, Lena Wik-ström," she said.

The door opened and Jana picked up her brief-case and went inside. A warder with a name tag that said Bengt Dansson and with a neck that was barely visible and earlobes big as wings smirked a stupid smile of recognition when she approached him.

Bengt looked at her identity card and smiled even wider when he handed it back to her, which made his chin pour out over his collar.

"A quick search too," he said.

Jana stretched out her arms and felt Bengt's hands move from her armpits down over her ribs and hips.

He panted when he crouched down in front of her and she rolled her eyes in irritation when he continued to search her from her hips down her legs.

"Which do you prefer? Metal detector or a body search?" he said and looked up at her with a desirous gaze.

"What do you mean?" said Jana.

"That you can choose. Detector or naked."

"You're joking, aren't you?"

"You can't be too careful when it comes to security."

Jana was speechless.

Bengt broke out into such loud laughter that his cheeks bobbed up and down. He put one hand on his knee and pushed himself up but couldn't stop laughing.

"Ha, ha, ha, haaa! You should have seen your face!"

"Very funny," she said and clutched her briefcase.

"You just…errr…" he said and showed a face that looked like a cross-eyed seal.

She felt a strong desire to thump him right in his face but reminded herself that the detention center was an unsuitable place to practice violence.

Bengt dried his tears. He shook his head and laughed out loud yet again.

"If you'll excuse me, I am in a bit of a hurry. You see, I have a job to do. Not play silly games," she said.

Bengt became quiet, cleared his throat and opened the door for her.

"You can enter," he said.

She stepped into the detention center corridor and nodded to the warder in the security office. He nodded back and then turned his attention to one of the three computer screens on the desk in front of him. Two warders were talking in a low voice next to the office. She couldn't help wondering if they were the ones who had been entrusted with fetching Gavril from his cell. She looked at her watch again.

08:45.

Fifteen minutes to go before he was to be moved. Her heart started beating a bit faster.

Bengt locked the door and led the way down the corridor which was lit up by strong fluorescent lamps in the ceiling. A bunch of keys rattled noisily with every step he took. The walls were painted a light apricot color and the linoleum floor was a weak mint-green. They passed a couple of detention cells, the doors white and reinforced with a wide band of steel at the bottom. They were all numbered.

At door number eight, Bengt stopped and lifted up the bunch of keys on the chain hanging from his belt. He looked for the right key, then he looked up at Jana again, laughed quietly and shook his head again. Then he unlocked the door and let her in. Before she went inside, she saw the two warders shake hands with two darkly dressed policemen and she immediately realized that the move would take place shortly.

"Stay outside," she said to Bengt. "This won't take long."

Then she stepped into the cell and heard the door shut behind her.

"What are you doing here?"

Jana gave a start when she heard Lena Wikström's rasping voice. She was sitting on the bunk bed with her legs pulled up to her chin. The sheet hung over the edge down onto the floor. She was dressed in dark green trousers and a dark green shirt. Barefoot. Her eyes were tired. The rings under them were wide and dark. Her hair was uncombed.

"What are you doing here?" she hissed quietly yet again. "Are you here to threaten me again?"

"No," said Jana. "I am not here to threaten you. I am here for a totally different purpose and I need your help."

"I'm not going to help with anything."

"You already have. By being here."

Lena didn't understand. And she couldn't be bothered to try to understand either.

"How much longer will it be?"

"What do you mean?"

Jana put her briefcase down on the floor.

"Until you lock me up?"

"I might remind you that you already are imprisoned."

"But this isn't for real. This is just a stage. A stop on the way."

"Two more days before the trial," Jana answered, and looked at her watch again.

08:52.

She crouched down in front of her briefcase, opened it and stuck her hands inside to hide them. She pulled off her Rolex and opened the back of the watch case. With her long nails she loosened a little tracking device that was in there, and then put the casing back on again. She quickly put the watch back on her wrist and with the tracker in one hand she closed the briefcase with the other.

"So in two days it will come to an end," said Lena almost inaudibly.

But Jana heard the faint words. She stopped just as she was going to get up. Lena has capitulated, she thought. She has given up.

"Yes, then it will come to an end."

Lena turned white in the face.

"Then it will be over," Jana went on.

"I want it to be over," said Lena and looked down at her hands.

She suddenly looked very small, slumped down and gray.

"I don't think I can take any more of this. I want to get away from here."

"You are here to stay."

"I don't want to be stuck in prison. I'd rather die. Please kill me! I know you can. Kill me!"

"Shut up!"

"I can't live like this. I must get away."

Jana stood up and looked at her watch.

08:59.

It was time. Now she would do it. She raised her hand to knock on the door but stopped when she heard Lena's voice.

"Please," she squeaked. "Help me…"

Jana sighed. She thought a few seconds before walking across to where Lena was sitting. She got hold of the sheet, bit a hole in the cloth and then tore off a long strip. She put it into Lena's hand.

"You can help yourself," she said.

Then she knocked hard on the door which was immediately opened by Bengt. She remained standing in the doorway a few moments. Waiting for the right opportunity.

Out of the corner of her eye she saw them approaching: the wardens, the policemen and then Gavril between them. Just as they passed her, she took a step forward and pretended to slip. She swung the briefcase, let one leg give way and affected to cry out. When she fell onto the floor her hand grasped Gavril's leg and quick as a flash she pressed the tracker on his pants pocket.

Bengt rushed up to help her up.

"Oh, sorry," she mumbled. "It's my heels. They are new."

The warders looked at her in surprise. The policemen almost disapprovingly. And Gavril, he smiled.

Jana couldn't help look at him. However much she tried to persuade herself to stop staring, she couldn't help it. Her heart pounded. She was so close to him but still so far away. Her hatred grew with every breath she took. Most of all she would have liked to have killed him straightaway. Most of all she wanted to stick a knife into his body, time and time again. He should die.

Die.

Die.

Die.

"You ought to be careful, little miss," he said with a smirk before he was taken along the corridor between the warders and the policemen.

You too, Jana thought.

You ought to be very, very careful.

"You do know what you're getting yourself into?" Danilo said from the passenger seat. In his hand he held a phone that showed Gavril's position on a map. On the floor of the car, between his legs, he had put a backpack.

Jana had her eyes glued to the road. She had one hand on the steering wheel and the other resting on the support in the door. The seat was soft and upholstered in the black Volvo S60 that Danilo had borrowed from a friend or rented at short notice from a local firm. She didn't care which. The main thing was that she didn't have to arrange a car and thereby risk being traced to it should there be a search later.

There was a pungent smell of disinfectant inside the car. They were outside the small town of Trosa. There wasn't much traffic and they were going quite fast.

"I know very well what I'm getting myself into," Jana answered, resolutely.

Never in all her life had she been so certain of anything, as she was now. Her entire body burned with desire to put Gavril against the wall—confront him. Then she would repay the wrong he had done to her. She would retaliate for his having killed her parents. And other parents. And their children. She would avenge their deaths if it was the last thing she did. There was no possibility to excuse his ill deeds, to move on and leave him be.

"You're risking everything. What if you get caught?"

She didn't answer.

She was well aware that the stakes were the very highest. She was staking all of her life on getting revenge. Despite that, there was nothing that could stop her now.

"Are you afraid?"

"I stopped being afraid when I was seven years old," Jana answered briefly.

Danilo didn't ask any more and silence enveloped them. All that could be heard was the sound of the tires on the asphalt.

They sat next to each other without uttering

a sound the entire rest of the drive. The tracker showed them the way via Järna to Nykvarn. After a twenty-minute drive Danilo straightened up.

"They've stopped," he said.

She slowed down. There was forest on all sides.

"How far away are they from here?"

"Two, perhaps three hundred meters," Danilo answered. "We'll go by foot the last bit so that they do not hear us."

"Where have they taken him?"

"We'll have to find out."

Fifty meters down a gravel road they found a discreet place to park the car. Jana turned off the engine and looked at Danilo who grasped the backpack.

"Perhaps it would be right to thank you," she said. "For helping me."

"Thank me later," he answered, and climbed out of the car.

The high gates were opened slowly.

A uniformed police officer waved with one arm and a police car slowly drove into the gravel drive. After it came a black minibus with tinted windows and finally yet another police car.

Phobos had butterflies in his tummy. He would get a new home. He looked quickly up at Papa who sat next to him on the backseat and then turned his head toward the large white house that towered up in front of them. A wall went all round it with bushes along the side. There were several scraggly trees and a fountain in the form of a mermaid where the rippling water had at some time formed brown lines on the light ceramic surface. Now the fountain was turned off. And ugly.

The house resembled a country mansion with two storeys and large windows. The front door was red and the façade was well lit-up by strong spotlights as well as weaker wall lamps. And there were pillars too. With cameras.

Wow, what a place.

Phobos squeezed the brown teddy bear he had in his lap. He was pleased with it. This was the first time Papa had given him a present. But he was absolutely not allowed to show he was pleased, that's what Papa had said. No smile or anything silly. He wasn't allowed to talk about the teddy bear either, only hug it. Like it. Like ordinary little boys did.

Now the house was close and the car drove up to the front door and stopped. Two uniformed policemen came forward and opened the car doors. Phobos climbed out on one side, Papa on the other.

"Shall we check the son too?" one of the policemen called to the other who was busy frisking Papa.

"No, he's only a kid," came the answer.

"Come along here," said the policeman to Phobos and led him toward the front door.

The chilly air pinched his cheeks. He walked with small steps beside the policeman, the whole time looking expectantly at what was to be his new home.

Phobos had butterflies again. He squeezed the teddy bear hard, and even though the teddy was well padded he could feel the hard steel inside it.

Jana stood leaning with her back against the high wall that ran around the house. The grass under her was damp. She felt how the cold found its way in through her tight black sweater. On her legs she was also wearing black and close-fitting leggings. She had chosen a pair of lightweight shoes, running type, for her feet.

Danilo was also wearing dark clothes with a large hood. He crouched down and dug out a Sig Sauer from his backpack. Danilo checked it carefully, then pulled out a silencer and screwed it onto the pipe with a practiced hand.

"You've still got the technique," said Jana.

Danilo didn't answer. He handed the gun over to her.

"I don't need a pistol," she said.

"What are you going to kill him with then? Your hands?"

"I prefer a knife."

"Believe me, you're going to need this. If nothing else, to get inside the house."

"Where did you get it from?"

"Contacts," Danilo answered briefly.

He put his hand into his backpack again and pulled out yet another pistol. This one too with a silencer. A Glock.

Then he got up and pulled the mask over his head.

"We'll wait until the police cars have left the area. Then we must work quickly. The quicker the better. In, shoot, out. Do you remember?" he said and smiled.

It was the first time in ages she saw that smile.

The police cars started and slowly rolled across the gravel back toward the gates. Four plainclothes but well-equipped policemen remained by the house. As soon as the gates had been closed, they moved to prearranged positions.

"You two on the sides, you in front of the house, and me at the back," said one of the policemen to his colleagues. "Understood?"

"Yes," they all answered in chorus.

"Right, to your posts. Report back exactly two hours from now."

And exactly two hours had passed before the wardens discovered her. The braided strips of cloth had tightened round her neck, cutting off the respiratory passages. Her first thought was a feeling of relief. Then came the panic but it was too late. You couldn't change your mind.

She had taken her final decision and there was no going back. It was impossible to get out of the noose. She knew that. Even so, she struggled. She kicked out, stretched her naked toes, put her hands against the strip of sheeting and pulled. She struggled to the very end.

When the wardens pushed into the cell they

just stood there and stared at her hanging from the bars on the window.

Lena Wikström hung there without moving and stared back at them, lifeless.

CHAPTER
FIFTY-FOUR

"Okay," said Danilo, and let go of the top of the wall. The cars had left the area.

He landed in front of Jana and pushed the backpack under a bush.

"You first. Here." He cupped his hands. "I'll lift you up."

She put her pistol inside her waistband at the base of her spine. She put her right foot in Danilo's hands and her hands on his shoulders.

"Ready?" he said.

She nodded in answer.

"Okay, one, two, THREE."

Danilo pushed up her foot and she got hold of the top of the wall with both hands and swung herself over. It was a long way down to the ground, and she made a hard landing. She crouched down beside a couple of almost bare bushes and made herself as invisible as she could, immediately tried to get an overview of the area, listened for sounds and looked for any movement.

Danilo landed with a thud. He immediately crouched down beside her and drew his pistol.

"Can you see the camera?" he whispered and pointed at a surveillance camera up on a pole opposite the entrance to the house.

"It's an IP camera which can see at a very long distance, roughly like a telescope. Never show your face for one of those, it registers details and facial characteristics at more than one hundred meters. So you must always knock out the cameras first. We didn't use to have to think about that, but it's new times now," said Danilo.

Then he pointed at the policemen who surrounded the house.

"There's one in front, one behind, two on the sides. Watch out for them. If they see you, you've had it, understand?"

She nodded.

"When I shoot at the camera, run to the house. Keep in the shadows."

"I know what to do."

"Okay, okay."

Danilo got up and pulled the hood further down over his face. He took a deep breath and then stepped right out onto the lawn with the gun aimed at the surveillance camera, and fired.

When Jana heard the shot, she quickly ran across the grass up to the house. Hardly out of breath she stood up against the façade and with a couple of steps disappeared into the shadows. Then she heard yet another muffled shot, followed by another two, then there was silence. She listened to her own breathing for a few moments, looked right and left. Peered toward the front and the back of the house. Listened again. Crouching down, she took a few steps forward, stopped at the corner of the house and looked out.

That same moment, a policeman came running. He had evidently reacted to the shot and ran with a drawn pistol toward the front. When he disappeared from view, she heard a pistol being fired again. And again. Then silence.

Jana peeped out a second time from behind the corner and immediately saw a rotating surveillance camera at the back. In her head, she counted how long the camera was pointed in her direction. Far too long. It wouldn't be possible to get inside from there. Not without being seen.

She released the safety catch on her pistol and lay down in the grass. Just as she was about to fire the gun, the glass on the camera was shattered by another shot. It came from behind her and hit the lens spot on. She quickly got up into a kneeling position and that same moment Danilo came up by her side. Under his hood he looked resolute with his lips pressed together and a cold gaze.

"Is the coast clear now?" he said briefly.

"Yes," answered Jana, and got up. "Have you killed the policemen?"

"I had no choice."

Danilo looked out at the rear and then half ran across to the back door. He bent down under every window he passed. With a steady hand he felt the locked glass door and then waved to her.

"Now listen," he said to her when she reached him. "Act fast. Don't think. Just complete your task. Okay?"

"Okay," said Jana.

"I'll stay here. If you're not out in ten minutes I'll come in." Danilo pulled out a lock-pick and forced the lock. A click was heard after ten seconds.

"Are you certain about this now?" he said.

"Yes," answered Jana. "I have never been more certain."

She held up the pistol in front of her face and squeezed it with one hand. Then she took a deep breath and opened the door.

She was inside.

The room was about five by ten meters in size. It resembled a large living room with a sofa, armchair and a glass table. Paintings with nature scenes on the walls. A white pedestal stood on one side. A flowery standard lamp next to it. No plants. No rugs. She sneaked across the floor and stopped in front of an arched opening. She peered slowly into the adjoining room which was lit up by a round table lamp, and noted that it was a dining room. Ten chairs were placed around an oval table. She quickly scanned the area and then moved on to the next room, the door of which stood ajar. She peeped in through the crack. It was a hall. The first she saw was a bench and a hat rail. The staircase was wide and there was a wine-red stair carpet. There were lights on upstairs.

Jana couldn't resist the temptation to go up. So she pushed open the door with her foot. That same moment, she heard a click behind her. Jana's heart missed a beat. She slowly turned her head and saw a little boy in the half darkness. His eyes were afire. In his hand he had a pistol, which he pointed straight at her.

She didn't move a muscle. The boy was close, far too close. At that distance he couldn't miss. He came slowly closer.

"Take it easy," she said.

"Throw your weapon away," said the boy. "Otherwise I'll shoot you."

"I know you will," she said and lowered her pistol. Held out her other hand in a gesture of surrender.

"What's your name?" she said.

"Fuck that."

"I just want to know what you're called."

The boy hesitated a moment, then said his name: "Phobos."

"Does it say that on your neck? Does it say Phobos there?"

Phobos looked astounded. Instinctively he put one hand up to his neck.

She went on.

"If you are what I think you are, then I want you to listen to me. I have also been like you," she said, and tried to gain his confidence.

"Throw away the gun," he said again.

"What you've got in your neck, that carved

name. I've got one too," she said. "Shall I show you?"

For a fraction of a second he looked confounded.

"No," he then said roughly.

"Can't I show you?" she said again. "Please, let me show you. I want to help you. I can help you get away from here, you don't need to be here any longer."

But the boy was not listening.

"Throw away the gun!"

"As you wish."

And then she threw it. The gun went high over Phobos and he followed it with his gaze. When it was right over his head she took a quick step forward, grabbed his pistol with her left hand, took a firm grip of his arm with her right hand, and forced him round. She put the pistol against his head.

"I'm sorry," she whispered. "But I had to do that. I know what you can do, and this is the only way to protect both you and me."

Phobos pulled with his arm to try to get loose.

She then took a firm grip of his neck and pressed so hard that he gasped for air.

"Calm down," she said. "I'll help you. But you must do as I say. If you don't, it is going to hurt."

He became still. There was a gurgling in his throat when he tried to get some air into his lungs. Jana released her hold a little.

"Just do as I say now," she said. "Do you promise?"

He tried to move his head in a nod. She loosened her grip a little more, and then looked around for the gun she had thrown. In the middle of the floor she saw a reflection of matte metal. But that wasn't the only thing she saw. There too stood a man staring straight at her. Despite the half darkness she saw who it was.

It was him.

Gavril.

"Bravo!" he said, and clapped his hands. "It isn't easy to disarm him, I can tell you that, so you did that well!"

His voice was calm and almost friendly from the darkness.

"I saw you come in."

"Give me your weapon," she said.

"I don't have a weapon."

"Your son has a weapon. So you must have one too."

"Yes, he does, but not me. Do you think the agents would let me bring a weapon into the house?"

"If your son could manage it, I presume you too have done it."

"No, it wasn't as easy."

"How did he do it?"

"Magic," he hissed and threw out his hand toward the light from the lamp.

A quick gesture, then the hand drowned in the darkness again.

"So you don't have a weapon?"

"No, little miss. I don't."

Jana tried to scan Gavril's clothes to see if he was lying to her.

"Show me your hands!" she said.

Gavril threw up his hands into the light and shrugged his shoulders.

"Hold your hands so that I can see them all the time. If you try anything I'll blow your son's brains out!"

"Sure, sure," he said, and smiled a not particularly convincing smile. "But if I may ask, what are you doing here?"

"I had to come here. There are so many questions."

"Oh really? Are you a journalist?"

"No. I just want to know why."

"Why what?"

"Why you do this?"

Jana nodded firmly with her head toward Phobos who made a gurgling sound with each breath he took.

He still had his hands on Jana's arm and he held on hard.

"Why is a good word. Why, for example, should I tell you?"

"Because you owe me that."

"I have debts to a lot of people."

"Above all to me."

"And what have I done to you?"

Jana felt the fury grow inside her, but forced herself to be calm.

"You used to call me Ker," she said slowly.

"What did you say?"

"You gave me the name Ker."

Gavril took a step forward. The light from the lamp fell on his face and revealed the scar.

He stared at her with his mouth agape. She stared back. When she saw his look, she felt calm. Her shoulders sank down.

"Well now. Ker. So you survived after all. Don't I get a hug?"

"Go to hell."

"Oh dear, we are angry, aren't we!"

"You stole my childhood, murdered my parents and carved a fucking name into me. Why? I want to know why? Answer me! Why do you do this?"

Gavril smiled.

Leaned his head back, exposed his teeth and hissed.

"Because it is so easy. After all, nobody misses people like you. Illegal kids, that's what you are. No papers, you don't exist."

"And that makes it more acceptable to kidnap and torture…"

"I don't torture!" Gavril cut her off with a raised voice. "I train. I give them all a second chance in life. A chance to become something. To become a part of something greater."

"Greater than what?"

"I don't think you understand how divine it is to govern a person's life and death."

"This is about children," Jana said in a hard voice.

"Exactly. Meaningless children. Perfect as murderers."

Phobos stretched a little and Jana tightened her grip around his throat. He responded by digging his fingernails even deeper into her arm.

"Why do you train them to do that? To murder?"

"What do you think? I have to defend myself. It's fucking tough in the market today. I have the best suppliers, middlemen and pushers. There are lots of buyers and it's a matter of ensuring I keep my income. Money is everything. Whatever people say, that's what everybody is after. What everybody wants. And when money is involved, there's a lot of dirty work too. If drugs are involved, there is even more. So you have to always make sure you have people around you with the same approach as you have yourself. Who want to protect me and what I have created—my market. Who want to cleanse away clumsy people, snitches, people who are unable to pay, who don't fulfill their obligations, so to speak. You see, it is difficult to recruit adults. They cost too much and when they have got a taste for the good life they only get greedy. Cheat you. Or they are totally stoned and utterly useless. Careless."

Gavril went on.

"From a crushed child you can carve out a deadly weapon. A soldier without any feelings, without anything to lose, is the most dangerous there is."

"Is that why you kill…"

"The parents, yes. The children are easier to

deal with then. More devoted. Aren't they? That's true, isn't it? You do agree with me?"

She didn't answer, clenched her teeth.

Gavril threw his hands out again.

"I make Sweden a better country. People might think that my activities are not acceptable, but I contribute to a better world by weeding out the weak. Partly, I do society a service by reducing the number of illegal offspring. Partly I let the migrant kids themselves clean up among the weak in society. It is like Darwin. Only the strongest survive."

"But you kill all of them."

"Children have always been murdered. In all ages. Even in the Bible it talks about the killing of children. Don't you remember the Gospel according to Matthew where King Herod after the birth of Jesus orders all the Jewish boys under two years of age to be killed because he has heard that a future king has been born and he doesn't want a rival."

"So you see yourself as the Herod of our time?"

"No, what I mean is that death is a weapon in itself. To convince everybody about who you are. I use children so I don't have to risk having rivals."

Gavril looked to the right and his scar wrinkled up in the movement and hung over his eye.

"Stand still, I said," Jana shouted.

Gavril turned his gaze back. His reddish-pink skin smoothed out again.

"I am still," he said slowly.

"And the drugs? Why all the drugs?"

"You must reward people with something. And

what could be better than to make everybody dependent? Not only on drugs, but on me too. Then they are less likely to run away too. You see, children do as you tell them. They look up to you. If you give them a dose of the right stuff, you can be a father for them."

"Like a god then?"

"Not really, more like his opposite. A devilish god you could say."

"Why carve names into their flesh?"

"So that everybody will feel they belong. A community. Like a family. All with unique names. But with the same content."

"Gods of death."

"Exactly. And I carve out the name so that you won't forget who you are. I gave you your real name."

"My name is Jana. That's my real name."

"But you are Ker."

"No."

"Yes, you are! Deep inside you are exactly what I trained you to be."

Jana didn't answer.

"What I do isn't anything new. In many countries there are young people who are deliberately recruited, trained and used in armed forces. I do the same here but I've taken it a step further. Anyone can shoot with a pistol, but not anyone can be an assassin."

"How many?"

"That we have trained?"

"If you look at it like that..."

"Seventy."

Gavril's answer hit her like a blow from a fist. She loosened her hold on Phobos's neck slightly. Seventy! His fingers stopped digging so hard into her arm.

"But we only chose the strongest from every batch."

"That's the containers, as far as I know."

"Yes."

"So you took seven children from each one?"

"Sometimes more, sometimes less. Then we selected the two best. Or just one. The rest were got rid of. You surely remember how we went about it?"

Gavril shaped his hand like a pistol and pointed it at Jana.

"Stand still!" she shouted.

The boy moved too. She tightened her grip around his neck and lifted him a couple of centimeters off the floor. He kicked with his legs before she lowered him again.

"It might be of interest to you that until recently I had a pupil on the island."

"Thanatos?"

"Quite right. He was unique."

"He killed Hans Juhlén. Why?"

"Goodness me, you are well informed. What should I say? Hans Juhlén interfered just a bit too much. He turned into a bit of a problem for us."

"By 'us' you mean you, his secretary, Thomas Rydberg, and Anders Paulsson?"

"Precisely!"

Gavril threw out his hand and Jana reacted by raising the pistol against him. He smirked and threw out his hand even further. As if to frighten her.

"Keep still!" she shouted. Her mouth was dry and she swallowed. "Go on, explain!"

"You've already worked it out."

"Go on!"

Gavril became serious.

His lower teeth were exposed in a weird grimace.

"Hans Juhlén managed to dig out a list of all the containers and put pressure on Thomas Rydberg for information. He threatened to reveal everything so we had to get rid of him. Thanatos carried out the mission to our great satisfaction. But Anders messed things up. When he was taking Thanatos back to the island, something went wrong. Thanatos tried to escape and Anders shot him, a mistake that was very costly for us."

"The container that I came in…"

"Was the first one we chose. It required a lot of planning. It still does."

"You're expecting a new one?"

Gavril made a grimace again. He raised his chin and hissed between his teeth.

"It is better to renew everything all the time. Then they won't have a chance to understand anything either. When they have carried out their task, when we don't need them any longer, we can let them disappear. There are new children coming along all the time after all. As you know, this has been so for more than twenty years. Thousands pass Sweden's borders every year. And nobody misses them. Nobody is looking for them. That's right, isn't it, there hasn't been anybody looking for you? Nobody, that's right, isn't it?"

"Shut up!"

"Nobody...who...looked..."

Gavril held up both hands toward her and waved them while he hissed. Like a snake.

"Sssssssssssss!"

"Keep still! I'll shoot!" she shouted and pointed her pistol at him.

Gavril calmed down. He lowered his head a little.

She felt her heart pounding.

"I know that you'll do it. I know exactly how you think. I've trained you after all," said Gavril.

"Not just you..."

"No, it wasn't just me," said Gavril loudly and took a step forward toward the gun on the floor.

"But the others are long since dead. I said that you must have people around you that you can trust. And you only want a few people around you, then there are fewer mouths to feed."

Jana swallowed. She squeezed the pistol hard.

"It's over now," she said with a resolute voice.

"It will never be over. Children are our future."

Gavril took another step forward.

She noticed his movement.

"Stand still! Stand still!"

He didn't listen, took yet another step forward.

"Stand still! Don't move! Otherwise..."

"Otherwise what?"

He took yet another step.

"Otherwise I'll shoot him," she shouted and pointed the pistol at Phobos instead. She pressed the pistol hard against his forehead and forced his head to the left.

Gavril stopped and smiled,

"Do it. He's worthless anyway."

"He's your son," Jana shouted and pressed the pistol even harder against Phobos's forehead.

His face was taut, he whined.

"He isn't my son, he is one of those worthless kids. Just as worthless as all the others. A no-body."

She looked at Gavril, unable to fully grasp his meaning. Then at Phobos, who was whining a lot now. She immediately stopped pressing the gun so hard and saw the red mark from the muzzle on his thin skin.

"You can shoot him, I'd do it anyway later. He knows that. Even so, he does everything I tell him. Don't you, Phobos? You do everything I tell you, don't you?"

Gavril blinked at Phobos, who immediately understood the signal and started to kick with his thin legs at Jana's. He hit her on the lower part of her shin and she gave a start from the pain without seeing that Gavril at that moment picked up the pistol from the floor.

She took a firmer grip of Phobos's neck and forced him up on his toes to keep him still. When she looked back at Gavril again, she saw the gun in his hand. She quickly turned round. And Gavril pressed the trigger…but the weapon just clicked.

He pressed the trigger again and again. Click. Click. The magazine was empty!

Gavril immediately started to laugh. Out loud.

Jana stared at the pistol he held in his hand. *That's my pistol*, she thought. Why is the magazine empty?

Suddenly a voice could be heard from the other side of the room.

"You're out of luck today."

Danilo came out of the shadows and stood a couple of meters from Gavril with a gun pointed at him.

"What the fuck are you doing here?" said Gavril.

There was something about Gavril's way of talking to Danilo that confused Jana. And Danilo just stood there, as if they were friends. Then she realized they really are friends.

"Let me do it," said Danilo and pointed his Glock at her.

"You see," Gavril said. "You have to surround yourself with people you can rely on."

"Yes, you are right about that," said Danilo. "But I'm not such a person."

Then he immediately changed the direction of the pistol and pointed it at Gavril again.

"What the fuck are you doing?" said Gavril.

Then he didn't say any more.

When he fell forwards and hit the stone floor he was already dead.

Danilo changed position. He went round Gavril and shot him again. In the back of his head.

Phobos stood absolutely still. His breaths were short. His eyes like saucers. Jana slowly moved the muzzle of her pistol from his head and pointed it instead at Danilo. He took off his hood and looked at her. His eyes were black. His gaze cold as ice.

"Jana," he said. "Little, sweet, lovely Jana. Why did you have to go and dig into the past? I said that you ought to let things be."

He walked toward her with the pistol hanging from his finger.

"I know what you're thinking. How could Papa recognize me? That's what you're thinking, isn't it?"

Jana nodded.

"Do you remember when I said that I pretended to be dead there in the forest, when Mama ran after me? And I said that I ran the other way? Do you remember that?"

Jana nodded again.

"You lied to me?"

"No, it was true. All of it. I ran but I couldn't run very far. Anders found me afterwards in a ditch. He pulled me into the van again. I thought I would die. But it was thanks to him that I'm alive. He took care of me. He has always been an old woman, soft as anything. But he knew his stuff. That's why I didn't think you'd manage him. I thought and hoped that you'd get shot there at his house."

Danilo moved in a moon-shaped path around Jana. The pistol in her hand moved in the same path.

"That's why you gave me his name," she stated quietly.

"Exactly," said Danilo.

"You are a part of it all," she then said.

"Right again."

Danilo was behind her now.

"But how…"

"How could I survive? I grew up on the island. Got to learn everything there. I was clever and got more missions. Not just one like all the others."

With dragging steps he was in front of her again.

"When I was seventeen I got to take over as trainer. Papa got rid of the other trainers. And all the other idiots too."

"I can't believe that you call him that."

"What? Papa? You did too."

"But no longer."

Danilo was to her left now. He kept on walking the same path around her.

"He is my papa. Oh no, I beg your pardon—I meant, of course, that he was my papa. And it was him, me, Lena, Thomas and Anders who took care of everything. Now they are all gone. Except me. It worked. Admittedly a bit earlier than I had believed, but it bloody well worked out."

Jana's thoughts whirled around in her head. She heard what he said. But even so she didn't understand what he meant.

"What do you mean? You planned this?"

"Planned, well sort of. I hadn't planned to kill Thomas Rydberg. Somebody else did that."

She looked down. Danilo was silent for a moment before going on: "When Thomas was out of the game, I saw that as a sign. That it was time."

"For what?"

"To step forward."

She suddenly understood the connection.

"You made use of me to kill Gavril," she said slowly.

"And you swallowed it."

"I trusted you."

"I know. And that's why it was so easy. I helped you to help me."

Jana stretched her back. The gun in her hand felt heavy.

She looked at Danilo, his ice-cold gaze back. Then he took three steps and kicked Gavril's dead body several times.

"I wanted you dead. You didn't think that, did you? That I wanted to kill you!" He kicked as hard as he could. The blood vessels on his forehead became distinct. His nostrils were extended, the tendons in his neck tensed like violin strings, and his teeth bared.

After a few seconds, he calmed down.

Jana didn't say a word.

Nor did Phobos.

Danilo sat down on a chair, flicked his hair off his forehead and looked at her.

"I'm sorry," he said slowly. "But you realize that you are going to die here."

She didn't know what she should answer so she

just nodded. Her hand shook and she struggled so that it wouldn't be obvious.

"To think that you didn't suspect anything."

"I ought to have done," she said and met his gaze. "I ought to have understood long ago. But it's not until now that I realize how it all fits together. You gave me a Sig Sauer. Thanatos was killed by one of those, and I realize now that what I got was the murder weapon. But you emptied the magazine so that I would die a simple death here."

Danilo laughed in answer.

"You wanted to leave me here so that nobody would suspect you," she said slowly.

The laugh became loud and nasty.

"Exactly!" He jumped up from the chair, and stood a few steps from Jana.

"When the police come they'll find you here and they'll come to understand that you are the one who has killed all my dear ones, my pretty prosecutor, and that you happened to get shot as well. Just think what a scandal there will be!"

Jana bit her lip. How was she going to get out of this? Her hand shook all the worse. The pistol was heavy now.

"And when they do an autopsy on your body they'll find the name on your neck. Then they will understand. That you are one of all those children from the island. They are bound to think that you wanted revenge on the people who had taken you from the container. Who had killed your parents. Simple, isn't it?"

Danilo took two steps back.

"You know what's best of all? The best thing is that you haven't suspected anything. I told you that you should be careful. I told you that. But you didn't listen to me."

He pointed the pistol at Jana, ordered her to let go of Phobos.

She refused.

"Okay," said Danilo. "Then I'll shoot you both." He aimed.

And fired.

That very same moment Jana cast herself to one side and pulled Phobos down too. They landed on the floor, she rolled round, pointed the Glock at Danilo and fired too, but she missed.

Danilo tripped over Gavril's dead body and lost his gun. He withdrew himself quickly out through the door. She was still on her back, breathing heavily with her gaze and gun aimed at the door. Then she got up and looked around for Phobos. To her horror she realized he was gone.

She went out to the hall, her eyes peeled all the time. She listened for sounds. In the hall she pressed her body against the wall, pointing her gun up the stairs, then to the side, then up the stairs again. When she reached the first step she heard a sound. It came from a door behind her. She crept up, waited a moment before opening the door. It led down into a cellar. A lamp hung over the stairs. She hesitated a moment. If she went down those steps she would be a perfect target in the light. Then she heard a click by her side, and twisted round. Behind a door she caught sight of a fuse box.

She smiled to herself.

Now we'll play a game, she thought.

An amusing game.

Jana Berzelius turned off the main switch and took a deep breath. Then she took one step forward and found herself stepping straight into another world. Straight into a memory. She was immediately transformed into the little girl in the cellar. The girl who wanted to survive. It was all happening again. But this time she didn't struggle against the dark. She embraced it. Now she was in control.

She stretched up her head and listened for sounds. It was still silent.

Numbingly silent.

She took a step forward, stopped and listened again. Yet another step, and still one more. After three steps she ought to be by the stairs.

Jana stretched out her hand to feel the banisters. She counted her steps in her head. One, two, three. Now she felt the banister in her hand. In her memory the handrail was rough and cracked. Now it was polished and smooth. Her feet worked their way slowly down the steps. On the last step she let go of the banister and felt with her hand in front of her. Then she heard a sound. Somebody was moving. Somebody was by her side.

Who? Danilo or Phobos?

She slowly turned her head to be able to register new sounds. But there was only silence. It was far too quiet. Perhaps Danilo stood and waited behind her back? A thought made her want to get out. To just get out of there.

Then she heard it.

The breath.

The signal.

She reacted instinctively and pointed the gun at the sound. Then she felt a powerful blow to her arm, lost her balance and fell backward. She ended up lying on the floor, perfectly still. Danilo was close now.

She made an attempt to lift her arm and point the gun up the stairs but the pain stopped her.

He suddenly kicked the gun out of her hand and she heard how it slid across the floor, behind her.

"You're not the only one who likes playing games in the dark," he said and kicked her hard in the side.

She groaned.

"It's fun, isn't it? Well? It's good fun, right?"

He kicked her again, so hard that something broke in her forearm and she shrieked in pain.

"It's time to finish this," he said and immediately sat astride her with his hands joined in a stranglehold.

She just managed to raise one hand and with her nails she clawed at his hands to make him let go. But he didn't. He pressed harder. She gasped for air. In the compact darkness it was hard to tell if everything was going black, but a nasty and familiar sensation came creeping up on her. She knew that she was close to losing consciousness.

Her other hand was firmly wedged under Danilo's legs, and her fingers worked desperately to get a grip on the knife that was on her hip. With a final effort she got a grip on the knife handle with the top of her index and middle fingers, and quickly coaxed the knife out and stabbed it straight into the back of Danilo's thigh. He cried out and immediately loosened his grip on her throat. She took a gurgling breath and then quickly swung up one leg. Danilo was knocked to one side and she pushed herself up. She pulled the knife out of his thigh and put the point of the blade against his chin.

"I told you that I prefer knives," she hissed loudly at him.

But she didn't have the advantage for long. He kneed her in the back and she was thrown to the side, landed on something hard and immediately realized what it was—the gun! She quickly picked it up with one hand and pointed it right out into the darkness. She heard his steps on the stairs and followed him. One step at a time up to the top.

Now she heard him breathing from the other side of the room. Although it was already black around her, she closed her eyes to focus. Then she fired a shot.

For a second time stood still.

After that she heard somebody groaning.

Her arm was quivering with pain but she ignored it. She felt her way back to the fuse box. All the while she had her focus on the groaning. With a quick movement she switched the electricity back on. She turned round to see the victim on the floor.

It wasn't Danilo.

It was Phobos.

CHAPTER FIFTY-FIVE

The handover of Gavril Bolanaki to the Security Services had taken place at nine that morning. At the same time they had held a joint press conference in the police station with the Security Service in charge.

Gunnar Öhrn had felt stressed by the crowd but with the help of the press officer he had nevertheless managed to convey what a good job he and his team had done. When he left the press room he had felt a certain emptiness.

The rest of the morning he had been busy successively informing the Security Services about the case. Dumping all the papers onto their table and leaving was not his style. When he realized that the case really was over as far as his team was concerned, he felt the emptiness even more. Now there was nothing more they could do.

At four o'clock, Gunnar had gathered the team together in the conference room. Henrik sat up straight in his chair and stared hollow-eyed in front of him. Anneli Lindgren sat leaning with her arms on the table. Ola Söderström chewed his pen. Mia balanced her chair on its back legs. Her hair was carelessly put up in a tuft. She looked pleased. It was a victory for her that the case was finished, and she smiled at the fact that she would no longer have to meet her antagonist, prosecutor Jana Berzelius.

"It's a pity," Gunnar had said, and looked out over the room.

The walls were now empty. The maps and the pictures of the victims had gone. The whiteboard had been wiped clean, the projector turned off.

"There are a lot of questions that still haven't been answered. And to top it all we've received a negative answer from Interpol. In their database there is no information about missing people from Chile."

Gunnar looked disappointed. The chances of identifying the victims from the containers now seemed to have vanished. But when he described Anders Paulsson's suicide, one could sense a feeling of relief. The relief lay in the fact that Gunnar hadn't wanted to hand over yet another murder case to the Security Services.

"Why did he shoot himself?" said Ola.

"Moral qualms, presumably," said Gunnar. "Conscience. The same with Lena Wikström. Nobody can live with crimes like that on their conscience."

The silence settled over the team like a lid.

"Well then," said Gunnar. "There is only one thing left to do."

"Thanks for everything," said Mia and got up from the table.

"Where are you going?"

"Aren't we finished?"

"No, we are not. There's still one thing left to do."

Questioning looks from all were directed toward Gunnar.

"We're going to the docks."

Five minutes later, Henrik Levin sat in his office and was fidgeting with the ghost drawing that Felix had made for him. It was a new drawing with three small ghosts on it. But that wasn't what he was thinking about. He didn't know how to react to the fact that he was to be a dad a third time. Deep inside he was happy but worries about the practical details overshadowed his happiness. He hadn't been able to sleep at all last night. And at the morning briefing he had been forced to concentrate to be able to follow it at all.

He looked up from the drawing of the ghosts and out through the window. Even though the case was finished, his head continued to process the events. His mind was on the dead children and he felt horror at the thought of his own children being kidnapped and trained as child soldiers.

He got the shivers.

The thoughts about Anders Paulsson made him reflect upon what drove a person to take their own life. He himself had created life. Twice. And now a third time.

He put the drawing to one side.

"What's the matter?"

Henrik gave a start on hearing Mia's voice. She stood in the doorway in full winter gear.

"You look dreadful."

"I'm going to be a dad," Henrik said slowly.

"Again?"

"Yes, third time lucky."

"So you have fucked after all! Well done!"

Henrik didn't answer.

"Anyhow," Mia went on. "Before I forget…"

She dug into her pocket and pulled out a crumpled one-hundred-kronor bill.

"Here you are."

"Keep it."

"No, I want to pay my way. I owe you for lunch and coffee. Take it!"

"Okay. Thanks," said Henrik and got up and took the bill.

"The least I could do," said Mia.

She wrapped her scarf round her neck three times.

Henrik pulled out his wallet from the pocket of his jacket, which was hanging on a hook behind the door.

He slid the hundred-kronor bill in with the other two already there.

Two?

Henrik was pretty certain that there had been three bills there before.

Mia noticed his surprised look and cut off his musings.

"Right, come on now. Let's get moving," she said.

* * *

Phobos was lying against the wall. His chest heaved up and down at a fast pace. He was taking short panting breaths. His dark eyes were like saucers and they stared in terror at Jana. He held his hand against his throat. The blood was pulsating out quickly, seeping between his fingers and forming a growing red patch on his sweater. The Glock lay by his side.

Out of the corner of her eye she suddenly saw a silhouette. Danilo passed three meters from her, ran out from the room and into the next. She reacted immediately and ran after him. The pain in her arm was forgotten. She would get him. He mustn't be allowed to escape. Danilo vanished into the dining room and just as she entered the room she saw him disappear into the next room. She rushed after him. But he was too quick and with a couple of long strides he was out of the room and she saw him throw himself out of the back. When Jana reached the door she couldn't see him any longer. She was now completely still and silent.

Ready to shoot from her standing position.

Her heart pounded and her blood pulsated.

He had got away.

The bastard had got away!

She unwillingly lowered the gun and put it into her waistband at the base of her spine. Slowly the pain came back to her arm. In a desperate fury she forced herself to turn back into the house.

Back to Phobos.

* * *

Henrik Levin stood in the docks and beat his arms around him but soon realized it was unnecessary. His down jacket kept him warm and he had thermal underwear and heavy winter boots too. He stopped midmovement and looked out over the quay. A large ship was approaching and now and then it released a muted signal. Large snowflakes fluttered down from the sky and formed a layer of white on the ground. The container area was cordoned off and the police ribbon danced in the wind.

"Shall we go closer?" said Mia.

She stood beside Henrik. Her hands were stuck in her pockets, her shoulders drawn up and her face hidden by a knitted scarf. Only her nose and eyes were visible.

"We'll wait until the ship docks," said Henrik and then nodded to Gunnar and Anneli who stood at the far end of the quay together with harbor staff and uniformed police officers.

They nodded back and then looked up at the ship which was now in the canal. The waves broke against the hull. A dozen or so seagulls were shrieking loudly and circling above the stern. Several sailors wearing green overalls were standing on different parts of the deck with mooring ropes in their hands.

When the ship was right next to the quay, the first ropes were thrown down, followed by the others, each flying in an arch over the railing. The long ropes were picked up by the harbor staff who fastened them round short iron poles. All the workers were wearing safety helmets and had large emblems on their backs.

The unloading started straightaway.

Henrik looked up at the hull where the containers towered up three storeys high.

Blue, brown and gray in turn.

"You are going to be all right," said Jana.

She crouched down beside Phobos. He had sunk even lower against the wall, his head now leaning on his shoulder. He was completely quiet. All that could be heard were his short panting breaths. His sweater was covered with the red stain. The blood ran down onto the floor and formed a puddle. His eyes were still terrified, but now he had a glazed-over gaze.

"It's getting lighter now," he whispered with a wheezing voice.

He coughed and some blood ran out of the corner of his mouth.

"You're going to be all right," Jana repeated, but realized how stupid it was to lie to him.

He looked her in the eye.

"Now it's all white...everything is...white..." he whispered.

And then his hand fell down.

He closed his eyes and took his last breath.

Jana immediately got up from his side. She grasped the Glock and wiped it carefully before putting it into his lifeless hand. Then she went up to the fuse box and wiped all the switches. Then she crouched down next to Gavril's dead body and ripped off the tracking device attached to his trouser pocket. She picked up the other gun from the floor and wiped that carefully too before putting it next to him. For a moment or two she sat there and looked at him. And then she did what she hadn't done for ages.

She smiled.

A genuine smile spread over her face.

After which she got up and realized there was yet another gun she must get rid of. Quickly and with a pained look on her face because of her wounded arm, she fished up the Glock from her back. She must leave that there too. With a practiced hand she wiped off all the prints and then carefully lifted Gavril's fingers and put them around the magazine.

She was still not satisfied. An important detail was missing.

The knife.

She went back down into the cellar, crouched down and looked for it. Under a shelf she caught sight of the bloody blade. She managed to slide the knife out and then put it back in the thin sheath inside her waistband. Then she went back up the steps and looked a last time at Phobos.

"I am so sorry," she whispered to him.

Then she left the house.

FIFTY-SIX

It was in the fourteenth container that they made the miraculous discovery. The container was blue and rusty. The snowflakes landed softly on the corrugated metal and immediately turned to drops of water which slowly ran down toward the ground.

The team stood four meters from the doors. Four galvanized lock poles went from top to bottom and a dockworker struggled to open the heavy padlock in the middle. In the end the lock gave way, and the dockworker immediately pulled open the doors. They were all expecting engine parts, bicycles, cartons, toys or something else that had been in the earlier containers. But in this one it was only darkness that met them.

Henrik Levin went forward to get a glimpse of the contents. He screwed up his eyes to be able to see better. He took another step and now stood with both feet on the edge.

Then he could see her. The girl. She looked at him with her eyes wide open. And she hugged her mother's legs.

* * *

Jana Berzelius drove fast along the motorway in the Volvo. She had been forced to wait a couple of minutes before she ran to the car. But Danilo was nowhere to be seen.

She turned up the heater to full. The windscreen wipers cleared the slushy snow from the windscreen. The radio was turned off. The adrenaline had worn off and she leaned her head back with one hand on the steering wheel. She rested her injured arm on her thigh.

Suddenly her phone rang. She looked with suspicion at the display which showed that somebody was ringing from a hidden number. She hesitated a moment or two before deciding to answer it. Henrik Levin politely announced his name, then went on: "Gavril Bolanaki is dead."

Jana didn't say anything, so he continued: "The Security Service couldn't get in touch with the policemen guarding the house. So they sent a special unit there and they found him dead. According to the first reports we've received, they shot each other, him and his son. But the policemen are dead too, so we don't really know how it happened. It was evidently quite a bloodbath. The unit found three guns in the house. They also found a torn-open teddy bear so the guns must have been inside that."

"Okay," said Jana.

Henrik was silent for a few moments.

"I'm in the docks now," he then said.

"Yes?"

"We found them. Ten families with children. They are all safe."

"Good."

"I hope it was the last one."

"Me too."

"The case against him is finished."

"It is definitely finished," she said, and then ended the call.

It was 18:59 when Jana raised her hand to knock on the mahogany door on the three-story detached house in Lindö in Norrköping. Then she changed her mind and rang the bell instead, letting the shrill tone signal her arrival. She took a step back and ran her fingers through her hair, still wet after her quick shower. In the windows the lamps with their cloth shades cast long shadows on the ground in front of her.

The door was slowly opened by a gray-haired man.

"Hello, Father," said Jana, and remained standing in the porch a few moments. So he could look at her.

Then she smiled her practiced smile.

Nodded briefly.

And stepped inside the house.

* * * * *

Acknowledgments

This story is fiction. Any resemblance between the characters in the novel and real people is accidental. The same applies to the characters' names. The locations in the book are real, but I have sometimes altered their descriptions so that they fit better into the action. Any errors that have found their way into the text are because of me.

I want to thank everyone who has helped me with this novel. All who have read and given me feedback, who have answered my questions and helped me with the facts, who have given me their commitment and time.

I want to say a big thank you to Mom, Dad and my younger sister, who have always listened to and encouraged me. Mother, your opinions have been important. And to my mother-in-law, thank you for your honest feedback.

Above all I want to thank my husband, Henrik Schepp, for your critical review, ideas and inspiration. Without you, there would be no book.

The police are zeroing in on the mastermind behind an entrenched narcotics ring. No one has ever seen him; he is like a shadow, but commands extreme respect. Who is The Old Man? Public prosecutor Jana Berzelius craves the answer, even as she struggles to put her dark past behind her. When her diabolical childhood foe, a cold killer who carries the same scars as Jana's, threatens to out her own criminal involvement, she must destroy him before he reveals her secret. As she prepares for the fight of her life, she uncovers an explosive, insidious betrayal that entangles her inextricably in the whole sordid mess.

Read on for an excerpt from Emelie Schepp's riveting second novel in the trilogy, MARKED FOR REVENGE,

available soon from MIRA Books.

PROLOGUE

The girl sat quietly, looking down at her bowl of yogurt and strawberries. She listened to the clinking of silverware against china as her mother and father ate breakfast.

"Would you please eat?"

Her mother looked at her imploringly, but the girl didn't move.

"Are your dreams bothering you again?"

The girl swallowed, not daring to lift her gaze from the bowl.

"Yes," she replied in a barely audible whisper.

"What did you dream about this time?"

Her mother tore a slice of bread in half and spread marmalade on it.

"A container," she said. "It was..."

"No!"

Her father's voice came from the other side of the table, loud, hard and cold as ice. His fists were clenched. His eyes were as hard and cold as his voice:

"That's enough!"

He got up, pulled her from the chair and shoved her out of the kitchen.

"We don't want to hear any more of your fantasies."

The girl stumbled forward, struggling to keep ahead of him as he pushed her up the stairs. He was hurting her arm, her feet. She tried to wrench herself from his grasp just as he changed his grip and put his hand around her neck.

Then he let go, his hand recoiling as if he'd been stabbed. He looked at her in disgust.

"I told you to keep your neck covered all the time! Always!"

He put his hands on her shoulders and turned her around.

"What did you do with the bandage?"

She felt him pull her hair aside, tearing at it, trying frantically to expose the nape of her neck. Heard his rapid breathing when he caught sight of her scars. He took a few steps back, aghast, as if he had seen something horrifying.

And he had...

Because her bandage had fallen off.

CHAPTER
ONE

There! The car appeared from around the corner.

Pim smiled nervously at Noi. They were standing in an alley, in the shadows of the light from the street lamps. The asphalt was discolored by patches of dried piss. It smelled strong and rank, and the howling of stray dogs was drowned out by the rumbling highway.

Pim's forehead was damp with sweat—not from the heat but from nerves. Her dark hair was plastered to the back of her neck, and the thin material of her T-shirt stuck to her back in creases. She didn't know what awaited her and hadn't had much time to think about it either.

Everything had gone so quickly. Just two days ago, she had made up her mind. Noi had laughed, saying it was easy, it paid well and they'd be home again in five days.

Pim wiped her hand across her forehead and dried it on her jeans as she watched the slowly approaching car.

She smiled again, as if to convince herself that everything would be okay, everything would work out.

It was just this one time.

Just once. Then never again.

She picked up her suitcase. She'd been told to fill it with clothes for two weeks to make the fictitious vacation more convincing.

She looked at Noi, straightened her spine and pulled her shoulders back.

The car was almost there.

It drove toward them slowly and stopped. A tinted window rolled down, exposing the face of a man with close-cropped hair.

"Get in," he said without taking his eyes from the road. Then he put the car in gear and prepared to leave.

Pim walked around the car, stopped and closed her eyes for a brief moment. Taking a deep breath, she opened the car door and got in.

Public prosecutor Jana Berzelius took a sip of water and reached across the pile of papers on the table. It was 10:00 p.m., and The Bishop's Arms in Norrköping was packed.

A half hour earlier, she'd been in the company of her boss, Chief Public Prosecutor Torsten Granath who, after a long and successful day in court, had at least had the decency to take her to dinner at the Elite Grand Hotel.

He had spent the two-hour meal carrying on about his dog who, after various stomach ailments and bowel problems, had had to be put to sleep. Although Jana couldn't have cared less, she had feigned interest when Torsten pulled out his phone to show pictures of the puppy years of the now-dead dog. She had nodded, tilting her head to one side and trying to look sympathetic.

To make the time pass more quickly, she had inventoried the other patrons. She'd had an un-obstructed view of the door from their table near the window. No one came or went without her seeing. During Torsten's monologue, she had observed twelve people: three foreign businessmen, two middle-aged women with shrill voices, a family of four, two older men and a teenager with big, curly hair.

After dinner, she and Torsten had moved to The Bishop's Arms next door. He'd said the classic British interior reminded him of golfing in the county of Kent and that he always insisted on the same table. For Jana, the choice of pub was a minor irritation. She had shaken her boss's hand with relief when he'd finally decided to call an end to the evening.

Yet she had lingered a bit longer.

Stuffing the papers into her briefcase, she drank the last of her water and was just about to get up when a man came in. Maybe it was his nervous gait that made her notice him. She followed him with her gaze as he walked quickly toward the bar. He caught the bartender's attention with a finger in the air, ordered a drink and sat down at a table with his worn duffel bag on his lap.

His face was partly concealed by a knit cap, but she guessed he was around her age, about thirty. He was dressed in a leather jacket, dark jeans and black boots. He seemed tense, looking first out the window, then toward the door, and then out the window again.

Without turning her head, Jana shifted her gaze to the window and saw the contours of the Saltäng Bridge. The Christmas lights swayed in the bare treetops near Hamngatan. On the other side of the river, a neon sign wishing everyone a Merry Christmas and a Happy New Year blinked on and off.

She shuddered at the thought that there were only a few weeks left until Christmas. She was really not looking forward to spending the holiday with her parents. Especially since her father, former Prosecutor-General Karl Berzelius, suddenly and inexplicably seemed to be keeping his distance from her, as if he wasn't interested in being part of his daughter's life anymore.

They hadn't seen each other since the spring, and every time Jana mentioned his strange behavior to her mother, Margaretha, she offered no explanation.

He's very busy, was always her response.

So Jana decided not to waste any more energy on the matter and had just let it be. As a result, there had been few family visits over the past six months. But they couldn't skip Christmas—the three of them would be forced to spend time together.

She sighed heavily and returned her gaze to the man whom the server had just given a drink. When he reached for it, she saw a large, dark birthmark on his left wrist. He raised the glass to his lips and looked out the window again.

He must be waiting for someone, she thought, as she got up from the table, carefully buttoning her winter jacket and wrapping her black Louis Vuitton scarf around her neck. She pulled her maroon hat over her head and gripped her briefcase firmly.

As she turned toward the door, she noticed that the man was talking on his phone. He muttered something inaudible, downed his drink as he stood up, and strode past her toward the exit.

She caught the door as it swung shut after him and stepped out onto the street and into the cold winter air. The night was crystal clear, quiet and almost completely still.

The man had quickly vanished from sight.

Jana pulled on a pair of lined gloves and set out for her apartment in Knäppingsborg. A block from home, she caught sight of the man again, standing against the wall in a narrow alley. This time he wasn't alone.

Another man stood facing him. His hood was up, and his hands were stuffed deep into his pockets.

She stopped in her tracks, took a few quick steps to the side and tried to hide behind a building column. Her heart began to pound and she told herself she must be mistaken. The man in the hood could not be who she thought he was.

She turned her head and again examined his profile.

A shiver went down her spine.

She knew who he was.

She knew his name.

Danilo!

Detective Chief Inspector Henrik Levin turned off the TV and stared at the ceiling. It was just after ten o'clock at night and the bedroom was dark. He listened to the sounds of the house. The dishwasher clunked rhythmically in the kitchen. Now and then he heard a thump from Felix's room, and Henrik knew his son was rolling over in his sleep. His daughter, Vilma, was sleeping quietly and still, as always, in the next room.

He lay on his side next to his wife, Emma, with his eyes closed and the comforter over his head, but he knew it was going to be difficult to fall asleep with his mind racing.

Soon he wouldn't be sleeping much at night for other reasons. The nights would instead be filled with rocking and feeding and shushing long into the wee hours. There were only three weeks left until the baby's due date.

He pulled the comforter down from his head and looked at Emma sleeping on her back with her mouth open. Her belly was huge, but he had no idea if it was larger than during her earlier pregnancies. The only thing he knew was that he was about to become a father for the third time.

He lay on his back with his hands on top of the comforter and closed his eyes. He felt a sort of melancholy and wondered if he would feel different when he held the baby in his arms. He hoped so, because almost the whole pregnancy had passed without him really noticing. He hadn't had time—he'd had other things to think about. His job, for example.

The National Crime Squad had contacted him.

They wanted to talk about last spring's investigation of the murder of Hans Juhlén, a Swedish Migration Board department chief in Norrköping. The case was closed and Henrik had already put it behind him.

What had initially seemed to be a typical murder investigation of a high-ranking civil servant had turned into something much more, much worse. Something macabre: the smuggling of illegal refugees had led the team working the case to a narcotics ring that had, among other activities, been training children to be soldiers, turning kids into cold-blooded killers.

It was far from a routine case, and the investigation had been front-page news for several weeks.

Tomorrow, the National Crime Squad was coming to ask questions about the refugee children who had been transported from South America in shipping containers locked from the outside. More specifically, they wanted to talk about the ringleader, Gavril Bolanaki, who had killed himself before anyone could interrogate him.

They'd be reviewing every minute detail yet again.

Henrik opened his eyes and stared out into the darkness. He glanced at the alarm clock, saw that it was 10:15 and knew the dishwasher would soon signal the end of its cycle.

Three minutes later, it beeped.